[THE MINISTRY OF SPECIAL CASES]

NATHAN
ENGLANDER

The Ministry of
Special Cases

ALFRED A. KNOPF
NEW YORK
2007

THIS IS A BORZOI BOOK
PUBLISHED BY ALFRED A. KNOPF

www.aaknopf.com

Knopf, Borzoi Books, and the colophon are registered trademarks of Random House, Inc.

Library of Congress Cataloging-in-Publication Data
Englander, Nathan.
The Ministry of Special Cases / Nathan Englander.
    p.   cm.
ISBN 978-0-375-40493-1
    1. Disappeared persons—Argentina—Fiction.   2. Missing children—
Fiction.   3. Human rights—Argentina—Fiction.   4. Argentina—
History—1955–1983—Fiction.   5. Jews—Fiction.   I. Title.

PS3555.N424M56 2007   2006048731
813'.54—dc22

Designed by Wesley Gott

Manufactured in the United States of America
First Edition

For my father

WOMAN Come, let me go at once and incense burn
       In thanks to Heav'n for my child's safe return.
                                    ——HERMIPPUS

The Doctor and the Gravedigger, they are partners.
                                    ——YIDDISH PROVERB

[PART ONE]

[One]

JEWS BURY THEMSELVES the way they live, crowded together, encroaching on one another's space. The headstones were packed tight, the bodies underneath elbow to elbow and head to toe. Kaddish led Pato through uneven rows over uneven ground on the Benevolent Self side. He cupped his hand over the eye of the flashlight to smother the light. His fingers glowed orange, red in between, as he ran his fist along the face of a stone.

They were searching for Hezzi Two-Blades' grave, and finding it didn't take long. His plot rose up sharply. His marker tipped back. It looked to Kaddish as if the old man had tried to claw his way free. It also looked like Two-Blades' daughter had only to wait another winter and she wouldn't have needed to hire Kaddish Poznan at all.

Marble, Kaddish had discovered, is chiseled into not for its strength but for its softness. As with the rest of the marble in the graveyard of the Society of the Benevolent Self, Hezzi's marker was pocked and cracked, the letters wearing away. Most of the others were cut from granite. If nature and pollution didn't get to those, the local hooligans would. In the past, Kaddish had scrubbed away swastikas and cemented back broken stones. He tested the strength of the one over Two-Blades' grave. "Like taking a swing at a loose tooth," Kaddish said. "I don't even know why we bother—a little longer and no sign of this place will remain."

But Kaddish and Pato both knew why they bothered. They understood very well why the families turned to them with such urgency now. It was 1976 in Argentina. They lived with uncertainty and looming chaos. In Buenos Aires they'd long suffered kidnap and ransom. There was terror from all quarters and murder on the rise. It was no time to stand out, not for Gentile or Jew. And the Jews, almost to a person, felt that being Jewish was already plenty different enough.

Kaddish's clients were the ones who had what to lose, the respectable, successful segment of their community that didn't have in its families such a reputable past. In quieter times it had been enough to ignore and deny. When the last of the generation of the Benevolent Self had gone silent, when all the plots on their side were full, the descendants waited what they thought was a decent amount of time for an indecent bunch and sealed up that graveyard for good.

When he went to visit his mother's grave and found the gate locked, Kaddish turned to the other children of the Benevolent Self for the key. They denied involvement. They were surprised to learn of the cemetery's existence. And when Kaddish pointed out that their parents were buried there, they proved equally unable to recall their own parents' names.

Harsh a stance as this was, it was born of a terrible shame.

Not only was the Society of the Benevolent Self a scandal in Buenos Aires, at its height in the 1920s it was a disgrace beyond measure for every Argentine Jew. Which of their detractors didn't enjoy in his morning paper a good picture of an alfonse in handcuffs, a Caftan member in a lineup—who didn't feel his reviling justified at the sight of the famous Jewish pimps of Buenos Aires accompanied by their pouty-lipped Jewish whores? But this was long over in 1950, when Kaddish found himself locked outside the gate. That terrible industry as a Jewish business was by then twenty years shut down. The buildings that belonged to the Society of the Benevolent Self were long sold off, the pimps' shul abandoned. There was only one holding that couldn't possibly fall into disuse. Disrepair, yes. And derelict, too. But, like a riddle, what's the only thing man can build that is guaranteed perpetual use? The dead use a graveyard forever.

That cemetery was also the only institution established by the pimps and whores of Buenos Aires that was built with a concession from the upstanding Jews. Hard-hearted as those Jews were when it came to the Benevolent Self, they couldn't turn away in death. The board of the fledgling United Jewish Congregations of Argentina was convened and an impasse reached. No Jew should have to be buried as a Gentile, God help them. But neither should the fine Jews of Buenos Aires have to lie among whores. They shared their quandary with Talmud Harry, who, as leader of the Benevolent Self, sat at the head of a board of his own. "You lie with them living," Harry said, "why not cuddle up when they're dead?"

Eventually it was agreed. A wall to match the one surrounding the graveyard would be built toward the back and a second cemetery formed that was really part of the first—technically but not *halachically*, which is how Jews solve every problem that comes their way.

The existing wall was a modest two meters, a functional barrier meant to set off a sacred space. The establishment of a Jewish cemetery in a city obsessed with its dead had signaled a level of acceptance of which the United Congregations only dreamed. They'd wanted to show their ease in its design.

But being accepted one day doesn't mean one will be welcome the next—the Jews of Buenos Aires couldn't resist planning for dark times. So atop that modest wall they'd affixed another two meters of wrought-iron fence, each bar with a fleur-de-lis on its end. All those points and barbs four meters up gave that wall an unwelcoming, unclimbable, pants-ripping feel. The United Congregations allowed themselves one hint at grandeur in the form of a columned entryway capped with a dome. Before any balance was achieved among the Jews, this was the one they'd struck with the outside world.

Two sets of board members stood watching the new wall go up. The Westernized Liberator's shul rabbi had declined to attend. It was the young old-country rabbi who paced nervously, making sure certain standards were met and horrified to find himself presiding.

When the mortar had dried, the governors of the United Congregations returned for the installation of the fence. They were surprised to find the pimps assembled on their side. It was a sight those upstanding Jews had hoped never to see again. A line of famed Benevolent Self toughs stood before them, including a still-robust Hezzi Two-Blades, Coconut Burstein, and Hayim-Moshe "One-Eye" Weiss. Towering over Talmud Harry was the very large, very legendary Shlomo the Pin.

"The wall is plenty high enough," Talmud Harry said. "A fence is an insult that need not be made." The Jews of the United Congregations didn't think it was an insult; they thought it would match nicely with the fencing all around. A number of ugly threats were already implicit. There was nothing much Harry needed to add. He pointed at the wall and said only, "This is as separate as it gets."

Their faces went long. They turned to the rabbi, but he couldn't support them. A solid two-meter wall was a separation by any standard: It would suffice for *mechitza* or *sukkah* or to pen a goring ox. While the finer points were being argued, Talmud Harry gave the nod. A jittery Two-Blades began to reach, and Shlomo the Pin rolled the fingers of his right hand into a tight cudgel-like fist. Feigenblum, the first president of the United Congregations and father to the second, saw this out of the corner of his eye. He took it as an excellent moment to declare the young rabbi's word binding, and a speedy departure was made.

The pimps didn't want to be second-class any more than their brothers who'd demanded a wall in between. When they put up the façade to their cemetery they commissioned a replica—but one meter higher—of the grand domed entrance that welcomed mourners into the United Congregations side.

Thank God again that it was settled. It allowed Talmud Harry to die in peace and be spared the sight of his own sons, lawyers both, facing Kaddish in the living rooms of their big houses and denying whence they came. It was the same when meeting with One-Eye's daughter and the son of Henya the Mute. All that these children had was fought for and paid for the Benevolent Self way.

It was Lila Finkel—whose mother, Bryna the Vagina, was said to have an incisive perspicacity as well as a cunt of pure gold—who took it upon herself to set Kaddish straight. "Take a breath," she said. Kaddish took one. "Do you smell it in the air?" she asked. Kaddish thought he might. "That's what good fortune smells like, Poznan. It's the season of our prosperity and it's never come this way before."

It was the heyday of Evita, of the liberated worker and her shirtless ones. Factories were rising up under Perón, and Lila drew for Kaddish a picture of the middle class rising with them and making room for the Jews. All she asked was that he join them in looking forward. No reason to dwell on ugly memories soon forgotten. Kaddish wasn't convinced, and Lila's patience began to wear. "Think," she said, and gave a good solid tap to her temple. "Which man is better off"—another riddle— "the one without a future or the one without a past? That's why the wall went up. So that one day the Jews might join together, so we could stand in the United Congregations Cemetery out of joy, not sadness, and all of us, looking toward that wall, might together forget what's on the other side."

Except that, for Kaddish Poznan, the future looked no brighter than the past. He'd not yet met and married Lillian; it was before the birth of his son. Without his mother Favorita's grave to visit, Kaddish had no one at all.

"So what?" Lila said. "In every people's history there are times best forgotten. This is ours, Poznan. Let it go."

Among the children who didn't acknowledge their parents' existence, someone else aside from Lila had been unnerved by what Kaddish said. When he went back to the cemetery bent on getting in, Kaddish found a chain had been added to the gate, a sloppy weld applied, and, for good measure, tar used to gum up the keyholes in both locks. He gave it a kick that echoed off the dome and sent a pigeon swooping down from above. Kaddish thought about what Lila said and went around to the United Congregations side. He entered through its always-open gate, he walked through its manicured grounds, and reaching it—reaching up, Kaddish scraped his shoes against brick as he pulled himself to the top of that wall. Perched there and taking in the

Benevolent Self, Kaddish wondered if there'd ever been a wall built that someone hadn't managed to cross. This one wasn't much of a challenge. It wasn't meant to stop the living but to separate the dead.

As a solution it was fine with Kaddish and, as word spread, with the rest of the Jewish community from both sides of the wall. Kaddish was occasionally spotted climbing over to the Benevolent Self or dropping back down between United Congregations plots. No one acknowledged he was there. If they could forget every last person buried in that ruffians' graveyard, it wasn't difficult to add one more. From then on, it was as if he wasn't. The Jews forgot Kaddish Poznan too.

This is how it stayed for a very long time. It was how Kaddish was treated after he fell in love with Lillian and when she, God bless her, fell in love right back. The Jews of Buenos Aires made room for her in their forgetting—no small matter, considering her family aligned itself on the United Congregations side. (Pity also the parents. What to do with a daughter who insists on marrying an *hijo de puta*? Why did Lillian have to find herself the only Jew proud to be a son of a whore?) This is how the situation remained for them when Evita died two years later, and in five, when Perón was driven off. Kaddish's visits to his mother's grave became ever more frequent after Pato was born. His mother was the family's single unbroken link to a past.

Not even Kaddish's name was family given; it was the young rabbi who'd picked it and, no more than a half kindness, it was the most the upstanding Jews had ever shown. Sickly, weakly, and grasping at survival, Kaddish barely lived through his first week. His mother—a faithful woman—begged that the rabbi be summoned to Talmud Harry's to save him. The rabbi wouldn't cross the threshold. Standing in the sunlight out on Cashew Street, he peered into the vestibule at the infant in Favorita's arms. His judgment was instant. "Let his name be Kaddish to ward off the angel of death. A trick and a blessing. Let this child be the mourner instead of the mourned." Assuming no fathering beyond the physical (and commercial) act, the rabbi gave Kaddish the last name that goes with the legend—it's from Poznan we know that a man's offspring through a prostitute will come to no good. Favorita repeated the name: Kaddish Poznan. She held out Kaddish and gave him a turn, as if trying

it on for size. The rabbi didn't smile or take leave. He simply stepped
out into the gutter, feeling he'd done right by the child. Let the name
Kaddish save him. And if the boy is righteous, let him get out of the
other one on his own.

Had Kaddish known the origins of his name, he wouldn't have felt
cursed. He was happy with his family. He believed in a bright future for
his son. And as creaky as his knees were when he climbed that wall, as
lightly and with as little *oomph* as he tried to land, he hadn't given up on
his own self either. If she'd acknowledged him in the intervening
twenty-five years, Kaddish would have told Lila Finkel she was partly
right. Hard as life got, there was something to living it with a little
hope. Maybe that was why Kaddish never needed his fellow Jews any
more than they needed him.

This was the balance maintained through the Montoneros and the
ERP and after Onganía was overthrown. During those two decades, the
community prospered and attained status. And Kaddish was convinced
he'd have prospered most of all had any of his schemes worked out.

The Jews didn't feel any great need to take stock when Perón
returned to power. It surely didn't make them think about Kaddish
Poznan's treatment all those years. The community did give a collective
twitch when, during Perón's welcome home, there was a small massacre
in the welcoming crowd. There were some in Once and Villa Crespo
who bounced their knees nervously throughout Perón's short reign and
two brothers in two big houses in Palermo who began to bite their nails
in earnest when he died.

Perón had left his nation with a dancing girl in the Pink House failing to run their lives. At this time of great uncertainty and deadly rumor,
a number of the fortunate feared that the envious and ill-willed might
start looking into the past. Though bodies mounted, there wasn't yet
any real burying. It was a period better defined by what was dug up.
So many secrets were being unearthed in Buenos Aires, anyone might
by accident stumble onto another. It was then that children of the
Benevolent Self acknowledged what Kaddish had always known—the
wall separating those two cemeteries wasn't so high. So desperate were
they then not to be linked to the Benevolent Self that they turned to the

only one who wouldn't let it go. They hired Kaddish Poznan to cross over the wall. They paid him good money to erase the names.

Pato crouched down behind Hezzi's marker. He planted his knees in the dirt and pressed his shoulder to the stone. Grabbing hold of its sides, he braced himself, ready for Kaddish's first blow. Pato was providing resistance. "The one thing you're good at," Kaddish had said. "We might as well put it to use."

It was a delicate job. Kaddish didn't want to knock that headstone over. And Pato was happy enough to take shelter from his father any way he could. He did not want to be there. He did not want to cross through the United Congregations Cemetery, did not want to carry the tool bag or climb over the wall. He wanted no part of his father's cockamamie and perverse and misdirected plans. At nineteen, a college boy, Pato was learning sociology and history, important things that can only be taught in a university setting. He had no interest in the thuggish world Kaddish came from.

To get anywhere with such a child, it's best to do as Kaddish did and take Pato's presence as acquiescence enough. Kaddish didn't expect much more. For a boy who wants to see himself as tough and independent, who wants to believe, while in the presence of his father, that he's a self-made man, certain emotions are confusing and shameful. Pato tried to keep them packed down. Despite the many traits that he couldn't brook, the infinite points of disagreement, and the day-to-day ways he and his father would collide, beneath it all and defying logic, Kaddish was the father he loved. "Swing," Pato said, pushing back against the marble. "Swing already. Let's get this done."

[Two]

IT WAS ALWAYS LIKE THIS for Kaddish Poznan, always something gone wrong. He shook his head and, acknowledging nothing beyond that, spit between mounds.

"It's a body," Pato said.

"We're in a cemetery. This is where they keep them." Seeing that they were on the United Congregations side, Kaddish stamped his foot. "We're standing on another right now."

"This one's different," Pato said, highlighting it. "You'll notice, unique in its positioning, this one's above ground."

"Where?" Kaddish said. He raised a hand to his brow to better see in the dark and knocked the flashlight loose from Pato's grip. After fifty-two years in that city, Kaddish's blindness was as sharp as his sight. He'd learned not to see any trouble that didn't see him first.

They'd chipped Two-Blades' name away and left his headstone intact. They were back over the wall and on their way home. All Pato had needed to do was walk a straight line. Instead, he'd taken them down a row they wouldn't have passed and had waved the flashlight around. Kaddish could have strangled his son right then—leave a second corpse with the first, God help him.

Pato fetched the light and headed toward the body. He was already leaning in when Kaddish grabbed him hard by the back of the neck.

"You're going to touch it now?" Kaddish said. "You want your fingers all over it, because it's so easy to explain how we came to be here in the middle of the night? Murdered—I see it same as you. But I promise, Pato, there's no murderer out there. Everyone would be more than happy to have us volunteer."

This is why Kaddish didn't want to see, and why he didn't want to walk down the row to the body, because half looking from a distance was so much different from standing right over this kid.

The body was a young man's, belly up and shirtless. Its feet touched the ground on one side of the headstone and its head did the same on the other. The throat was slit clean and the body drained of blood. There wasn't a drop to be found.

"Somebody moved it here," Pato said.

"You think they've been moving themselves around the city? You think they pop out of the ground like tulips? The police kill them and dump them and the paper reports nonsense to go along. It's a tragedy among tragedies. Now let's get home." Kaddish slipped between graves. Pato didn't follow. "This is the single worst place in Buenos Aires to be standing."

"For us, yes," Pato said. "And for this boy to be lying." He then raised the flashlight and lit the Jewish stars and etched hands and Hebrew dates on the headstones.

"Should we drag him to the car and drop him off in Pompeya? Is that the plan? Trust me," Kaddish said, "if they want to start slitting Jewish throats, they won't bother drumming up an excuse."

"How do you know he's not Jewish?"

Kaddish snatched the flashlight and brought it close to the murdered boy's head. "Such a nose as this God hasn't set on a Jewish face in two thousand years. It's smaller than yours on the day you were born." Bringing the lens up to his chin, Kaddish lit his own face like a sundial. In the Poznan family it was understood (and oft pointed out) that Kaddish's ample snout was the smallest of the three. Unscientific a proof as it was, Kaddish thought his point was made. He lowered the flashlight and took Pato by the arm. "Time to go home," he said. "Let

Feigenblum and his board deal with the Jews on this side. We, my *hijo de hijo de puta,* have Jews of our own."

Kaddish coughed his morning cough and scratched the parts that needed scratching. He made his way into the kitchen, surprised to find his wife still there. The paper was spread across the little table, and Lillian, holding a section, looked up at him over half-glasses.

Kaddish kissed her on the cheek and sat down at her side. "It won't be in today's papers."

"How do you know what I'm looking for?" Lillian said.

"An ambush is my only guess if you're not at work."

"Everyone is always against you."

"They usually are," Kaddish said. He patted at the newspaper on the table. Lillian brought out the ashtray from underneath.

"You're going to get yourself killed," she said.

"You're opposed then?"

Lillian reached underneath a second time. She passed the lighter to Kaddish but she didn't let go, his hand clasped over hers.

"I'm worried for my son."

"The greater everyone's fear of the future, the more they want the names gone."

"At some point it becomes too much."

"I'm finally bringing home real money and now you want me to stop? But you don't, not yet, do you? The line hasn't been crossed."

"It has for Pato."

Pato stood in the doorway in his underwear. "I don't want to do it anymore," he said.

"And I don't want him to," Lillian said. "And I don't want you to either. This time you find a body. Next time," she said, "who knows?"

Pato slipped behind his father and went over to the stove. Kaddish turned and stared at him while he spoke. "So the police kill the rebels who would otherwise kill each other and terrorize us. It's a tragedy for someone, but it's not ours."

"You saw him same as me. That wasn't a rebel," Pato said. "It was another kid. I'm telling you, they kill for no reason. Innocents shot dead."

"His throat was slit, first of all. And second, if he was innocent, all the better if we keep at it. Let's stay guilty and then we'll be safe."

"It's not a joke," Pato said. He shook the empty kettle and stuck it under the faucet. "Things are spinning out of control."

"Jesus, what do you think out-of-control will look like if this isn't it? The government is cleaning up and when they're done things can only improve. You'll see, safer is the way this country is heading. Safer—and you and your stupid friends better watch it—for those who don't make trouble and keep their big noses clean."

"You're a fascist," Pato said, setting the kettle on the fire.

"Good for me," Kaddish said. He put out his cigarette and blew a cloud of smoke.

[Three]

PEOPLE DIE EVERY DAY, their houses burn down around them, they tumble from ladder and rooftop, swallow fat olives down the wrong pipe. They are also found murdered in many original ways. But a lot more people are afraid of a gory, violent, untimely death than manage to get themselves killed. This is how Lillian's office made its money. She worked in insurance. People paid them premiums against their worst fears.

Lillian always found it disappointing when she was processing claims. It wasn't about the money paid out, as none of it was hers. It was the inevitable emptiness in trying to replace property or human life with a company check. It was a sleight of hand that wasn't. Everyone signed up knowing what they never seemed to understand: You don't get anything back. The only thing fire insurance has ever extinguished is a nagging doubt. The house goes up in flames just the same.

She liked to think that she worried with an actuarial specificity, light on emotion and in proportion to actual occurrence. Lately she'd been worrying more and more. And that body—poor child—was simply too close to home. Lillian felt it was time for protection, real and solid to the touch. She wanted a policy of her own.

Lillian went into the kitchen and took a carving knife from the drawer in the counter. She pulled open the refrigerator and then the freezer door inside—revealing the block of ice that had formed in the compartment within weeks of Kaddish's bringing it home. When she'd told him, he'd said, "Broken means no ice. This is the opposite, it works too well." And that's how it had stayed ever since.

Lillian raised the knife and drove it into the thick knot of ice that left the freezer in a pucker. The blade cut frost. The tip buried itself a centimeter deep, and Lillian's hand slid a fraction too far, nicking her palm.

She worked the knife free. She wrapped a towel around her hand and struck again, this time more carefully. She built up a rhythm, sent fissures through the block, and, with frozen fingers, pulled free loose chunks. Her knife palm burned from the friction, her other hand from the cold. Here and there a swirl of pink clouded the puddle on the floor.

"You can do better in a house full of chisels," Pato said.

Lillian was startled to find him watching. She looked at her progress and said, "Fetch me your father's tools."

Pato sat at the table while his mother attacked the freezer, covering the floor with ice in quickly melting hunks. She didn't stop until what she searched for was free. Buried in the back corner was a small square package wrapped in silver foil and abandoned with all the others when the ice had formed.

She ran it under water. Steam rose up. Ice crackled and slid away, the foil shining as if polished. Lillian peeled it back, revealing a tin, rusted at the lip, its sides bulging outward. She flipped the top. She squeezed hard so the tin warped further and worked out the thick wad of bills jammed inside.

"Best hiding place in the world," she said. "Even before the freezer froze over."

Pato stared.

"There are others in the apartment," she said, and pulled another roll of bills from her pocket. "I've been to those too."

She handed the money to her son.

"A fortune," Pato said. He licked his thumb and started counting.

"A lot of paper. It's not much in the way of money these days."

Pato didn't seem to agree.

"A secret," she said.

Pato crossed his heart with a handful of money.

"I used to dream of buying you an apartment," she said. "Since that won't ever happen, the least I can do is buy you the door."

They stood on a patch of cobblestones where the pavement had worn away and old Buenos Aires pushed through. At the end of the block, in front of a store with chandeliers in the window, two men unloaded Turkish carpets off the back of a truck, laying them out on the sidewalk. Otherwise the block was silent and the security shutters on the businesses pulled down. The storefront they were looking for was lifeless. "You'd think they'd have a decent door," Pato said. Lillian had thought it was closed.

The interior, though, was a wonder. The whole place consisted of one giant room crowded with stock. The doors, cheaper, lighter, were stacked six and seven thick all along the walls and standing unbroken end to end. Lillian turned back to the entrance and for a moment could not tell through which one they'd come.

Looking up, Lillian and Pato found two-by-fours crisscrossing the ceiling and between them, lying flat and edge to edge, end to end, door after door after door. The lights in the ceiling were hidden by the stock below, and a cold blue glow lit the room. "This is a sensible place," Lillian said. "Nondescript on the outside, asking no trouble, and all its flair packed neatly inside."

Pato headed for the deluxe models on the far side of the showroom, where doors stood upright in their frames. Lillian followed him over and the manager made his entrance, stepping through the one Pato tested. He was a young man with straight hair to his shoulders and a handsome face gone ragged from drinking or drugs or a worry so great as to leave black lines under sunken eyes.

"Still looking," Lillian said. The manager was already backing off, no pressure at all.

Lillian moved through the rows, sizing up. She opened and closed, tapped against wood, pulled latches, turned knobs. When Lillian slapped her palm hard against a panel, the manager turned to her from his desk across the room.

"I'm ready now for help," she said, and he made his way over. Lillian pointed out a lovely pine model with six windowpanes set in a delicate sash.

"Beautiful choice," he said. "Elegant."

"Flimsy," she said. "An invitation. This is exactly what I do not want."

Pato shook his head. "You can't win with her," he told the manager. "You can't get the answer right."

"I'll try," the manager said, fake eager.

"Then listen careful," Lillian said. "No beauty. I don't want anything designed with an eye toward the aesthetic, not a cent spent on rounding an edge or fastening trim. I want density. I want a door that won't kick in, a hunk of wood that will not splinter. Give me something that will swallow a knock."

"Security, ma'am. Is that what you're after?"

"I put a lot of weight on doors."

"Security is the rage. You're not alone." He said this in grave tones and then winked one of his receding eyes. "A woman like yourself needs to know she can keep the men from beating down her door." The manager gave a sheepish look to Pato.

"I think the man is flirting with you," Pato said.

"Do you see the things money can buy?" Lillian said. She put a hand to her hip, making a cursory acceptance.

The manager led them to a door in the last row. "How about this," he said. "Not wood but steel."

"Steel?" Lillian said. She honestly hadn't thought of it.

He fanned out a stack of cards that hung by a chain from its knob. "Veneers," he said. "Colors and styles. Black, white, brown, wood-grain. Your choice." He let them drop.

The knob was industrial and oversized. There was no spring to its mechanism. It had to be turned, two, three times. Unscrewed. "An extra bolt," he explained, pulling the door open. The lock was in the center of the door, the key in it. When it was turned, rods extended from top, bottom, and sides. Sixteen dead bolts reached in four directions. "Four sets of four rods," he said, "plus the bolt in the knob. All steel. A stainless steel cross with a lock for a core." The manager turned the key and the bolts withdrew. The key was flat and grooved on both sides, a series of bumps and circles carved to its base. He handed it to Lillian. "No skeleton in the world to match this. And that lock can't be picked. If you need an extra key, the locksmith won't even make a copy without a registration card and ID." He took a step toward Lillian. He turned and joined her in admiring the door.

"Impressive," Lillian said.

The man slapped a hand against it. It did, indeed, swallow the sound.

"Security in these times is not cheap," he said. "But"—and he winked at her again—"I could be convinced to jew the price down."

"Well done," Pato said. He laughed and clapped the manager on the back. "I think you just made yourself a sale."

[Four]

ABSENT A CORPSE and absent any sign of its presence, it was hard to believe that the body had been there. Kaddish had agreed to check for the slit-throated boy on their way over the wall if he could have an extra stop of his own. It was against his better judgment and he wasn't even sure why he'd negotiated, since he'd have dragged Pato along regardless. The two of them stood staring at the spot, and Pato again raised the flashlight to better light the stones nearby.

"What if it was still here?" Kaddish said.

"Then we'd bury him," was Pato's answer.

Kaddish thought they might as well bury themselves while they were at it but decided to let it pass. There was no need to worry over a solution to a problem that wasn't. There was also no need for Pato to stand there, slack-jawed, trying to decide how sad he should be. "Our part in this misfortune is finished," Kaddish said. "For once we get some good luck." When Pato didn't respond, Kaddish said it again, adamant. "Good luck—how else can we take it?" It was a shortsighted stance. Kaddish would soon be wishing for a time when there were bodies yet to be found.

Dropping down onto the Benevolent Self side, they went straight for the old oak and counted four rows past. Kaddish helped Pato step over a marker and then gave him a shove forward. He followed behind until they reached his mother's grave. Here lay Favorita Poznan, with a first name she'd hammered out from the Yiddish and a last name taken from her son. If Kaddish could offer nothing else in the nine useless years he'd had before his mother died, at least he'd had a name to give back. On Favorita's left the madam, Bluma Blum, was buried. On her right rested One-Eye Weiss—though no one would know it from what was left of the inscription. Kaddish had already been.

Kaddish never learned the circumstances that settled his mother at Talmud Harry's, and he never judged her for the sad work she'd done. As for Favorita's seeing to it that she was buried a Poznan, Kaddish always assumed that long before the children of the Benevolent Self had thought to become ashamed of their parents, his mother had decided to protect her family from a disgrace of her own.

It wasn't dishonor that drove Favorita to adopt Kaddish's name. The moment she set foot on a ship bound for Buenos Aires, she knew word of her doings would never reach home. And if by some chance her family learned of her situation, it wouldn't have surprised. While the ship was moored at Odessa's port, Favorita stayed belowdecks, ignoring the last whistle. She pretended she hadn't heard. This was the only deception she'd allowed herself; it was the one she needed to start her on her way. She went back on deck, intending to disembark and return to her family, and got there in time to see Russia recede. Favorita could still make out the local children, glistening like seals and diving from the piers.

It was irreversible now and she consigned herself to whatever waited on the ocean's other side. Favorita made her way toward the front of the ship, toward her husband, who stood at the railing surrounded by his other nineteen wives.

He was a smooth-tongued and smartly dressed alfonse who'd gone from town to town with a satchel stuffed with marriage contracts and money, making promises and taking brides all along the way. He was right then busy tearing up those contracts and sprinkling *ketubas,* like confetti, out over the budding waves. So ended Favorita's marriage, unconsummated and wholly unconsecrated. As for her status in Argentina, other papers had already been arranged.

With the aid of quick hands, low light, and countless pigeon heads, Favorita spent her first months at Talmud Harry's marking the bedsheets, a virgin for all who were willing to pay. She didn't want to look at the men but always kept her eyes open. When she closed them she only saw home. Hardest for Favorita was the memory of her mother kissing her cheeks, saying good-bye to a daughter who'd sold herself to feed them, her mother who would die from the guilt of it and the necessity of it and from forever missing Favorita, who was then still called by her Yiddish name.

Home is what Favorita would see when she closed her eyes until the day she died; it is what she dreamed during daytime sleeps after working through the night. And as unwilling as she was to forget from where she came, she was equally unwilling to forget who she herself was. She held on to the good *midos* with which she'd been raised. She remained a moral girl, despite what her life had become. Favorita kept kosher as best she could and, if she wasn't working, never missed a service at the Benevolent Self shul. When Kaddish was born to her, she wished what all mothers do. She wanted to provide better for her son.

She also wanted to give him the new start that she couldn't manage for herself. It was for Kaddish that Favorita became a Poznan. It was for her son that she kept silent about who she'd once been. Because Favorita saw her own life as a bridging, a continuation of what was: It had a beginning followed by a journey and it would come, she always knew, to a bad end. As much as her adopted country would one day try and split the present from what precedes it, a person put on this earth lives her life straight through. With a child, though, Favorita believed, a new line could be started. The rabbi had his wish for Kaddish and this was Favorita's. She wanted him to have a future as limitless as his past.

This was another reason beyond loyalty and love that Kaddish wouldn't give up on his mother. Not only was she his connection to the past, she was also its start. Favorita was as far back as the Poznan name would ever go.

For his grandmother, Pato mustered a little reverence. Since it was important to Kaddish that he did so, it was as close as he got to showing his father any respect. This was all Kaddish wanted. He didn't ask it often and, when he did, Pato always came through. They each picked up a rock and set it upon Favorita's headstone, as is the Jewish custom. Then, in deference to Western fashion, Pato reached into the tool bag and pulled out fresh flowers. It was a small bouquet to leave on his grandmother's plot, and it was the only blooming bunch in the graveyard.

"Hammer," Kaddish said, and put out his hand.

Pato looked at it. "It's a desecration," he said, and then did as he was told.

Kaddish took a breath as he raised up the hammer and exhaled into the swing. The chisel struck and the energy, like a shock, didn't transfer to the stone but raced back up into his arms. He'd hardly made a mark.

"No one is desecrating anything," Kaddish said, and wiped a forearm against his head. "We are here to prevent further damage. I'll tell you what this job is. It is work that needs to be done in a world that runs on shame. Guilt feelings or no, they'd have smashed this place to rubble without us."

Kaddish took another swing at the stone, thicker and darker than the others around it. It belonged to Babak "the Sephardi" Lapidus, and it was the nickname that Kaddish started with. He hit, the chisel slipped, and he scraped his knuckles.

"Losing your touch," Pato said.

Kaddish offered his son the tools.

"I won't have any part of it," Pato said.

"You already do. Unless you've got another way to feed and clothe yourself against three-hundred-percent inflation?" Kaddish shook out his aching hand.

"It's extortion," Pato said.

"It's called work."

"No," Pato told him, "not when it's against my will."

"All work is against your will. Some Marxist you are. So quit working. Go eat one of your books."

"I hate you," Pato said.

As with so many conversations of late, it ended as it began. Nothing accomplished, nothing understood. Father–son time, Kaddish appreciated either way.

Kaddish took another useless swing. "It's a stone that would do better shoring up a chimney. Better suited," Kaddish said, "than sitting on the Sephardi's head. He was a good man."

"He was a pimp and a murderer and a thief like all the rest."

"How would you know except if I'd told you?" Kaddish pushed Pato aside and took out the heaviest hammer. He set the chisel against the slab at a sharp angle and set his feet wide apart. He didn't want to make too great a noise but raised up his arm and struck with force. The blow took all of *Babak* away. With the name freed, a stink filled the air, a fetid odor that made Kaddish turn his head. It was there and then gone, like tracking a burst of sound. He struck again, and with the chip came the smell.

"You've stirred him up," Pato said.

"Nonsense," Kaddish said. "It's the stink off the stone."

"You've unleashed something. You've finally done it. You let loose the pimping stench of the dead man's deeds."

The whole office consisted of two rooms. Lillian and Frida shared the central area and Gustavo had the back. In the central area, two extra desks faced the ones in use, ready for the new hires that Gustavo never made. Lillian and Frida's work spilled over onto those desks, as is natural. A visitor to the office could only assume that Gustavo had in his employ a staff of four. No one was ever disabused of this notion.

Lillian had started as Gustavo's secretary and over time he'd taught her the business. She'd learned it, mastered it, and finally turned Gustavo into the man of leisure he'd always wanted to be. He lunched with his favorite accounts and wooed new clients, neither of which took that much time. To fill it he played golf every Wednesday, and on Monday mornings he swam and then took a late breakfast at the Equestrian Club. He'd brought in Frida a decade ago to answer phones and manage the office and to assume all administrative duties from Lillian. And from this promotion, Lillian had kept her chin up for the last ten years.

Gustavo rubbed a palm across the top of his head, smoothing and resmoothing his hair. "We'll count it against your vacation," he said, and gave Lillian a smile. Lillian had saved up a thousand early afternoons and still sounded apologetic in asking. She knew Gustavo took advantage and that without her he was lost. But since Gustavo knew that as well and was sometimes cowed by it, Lillian saw his selfishness as a harmless personal flaw.

Lillian kissed Frida on her way out and walked quickly toward home. Despite her rush, she paused outside a bar to watch a street performer play. Two men drank beers at a sidewalk table, and the musician sat at their feet on an overturned crate, his hat on the ground at his side. He played the guitar beautifully. Lillian rested her briefcase on an empty chair, listening with the men until the owner came out and told the musician to move on. "Take it into the subway," he said. "They'll adore you down there." Lillian dropped all her change into the hat and walked off. She arrived at the apartment well ahead of the workmen coming to install the door.

She made the two workmen maté before they'd even thought of a break. Then she set out her files on the kitchen table, slipped on her half-glasses, and set about her business as on any other day. When they called for her, she straightened her skirt and went out, handing the older of the two the tip. Lillian took a good look and decided they were brothers. The younger one lifted the old front door as if it were made of cardboard, flimsy thing that it was.

They left and Lillian locked her new door behind them. She felt secure and she felt relaxed—partly because she had the apartment to herself and partly, guiltily, knowing no one could get in. It was the first time in her life that she was alone in a house, the only one holding the key.

She went back to her files, waiting for that first knock. When it came, she was on her feet, ready to face Kaddish and explain how and why she'd paid a fortune to buy a door for an apartment they didn't own. She peered through the peephole at the bubbleheaded man outside. It was her neighbor Cacho from across the hall. It's never who you think.

"This is really something," Cacho said, when Lillian let him in. He stuck out his bottom lip and gave the door a playful kick, as if testing the tire of a car. He ran his fingers along the frame, this time more serious, brows knit. "I'd say it'll serve its purpose. It should safely drive intruders across the hall." He signaled his own apartment with a tilt of the head.

"God forbid, Cacho," she said. "That's not my intent."

"I'm kidding, of course," Cacho said. He laughed to prove it and then averted his eyes. Lillian's gaze followed Cacho's to the small scalloped shelf mounted on the wall behind the door. Her mother had carried it from Europe, and it was the only keepsake Lillian had taken from her old life when she'd left to marry Kaddish. It's where they left their keys. The new ones rested there. They were large curious things.

"I'd have broken in myself if I knew you'd go to such lengths to protect what you had."

"Yes," Lillian said. "Great treasures. And I worry that someone will run off with my Kaddish in the night." Lillian ushered him out and then leaned back against the door, feeling it twice as thick.

It took her a long time to relax again after Cacho left, but when she did the calm felt deeper than before. She made herself tea and cooked dinner for one, assuming Kaddish and Pato would miss it. Then, utterly unlike her, she stretched out on the couch to watch television. She turned the volume low. She adjusted the pillows and wiggled her toes, and, as she had seen Kaddish do on a million nights, she let herself fall asleep fully dressed, one foot on the floor.

Kaddish sent Pato upstairs with the tools, and for the first time that night his son was happy with the arrangement. Pato was glad to be rid of him and Kaddish knew if he raced up to the apartment right then, Pato would already be safely ensconced in his room, headphones on and needle dropped.

Kaddish had kept on across the narrow lobby, past the stairs and the elevator and through another door onto a crumbling patio. A Moorish tile bench ran along one of the building's walls. Because of this, Kaddish referred to that space as the courtyard, though to the rest of the building's residents it was the bottom of the air shaft and nothing more. Kaddish leaned back against the wall and smoked a cigarette. It was the highlight of his day.

He watched the shifting lights from the apartments and the eerie shadows thrown by the laundry overhead. He could see his underwear drying on the highest line and Mrs. Ordóñez's gigantic bloomers hanging below them, waving in the breeze as if she were trying to signal her surrender. Kaddish had sat out there at all hours, and there was always life in that building. Beyond the lights there were the noises, general and specific, the telephone rings and barking dogs, the nightmare yells and late-night fights, all the wafting farts and flushings.

Kaddish walked back into the lobby and just missed the elevator. A neighbor was getting home late. He rounded the first landing and the hallway lights went off, leaving him in the dark. He grabbed the banister, gave himself a pull, and took the last flights in blackness.

He fished out his keys. He reached for the keyhole and—accompanied by the sound of metal against metal—discovered that there was no hole to be found. Kaddish ran the backs of his fingers against the door, ran the key along it to catch the lock's edge. He fumbled for the button to the hallway light (the switch had long ceased to glow). Squinting now, half blinded, he looked back down the stairs and then up toward the roof. Kaddish was on the right floor—after twenty years, how could he have made a mistake? He looked over his shoulder at Cacho's apartment, exactly where it belonged. Kaddish then faced forward and squared off. With the key between thumb and forefinger, he let his hand drop to his side. Kaddish's home, Kaddish's apartment, and there it was, moved out of place. There was a lock, like a heart, in the center of the door.

[Five]

IT WAS IN THE SPANKING-WHITE private clinic of the illustrious Dr. Julio Mazursky that the good doctor, looking through the window as if reading from the sky, shared with Kaddish Poznan an intimate detail or two. Kaddish, standing—not invited to sit—wrote the names in ballpoint pen on the nubbly sanitary paper that covered the examination table. The table itself was upholstered in fine leather and padded, so that in jotting down the names twice Kaddish's pen poked through. There was a knock and Kaddish vaulted up onto the table. He planted himself at the foot end, sitting on his details, an open pen in his hand.

A nurse entered—having waited for a moment to pass but not for an answer—and there was Kaddish grasping the edge of the table, swinging his legs. The doctor looked out the window as if alone in the room, hand holding hand behind his back.

Kaddish thought this must be a popular position, that the doctor did his thinking this way, as the nurse approached him with a chart and wordlessly he took it, still not turning round. The doctor flipped a page. The nurse gave an order into an intercom mounted on the wall.

"Take your shirt off, please," the doctor said.

Kaddish stopped his legs.

"My shirt?"

"Your shirt, yes, please," the doctor said, with the confidence of a busy man.

Kaddish took his shirt off and threw it onto a chair.

Now it was the nurse's turn. Looking up at him, she said, "Your undershirt as well, please." Kaddish took off the undershirt and sat up straight. He had strong arms and shoulders. He had a gut, but it looked solid. The nurse gave it a glance and dismissed him.

"I'll be in four," she said. The doctor nodded to the window and the nurse left. Kaddish followed her out with his eyes, jumping from the table before the door had closed behind her.

With the particulars down, first pulling the left side, then the right, Kaddish worked the paper through the metal guide at the foot of the table. He gave it a yank, jamming all the paper to one side, and coming away with a jagged strip. He reached back and yanked off the rest, a tail of paper with the last of the names. "Fat fingers," Kaddish said.

The offices had a commanding view and the doctor lowered his gaze to the city below, Buenos Aires spread out before him like a puzzle. Something wasn't right. Dr. Mazursky hadn't noticed anything on his way to work that morning. He'd walked from his house to the open car door. There was a book in the backseat that he left there for his commute. And, as he did every day, he read it as he was driven to his office, sometimes sharing a smart passage with his driver. Dr. Mazursky hadn't been aware of anything beyond the time. He'd said, "What is taking so long?" and received the answer—"Detours, sir"—in reply. Looking down at the city he saw that the puzzle had shifted, traffic patterns switched. A great swath of empty city was visible where it should have been congested. There was too much military green and too many helicopters in the sky.

"The list," the doctor said, "would you please, Mr. Poznan, read it back to me."

Kaddish tried for the same tone the doctor had used, as if he were ticking off the names of a disease in all its forms. These are the names as Kaddish read them: "Pinkus Mazursky, Toothless Mazursky, Happy

Mazursky, and," from the second piece of paper, uncrumpling the scrap in his fist (a smile and cough, acknowledging), "Pinkus 'Toothless' Mazursky."

"Mazursky," the doctor said, as if there had been an error in pronunciation. There was no difference to be heard. "I apologize for the variations. I wasn't at my father's unveiling. His associates," and this with disdain, "his coterie arranged for the monument and its inscription. I've never myself set eyes on the stone."

The doctor finally turned. He was a plastic surgeon and Kaddish sensed that the doctor was seeing not a whole man but only the collection of faults of which Kaddish was constructed. Stopping when he caught Kaddish's eye, a sexy eye, he'd admit, but too close to the broad bone of that horrendous nose, the doctor approached. Coming closer, he said, "A figure? How much?"

He bent at the hips and brought his face near to Kaddish's ribs as if something suspect had crawled into his line of sight. There was a scar there, raised and long, a childhood accident. The doctor reached out with three fingers pressed together and his thumb tucked. It was a papal gesture. He applied a little pressure, moved Kaddish a step back into better light, and did it again. He straightened up for his pronouncement.

"That scar could be hidden."

"It is," Kaddish said, "when I'm wearing a shirt."

The doctor didn't miss the point. He had made Kaddish strip down. "For discretion," the doctor said, explaining.

"For discretion, of course. I should be thankful you didn't go for the pants."

"I still might," the doctor said, and Kaddish picked up the shadow of a smile.

"Even a first-day prostitute keeps her shirt on until some money has changed hands," Kaddish said. He resisted crossing his arms.

"You were going to quote me a figure."

Kaddish was, but it was essential, he believed, that it be done from the right position. It is always better to be embarrassing than embarrassed.

"If you're really interested in scars, there is something that I've been wondering about." Kaddish opted for the pants on his own. He undid his belt and dropped them to his knees when the doctor stopped him.

"We can schedule a proper appointment," the doctor said. "I'd be happy to see you in that context." His eyes displayed a warm bedside manner, but he was looking at Kaddish's nose.

"Sure," Kaddish said, buckling up and scanning the room. He'd had a number in mind in the waiting room, and another when he was led into this fancy consultation room with its feeling of polished surgical precision—not a bit of personality in it except for one heavy-looking mask up on the wall. An old framed print leaned against the wall below it, a woodsy scene with a man on a horse marked, in English, THE HUNT.

"Nice piece," Kaddish said, signaling the mask and not really caring. He was figuring his sum.

"I was in Asia fixing cleft palates." The doctor looked at the mask and to his picture on the floor. "After months of taking nipples off and sewing them back on, the palates are a salve. They fly you over to fix the poor kids, to put their heads back right. It's funny there. They only bring you boys." He paused to consider his own statement, as if someone else had brought it to his attention. "I stopped in Hong Kong on the way back and picked the mask up there."

"Looks expensive."

"It's from the New Year's festivities. They celebrate just now. In China the new year comes late." Again the doctor seemed friendly, and again he considered his own statement, rapt by his observations. "The Year of the Dragon and their first in forever without Chiang Kai-shek. I was lighting off firecrackers and thinking, *We should be so lucky. Isabelita should choke on a bone.*"

"Looks like you'll get your wish."

"It's no wish of mine. To dream of one government ending doesn't mean you'll want the one that comes in its place."

Kaddish pictured the before-and-after photographs from the album in the waiting room: mug shots of rejuvenated cheeks and chins, breasts and thighs. Taking it all into account, he doubled the figure in his head.

Kaddish moved to the middle of the table. He wrote the number in the center of the white paper, this time careful not to rip. It was another of Kaddish's rules: a verbal agreement, deals closed with handshakes, should always be made over figures written down. Dr. Mazursky circled to the other side, planted his hands against the paper, and, leaning in, read the number upside down and raised his head, eyes wide.

The doctor had a wronged look about him. Kaddish couldn't tell if he'd gone too far, so he halved the number, crossing it out and writing down the new figure. "Half off today," Kaddish said, backing up to his initial price.

"So much?" the doctor said.

"So much is much less than the first figure." And then he used the name he was being hired to save. "You'll agree, Dr. Mazursky?"

"It is hardly a few minutes' work."

"What you are paying for is the discretion that you so prize. I provide respect for the dead and confidentiality for the living." With some flamboyance, Kaddish tried out, "Dr. Mazursky, what I offer is a face-lift for the family name."

The doctor seemed to be considering. It was a considerable sum.

"With inflation," Kaddish said, "by the time I get downstairs, I'm already losing money."

The doctor stepped over to the counter. He lifted the top off a jar and fished out a cotton ball. "All right," he said, pressing the cotton to the mouth of a bottle of iodine. "Hold still," he said. Mazursky swabbed the iodine across the base of Kaddish's neck, carefully painting a cut that was not there. The doctor blew lightly on the tincture. He put a plaster over the spot, the red of the iodine reaching out from underneath on all sides, and called for the nurse.

"One more thing," the doctor said, taking a finger and smoothing the edge of the bandage down.

"Yes."

"About Toothless Mazursky. About that name in particular. My father, until the day he died, had, but for a single gold crown, a full set of teeth."

"I wouldn't doubt it."

"I am a cosmetic surgeon."

"A national service in Argentina."

"A ruckled mouth, my father would never have."

"A nickname is all," Kaddish said. "It's only a nickname."

"Quite," said the doctor.

Pulling on his undershirt, Kaddish poked his head through with a ready idea. "They were a tough bunch, the Society members. Maybe he left the other guys toothless, is what it was." Kaddish threw an uppercut and checked it mid-swing.

"Maybe so," the doctor said. He was not amused.

The nurse returned, this time without knocking. Kaddish started on the buttons of his shirt and the nurse headed straight for the table. In a practiced motion she pulled a length of paper as long as a man. The roll whistled as it unfurled, and then she zipped the paper across the metal teeth. Already in a ball—no joy on her face—she stuffed it into a garbage built into the counter. Kaddish watched his numbers disappear.

The nurse replaced the lid on the jar. There was a chart next to the jar that didn't have Kaddish's real name.

"Charge him for a biopsy and an office visit," the doctor said. Kaddish raised an eyebrow. He pressed at the bandage on his neck and then at Lillian's checkbook in his pocket. He didn't currently have his own.

The nurse looked from the counter to the examination table and back to the counter.

"The specimen, Doctor?"

"I'll label it myself."

The streetlights were on before dark, and Kaddish wondered if they came on earlier over here. He walked along the doctor's tree-lined street, on the fancy side of town, far from Once and his apartment and the rest of the Jews—Jews that came here to visit Dr. Mazursky because they heard the Gentiles visited him, and the Gentiles visited because they like a Jewish doctor on a high floor. A beggar sat in a doorway. In this neighborhood he looked twice as poor. Kaddish fished for change but had passed before he came up with something small. He walked on and spent the money on a *Clarín,* scanning the front page and shaking his head. Everything is coming apart around them and his newspaper runs a picture of an Uncle Sam up on stilts; the Yankees always happy to throw a party for themselves. The only thing Argentina will have to celebrate on its two hundredth anniversary is the miracle of turning back the clocks. The Stone Age would reach Buenos Aires before the future did, of this Kaddish was sure.

There was a breeze but it only blew heat. The street was quiet and then a Ford Falcon trolled past. The driver had his elbow out the window, like he was cruising for girls. There were no plates on the car and it kept moving slowly. Two men in back both turned their heads, giving Kaddish the once-over. He crossed the street in the wake of the car and flipped his paper to the sports.

In the United States they celebrate a bicentennial, and in China they ring in the Year of the Dragon. Kaddish kicked a bottle along the curb. Here all we get is the Year of the Falcon. A bird of prey. A Yankee car.

[Six]

AS FOUR MEN FROM THE NAVY threw a career army man from the window, he was thinking his last thoughts. A retired colonel, his uniform covered in the ribbons and medals of a military regime—all those decorations were upended along with him as the blood rushed to his head. A medal came loose and clanked against the street. A chest full of honors and what good did it do him? *I should have served in the air force,* he thought. *Then I would have wings.* With that, not even the time for a cynical upturn of the lips, he hit the Avenue of the Liberator; and along with the countless motions that make up a late night in Buenos Aires, that together are the heartbeat of any city in the world, Lillian Poznan turned her head on the pillow to have her last deep sleep before her fears turned real.

Lillian didn't feel the city was light one resident when she woke up. She didn't feel, as she often did in the kitchen with her bills, that the country was united in spinning out of control. Looking into the street, she didn't sense that there were right then a million more working stiffs in front of a million more windows, all in it together—all but the colonel, his window still open, a cat curled up on its ledge.

Lillian had slept well. She'd woken up rested to find that Kaddish still hadn't come home and, miracle of miracles, Pato had already left for school. She took her time getting ready. *El Golpe,* "The Sting," played on the radio, and she tried to remember what theater she saw the movie in. She stood in her stockings eating a pastry over the sink as she decided on the Beta—the Beta on Lavalle.

Lillian waited for the old cage elevator that ran up the center of their building like a spine, the staircase snaking around it. She waited with a hand on the gate, one knee locked and one knee bent, to compensate for the weight of her briefcase.

The door to Cacho's apartment opened. Her neighbor was still in his pajamas and had a worried look on his face. He scratched furiously at one of his eyebrows, and because of this Lillian noticed that the other one was chapped and red.

He was an early riser, a militant in his lifestyle. She'd never before seen Cacho in his bedclothes, never with a wrinkle in his shirt, even at the end of the day. She'd always felt he must keep an iron at the office hidden in his desk.

"Are you home from work today, Cacho?"

"Work today?" he said, and went back to scratching. "Work today," he repeated, standing up on his tiptoes to look behind Lillian and keeping an eye on the stairs. That's when the question turned entertaining, the best thing he'd heard in a while. Cacho gave a quick laugh. "Work today. Would you?"

"Obviously," Lillian said, and held up her briefcase, heavy with files.

"It's rhetorical," Cacho said, almost screaming. "The question is, would you go to work if you were me? Would you go out this morning if you were me?" Lillian had never seen Cacho like this, and, waiting for an answer to his rhetorical question, he switched to the other eyebrow and she saw that on the first there was blood. He had scratched himself bloody. "If you were in my position, would you even leave the house today?"

"I don't know," Lillian said. "What is your position?"

"What does it matter? You're already in it and still you go." With this he dropped his hand from his eyebrow, only to throw both arms up in frustration. He retreated into the apartment and slammed the door.

Lillian was so intrigued by this she didn't notice for another couple of minutes that the elevator was out again. She had slept well. She was happy and took the stairs.

It wasn't long before Lillian understood the position she and Cacho were in, the one Kaddish and Pato were in, the position they all were in, especially—but not really any more especially—that their leader Isabelita was in—or already out of—that morning. Lillian was walking down Avenida de Mayo toward the Pink House and the plaza in front of it, the route she took every day. Except there was a roadblock up ahead and beyond that a tank, a tank in the middle of the city. It was preposterous, and Lillian looked to her right and her left to see if there was anyone to share this with. She saw a man going the other way who would not make eye contact, and then in an empty parking lot a little way down she spotted a Dodge pickup. In it were eight soldiers in uniform, in helmets even, crouched down, covering the directions of the compass. Three were facing her from the back end where DODGE was stamped in large letters and a pickax mounted across the name. The muzzles of the boys' machine guns stuck out over the truck's rear. Lillian looked behind her for the war, for the onslaught, and then again at these young boys, the kind that came knocking on the door for Pato and then slunk off with him, record albums in a stack under their arms. These boys were neater, short-haired. And they were crouched down, guns at the ready.

A flatbed truck with a tank on its back crawled across the next avenue. Another one followed behind. These trucks, moving through the city at a speed fit only for funeral processions, lumbering along. Where is the surprise at this speed? Trouble does not break out anywhere in the world, Lillian thought. War is not unleashed. It is slowly, it is carefully, installed.

Lillian looked toward her neat little soldiers in their parking space. It's almost as if there should've been something to say. If they were not pointing guns—that is, if they were not in the military—she'd have said, *There are tanks up ahead.* But they probably knew that—could see them just as well as she did. Lillian turned around and went back to the last corner and took a different way to work.

It seemed they were having a coup.

It seemed they were having a coup, and for this Cacho stayed home to scratch out his eyes.

Frida was at her desk when Lillian walked in. She said, before anything, "Isabelita is trapped in the Pink House. It'll be over before it starts. A day at the most, Gustavo is saying. We're going back to a military government."

"You'd think they'd have come home," Lillian said. "Kaddish was gone and Pato off to university before I got up. Classes must be canceled. Where would the kids go?" Lillian shook her head. "When do I ever sleep late?"

"Adaptability," Gustavo said. He was out of his office and inserting himself into the conversation as if Lillian had been talking to him. It was Gustavo's way of being boss, of owning everything there. He stood between them and smoothed down his hair. "We have inbred ourselves into supreme adaptability, and now it's become a detriment. We'll get used to this government same as the last—and if it turns on us we won't even see it coming. We'll go down, thinking *All is well.*" Gustavo said this as if the three of them were observing it from Switzerland. He spoke with a certain glee.

Lillian nodded a thank-you and turned her back to him and said, very clearly to Frida alone, "A truckful of men point their guns at me, and still I go on my way."

Gustavo circled around and returned himself to the conversation.

"After the soldiers, who else should come to work more than you? We sell insurance. Today is what we are about. It's our big gamble. We pay out. Others pay in."

"And?" Frida said, dragging out the word.

"Life. Property. All the values shift. You'll see when things settle; much will have become precious, and many will have no worth at all."

Frida gave up. She asked for the advice that he'd dispense regardless. "So then what do we do? Sit here and wait?"

"We get down to business," Gustavo said. "Life and death you can't control now. It is only profit that can be arranged absolutely during a war."

"Who are we having a war with?" Frida said.

"That's the point. Figure out the sides and begin to earn."

With that, Gustavo went back into his office.

Lillian took Frida's hands.

"You'd think Pato—he's very sensitive. You'd think he'd have turned back from school."

A glass floated above the floor, held steady by five fingers pressed, from above, around the rim. The fingers were of a hand, the hand of an arm, and the arm hung disembodied behind the back of the couch.

Lillian dropped her keys on the little antique shelf. She dropped her purse, loudly, by the wall underneath. The glass held steady; the arm did not move. The television visible beyond the couch showed the Liberators Cup, River Plate vs. Portuguesa. The little men ran back and forth. Lillian couldn't see the ball through the smoke, a thin gray cloud in front of the black-and-white of the set.

Lillian approached, leaning over and kissing Kaddish on the head. He put his cigarette in the ashtray resting on his stomach and placed the glass on his chest.

"I'll know you're dead," she said, "if I ever come home and find that cloud missing or that glass knocked over on the floor."

"What's wrong with ritual?" Kaddish said. "It doesn't hurt for some things to stay the same."

"No," Lillian said. She agreed.

Kaddish sat up with his back against the arm of the couch, his legs stretched out. He moved the ashtray to the floor.

"Crazy day," he said.

"Very crazy." Lillian smiled and went to sit. Kaddish raised his legs and Lillian slipped in underneath, then patted them down. She closed her eyes and let herself relax. She listened for the music that was always on and always too loud, emanating from Pato's room. Lillian couldn't hear it, and that only meant headphones or a grinding needle when the boy passed out. Creatures of habit, her husband and her son. They shared a great love for the comfort of sameness.

"He asleep?" Lillian said.

"Out," Kaddish said.

With a tilt of her head, screwing up her face, she stared hard at her husband, trying to understand.

She stared hard at her husband and was already mad at herself. On Coup Day, on this day, how had she not raced straight for his room to check? Then there was Kaddish, this man who understood nothing, whom she could not for a few hours trust.

"Out?" Lillian said.

"With the hairy one. That kid that looks like an octopus—all head."

"Rafa," Lillian said. Then as an afterthought, distracted with worry, "It is time you learned your son's friends' names."

"He came by, Rafa did, and they went off to some bar."

Lillian pushed Kaddish's legs off her lap so that he sat up straight, so that she could stand up and face him.

"What bar do you think is open tonight? How could you let him leave?" She looked toward the door, as if Pato might come through it. And then she asked Kaddish, quite calmly, "Don't you have any sense of your own?"

"I told him. He doesn't listen."

"Then tie him up. Hold him down. If your son doesn't listen, why didn't I find you by the door sitting on his back?"

"Uncontrollable," Kaddish said. "By his father, uncontrollable. Rebellious Jewish boys only listen to their mothers. For fathers they have no use."

[Seven]

IN THE FIRST WEEKS after the coup, Lillian's office received the people who had what to insure and the money to do it. Business rose steadily, and the caliber of the clientele rose with it. Gustavo was the epitome of Argentine politeness as still-stunned citizens took out policies on themselves. They repeated questions, asked the obvious, and all touched upon the central point: *What happens if I die?*

"Covered," Gustavo would say. Then, after a *God forbid,* he'd offer a withered smile. When asked about the money, Gustavo spoke with a comforting detachment. "The insurer issues the payment," he would say. "You—that is, the surviving family—send us proof of death. We alert the company, and then. . . ."

And then Gustavo would make one hand motion or another, signifying ease and flow and continuity. He was not deceiving them. The process was to be that smooth—that is, for those with proof of death. Gustavo had heard whisperings of his own. That is why, in each instance, he made sure to state this point out loud. The customers noted it or they didn't.

It was Lillian writing up these policies, and Frida typing the forms, who dealt with the addresses where payments were to go. In the event of misfortune the beneficiaries were in Havana and Miami, Manhattan and Rome. Every foreign street name depressed Lillian more. It did not bode well. The men and women who'd fallen out of favor had already sent their families away.

Lillian watched Gustavo lead one of these people out of his office, a *diputado* she recognized from the TV. Without the lights and the pancake makeup he simply looked old. Gustavo walked close to this man with his arm raised as if he were about to hug him. But the arm never came down. It served as a guide so that, when his client bumped into it, he redirected himself as he shuffled to the door.

As delicate as Gustavo was when dealing with truncated prospects, he was equally deft when managing windfalls, the steady stream of acquisitions that were hard to explain. That is why, more and more, the upper crust turned to him as an agent.

There was also the matter of his parentage. With a change in government comes a change in fashion. Though he'd done little with it, somewhere—generations back—introduced into Gustavo's line was a very fine, very un-Perón last name.

Some sounds are unmistakable even if you've never heard them in real life before. With the first gunshot, Lillian knew she'd been waiting. She sat up in bed, not yet awake and absolutely sure. There was another shot and then a steady burst. Kaddish snored through it and Lillian let him. She got low out of bed and crawled to Pato's room, though there were no windows anywhere in the hall. Pato was under the covers and asleep and Lillian crawled over to his window. She peeked out through the space under the curtains, too afraid to pull them apart. There was no yelling or footsteps. She couldn't hear any cars. Then it would come, another tattoo of it, and Lillian tried to figure if it was people taking turns—a shootout—or if it was one man with one gun taking his time.

So many waves washed over their beautiful city. There'd be a wave of quiet before a wave of crime. They'd get a wave of kidnap and ransom, of political promise, then leftist terror followed by rightist death squads. With the new government, the clean streets, and a safe high-strung city, Lillian had been waiting for this. This was the wave of scores settled, and maybe of what Lillian feared most. Pato had said it after they'd found that boy murdered. What if this was the wave of innocents shot dead?

You cannot ever let your guard down in Buenos Aires. It's like standing in the ocean and facing the beach. It's up to you to know what's behind you. Always there's another wave coming, building in force and crashing down.

The shooting stopped. Lillian looked toward Pato's clock. It was barely after midnight. The whole incident couldn't have taken more than three minutes or four. And as agitated as she was (or maybe because of it), Lillian fell asleep there on the floor between her son's bed and the window. She awoke again after dawn. She got showered and dressed and went down to the bakery and to pick up the news. This time, she didn't know how, it was already in the paper that morning. Seven bodies of seven rebels were found dead on different streets. Lillian wondered how far sound could travel. None of them was discovered on their side of town.

Lillian often tried to imagine what her parents would say if they weren't already buried in respectable United Congregations plots. No great success, her life no better or worse than the one they'd struggled to give her. But together she and Kaddish had produced a wonderful son, tall and handsome and smart, and ten times more independent than she'd been. And even if Kaddish didn't stop as he went by, no son-in-law spent more time around his in-laws' graves. "Such beginnings," they'd said, when she started seeing Kaddish. "Such a past." They'd harped on this while Lillian pointed out in each and every argument that the past they abhorred wasn't his.

With all her years in insurance, Lillian had become a great believer in statistics. Anything could happen to anyone anywhere, but if you didn't want your car broken into, Lillian could tell you on which block not to park. That said, Lillian still made room for possibility. When she was young and Kaddish was courting her, it was his ambition that had won her over. Not only did he dream without limit but he got Lillian to believe as well. And from their first date onward it had always been a *we* from Kaddish. All those dreams realized included her at his side. When Lillian flipped through women's magazines, she couldn't stand the photos of the mousy society wife on the corner of a settee, ankles crossed, with a fat-and-happy husband smiling for the camera and looking like he was a meter closer to the lens. The cheerfulness of those ladies' interviews was what maddened her. How delightful the hard years were. Lillian believed every great success and wondrous achievement was based on bad judgment and recklessness, and more often than not on selfishness and the endangerment of more than one life. The successful ones were simply afforded better chances or had better luck. After spending as many years with Kaddish as she had apart, somewhere in herself Lillian still believed he could do it. What were the choices (what was her life) if she believed he could not?

In any new friendship, the question that accompanied the first trace of intimacy was always the same. They wanted to know why she'd married him. (Lillian, who'd sneaked off to find a rabbi who'd rejoice in their union and who didn't know the Poznan name.) She always answered with a question of her own: "What would you ask me if his dreams had come true?"

This is why, even with the head-splitting pressure she felt during the change of regime, it was at these times she loved him best.

"They don't order my services yet," Kaddish said, "but when they feel safe enough to whisper the names again, I'll be busy like never before. A government fifty times more Catholic than the last and a civilized class being built around it. To be part of it they'll pay me the same and fifty times more."

"I hope you're right," she said.

"When it feels quieter at night I'll finish with the doctor's job and then you'll see the kind of cash I bring home. The shame industry is about to bloom."

He was a man on the cusp and acted like it. Lillian had come home these last weeks to find that Kaddish had been to the vegetable man and the butcher. She'd step in the door to find Portuguese rolls laid out in a basket with a napkin underneath. She'd find Kaddish in the kitchen, his glass of vermouth covered in greasy fingerprints on the counter, bent over a skillet flipping croquettes. He'd even defrosted the freezer himself. Kaddish was a pleasure, full of compliments and kisses, and if he still watched the same amount of football, it was while sitting up and leaning into the television, chanting and full of good humor, not flat on the couch as if someone had aimed the set at a corpse.

Lillian felt guilty about enjoying her son in the same way. She was happy to see that Pato wasn't totally senseless. During this same period, he actually listened to his mother. He didn't stay out late, didn't talk too much on the telephone. He got up early each day like honest people do and went to fetch the pastries without fail. At night he made it home for dinner and didn't much bother his father, who hadn't much been bothering him. She didn't want to get hopeful, but outside the financial pressures that threatened to put them on the street, and the political uncertainty that kept them locked inside, it was the best in a while that their lives had been. With debts and threats and all their troubles rolled up together, she didn't miss the opportunity to see the good. There was a roof over their heads. There was food on the table and her family around it. Worse or better, now was good. And when she was feeling anxious, she'd only wonder if she'd overdone it with the door.

Pato was over at Rafa's apartment, where he and his friends mostly hung out. Rafa's mother had long ago decided she'd much rather accept the kids' lifestyle and keep them home. In terms of motherly rights, she knew she lost much in the trade. They smoked pot in her living room and made out on her couch. She couldn't get into her own bathroom or leave cash lying around. More than once she'd found some girl in her clothes, so that upon introduction the first thing she did was check what they wore.

It was not a big apartment, a touch smaller than Pato's and exponentially so if one accounted for her father and her daughter as well as her son. The master bedroom had gone to them, where she'd fit a bunk bed and two trundles, one on each side. The room slept Rafa and his younger sister Mufi, as well as her own father, their grandfather, who'd moved in sometime after her husband moved out. The kids didn't think he was a bad roommate for eighty-two. He slept through anything and didn't fight for space in the bureau that ran along the fourth wall.

Rafa was rummaging through the top drawer of that bureau, while Pato sat on one of the trundle beds. Their friend Flavia made pleasantries with Rafa's mother and they heard Flavia laugh from the other room.

Rafa was looking for a new screen for his pipe. The last one, now discarded, kept popping out and so he'd glued it in place. It was a solution whose ramifications Rafa hadn't considered until he'd taken a deep glue-laced hit and understood his mistake. Flavia and Pato had held him down until what they guessed was a sort of temporary psychosis had passed. Strolling through San Telmo the next morning, he'd bought them all matching rings as thanks. Rafa wasn't sure for a number of days if how he felt in his head when he thought was how he felt thinking before.

The three of them sat on the living room floor. Rafa's mother completed the circle, sitting on the couch. The pipe moved around. Rafa's mother ignored the pipe and accepted a glass of Coke with a nod.

Pato thought he should call home. He was going to and then he lay back and watched the bubbles of paint on their ceiling where the rain came through.

Pato forced himself to stand and was about to ask if he could use the phone (he was the only guest who still made overtures toward manners). Instead he said, "Where's your cigarette?"

"I don't have one," Rafa said. To prove it, he showed Pato two empty hands.

"You were smoking," Pato said. "You changed your socks and then you were smoking."

"Definitely maybe," Rafa said, considering. Rafa's mother gave him a little kick and he got up off the floor. The boys went back and searched the room and then Rafa remembered the screen. He pulled open his top drawer, and a little cloud escaped. "Shit," he said, fishing out the lit cigarette and making sure his socks weren't on fire. He put the cigarette in his mouth and they went back outside.

"You'll burn the house down," his mother said. "You make yourself retarded from smoking drugs. What kind of person forgets a cigarette in the drawer?"

"It wasn't in the drawer," Rafa said. "It was in the ashtray. Ask Pato."

She turned to Pato and started laughing. She reached up and pinched his cheek.

"If only my own son couldn't lie."

Lately their stories had turned odder and more sinister. When they switched fully to politics and their conspiracy theories, Rafa's mother would get up and leave the room. She hated when they stopped talking in front of her and always tried to excuse herself before they did. Rafa's mother listened to this last story from the edge of the hallway, ready to move on.

"They switched out my sociology professor," Flavia said. She was lying on the floor with her head propped against the base of the couch. She stared up at Rafa's mother while she spoke, half looking for help and half holding her responsible, *all adults the same.* Rafa's mother held her ground. "We were waiting around in lecture hall and he just doesn't show. Right after the first kid stands up everyone else grabs for their bags, and that's when this moth-eaten man comes in. He's maybe two hundred years old. He says he's the new professor while he's still shuffling toward the blackboard. Then he starts reading his lecture word for word off a stack of yellow cards."

"You sat quiet?" Rafa said.

"I didn't talk when I *liked* the professor. It was Matalón—he screamed it out. 'Where's Professor Gómez?' he yells. 'Where's Dr. Gómez?'"

Pato stared wide-eyed, as if he was watching this on TV.

"So what happens?" Rafa said.

"Nothing. The old guy doesn't stop reading. And Matalón gives up, and then this other girl screams it out. And then another couple of kids chime in. And finally the geezer—he's nearly blind, the cards are pressed up against his face—he puts them down, and looks around as if he's surprised to find us sitting there. He says, 'I'm the teacher in this class.' We all just shut up then. It was clear. The guy is our teacher now."

Lillian was at the table in the kitchen sitting over a folder, an adding machine on one side, a cup of tea on the other. Kaddish came in and kissed Lillian on the top of her head.

"You brought home work with you?"

"When do I not anymore?" Lillian said. She was wearing half-glasses on a beaded chain. She put them on when her eyes felt tired. Lillian looked too young for them, and they complemented her in the contrast. Kaddish rubbed at her shoulders and Lillian took the glasses off and let them dangle.

There was a split lemon Kaddish had left on the counter. He fixed himself a fresh drink and stirred it with a finger.

"Where's Pato?" he said.

"Out with Rafa, I guess."

Kaddish raised an eyebrow. He disapproved. "That head is too big," he said. "Too big to be of any use to anyone."

"He's a bad influence, it's true. But no worse on Pato than Pato is on him." They both smiled at that.

"It's not so easy to keep the boy in the house," Kaddish said. "You didn't do so well yourself."

"He was gone when I got here."

Kaddish took a sip of his drink and then held it up to the light, looking through it.

"I'm going to take him out when he gets back."

"Leave him alone, Kaddish. He hates the work. It helps no one to drag him along."

"What helps no one is a university education. That's what's a waste."

"It's an indefensible position. You know it's not so."

Kaddish put his glass on Lillian's folder and sat down across from her. "The university is the worst place to be right now. You think I don't get it, but I do. The men who run this country are more like me than like Pato."

Lillian laughed out loud.

"Seriously," Kaddish said. "Angry intellectual types make them nervous. I know it, because I feel the same way. If they're as afraid of the boy as I am."

"You do a fine job of torturing him for someone who's scared."

"When a government is scared, do you think it's any wiser? I tell you, they're not messing around this time. Order is what they're after, and order is being restored. They've got everyone working double shifts, the goon squads and the garbagemen both."

"And that's the night you want to sneak off into with your son? It makes no sense. You contradict yourself all the way through."

Kaddish adjusted his legs at the table. His knee passed Lillian's, and she moved her feet so he could extend his leg between hers.

"It's safe for us," Kaddish said. "Safe for people who mind their own business and dangerous for the ones who threaten them."

"Like university students," Lillian said, taking Kaddish seriously, thinking it through.

"Yes," Kaddish said. "Politicals and revolutionaries and hippies and university students." He reached across the adding machine and pressed at the keys. He liked the clicking of the paper roll.

"What about bogeymen who roam the graveyards in darkness?"

"Not even on their radar," Kaddish said. "The only danger from that cemetery is to those who don't protect their names." Kaddish could see that he was losing Lillian's attention, problems appearing in her head. "I want to give him something, Lillian. The world flips: Good people with everything, comfortable people in a flash out on the streets. To survive one must have a skill. A bunch of facts won't protect Pato, not if he reads every book in the world."

Lillian didn't need to hear this from Kaddish. She knew better than him what a person could lose. Every permutation of bad fortune made it across her desk. She was also the one whose parents were both struck down by illness within the same month—her parents gone, and she'd never gotten to reconcile. Not once had they seen Kaddish with her as her husband. She couldn't match him for sad family history. This didn't mean she was oblivious to the hardships in the world.

"I'm taking him with me tonight," Kaddish said.

Lillian stretched out her fingers and stared at her hands.

"That Rafa is too fast," she said. She put her hands on the table, her fingers spread wide. She raised her eyes to Kaddish. "You should take it more seriously, who your son hangs out with. It is no good these days to mix with the wrong crowd."

"You want me to tell him, his father with a whorehouse education? This is what strikes fear into a college boy? He didn't listen to me when he was six and thought I was the greatest thing in the world."

"He didn't think it at six." Lillian replaced her glasses and straightened up her papers. Kaddish lifted his drink. "If you can drag him to that cemetery, you can convince him of this. Anyway, he is your son. Still you should try."

Kaddish bit an ice cube in half.

"Trying is the one thing I'm good at. When have I ever stopped trying?"

[Eight]

THE DOCTOR'S INFORMATION was as good as his name. The stone read PINKUS "TOOTHLESS" MAZURSKY in Spanish and had an epitaph in Yiddish underneath: *Hang a scarlet cord from the gates of Heaven, as Rahab did from her wall.*

Pato dropped the tool bag and it hit with a clatter. Kaddish asked for nothing. He got down on his knees. He pulled a chisel with a crenellated end and then switched it for another.

"A toothless chisel for a toothless job," he said. And, like a *shochet,* Kaddish ran his thumbnail along the cutting edge, searching for nicks. "An inscription half again as old as you are, Pato. Not a very long life for such a thing."

When there was one good swing left to the job, Kaddish turned to his son and offered him the tools.

"I won't do it," Pato said.

"I'm pretty sure you will. You're an easy mark, Pato. Always you say no, and always you come along."

"Fuck you."

"That you always say too. I'm your father, and I don't even feel it anymore. Come, this is a big money job. Finish the name and this time I'll give you real cash, a real cut." Kaddish held out the hammer. "By the looks of you, it'll be painless—stoned out of your gourd." When Pato wouldn't take it, Kaddish placed the tools at his feet.

"It's like you don't hear me at all," Pato said. "I won't live your life, and I don't understand why you're living theirs."

"Whose?" Kaddish said. He had no idea.

"The Jews," Pato said. "They reject you since birth and you still play the role they gave you. A son of a whore for your own self is your concern, why would you want to be that for somebody else? Why not be done with them completely? Get out of this business and out of the neighborhood and start a new life."

"You'll see in time. There's no running away," Kaddish said. "If you do, when you're old it's much worse. You'll forget your name. You'll forget what you're saying as the words come out of your mouth. Then, without anything left, you'll remember who you are and you'll find yourself afraid and alone among strangers. Better to struggle at home."

Pato pointed up through the fence in the direction from which the sun would rise. It was almost dawn. "Why not finish before we get arrested?" he said.

Kaddish switched off the flashlight and dropped it in the bag. "Swing or we stay. We can go off to jail together for all I care." He stood face-to-face with his son. "Take the swing and we get home safe and tomorrow you'll have money to spend."

"You can't make me," Pato said.

Except Kaddish thought that he could.

He snatched his son's wrists and, with embarrassing ease, turned the boy around and pushed Pato down beneath him. He got in position before Pato had the sense to struggle.

Kaddish squeezed Pato's narrow rib cage between his legs and put his whole weight on Pato's back. He slipped his strong hands off Pato's wrists and up around his son's hands and, clamping down with those thick fingers, Kaddish forced Pato to pick up the chisel in one and the hammer in the other.

With all his strength, Kaddish forced Pato to move the tools in place, and with all Pato's strength, Pato kept his father from wielding them.

"You're insane," Pato said.

"Swing and it will be over."

Pato pushed one way and Kaddish pushed the other and neither one moved. "It's a deadlock," Pato said. "Let's both let go on the count of three."

"Then it wouldn't be a deadlock anymore. It would be that you'd won. How about on three you finish chipping away at the name?"

"I know why you're doing this," Pato said. "I'm not going to be like you. I won't live your life."

"Swing," Kaddish said. "Swing and it's over, and you can play psychologist the whole way home." He pressed his chin against Pato's skull. "It's for your own good," is what Kaddish said.

They'd maximized their respective positions and both understood they'd arrived at the point of action. Their muscles were so long tensed there was almost a hum.

In the instant when Kaddish yanked the hammer hand back with all his might, Pato knew he'd been overpowered. His smart son, his university son, already had a strategy prepared. Stronger arm to stronger arm, he'd never defeat his father. But two hands against his father's weaker, this he could win. When that yank came, Pato let his arm go without resistance. He let it go so limp that when the hammer reached its apex and he gave his hand a yank straight down, Pato managed to pull it free. While his father bobbled the hammer in that crucial moment, Pato moved his right hand over his father's left, trying to free his other arm and run. Pato felt a boy's nervousness. He nearly giggled as he peeled his father's fingers back.

Pato's left hand was coming loose when the hammer met chisel. It hit with so much force that the blade sunk into the stone, and the chisel rattled like a saw. A divot of marble came flying off. Pato's body went limp, as did his father's behind him. Both of them lay there in the dirt, side by side, Kaddish panting in Pato's ear.

Kaddish got to his knees, trying to prove he had some fight left. "Come," he said. "Let's hurry, it really is getting too light."

Pato didn't respond. He remained curled up as Kaddish retrieved his hammer and surveyed the mess he'd made out of the stone. Kaddish worked the chisel back and forth. That's when he felt the stickiness of the blade.

Pato didn't resist when Kaddish turned him over. He let his father take hold of his hands, still cupped together. He let Kaddish open his left, which was tightly curled around his right, and the right hand was clamped shut on itself. With some effort Kaddish forced that slippery hand open. In the wash of blood that ran out, Kaddish glimpsed the white of bone.

On a long flat chip of marble already pressed down into the ground Kaddish found what he was hunting for. Pato's perfect fingertip rested on that sliver of rock. Kaddish snatched it up. He held it tight in his palm, as if it were the only proof of what he'd done.

Kaddish pulled at the weight of Pato with one hand. With the other, the tool bag heavy around his wrist, he held what he'd found. "We'll go to the hospital," he said. "I'll get you put right."

Pato cradled his wounded fist and the two moved slowly along. As horrified as Kaddish already was, he was further distressed by Pato's expression. It was the look of a son who saw true fear on the face of his father, a fear that unmasked something beyond fatherly concern. Pato knew Kaddish was already worried over what Lillian would say.

"I won't tell," Pato said.

"No," Kaddish said.

"An accident," Pato said. Then they reached the wall and Kaddish helped Pato over.

On the way to the hospital, Kaddish drove the car with his hand shut tight. As tightly, he was sure, as Pato clutched the one where the hot prize he held was supposed to go.

"Jesus," Kaddish said. "Jesus." How much of his life did he have to spend asking himself, *What have I done?*

Pato spread himself out across a row of chairs in the waiting area of the emergency room. Kaddish paced the length of it, a cigarette in his endlessly moving hand.

An elegant lady sat across from Pato in the opposite row of seats, a Recoleta-type lady who kept smiling at his son. A nurse had given Pato a towel, which he'd wrapped around his fist. He sometimes stared back at the lady and sometimes pressed his face into the towel, so that there were now patches of blood on his cheeks.

The woman's foot was raised up across a young man's lap. Kaddish wasn't sure if it was her very young boyfriend or very old son. It was obvious why she was there; a shard of wood, a giant splinter, was sticking through her foot. The woman's wound, like the woman, was elegant. Nothing out of place, just the shard—like an arrowhead—poking through.

When the doctor finally arrived he attended to the woman first. He tucked his stethoscope into the pocket of his coat and leaned in to study the woman's foot where it rested in her companion's lap. Straightening, the doctor replaced the stethoscope, draping it around his neck.

"That won't pull out," he said. "A good tug, and instead of one you'll have a hundred splinters moving through that foot. I think we'll split the bottom." He made a cutting motion across his hand to demonstrate. "It'll come out cleaner if we cut across the sole and lift the splinter clear."

A wheelchair arrived for the woman. She smiled at Pato, and Kaddish saw the strain in Pato's smile back. "Never go barefoot walking on a dock," she said. "Even shod, one should never run by water." Advice from the stranger and then the orderly rolled her away. Kaddish liked what she'd said. Advice so limited in scope that it never needed challenging. She'd addressed his son in the way Kaddish dreamed of doing. Never had he managed a bit of wisdom so sound.

The doctor approached Pato. Kaddish stood there with his closed fist extended, ready to present the segment of his son.

The doctor pulled off the towel. There was a doctorly, "I see," and then he mumbled something into Pato's hand as if he were talking to the wound. The doctor wrapped it tight again. "Fingers and toes today. You wouldn't think they come like that, in groups, but they do. One day it's all stomachs, and the next everyone's getting poked in the eye." He helped Pato up and, seeing that he was steady, let him go.

Here Kaddish came to the rescue. He unfurled his fist, and there it was in his blood-red palm, a small fingertip set in the middle. It wasn't horrible like in the cemetery. It was more like Pato was there sprouting from him, as if the world had never changed and the ancient rules still held. As if this was how sons were born to fathers, from ribs and hands, from parts taken and shared.

"What's this?" the doctor said, sloping his shoulders and looking into Kaddish's hand. Curious, he lifted out the fingertip, peered at it this way and that. "No good to me," the doctor said. He then tossed it unceremoniously into the ashtray, a slice of Pato stuck in the sand. "I'll take him back and sew him up. It shouldn't be more than a few minutes." The doctor led Pato away, holding the boy's good hand.

Pato was gone for a lot longer than a few minutes so that Kaddish began to worry about complications. He was caught off guard when Lillian walked through the sliding doors.

"How?" Kaddish said.

"Motherly intuition."

It had been a tough night and a tough morning and Kaddish, frazzled as he was, took this to be true. Lillian recognized his confusion.

"Pato had the sense to have a nurse call." She sat down beside Kaddish. "Where is he?"

Kaddish didn't answer. He stared at the handful of money that Lillian dropped into her purse.

"I raced over in a taxi," she said.

Kaddish nodded. He was sick with worry about Pato and sick with guilt over what he'd done. With Lillian next to him, he thought he might pass out from the pressure of that ashtray. God help him if Lillian turned to look in the sand. He wondered what they'd told her on the phone.

"He'll be done soon," Kaddish said.

Pato came out of the emergency room with a modest bandage on his ring finger. The bloodstains on his shirt had turned brown and he was a shade too pale.

Lillian ran up to him and took hold of his face.

"How many stitches?" she said.

"A bunch," he said, very calmly. "I lost half the tip and part of the nail."

"Lost?" Lillian said. "Your fingertip?" She turned to Kaddish and looked as if she might yell but simply shook her head once. Everyone was on best behavior. Lillian for her son. Pato for his mother. And Kaddish guessed he'd be on best behavior for his own miserable self.

"Will it be fine?" Lillian said. "Will it be perfect?"

"What's perfect?" was Pato's answer. "They said wait and see. Maybe a bit stubbier but the same, more or less." After considering and with a bitter laugh, Pato added, "I guess that would be less."

"My fault," Kaddish said. "I'm sorry," he said. Lillian was wiping at everything while Kaddish drove. The front seat covered in blood.

Pato was laid out in back, his head touching the door. He watched the tops of the telephone poles, measuring the car's slow progress along the telephone wires and the tops of buildings floating against the sky. He didn't say a thing.

"You feel strong enough to drop me at work?" Lillian said. Kaddish, who was happy to be addressed, nearly answered.

"Sure," Pato said. "Absolutely."

Kaddish's family ignored him but he was the one steering them along the lush avenues of Buenos Aires and was in this way involved. He loved these avenues, the very widest in the world. Kaddish believed in their greatness as a real and palpable truth. A city built around such avenues always held promise. What couldn't such streets manage to carry; what wouldn't be raised up in estimation by lining their sides?

The traffic slowed and Pato came forward from where he lay, resting his chin on the front seat. There was a roadblock nestled in a crook of the avenue. Three jeeps were parked on each side of the road, closing off the lanes. Columns of flares had been lit. Patches of lava sputtered on the pavement. Because of gawking, because of the way people are, the traffic continued beyond the roadblocks as well.

Kaddish pressed in the car's lighter. He'd already gotten a cigarette into his mouth.

Lillian fought off panic. It was an unlucky morning already. She looked around that front seat and prayed that no one would notice what was left of the blood. She stared out Kaddish's window and saw a man on the other side of the road being beaten with the butt end of a gun. Two hits and he disappeared down between the cars. The soldiers circled around him.

This was not Lillian's first military government. It was not the first roadblock in her life. This one Lillian could tell was a danger, and not only because of the beating. The roadblock soldier has its own personality, and each pack of soldiers, Lillian believed, could be read by its leader. From the last fifteen meters it was already clear. She could tell by the look of the young officer, spread out on the hood of his jeep, his shirt open, and catching the sun on his chest. It was a position that no one with a real enemy would hold, a lazy bullying stance. There was a jumpiness to the soldiers in motion that gave Lillian a very bad feeling about the one they approached.

"War," Lillian said. This was addressed to Kaddish, and he nodded and picked a fleck of tobacco off the tip of his tongue.

It was a war they were in. And this, Lillian felt, was its form of combat. The endless battles of Argentina. And how many of them did they fight against themselves? This is what set loose the panic in her, a reverse progression she'd been caught up in before. First the government declares victory, next comes the fighting, and then—as an afterthought—an enemy is picked up along the way. If a country wants to go on the offensive, always there are takers. Always there is an enemy who will step up to be had.

"ID," Kaddish said, holding the wheel from the top so that both arms were in view. He'd heard of a man shot for reaching down to scratch his leg. Lillian opened her purse; Kaddish quickly pulled his wallet and tossed it up on the dash. Lillian held their two ID's together.

"Pato," Kaddish said.

And Pato said, "At home."

"What?" Kaddish said.

"I didn't bring my wallet to go vandalizing with you."

"Not an excuse," Kaddish said. "You know the rules of this city. You know there's no fucking excuse."

Lillian fought to keep a tranquil expression on her face.

Kaddish raised his voice. "What do we do now?"

Lillian surrendered to a fear that springs from helplessness. She'd felt it from the first glimpse of those jeeps. In Kaddish it welled up with Pato's irresponsibility and turned right into anger, into a rage that overtakes fathers who only want to protect their sons.

Kaddish looked as if he might tear the wheel from the car. She did not pity him. She had married him and his thick neck for the strength they promised, for exactly the things he hadn't delivered. Let him explode if he was going to. Let him suffer over this roadblock and over the bandage on their child.

She looked out the side window. She watched the people in the next car as they attempted to look innocent. Even with Kaddish yelling, she wasn't sure how much better a job their neighbors were doing.

"You're an idiot," Kaddish said. "The stupidest college boy there is. Do you want them to ask about the tools in the trunk? Do you want them asking where we've been?" Kaddish flicked his cigarette out the window. "Tell me," he said. "Do you want to be dead?"

Pato said nothing. Lillian wanted to turn and look at her son; she wanted to silence her husband. Lillian kept her gaze steady, staring out the window. She could not see what Kaddish did. She didn't note Pato's lip shaking as it had when he was a child, the tears pooling in his eyes. It was scary for Pato too. It was his ID that was missing. And, fuck him, his finger was missing too. But Kaddish wouldn't stop.

"Say it once and I'll know. Make it clear if that's what you want. Tell me," Kaddish said. "Are you trying to get dead?"

He went on with a forced calm added to his voice, guarding against anything a soldier might hear through windows rolled down. He cursed his son with all the love that he had.

Lillian knew Pato was afraid of his father, and afraid of the soldiers, and even with the windows down their small car was filled with dread. Lillian watched as the trying-to-look-innocent people beside them were simply waved on. She didn't stop Kaddish's berating, and neither did she shush her son's crying. She did not coo to Pato, who started to sob deeply with sounds that took her back even farther than his boyhood to the long nights of colic when Pato was only a slip of a thing.

Kaddish drove between the jeeps, keeping the car in first. When the jumpy soldier Lillian had been eyeing stepped in front of the bumper, Kaddish slammed the brakes and the car stalled. The soldier, who had not signaled, just raised his gun and aimed it at Kaddish, while another soldier shielded his eyes with a hand and brought his face up to Lillian's door as if it were night and the windows were closed. He circled around, said, "Trunk," and Kaddish popped it. They did not hear the clank of tools, the only thing in there. Then he came back and asked for the ID's.

Kaddish handed him two, which he checked.

Then he said, "Where's the boy's?"

"Forgot it," Kaddish said.

The soldier, again with that face close, studied Pato—bawling, shaking and runny-nosed, and way too big to be in such a state, even with the bandaged hand.

"Why is he crying like that?"

"Forgot his ID," Kaddish said. "And his finger. A delicate flower, my son. We have come from the hospital just now."

The soldier considered and, looking back to Kaddish's ID, said, "What kind of name is Poznan?"

"Polish," Kaddish said. "It's the name of a town."

"You don't look like a Pole."

"Not my father's name," he said.

The soldier seemed satisfied with that. He straightened up, motioned with his chin to the soldier with the raised gun. The soldier lowered the barrel and moved aside, and for no reason he spit on the hood of their car.

Lillian shifted in her seat so she could stare at her son.

She found him watching his father, staring at the back of Kaddish's head. She could see in the way Pato looked at him that he'd rather have been shot right there on the road than cry his way to safety. He was embarrassed and he was angry and she wondered, too, if he might be in shock. Pato blamed his father for it all. Considering why they were in the car right then, maybe there was a trace of that feeling in Lillian too. Maybe that's where Pato found a vote of support for vengeance and that's why Lillian didn't stop him, why she let her son unleash a tirade more serious than the ones he'd long trained on his father. Pato went at him as soon as the car made a little headway in the traffic. "You're lazy. You're a failure. You've kept us down. You embarrass us. You cut off my finger. You ruined my life." In the grand Jewish tradition of the *dayeinu,* it was a list of his father's deficiencies, each one building on the last. And central to the form is the notion that each accusation, if that had been Kaddish's only shortcoming, still it would have been enough.

Lillian hadn't gotten involved at the start and chose to stay out of it now. She took another glance, though, and saw Pato looking her way while he laid into Kaddish. Pato was testing her as well, feeling out his mother to see if she'd allow such an unbridled assault. He wanted to see if she'd let him go at his father with all that he had.

It was between them, is how she saw it. Though it wasn't just. It was between the three of them, between a family—the same one the soldier had studied over the end of his gun.

Unwise in the ways of the world, Pato didn't yet know his own strength. The only thing he was expert in was his father's weakness.

Kaddish told the boy to stop. He yelled at him to stop. Pato continued long enough for Kaddish to give up his yelling and go silent, and then—Lillian tried to deny it—Kaddish drove on, weeping even more loudly and woundedly than Pato had. Kaddish cried and drove and wiped his eyes on a sleeve. Lillian understood that it had gone too far and decided to bring it to a halt.

She was really about to when Kaddish pulled the handbrake, stopping their lane completely, and, engine running, got out. "Too much," he said, through tears. He then wove on foot across that wide and beautiful avenue he'd been admiring. He maneuvered the lanes, slapping at the hoods of cars, directing himself out.

She and Pato sat dumbfounded, thinking Kaddish would turn back. Kaddish's keys were in the ignition, his ID still on the dash. When he didn't, Lillian got out of the car and walked around to Kaddish's side. She sat down in the driver's seat and pulled Kaddish's door closed.

"Should I get in front?" Pato said.

"No," Lillian said. He shouldn't get in front. He should stay right where he was in the back. Right where children belong.

[Nine]

"DO YOU DROWN IN YOUR DREAMS?" Dr. Mazursky said. "Do you die in your sleep?"

Kaddish did. The nightmares were vivid and he roused Lillian with his starts. Still only half-conscious in her waking, he never needed say more to her than "Bad dream." With that, Lillian would sleep.

"Hands round the throat," Mazursky said, pantomiming. "Do you wake up struggling to pull them free?"

They took their dinners together in relative peace: Lillian and Pato and Kaddish, all casting blame. The stitches were out and Kaddish's heart broke every time he saw that raw pink fingertip, covered in tight skin. It really wasn't much shorter than the rest, and barely noticeable. If one was looking for it, if the boy held his fingers to his lips, one might see. Kaddish couldn't keep his eyes off it. When Pato caught him staring, he'd always ask about his share.

"Where's my cut of the money?" he'd say. "When do I get my split?"

"It's on its way," Kaddish said, never giving him a day or telling him an amount. During one dinner, holding up a bowl of peas for his son, Kaddish said, "I have a meeting with the doctor on Friday." When the doctor pushed the meeting off until after the weekend, Kaddish told Pato he'd canceled it himself. "I tell you, this house will soon be over-flowing with cash."

Kaddish had come to collect. He'd found the doctor at his clinic, som-ber and lacking good cheer. The nurse who'd barged in the last time led Kaddish to the same examination room as before. He didn't sit up on the table when left to himself; he stood in front of the mask brought back from the doctor's travels and wondered what all the patients wait-ing for new faces thought of such a thing—and if the doctor had thought about it himself.

When the doctor arrived, the two of them took the same positions as when they'd closed the deal. They stood at the foot of the table and the doctor stared at Kaddish's nose.

He brought down the steel bowl of an adjustable light and took Kad-dish's chin in his hand. There was no surprise, just, again, his slow doc-torly reaching. He turned Kaddish's chin this way and that in the light.

Kaddish couldn't figure what it was in the doctor's reach—the confi-dence or boundarylessness, the entitlement to touch—but it made him ashamed of the way he'd snatched at his son. Kaddish took the man's hand from off his chin and did not immediately free it, but with steady grip (and still steady pulse) lowered it for the doctor to the doctor's side. He did not like that the doctor knew how he dreamed.

"It's just," the doctor said, "your fee. I don't keep such sums in my office. It's a lot of cash to have around." He smiled. "You must under-stand?"

"Not very well," Kaddish said. "You'd think exactly such a sum might be here waiting when you knew I was coming to get it."

"Next Tuesday night. Come to my house. That's where my safe is, and your money."

"It sounds like a very complicated combination if it takes a week to open it."

"Not a week to open. But a week to find the right amount inside."

. . .

The doctor's private study was all heat. Wood and heat and low to the ground. Hatchet-marked beams pressed down from the ceiling, bucket chairs with leather buttons kept guests close to the floor. The fireplace was empty. Three birch logs, peeling back on themselves, sat out next to the andirons.

Kaddish had waited patiently until Tuesday and come out to the doctor's fancy house in his fancy neighborhood expecting to be paid. He'd imagined it all week and didn't think the doctor would really open a safe in front of him, cupping a hand around the dial. What he'd imagined was a desk just like this one, at least the formality of it. And he'd also imagined a drink (that hadn't been offered), the fake camaraderie of it, and then an envelope fat with cash, not handed to him but slid slowly his way.

The doctor was already harping on the same questions from his office the week before. Was there congestion; was there choking: "Do you feel as if your heart forgets to beat?"

Kaddish was seated lower than the doctor and looking up at him across a deep wooden desk, looking beyond at the oil painting behind him on the wall, he saw them: four horses flying across a field with jockeys on their backs.

He still wouldn't tell the doctor about his sleeping, but those horses on the wall were enough to get his heart to skip a beat now. In the next thump, with the tock and retick of it, an adjustment in Kaddish's rhythms was made. Kaddish felt awake. The droopy-eyed warmth of the room no longer affected him. And, more important than awake, he was aware. He'd been down and out too many times not to see where this was headed.

Kaddish recalled the picture from the other office, the frame leaning against the wall. A horse with a hunter saddled on its back. He knew he wasn't getting paid today. The doctor wouldn't be pulling open any drawers; no envelope fat with cash would be pushed his way. A gambler. It hadn't crossed Kaddish's mind. And Kaddish knew why. He'd been too impressed by the name he was being paid to protect.

The doctor asked finally, "Do you snore?"

"Do I snore?" Kaddish said, his patience worn down.

"Yes, when you sleep."

"To wake the devil," Kaddish said.

"I think, from the size, from the width of that bone—your nose does not break, does it, when hit in the face?"

"This is not about the width of my unbreakable nose—though it's true, I'm quite proud, it withstands. It's about money for a job well done."

"A job well done indeed. And that's what I want to talk about. This *is* about your nose actually. This meeting is about that big fin of a kosher nose."

Kaddish was less offended than confused, trying to figure out how, when he was trying to puff himself up, he was losing so much ground. Kaddish leaned farther forward as the doctor melted back into his chair, unimpressed. Kaddish did his best. "This meeting is not about anything but getting paid."

"There is no money," the doctor said, matter-of-fact. "I promised you a fortune to erase my father's name because that's what the service was worth to me. Now I don't have a cent to give you for your fine work."

"How can you not have any money? You're a goddamn legend of a plastic surgeon in the land of limitless plastic surgery." Kaddish's voice was all desperation. "There isn't an adult left in this country with an original part. I passed a dog on the street today that had its ears clipped."

"They do that with certain breeds. Tails as well. The tails are docked."

Kaddish raised an eyebrow. He took hold of the edge of the desk.

"I thought I was protecting your good standing. Where are all the millions? Sell something from that clinic of yours. Take another picture off the wall."

"You were hired to protect the name, exactly that. And why do you think an assault on my very good name is feared?" He gave Kaddish a moment to answer. "Because there's nothing behind it," the doctor said. "I've lost it all. If I was at my best, I wouldn't need help from you."

"Horses," Kaddish said.

"Among other things," the doctor said. "A special love for the horses. But a fine résumé of other interests." The doctor shrugged. "You're not the only one with a taste for high risk and bad business. Lately it's been football, if you want to know where your money went. There was no intent to defraud. You were going to fix me from the outside and our national team was going to fix from within."

"But I did my part," Kaddish said.

"That's not in dispute. It's the national team that didn't do theirs. I had a fairly gargantuan double-or-nothing in place for Poland. And the upside for me was the chance to owe nothing."

"But they won," Kaddish said. "What more were they supposed to do?"

"Lose," the doctor said. "They could have managed that. It was an away game on the day of a coup. What kind of national team, playing in a foreign city, when there is chaos at home and their loved ones far way, with that on their shoulders and evenly matched, who pulls it together to win on such a night? What kind of disconnect does it call for?"

"The blue-and-white sort, it seems. The magic of *la Selección*."

"There's something wrong in this country," the doctor said. "Something in us has gone dead for that to be possible."

"You could have told me the same last week."

"Every debt can be doubled. I made a wager on Atlanta. I thought, Who better than an Argentine team with some Jewish blood?"

"So when do I get paid?"

The doctor straightened himself up and leaned across the table, his face very close to Kaddish's, who was already leaning in. "Tell me this. Look objectively. Am I a handsome man, Mr. Poznan?"

"No," Kaddish said. "You are an unattractive man."

"Good, good. This is my point. I spend my days changing people's appearances but no one asks why I haven't changed my own. It's more than the shoemaker going barefoot. It's because only failure comes out of it. The work that I do is futile. I'm a failure before I start."

"Instead of paying me I'm getting a lesson that will send me out of here more satisfied than if I had been paid."

"I will send you out feeling more than satisfied and more than paid. I promise."

"More than paid?"

"Feeling it," the doctor said.

"Do you know what this job cost me?" Kaddish said. He raised his voice. "Do you know what I already can't get back? An injury. My son lost a finger doing this."

The doctor thought for a second, then said, rather brightly, "Do you want me to put a toe there? Fingers can be traded. It works very well with the thumbs."

"It was only the tip," Kaddish said. And, holding his hand up in the doctor's face, he wiggled the corresponding digit.

"No, nothing for tips. In that case there's nothing really to be done."

"There's one thing. You can pay me what you owe. You can send me home with the money we need to live. I'm afraid of being put out onto the street," Kaddish said. He looked around the room. "Being ruined doesn't seem to hamper your quality of life."

"Have you been to the misery towns on the edge of this city? There is a necklace of poverty that chokes Buenos Aires tighter every day, and I can swear to you, Poznan, the *porteños* in those shanties would think your rock bottom looked mighty good too."

"Money, Doctor. I want what I'm owed."

"I've got something better," the doctor said. "I've got something that can fix us both. Until you, Poznan, everyone who came into my office was trying to repair something inside when they asked me to fiddle with the out. But you, my fake patient, are the chosen one. Now follow me here, Poznan: It's not a matter of how far an ear sticks out from the head and how close I pin it back. The failure has nothing to do with my more than prodigious skills. It's that the person is so bothered by a healthy hearing ear that she's willing to risk death under my care to have it pinned down. No matter how superior my work, I can never get it close enough. As ridiculous as it sounds, those ears stick out in the soul."

"And this drove you to gambling the way some are driven to drink?"

"I'm not driven to anything. I'm admiring of it. Gambling offers the opportunity for perfection. One step into the future, there is already a winner. Somewhere else in the continuum all the races are already run."

"Then you really are pitiful," Kaddish said. "Because you're a failure at that too."

The doctor was energized.

"True. So far. Until now. But that's why I love it. At any time I could figure it out. From tomorrow on, maybe, I will never lose again. It's possible," the doctor said. "All I ask for in life is a fair chance and decent odds. This is what good countries offer their citizens—possibility and nothing more."

"That's touching," Kaddish said. "It fills me with hope. Now if we focus on the more immediate and pressing matter of your failure to pay, how do you get out of your debt to me?"

"Through your nose," the doctor said. "That's what I've been driving at." He pulled open the drawer as Kaddish had hoped. He pulled out a hand mirror and pushed it Kaddish's way. "Through that horrendous ax of a nose."

"Aside from the insult—"

"A point, yes. This is the better-than-paid part. This is where I change your life. The nose, I admit, is likely one of a kind, but your symptoms are a medical cliché. A deviated septum, for sure. Trouble sleeping, I'm absolutely convinced. That's likely from the size of that neck, but, I'd put money on it, it's got to be aggravated by that tumor you've been breathing through. You must wake, I bet, a thousand times a night. The airflow stops, the heart freezes for a beat. It's in those frozen moments that the dangers lie. It could be fatal at any time."

"Fatal? And you can fix that?"

"Take up the mirror." The doctor pushed it another centimeter. Kaddish picked it up. "Look at yourself. Look at that monstrous thing. I can take it down a few sizes. Lighten your load. Let me correct the medical malady and make you handsome to boot." Kaddish looked at his reflection, turning his head from side to side. Handsome—he'd thought he was. He put the mirror down.

"You said it's always a failure. You said, even with plastic surgery, it can't work."

"I said, until now. I said, in my experience it will always be imperfect even when made perfect."

"So why offer?"

"Because I came to you. You live with enough nose for ten men and yet you accept your deformation. I've never met anyone less self-conscious." It's the doctor now who raised his voice nearly to a yell. "In you, my friend, is the possibility of success. You have the flaw without the failing. A pure specimen."

Kaddish considered the offer. He picked up the mirror again, studying his own nose as had the doctor, taking in what he'd thought was its regal length with the regal and unfamiliar background of the study wall and the empty fireplace behind him. It doesn't take much to convince a person of the negative when he's studying his own features and the idea of deformity has been put into play. It helps when a doctor of renown has made the diagnosis. Horrendous, the doctor had said.

Scrutinizing himself in the mirror, Kaddish was pretty sure his nose wasn't as bad as Lillian's. He'd never thought—never seriously considered fixing it. It sounded vain. But if he was already handsome now, he wondered. Really, it was more about the sleeping and the saving of his life.

"You're honestly broke?" Kaddish said.

"Destitute."

"And the breathing?"

"Breathing, sleeping, snoring. I bet you think you have allergies that aren't. I bet you never set foot outside the house without a hankie, forever draining that nose."

Kaddish didn't, it was true. One in each of his back pockets: two clean hankies every morning, like putting on socks.

"You could leave it at home," the doctor said. "You may even see the world differently, attain binocular vision. Right now, you see like a toucan, turning your head to get the whole picture. We could combine the two worlds for you."

It was not that bad, Kaddish thought. It may have been close.

"I've always been happy this way," Kaddish said.

At that the doctor guffawed and threw his weight back against the chair. The chair tilted with him and, just when it seemed it would flip, it righted itself, setting the doctor back where he was.

"You can't possibly be happy like that," the doctor said. "The days of melancholia and black bile are over, the source of happiness finally isolated. It's right here," the doctor said. He poked at Kaddish's face.

"Happiness is contained in the nose. Like a diamond, it only crystallizes under pressure. In so much space"—he took another swipe—"happiness cannot form. This is why Jews, as a people, are dysthymics. In those ample noses happiness moves around like a firefly in a jar. It must be contained more exactly. One must keep it in place. Like a butterfly pinned to velvet, happiness run through. We can cure you, Poznan. We can liberate the man trapped inside the Jew."

"What is it worth?" Kaddish said. "How much in dollars?"

"You said yourself, I'm the best there is."

"You owe me a hefty sum."

"And that's quite a hefty nose. If I charge by the kilo you'll end up paying me. It's a fair trade."

"Who wants to trade anything?" Kaddish said. "I came here for cash."

"Be selfish then. Keep it on your face. Understand, though, from that single nose I could make many to distribute to the poor and needy."

"Are you even allowed to talk like that?" Kaddish said. "You're a fucking doctor."

"How many patients come in and I can say nothing? It's rare I get to be the client. You're the professional here today. Take the deal, make me your physician, and—considering that nose—I'll do the best I can."

"How about the operation in exchange for the interest you'd owe?"

"Please," the doctor said. It was a dismissal, not pleading. "You can't imagine how much debt I hold. Some of the capital has got to go."

"Debts of my own," Kaddish said. "We're all feeling the strain." He wanted to reach for the mirror again; he was sorry he'd put it down.

The doctor had been rude, and the doctor had swindled him, but beyond that, as restitution, this was the kind of rich-person luxury Kaddish could never consider. It was an extreme indulgence offered by the best there was. Then it hit him. And he chided himself in the moment, knowing Lillian would say he was selfish and thought it too late. This was also the kind of indulgence he'd never been able to provide for his family. Kaddish took a long breath. He was feeling magnanimous, like he was finally doing something right. "My wife," Kaddish said, "is similarly well endowed. My son, as the fruit of such a union, is blessed from both sides with the attribute."

"Don't even—" Mazursky said. He waved a hand. "The whole debt and much more. You'd have to pay me."

"Thirty-three percent," Kaddish said. "One third for each nose. A clean slate for the set."

"I couldn't." Mazursky took back the mirror. He returned it to the drawer.

"That's what I'm asking," Kaddish said. "Or we go back to the old deal."

"From the old deal you get nothing."

"I'll sell the debt," Kaddish said. "I'll hawk it to those who'd relish beating it out of you."

"And who do you think I owe my money to? Notwithstanding that, I couldn't do three unbilled noses in my clinic." The doctor paused and fixed his eyes on the middle distance over Kaddish's head. Then he grimaced as if crunching numbers and consulting with himself. "For my fellows, for my class—if you let me do it at the hospital where I teach, it could be managed." The doctor extended his hand and Kaddish shook it. "It really will change your life."

Kaddish was convinced he'd found his way out of a rotten situation and negotiated better terms. He pictured his family seated at a center table at La Estancia, laughing and pouring wine; then, after a particularly smart remark he'd made, Kaddish would fork a piece of steak up under his tiny but masculine nose. Kaddish turned the deal upside-down in his head. He tried to find an angle, something he'd missed, where it could possibly go wrong.

When Kaddish got up to leave, Mazursky asked him one more question. "The name," he said. "It's really gone?"

"From everywhere but here," Kaddish said, and he tapped two fingers to his temple.

"Coming home empty-handed is one thing," Lillian said, "but to come home at your proudest!" Her dismissal would usually have struck Kaddish to the core.

It wasn't a restaurant, but Kaddish couldn't have been any more content sharing dinner with his family. He'd brought home a celebration, right down to a half kilo of Freddo: *frutilla* on the bottom and chocolate *suizo* on top. For himself, he'd opened a good bottle of wine. "I *am* proud," he said. "And it's not empty-handed at all."

"No," Lillian said. "It's worse than empty-handed. How is it that your finest hour will leave us with less and not more?"

"I've lost enough on this deal already," Pato said. He waved his pink finger at Kaddish. "The nose stays. It's enough what this government forces on us already; we don't need to volunteer to make ourselves look the same."

"You shouldn't even consider it," Kaddish said. "With a nose like that, you could qualify for disability. A person could retire off such a thing."

"Leave him alone," Lillian said.

"He doesn't have to leave me anything," Pato said. "I want to know why he thinks it a wise idea for the whole family to go out and get a new face. Even a top-of-the-line, first-quality, next-season's-model face."

"It's a great deal, that's why. It's a small fortune's worth of work. Not to mention the overhead. For you he'll need to hire outside contractors, rent industrial tools. Let me tell you," Kaddish said. He raised up his own accusing finger. "Princes fly in from Saudi Arabia. Fine Yankee ladies come down from New York. From Manhattan! This for the service of our doctor." Now he whispered. "It's said that, before she passed, he did the eyes of Evita. What is being offered is offered by the best."

"*¡Hijo de puta!*" Pato said. "The best of your sons of whores."

"And so what about it," Kaddish said. He thought about slapping his son. Instead, Kaddish wiped his mouth with his napkin and then his forehead and then his face—everything short of putting it over his finger and corkscrewing it deep in each ear. Kaddish lifted but did not drink from his wine. "You cost us money if you don't get one," he said. "You sour the deal by a third. It's ungenerous. It's ungrateful."

"You're a sick man," Pato said. "Go get someone else."

Kaddish considered this. Maybe he could trade it for cash, or at least give a gift to one of their own.

"What about Frida?" Kaddish said to Lillian. "Last time I was by the office I was thinking she could use a little off the top."

"I'm not offering my friend a nose job," Lillian said. "It's insulting."

There was an audible yelp from Pato, frustrated to an insane degree.

"Then why aren't you insulted? Why isn't it rude and insulting and barbaric to offer it to you?"

"Because we're family," Lillian said. "There's a difference."

"No," Pato said, "there isn't." He turned back to his father. "Why is it acceptable with us?"

Kaddish looked at Lillian and then down at his plate. "Because we're ugly," he said quietly. "For exactly the reasons you complain about. Because we look different and this is our chance to look like everyone else, to look better than everyone else. We can, with this, fit in."

"You're hateful," Pato said. He stood up from the table. "You mangled my finger and you owe me my share."

"You'll have your cut," Kaddish said. "Maybe you misunderstood, since you've never done any real work. The nose jobs are nothing more than interest paid against a debt. It's vig on the money he owes me. In the loan business, they set up such payments all the time."

"That's not what you said before."

"Well, it's what I meant. You think I'm stupid, Pato? You think your father would walk out with nothing?"

Pato turned to his mother. "Do you believe him? Do you even believe a word of it?"

Lillian pictured Kaddish's keys in the ignition and him crossing the avenue, running between those cars. She looked at the proud face he had on now.

"Are you telling the truth?" she said. "Did you mean he was paying the interest and then will provide us with cash?"

"Absolutely," Kaddish said.

Lillian turned back to Pato. "Then I believe him," she said.

"The perfect couple," Pato said. "Who would think there could be a woman so perfectly matched to such a man?"

Pato went down the hall to his room and slammed the door. Then there was music. Loud, loud music. Pink Floyd blasting out of the speakers and through the door and down the hallway, Pato's music from a high-end high-fidelity stereo that was bought with part of Kaddish's payment from the Habenbergs, one of his earliest jobs. This Pato would take.

"Everyone has a price," Kaddish yelled into the music. Then, to Lillian, he said, "Everyone, for everything, has a value. Even for themselves."

"We must be worth a lot, then," Lillian said. "For our noses alone you give away a king's ransom."

"The noses are big," Kaddish said. "I didn't mean to say ugly. I don't know how that word got into my head."

"It's out of your mouth that's the problem. It's what you say."

"You're a beautiful woman," Kaddish said. "Pato is a handsome son. He presses my buttons, that boy."

"Since he was born," Lillian said. "A shame you can never manage sense when he's in the room. I'd fetch him back if I thought you could repeat that with feeling."

"Not worth it," Kaddish said.

"No," Lillian said. "And the offer, he's right, is insulting."

"My apologies," Kaddish said. He drank from his wine.

Lillian moved a spear of asparagus across her plate.

"Against my better judgment," she said. She cut the asparagus in half and raised her eyes to meet her husband's. "Somehow I'm looking forward to my nose."

[Ten]

KADDISH WAS SURE HE WAS CRYING but he couldn't feel the tears. There were two steel rods up his two large nostrils, and the good Dr. Mazursky stood over him, holding their ends. The doctor pressed down on those rods and began to push across. It was as if he were trying to loosen a bolt, turn on a hydrant, as if the doctor were gearing up to turn those rods the whole way around. It was the Mazursky method he was trying, engineered for the extra-walloping nose.

They were not up on stage as Kaddish had expected. He thought dozens of students would watch from a gallery, taking copious notes and peering through glass. There were only five students, two girls and three boys, gloved and masked and looking like children. Lillian was among them. She was also in scrubs, and, not counting the nurses and the anesthesiologist, she rounded out the audience to six.

The doctor turned to face the students. "It's a steady motion," he said. Then he raised up his elbows and shoved.

Before the operation, the doctor had come into the room where Lillian and Kaddish waited in surgical gowns. Those five children in white coats were standing behind him. "Do you want to draw straws?" he'd said. "As dexterous as I am, I can only do one nose at a time." Lillian looked to Kaddish and gave a quick and panicked shake of her head.

"I'll go first," Kaddish said. He kept his eyes on Lillian as he said it, making sure he'd read her right. The doctor then asked Lillian about the strength of her stomach. Fortified, is what she told him. "Then come watch me make history," the doctor said. "A rhinoplasty like this is as serious as detaching Siamese twins. There is a chance," and for this part he addressed the students that trailed him, "that we may lose one of them after separation."

Lillian watched it all until the insertion of the rods. When the doctor gave that push, Lillian turned to the side. The student beside her was up on her toes.

Kaddish blinked quickly. At least he thought he had, the view was so wet and fuzzy, he wasn't sure if his lids had moved. Again there was the question of tears. Kaddish still wasn't sure if he was feeling anything, though he thought maybe his head had split in two. He felt a line up the middle of his forehead, a soft separation or something like. It made the oddest noise, so very distinct—an internal sound. He wondered if this was what deaf people heard, if, with the world around them turned off, they got such wonderful sound from within. It was like an egg cracking. And that's what Kaddish saw. It was as if his eyes were in backward, peering into the blackness of his empty head, and in its very center floated a large white egg, so white as to be throbbing in its whiteness, so that against the blackness its edges seemed to glow.

A three-minute egg floating in the middle of his head.

When the doctor had given his quick turn, a heavy silver spoon came down into the darkness. That was the sound Kaddish heard emanating from the inside of his head: the perfect echo of spoon against shell.

He was sure he was crying, or that blood (the egg still glowing but now red) was running from his eyes. He said something, a joke, but even Kaddish wasn't sure what it was. Then, "Bad dream," he slept.

When the rods were out the doctor said, "Second nature. Like making your way into a lobster claw." The doctor's trusted nurse held forceps at the ready while the doctor worked his scalpel up inside Kaddish's nose. He put out his hands for the forceps, inserted them, pinched, gave a little shake to the wrist, and pulled them back out, holding them high. "And there's the meat—all but the butter." He held aloft the bump from

Kaddish's nose. Lillian kept her eyes averted and felt nauseated nonetheless. The more she tried to get it out of her head, the more she saw butter trickling down.

Kaddish was out cold but would surely have enjoyed hearing the doctor. Two peas in a pod. Both thinking of food. That is, one thinking of an egg and one of a lobster—both thinking of things that we crack open and eat.

The doctor lifted his arm a bit higher when a student interrupted.

"Crab," the student said. Eyebrows arched over the mask, the doctor's eyes darted around trying to isolate the source of the comment, as if his students were dressed this way to confound him.

"Bracchi," the doctor said, "was that bit of profundity from you?" Still the arm, and Kaddish's mangled cartilage, aloft.

"Yes, sir," he said. Then, "Yes, Doctor," to replace it.

"What is it then?"

"It's not so much like lobster, Doctor, as crabmeat. That is, from back here."

Dr. Mazursky considered and then raised his voice.

"I'm educating," he said. "It's more important that the feel to the rods is that of breaking open a lobster claw, not a crab leg, than that the meat tends more to the latter." As if to punctuate his statement, he flicked the forceps toward the bucket and Kaddish's nose, his most defining characteristic, clanged against its side.

There was additional cutting and sewing and then a final length of white tape laid down across the bridge of his nose. "Voilà," the doctor said. One student clapped and Lillian peeked over to see the master's work. It looked as if her husband had gone through the windshield of his car.

"Who's next?" the doctor called out.

Lillian raised her hand. "Me," she said.

"Who, me?" the doctor said, confused as to who was behind the mask.

"Me," Lillian said. And the doctor understood.

"Well, of course you're next. I mean, who's doing the procedure?" The doctor looked into the other faces. Lillian's was still the only arm up.

"Bracchi, then," the doctor said, pulling off his gloves. "Full of wisdom, let's see if you can translate it into nice work. Let's see how keen that eye is from up close."

Lillian looked to Kaddish. When did he do any better than this in an emergency—at her side and out cold?

Bracchi had already stepped forward. An orderly was wheeling Kaddish away on a gurney.

"Shall we sedate you now?" the doctor asked.

"No," Lillian said. She pointed to her husband as he was slipped through double doors. "Not Bracchi," she said. "Not the students." She was aghast. "Three for all was the deal my husband told me," Lillian said. "Me and him. That's only two."

"I explained to your husband," the doctor said—this in front of everyone, he didn't seem at all troubled, didn't seem to care—"his nose alone is a fair trade. I made it crystal clear. The only way I could afford his terms was in the teaching hospital."

"Yes?" Lillian said.

"Well, what did you think it meant? What could it possibly be but that I teach here? It's surgery, not arithmetic. The only way they learn is to touch. Isn't that right, Bracchi, my wunderkind?"

"Gospel," Bracchi agreed.

"You've done it before?" Lillian said. "He's done it before?"

The two men answered in unison. "No."

Lillian stood silent.

"Someone has to be the first nose," the doctor said.

"I've read the chapter," Bracchi said. "Irene and I went over it together last night." One of the two girls nodded, her eyes small and steady above the mask. "I've just watched it performed by the best."

"He's already a doctor," the doctor added. "This is a specialization. They are more fellows than students. He's not an urchin dragged in off the street."

"I'm not," Bracchi said.

"Lie down," the anesthesiologist said. He was watching the clock.

Lillian looked in the direction they'd taken her husband. She looked into the eyes of the doctor, so much coercion in that strip of face over the mask. She felt her nose pushing out against the fabric of her own.

She lay down on the table.

Before the anesthesiologist even moved, the doctor said, "Take a good long breath. It's the last time you'll get so much air with such ease. The rest of us," he said, "do a little work to breathe."

Lillian wasn't sure what she should and should not be hearing and should or should not be feeling. Being invited to watch her husband's operation, she knew it was something she was definitely not meant to see. At the start of the procedure she'd thought she was asleep. She believed she was dreaming exactly what was happening but that what was happening was not real. Then she remembered why she was sleeping and understood that she was awake, that there really was a tight circle of baby doctors around her—everyone standing so much closer while Bracchi worked. She was then for some reason thinking about driving: Kaddish through the windshield, cars and accidents, and a young doctor behind the wheel. It was with the rods in her nose that a form of clarity returned.

She could not feel that the rods were hard or that they were cold. But she felt a serious pressure building as Mazursky instructed. She did not trust him at all, not a bit, except when he was doctoring. How nicely and smoothly he had wielded his tools over Kaddish—even when she'd turned her head to the side she'd felt his ease. How nice he sounded while directing Bracchi, as if he were moving the rods with his voice from afar.

Lillian saw the bright lights and knew her eyes were open. She closed them but they didn't move, the lights still there along with the motion around them. Thinking them closed, her eyes immediately did, and then it was only the doctor talking and the pressure, which had decreased momentarily, increasing again. "Good God, man," Mazursky said, and now his voice wasn't so smooth. "Do it already. Down and over, down and over. Nothing gets done in this world without follow-through."

Lillian exhaled through her mouth and the down and over came. There was the twist and turn and the release of it. Though there were many sensations missing beyond the lack of feeling in her face, a single dominant impression remained. The one thing she could feel perfectly well was just another thing that wasn't there. Along with the follow-through, Lillian felt a sharp, a clear, a prominent absence of grace.

[Eleven]

"THEY'VE GOT TO GO," Lillian said.

"There are rumors," Kaddish said.

Pato couldn't believe this was happening. Seated together on the couch, their knees touching, his parents had actually formed a united front. They sat there with their swollen cheeks and black eyes and masks of white tape across their noses looking very much punched in the face.

"They're my books," Pato said. "How can you even ask such a thing?"

"You're the one full of conspiracy theories; oppressed long before it was in style. Now it's in vogue," Lillian said. "Good for you. A trend-setter. Only, the books have become dangerous. You've got to get rid of them. No one wants to be rid of you."

"Just because you're paranoid, don't take it out on me. The door I went along with. Who cares about changing keys?"

"We're both paranoid in different ways," Lillian said. "My way and you may live to be anxious until a ripe old age."

"I haven't done anything wrong."

"It doesn't matter if anyone's really coming or not, it's your lot as a Jew to fear it. We are bred for the waiting."

"You're as crazy as he is," Pato said.

"And you don't show enough fear. Take yourself seriously and accept that the books are finally as subversive as you want them to be."

"Honestly, I'd rather give you my nose. I should have shown my loyalty with that when I had the chance."

"No one's offering that now," Kaddish said. "It was a mistake in the first place. Who's going to breathe for the family without you? What if there's a gas leak? You're our canary, Pato. We need you to test the air."

"If I had the money," Pato said, "I'd take my books and move out and never speak to either of you again."

"By the time you have the money," Kaddish said, "you won't need it because my life insurance will have long ago paid out. You can just move into the big bedroom."

"Enough," Lillian said. "The books are going. Either choose the ones you know to be troubling or get rid of them all."

"I read half of them for classes given by the university of this city, which is run by the state. There is nothing wrong with having books."

"But you have heard," Lillian said. "You've heard that they're dangerous. That they're guilt. Don't tell me you and your friends don't know of the craziness going on? Frida's niece was interrogated for ten hours straight, no bathroom break, no water, her mother kept outside. They wanted to know about her organizational affiliations. She's sixteen, Pato. She's captain of her volleyball team."

"Who knows what stories are true anymore? The honest mouths are shut. The graffiti is gone. This whole country has been whitewashed. Go look," Pato said. "The walls have been painted over. There's a ring of white as high as my head around every tree."

"I've seen the trees," Kaddish said.

Lillian bit at a nail. She'd somehow missed the whitening of the city.

"They're cowards," Pato said. "They're supposed to burn banned books in the street. That's how it's done, with big bonfires and evil intent. This is the only ruthless, coercive system that expects us to destroy them ourselves. Do I have to ransack my own room while I'm at it? It's like—" Pato said, looking around for an example, "it's as if—" and he looked down at his parents, together on the couch, Lillian's hand on Kaddish's knee from where she put it to still him. "It's like what you've done to your faces. It's like the horror of a nation with one acceptable nose."

"Except that we had a choice and you don't. There'll be plenty left for you to read."

"I do have a choice," Pato said. "Whatever the threat, I'm keeping my books either way."

"Tough guy," Kaddish said.

"You're at a dangerous age, Pato," Lillian said. "You look like a man, you think like a man, but you still have the idealism of a child. Why do you suppose all those soldiers out there are also nineteen? It's because they're the only ones stupid enough to die for a cause. After that, a little older, and the high-mindedness will melt away like baby fat. It's only the generals, only the generals and rebel leaders and rock stars, your military men and your outright morons, that go boldly on after adolescence looking for a reason to die. Your hippy mottoes are right, Pato. Don't trust the grown-ups. Don't trust any adult with a cause."

"Not unless they make sure to die before you do," Kaddish said.

"Not even then," Lillian said.

"The books go," Kaddish said. "The dangerous ones get torn up and all the rest can stay. If you want, I'll buy you a new book for every one you lose."

"The ones you want me to get rid of are the ones I most want to keep. And," Pato said, "I'll buy whatever I want when I get the money I'm already owed."

"We're serious," Lillian said.

"Then be serious with each other." Pato grabbed his jacket. "Keep the books and the door and your bloody noses and have a second honeymoon. It'll be great—I know how you two so enjoy time alone."

Pato stormed off, slamming that heavy door as best he could. With the dead bolt in the door handle, he didn't even manage to lock himself out.

It was a happy home for Rafa's mother with so many kids sleeping there. She made a big production of pulling out the trundles and making up the extra beds. The one next to her father for Pato, and the one next to Mufi for Flavia. The kids all came out of the bedroom laughing.

"What?" she said. "What?"

"We're not sleeping like that," Rafa said. "You can slide the trundles away."

"That's how we've always done it."

"Poppy is eighty-two. He announces his presence in a way that makes it unpleasant to share the bed."

"He's your grandfather!" she said. "Respect."

"I respect him, as do my friends," Rafa said. "And here I pay homage to his pungency. Pato will get the top bunk."

"That mattress is shot. There's a hole right through it."

"Good, then he'll have somewhere to stick his nose."

"And what's wrong with your sister?"

"Nothing's wrong with her," Rafa said. "It's just that my penis won't reach Flavia from across the room."

"Disgusting," Rafa's mother said. "Save such jokes for your friends."

"It's a valid logistical concern."

"Since when is Flavia your girlfriend?" his mother said. Again she'd fallen out of the loop. "We didn't discuss letting girlfriends share a room. It's one thing, a lady that is your friend. A girlfriend is another." She gave Flavia a disappointed look.

"She isn't my girlfriend. That's the wonder of my generation. We've dispensed with such formalities."

They waited out Rafa's grandfather, which wasn't difficult since he was always asleep by seven. Mufi was another matter. She wasn't much of a pain for a twelve-year-old, but they knew she'd stay up until the last one of them had gone to bed. They simply waited until she pretended she was asleep, forcing her to balance the thrill of eavesdropping with what had to be an exhausting performance. It looked like she was playing dead.

Flavia and Rafa were squished into the bottom bunk and Pato was above them on the thin foam mattress, which indeed had a tear all the way through.

"I might be better off with your grandfather," Pato said, at which point, as if on cue, Rafa's grandfather rattled the bed with a fart that put an end to the proposal. They laughed hard and stopped suddenly, trying to catch Mufi making a noise.

"She's good," Pato said. And they gave her another minute to break. "I wish you guys could see my parents. It's like letting someone hit you in the face with a shovel."

"Who cares what they do to themselves?" Flavia said. "You have a nice room at home, you should sleep in it."

"I'm not here because of the nose jobs," Pato said. He tried to prop himself up and banged his head on the ceiling. "It's because of the books."

"I got rid of mine," Rafa said.

"If you'd read any of them you might have felt more attached. And you have a little sister," Pato said. "There is a child in this house to protect." They paused again. Mufi rolled over and let out a little snore.

"What's the difference? I'll replace them when this is over."

Flavia took Rafa's side. "A little perspective wouldn't kill you, Pato, when so many other things might."

"To fuck him is one thing," Pato said. "To agree with him is another. It's actually hard to believe."

"I'm keeping my books," Flavia said. "But, in an alternate universe where my parents were remotely communicative, I wouldn't get into a battle with them over it. I don't want to sound like your mother, but if I could sleep in my own bed in my own house, I would."

"So go home," Pato said.

"I don't think that's an option anymore," Flavia said. "I went to therapy this morning and my shrink wasn't there."

"Gone—not there?" Pato said. "How do you not say that until now?"

"She told me," Rafa said.

"Rafa's mother doesn't have to know every last thing," Flavia said. "She got enough news about my life today."

Pato was jealous that Rafa knew before him. And feeling jealous when they were talking about a kidnapping made him feel petty and small. He also resented the sex his friends were having, and this made him feel smaller still.

"I waited around for the whole fifty-minute hour," Flavia said. "For most of it the shrink in the other room is giving me the evil eye—and he's the one that must have buzzed me up. There wasn't anybody else there. It's when I'm leaving that the guy gets off his fat ass. 'Friday,' he says. 'They took her right out the front with a canvas sack over her head.' I said to him, 'Who took her?' And he looks at me like I'm an idiot, like I'm too greedy to be satisfied with what's been given. 'Who took what?' he said, all formal. 'This isn't a bus stop. If you've got no business here, go loiter somewhere else.' Then he went back into the other room and slammed the door."

"Two people in two weeks," Rafa said. "You're like lady luck."

"Fuck off," she said.

"So you're never going to go home?" Pato couldn't imagine it, though he'd claimed to be doing just that.

"They've got the patient lists. They can't not have them. I might as well be a member of the ERP."

"I still can't believe you didn't tell me before."

"It's because his mother is crazy," Flavia said.

"It's because my mother is crazy." Rafa seconded the thought. "She'll go nuts. She'll think we're all headed for the firing squad."

"What about classes?"

"I'll keep going for now, I guess. I'll see how it feels. Otherwise I'll hide out here for a while unless Mufi tells."

"Yes," Rafa said. "Unless my sister tells."

"I won't," Mufi said.

"All right then," Rafa said.

They all proceeded to feign sleep. Rafa and Flavia believed the others really were so that they could effect a privacy they, in reality, rarely managed. Mufi stayed awake, banking on more secrets. And Pato lay up on his thin foam mattress, listening to the sounds of struggle and the positioning and repositioning below him. He decided to spend another night or two at Rafa's to spite his parents and to prove he wasn't sure what to Flavia. He'd take at least another night before going home. Pato considered all these things as the wood began to creak and his bed began to sway. He closed his eyes and drifted off. Pato's friends kept up their slow rhythm below, rocking him to sleep.

[Twelve]

CACHO CALLED OUT FOR THE ELEVATOR to wait and Lillian held the gate for him. She was wearing sunglasses that sat high up on her bandage. She took them off, revealing black eyes.

Cacho winced when he saw her and, recovering his composure, said, "It looks to be a bright morning, but the paper says rain."

"Since when are newspapers interested in the truth?"

Cacho tried to agree enthusiastically but nothing coherent came out. His overcoat was thrown over one arm; he switched it to the other. There was an envelope in the uncovered hand.

"You look very smart in that suit, Cacho," Lillian said. She gave it a tug, straightening his lapel. "It makes you look tall."

"I got a summons." He showed her the envelope. "I think I'm headed your way."

"Routine, I hope," she said.

"There's nothing routine about it," Cacho said, and his voice cracked. "It's because of my trip to Punta del Este. Now they've called me down to the Ministry of Special Cases. I already registered my return—there's no call for it."

"Maybe they think it's a bit late for the beach."

"My brother's business is there and he stays year round. It's his business. It's travel related. I really don't know what he does. And I can't stand missing work."

"Calm down, Cacho. You're a model citizen."

"I can't calm down. These things terrify me. That's what makes me a model citizen: I'm too afraid to do anything wrong."

"I never thought about it like that."

"That place was bad enough before the coup. Since then, it's the ministry of last resort. It's a bureaucratic dumping ground, a loony bin for those with no redress."

"We all hear the talk, Cacho. But it's likely only that."

"Have you heard about the *chupadas,* then? Families are sucked up into a vacuum, never to return. I've been told they go into that ministry and never come out."

"That's not very logical, Cacho. Every ministry deals with big business and small. It's a nothing reason you've been called in for. And I promise, you'll come right back out."

"You promise?"

"I do."

"It's a matter for the judicial system, if anything. I should've been summoned to the police or to court. It makes no sense to start me there. I know they want us to be afraid. But why bother me? I was afraid already."

They walked Avenida de Mayo together, toward the plaza and the Pink House, the ministries and Lillian's work. It was a beautiful day, not a cloud anywhere in the sky. Lillian switched the subject back to the weather, then their jobs, and Cacho asked about Pato.

"I haven't seen him lately," Cacho said, "He must be studying hard."

"He was staying with a friend for a few days, is all. I assume you hear both my men screaming now and again. The apartment gets small as my son gets big. I hope last week wasn't too loud."

"I go to sleep very early."

"That's good," Lillian said. "Only they don't always fight at night."

"I'm only guessing for not hearing," Cacho said.

"Maybe it's the new door." It was then Lillian remembered to look: a nearby wall, the tree at her side. They were whitewashed.

Police sirens hit them and the two froze in place. A cruiser raced in their direction and behind it ran a soldier on foot. The police car passed, and then the soldier, without even a look their way. Lillian and Cacho hadn't moved, except that her hand was in her purse and Cacho's pressed against his pocket, holding his wallet from the outside. They were reaching for their ID cards, a reflex like blinking after a boom.

"I should hurry," Cacho said, motioning toward the ministry. "Thanks for the support," he said and turned.

"Cacho," Lillian said. Lillian pulled her sunglasses out of her bag, as if that's what she was after when she reached. "It's not only Pato," she said. "You haven't seen me in some days either." Lillian did her best to grin. "I've had some cosmetic surgery."

"Oh," Cacho said. Then he said it again, more loudly. "Your face," he said. "I see," he said. "Now that you mention it, I can see you've had something done."

Standing at the kitchen sink, Kaddish tore off his bandage in a single pull. He dropped it in the pail underneath and, while prone, pulled the plugs of gauze, absolutely foul, from his nostrils. He washed his face with dishwashing liquid, much to Lillian and Pato's dismay. Using a dish towel, he wiped it harder than one would think sound and turned toward them—letting the towel drop.

His drink he'd already prepared. Smiling wide, he toasted the air, took a sip, and said, "What do you think?"

"Oh my God," Lillian said.

"Still swollen," Pato said.

"You look gorgeous," Lillian said. "I mean really, really handsome."

"You look like everyone else," Pato said. "A stranger to me."

Kaddish's smile only widened.

"Gorgeous?" he said.

"You really do." Lillian put on her reading glasses, perching them on the bandage she still wore. "A fabulous nose. Small but strong." Her excitement for him was pure, and it blossomed as she touched the tape

on her cheek. "You look like Hugo del Carril. You're a movie star!" She
*tsk-tsk*ed him and shook her head. "How can you trust my opinion and
not run to see?"

"Your reaction is enough of a mirror," Kaddish said. He reached
toward her face. "I'd rather see what you're hiding."

Lillian drew back. "At the doctor's," she said.

"It's only a piece of tape."

"It's only tape," Pato said.

Kaddish's eyes were fluttering. He leaned against the counter and put
two fingers to the bridge of his nose.

"Still can't breathe," he said. "I think maybe he sewed it shut."

"Maybe there's some seal you're supposed to break," Pato said. "Like
a hymen in your nose."

"The wit of a boy who makes love to the sheets."

"A hot shower," Lillian said, "and I'm sure it will clear up."

"We'll take one together," Kaddish said. "You lose the bandage, I'll
lose the kid, and we'll see what we can arrange."

"The two of you with runny noses and black eyes. It's the height of
romance!"

"Boundaries," Lillian said. "We're still your parents."

"Come, my parent," Pato said. He led his mother back to her chair.
"Let's see if it's cooked."

Lillian lowered her glasses. She turned her chair out from the table,
and said, "Maybe I should wait."

"I'm not looking in that mirror alone," Kaddish said.

Lillian studied his fine new face, striking even with the swelling. "So
handsome," she said. "All right," she said. She straightened up, tilted her
head back, and put her hands on her knees.

"Ready?" Pato said.

"Ready," she said, smiling. "Peel it slowly. One fell swoop and I'm
afraid the nose will come off too. It's a lady's nose, remember. More delicate than the one on your father's face." She bit her lip even before Pato
started. Partly for the pain and partly to keep down the smile until it
was done.

Pato worked the tape free. He peeled the gauze pad down from the top. It was sticky and had fused in the middle, so he warned her, "Deep breath," and yanked it off the rest of the way.

"Oh my God," Pato said, stepping back.

Lillian smiled wide. "Gorgeous?" she said.

"Oh my God," Kaddish said.

"Stunning?" Lillian said.

"Give it a minute," Pato said.

"A minute?"

"Absorbing," Pato said.

"Roman," Kaddish said.

"Romanesque is nice," she said. "Like Elizabeth Taylor as Cleopatra." Lillian had seen Cleopatra at the Premier on Corrientes. She touched her nose gingerly, feeling its shape. Kaddish held the bridge of his own. He put down his drink. He wasn't getting enough air.

"It feels so different," she said, getting up. "Come, Kaddish, let's go see." She took his hand and pulled him down the hall. Pato, shaking his head, went along. Kaddish started into the bedroom. "The bathroom mirror has the best light," she said, continuing on.

Lillian flicked the switch as if she were at a surprise party and the guest of honor had arrived.

She saw her husband's face in the mirror alongside her own. She couldn't understand. She didn't—*give it a minute*—understand.

"I'm sorry," Kaddish said.

"Roman ruin," Pato said.

"Oh my God," Lillian said, and was struck dumb. When she could speak it was to spit out the name of the young doctor like a curse. "Bracchi," she said. Lillian turned her head this way and that. "Kaddish?" she said, despairing.

Lillian started her survey again. She began from the front where her nose, so thin, was nearly invisible. The prominent bump on the bridge seemed to have been lowered to the tip, where it floated, mottled and clownlike. It looked as if a gumdrop had been affixed to the end of her face. From the side, she was surprised to discover, the profile was even worse. That sharp bone came out from between her eyes and then dropped straight down, a crag that jutted out where the gumdrop began. What she settled on was the image of a carcass—it most reminded Lillian of a chicken's breastbone when the bird is picked clean.

And then it hit her. Lillian reached up. She touched it. She looked at her handsome husband. She looked at herself.

"Worse off," she said. "Always worse off."

[Thirteen]

KADDISH WAS AT THE BOOKSHELVES trying to set things right. Lillian wouldn't speak to him, which he didn't think fair. She was the one who wanted him to go first.

If anything, things had been better with Pato since he'd come back from Rafa's. Now that Kaddish was getting normal airflow through his nose, now that he could eat with his mouth closed and nod off on the couch in silence, it seemed a great relief for Pato not to have to hear the sound of his father breathing. Kaddish, who didn't consider himself very sensitive, had always pretended not to notice the pained look on his son's face with each exhalation, with every reminder that Kaddish was alive.

He pulled a Marcuse off the shelf. He was embarrassed and quickly turned as if Pato was right there behind him. Only Pato could make him feel inadequate in this way. When Pato shook his head at the holes in his father's knowledge, Kaddish felt sorry for himself and felt stupid before his son. He didn't have the slightest doubt about what he was doing now. It was only his ignorance that unnerved him. This wasn't the cemetery. Running his fingers along a name pressed into the spine of a book, Kaddish had no idea about the man behind it.

For Kaddish, the shelves were a sign of what he'd done right with his son. And this is where Pato misunderstood him. The books made

Kaddish proud. He loved that Pato was educated. It was Pato's educated attitude that made Kaddish want to wring his neck. He could dump them all if he wanted, every last book. Simpler. But he wasn't an animal, he wasn't being cruel. As always, as forever, Kaddish was trying his best.

That's why Pato should have been there doing it. Not solely because he could pull the right titles with ease, but because, if he really loved those books so much, they should be disposed of with proper respect. Kaddish remembered when there was a fire at Talmud Harry's house and his library damaged. Talmud Harry left the unsalvageable books boxed up at the rabbi's door. As proud a man as he was, he wanted his *shemos* buried with everyone else's.

Kaddish took down anything that mentioned Che Guevara in the title and then he added a Lenin and a Lermontov to the stack. The Lermontov was a thin little novel but there was a portrait of the writer on the cover and Kaddish thought he had the face of a rabble-rouser. The only book he opened for pleasure was a survey of Argentine poetry. He read "Martín Fierro." He could still pretty much recite the first page by heart.

Kaddish pulled out a psychology textbook. Hidden underneath it was a mimeographed pamphlet with sentences crossed out and additions made by hand. Kaddish flipped through it. There were jokes and political cartoons, a couple of reviews, and some left-wing nonsense. The last page was a nest of famous quotes that sounded more or less the same. This just the sort of thing they'd kill you over, some student's after-school project.

Kaddish went down the hall and checked Pato's nightstand and the books strewn on his bedroom floor. Then he went back to the living room to give the shelves a once-over, to see if his selections held up.

A Hebrew Bible Kaddish left. He took down a Spanish copy of *The Art of Loving* and *Reflections on the Jewish Question* and a *Mein Kampf* he'd never seen. He'd wondered how his son had come to read it. If Kaddish had asked him, Pato could have led him the whole way: how *Ward Six* had gotten him to *The Cherry Orchard* and that to *Onegin* and on to *A Hero of Our Time*, which led him by fluke to Voltaire. Each book begat another. For a boy whose entire family history dead-ended on his father's side, this is how Pato traced his line. It was Pato's proof of how he came to be. If there was any conspiracy to follow, this one left a trail.

Such a big ruckus over thirteen books. Two trips, two piles on the bathroom floor, and then Kaddish fetched the kerosene from the service balcony and brought it inside. The bathtub had seemed the most sensible place to make a fire indoors when the intent wasn't to burn the house down. There was water at the ready and nothing flammable in reach. Kaddish unhooked the shower head from its clamp and let it hang outside the tub. He cranked open the slats to the small bathroom window, and peered out with the lights off to see if anyone was in his courtyard or if he could spot any neighbors hanging laundry who might see the smoke, might call the fire department and the police, and, as with so many of his plans (even he understood after Lillian's nose), bring about the exact opposite of what he'd intended. Kaddish had waited until dark. Every passing hour made it safer with the neighbors, but he had to beat Pato and Lillian's return. Lillian was working late these days and his son, likely off causing trouble, rarely got home before his mother.

One book at a time, and Kaddish figured the smoke would be no worse than a dinner gone awry. Kaddish knew there'd be aftermath. He also knew he was protecting the family, securing them better this way than Lillian ever could with a door. She might not show it while Pato was still seething, but Kaddish knew it would redeem him; at night she'd roll over to his side of the bed, put an arm around him, and kiss him on the back of his neck.

Kaddish used the Lermontov as kindling. He poured the kerosene. He pulled a cigarette from a pack with his teeth, lit it, and tossed the match onto the book in the tub. Flames rose up.

The match made a small stain on the book's cover, a cradle for the match head, and then, around it, all this benign yellow flame. In the dark of the bathroom Kaddish found it calming. He enjoyed this window of time when he'd done what needed doing and there wasn't yet any harm. He'd never expected a happy life, only moments of joy to carry him through. This he would cherish. For one perfect moment the book was on fire and did not burn.

The cover caught first. Then the pages inside began to curl. Kaddish knew Pato would be furious but, watching the book burn, he realized he'd maybe underestimated to what degree. There's something about the singular, Kaddish thought, that is always more distressing. He believed this about all things. Kaddish tossed the pamphlet on top as a remedy. It is why war and disaster were always spread across the front of his newspaper. It's not just magnitude. It's the ease of calamity on the conscience. A single death is too much to look at for long. Better the way Pato wanted it, like a bonfire, a mountain of books blazing in the town square.

Kaddish took another book, fanned its pages, and balanced it as if on display. The smoke turned acrid with the addition. Kaddish cranked open the window the rest of the way and the smoke was drawn out, its path almost geometric as it rose up, then funneled into the air shaft before rising again. Bits of burning page flew over his head and circled around the bathroom like fireflies. The smoke became heavier; recognizing the ridiculousness of his cigarette, Kaddish tossed it into the tub. He used the biggest book to break up the embers of the last. He poured on more kerosene, hoping for that gentle flame. It didn't work that way a second time. The pages turned wet and then burned faster, so he added another book, hoping it would somehow exhaust the fire. Kaddish got down on the floor. It was hot and he began to worry about real damage to the bathroom as the tub and the wall tiles blackened. He'd planned to scrub it clean after, to wipe the ash away. He got into a rhythm and burned the books at a steady pace. As if saving best for last, the final volume turned out to be his son's favorite. Kaddish didn't intend for this, but it showed good instincts just the same.

He was pushing at that last book with the handle of the plunger, as if tending to a hearth, when a gust of clean air nearly bowled him over. This was precipitated by the swinging open of the door. Looking up, trying to get his bearings, Kaddish turned his eye to the mirror, which held in it a reflection from the hall. The air was still hazy and the mirror glass smoky, and Kaddish's eyes were adjusting while the remains of the fire flickered in the tub; all of this together made for a face hard to read. If one stared carefully, though, looked hard into that mirror—if one used a bit of imagination and applied it to those ghostlike features— a face could be made out. From the nose alone. From their lone nose.

The last book wasn't done yet. It would need some attention. But Pato was already at his father's side, a hand on the edge of the tub to steady himself, the other grabbing the book. He pulled it out and dropped it to the floor. It made a puffing noise and there was a flurry of sparks. Pato rushed his burnt fingers into his mouth.

"No," Kaddish said. He reached into the tub and turned on the water. "Here," he said, pointing through smoke and, with the water, steam. "To the kitchen," Kaddish said, "you can still get at the ice."

Pato already had his hand out and was looking at his fingertips, waiting for the blisters to form. He lowered that hand to stare at his father. How many times had Pato raced down the hall trying beat his father to the bathroom, the only room in the apartment with a lock. How many times had Pato feared that Kaddish—as Pato himself just had—would burst through the door? And Kaddish had tried. There were the cracks to prove it from Kaddish throwing his shoulder against it in a rage. Though the roles were reversed, they'd never been in there with all that fury before. Kaddish may have banged until the wood cracked, but he'd never gotten in.

Recognizing this reversal, Pato understood why his father never made it all the way. He'd been chasing without enough chase, breaking without enough break. Kaddish hadn't ever really wanted to follow through.

Pato lamented this as his burnt hand became his swinging hand, as he made a fist and hit his father right in his brand-new nose. It didn't fracture—solid work from Mazursky, the foundation of that strong bone left as it was.

Kaddish also had a good thick neck to keep a skull from rocking and a brain from bobbing. He had a sturdy jaw and a tough nose and a cannonball head. Kaddish wasn't knocked out, only knocked down. He stood up slowly, dizzily, and he went to the mirror and looked in, though with the soot and smoke, and Kaddish a bit bleary from the hit, there was nothing but shadow to see. As Pato waited for the blisters, Kaddish, who had scarcely finished healing from his nose job, waited for his eyes to turn back to black.

"I'd rather it had been someone else," Kaddish said. "A scuffle in the playground or a brawl with your gang. Still, I'm glad to take a punch off you and see that you're not such a pussy after all. It's a hard world we live in."

"We don't fit together and never have. It's time that I free you up officially," Pato said. "Let's pretend this never happened—that I never happened. We can go our separate ways. I'll have no father, and you'll have no son."

"You can't make me dead to you, if that's what you're proposing. That's not how it works." Kaddish patted Pato gently on the cheek. "You're not the first son in such a predicament. So I tell you, some things aren't so easily achieved."

"What would you know about having a father?" Pato said. "You have no clue."

"That's what makes me expert on the matter," Kaddish said. "Without ever having met, without knowing a thing about him, I tell you it's work to see a father undone."

"Always you know better," Pato said. "If there's enough hatred, I bet it can be managed. The one thing you taught me is to give it my best."

Kaddish said, "Fine," as if accepting the terms.

Pato considered taking his book from where it smoldered on the floor. He opened and closed his burnt hand. Then he looked his father in the eye, full of disappointment.

He did not, in his anger, take keys or wallet, left up on the scalloped shelf. He did not take the jacket, inside out, that he'd pulled off on his way down the hall. He had nothing to protect him against the wind and the rain that hit him outside. Pato held up his hand and sighed, his feet already wet. He pushed on toward Rafa's. It was his intent never to come home.

[Fourteen]

THEY SAT TOGETHER IN CLASS at the university. They were in the tiered lecture hall used for social psychology, getting their exam grades.

Names were being called in alphabetical order. Pato was caught in the middle of the alphabet but he was the first of his trio to be summoned to the front. Rafa moved his legs so his friend could slide by.

Pato felt ridiculous for worrying over his grade. He already knew that only one person in that lecture hall would be given a pass. Insane as it seemed, these were apparently the rules handed down from above. It was another way to intimidate them and an attempt to split their ranks. A whole class full of failures and Pato couldn't help it. He wanted the decent mark.

His parents could deny it, but they might as well have strewn rose petals on the street to lead in the junta. This was the kind of government a troubled nation ends up with when quiet is sought at any price. What his parents weren't yet getting was the difference between terrorism and terrorized. A regime that worried over minutiae was more troubling to Pato than one that hunted and killed its enemies in cold blood. It filled him with a greater dread, the thought of some general worrying over their scores.

Professor Schuster held her pen to his name on the class list and had a hand splayed across his test. "Mr. Poznan," she said, and handed him the paper. He'd studied hard for this exam and he'd failed.

Three failures sat in a café and drank coffees, looking out on a block of university buildings. They compared right answers marked wrong and theorized about who got the lone pass. Pato stirred a shaving of lemon peel into his cup. Flavia watched the birds on the other side of the windows. She thought, if she and Pato and Rafa were sitting outside, she'd toss the birds her crumbs.

"Crash at my mom's if you want," Rafa said, "but it's the dumbest thing I can think of. You don't need to look like you're on the run if you aren't."

"Flavia looks like she's on the run," Pato said.

"A brilliant point," Rafa said, "except that Flavia *is* on the run." He reached for his coffee and knocked his saucer to the floor. The whole room turned and Rafa raised up his hand. "Go back to your business," he said. "Everything is under control."

"I told you even before your father torched them," Flavia said. "You're turning into a fanatic. It's not worth a war over books."

"Anyone more extreme than you is a fanatic," Pato said. "And anyone more conservative, a fascist."

"You should go home," Rafa said.

"He should go home." Flavia's pigeons took off and she followed them skyward. That is why she was the last of the three to stand up and press her palms to the glass.

The birds dipped together and then scattered again. A horse came into view, moving at a canter. A police officer, helmeted, black-booted, was mounted on its back. It was shocking enough, the sight of him with the university buildings behind. It was made worse, Flavia thought, more incomprehensible, by the way the policeman was leaning over to one side, by the gloved hand he had lowered, by the blond hair it held, spilling over, blowing back. The policeman was dragging off a student by the hair of her head. The student was sometimes running, sometimes falling, as the horse came their way.

The girl held on to the policeman's wrist—almost as if she didn't want him to let go.

There's nothing you don't see when your world is coming apart. Things you'd never assemble, events that before a certain point you couldn't have imagined imagining. A year before becomes a different life. Now Flavia was looking, now the policeman pulling, now this poor girl was passing the café on the day their exams were returned.

Flavia looked to Pato and Rafa. She couldn't believe it even as she was believing. She put her arms around the boys and they responded in kind.

Rafa searched for their concert tickets. Flavia passed Pato the joint. When Rafa found them, Pato took charge. He held the smoke in and sat on the floor cross-legged, elbows to knees, the roach in one hand and the tickets fanned out in the other. In their poverty there were certain things they made sure they weren't too poor for. Beyond this, Rafa and Flavia were bankrolling Pato. He'd have to go home, at the very least, to get his stuff.

"We should get moving," Rafa said.

Flavia licked her lips, taking stock. "I'm still not high enough. You better roll another before we go."

Rafa did. And he pulled the middle cigarette from a fresh pack, replacing it with the joint.

"*Vamos,*" he said, and they were gone.

The gels slid over the lights and the lights, in endlessly changing colors, washed over the club. They were screaming their heads off, singing themselves hoarse. Everybody there knew the words by heart. They were one with Invisible, up on that stage. When the hall went dark but for a spotlight on Spinetta, the sound of the clapping turned deafening and Rafa put his hands over his ears. Flavia passed Pato the joint. Spinetta sang into the microphone, his face framed by his hair and a silver haze of sweat and spit around him.

This place was a miracle for Pato. To be both anonymous and make himself heard, it was the one place where the bitterness left his mouth. Pato had tears in his eyes the whole time, from beginning to end.

Pato and Rafa and Flavia worked their way closer to the stage. The bass put a solid throb into Pato's head, while the joint took the knot out of his stomach. Pato passed it to Flavia. As she passed it back, a flashlight's beam rolled across her face. Flavia pointed to a security guard standing on a corner of the stage. Pato followed that light around the crowd until it settled, and when it did, the flashlight steady, a walkie-talkie came up, and the security officer yelled into it. Pato couldn't hear, but he could see the man's thick neck—like his father's—go taut.

The music continued, they sang along, but Pato watched the security guards. They came from different directions, men bigger and wider than the other concertgoers, the only ones moving against the grain, splitting up the perfect unity of the crowd. Pato watched until he got a glimpse of the boy that was caught in the flashlight's beam. Rafa pulled the joint from Pato's hand. Before Rafa put it to his lips, he screamed into Pato's ear, "Eyes front. Eyes on Spinetta. We're having a good time, so sing."

Pato wanted to see what happened. He listened to Rafa and looked at the stage. He watched his Spinetta. His hero.

Pato sang his heart out.

They all three had a wonderful time.

They discussed the merits of the concert afterward. The three of them and a hundred others piled into the closest pizza place to recap, creating a happy and considerable din.

For Rafa it was simple: With every other outlet of free expression corrupted or co-opted, the musicians were the only ones who managed to tell the truth. Rafa was convinced that rock music survived because the adults didn't understand a word. It must really sound like noise to them, an indecipherable ruckus.

"It's all thought out," Flavia said. "This and the football stadium—they give us two places to scream and curse and stamp our feet. They're not stupid," Flavia said, "they're evil. They know they have to provide an outlet. Without a valve to release the pressure, this country would explode."

"If they knew what we were singing," Pato said.

"You think they don't?" Flavia said.

"I believe they don't," Pato said.

"I don't think any group of people has been marched to their graves without a song to keep time."

"I'm with Pato," Rafa said. "If they knew what the words meant, they'd never let it go on. Look at this." Rafa motioned to all the other concertgoers around them. "This energy could be harnessed."

"Apparently not," Flavia said. The police pulled up outside in force. They'd brought along two regular city buses with the windows blacked out. Some kids ran, most didn't dare. It was the usual harassment, practically part of the ticket price. Rafa pulled out the nub of their joint, popped it in his mouth, and, with a swig of Coke, washed it down. There was, after all that excitement, total silence but for the sound of shuffling feet as the police began herding everyone in.

The atmosphere was closer to that of a principal's office than a police roundup. There was a distinctly disciplinary feel. The stakes were low and the interaction for many of them had become commonplace. Young people congregate. The cops round them up. A fear of God and country is instilled in them before they're sent home, and then the cycle starts again. Everyone seemed pretty resigned to the routine.

A strip of tassels hung along the front window of the bus the three of them were forced onto. Photos of Gardel and the Boca Juniors were stuck to the ceiling, and little plastic dogs, the kind whose heads would shake when the bus stopped at a light, were lined up across the dash. Along with the other touches, the name Graciela had been painted in *fileteado* script on the rearview mirror. There was a photograph of a girl taped next to it: Graciela, Pato presumed.

There was a sort of nighttime bus-ride ambience that Pato usually loved. But this was not a regular bus. The windows were painted over. And whichever driver was sweet on Graciela and liked to make his little dogs shake at the stoplights—the policeman at the wheel wasn't him. Before they drove off, another officer climbed on with two plywood boards. He moved the kids out of the front seats and, sliding in one board and then other, he made a temporary wall so that none of them could see where they were headed or get out the front door. Rafa and Flavia and Pato sat together. Rafa had his feet stretched out as always. Flavia leaned her head on Rafa's chest. Pato sat on the edge of the seat, leaning forward, and was jostled with every bump in the road. This was his first time; it was Rafa's third. Pato tried to affect the calm—or at least the surrender—he was reading on everyone else. Flavia and Rafa tried to include him in their argument over how many policemen there had been. Pato had nothing to add. He tried to breathe deep and kept craning his neck as if it would otherwise fuse. He really wished he wasn't stoned.

They drove around for some time and didn't seem to be headed anywhere in particular. A police car had used its siren when they'd pulled out from in front of the pizza place. They hadn't heard it since. Pato wanted to know if Rafa thought they were still in the city. He'd whispered the question. Half a dozen people answered. They thought that they were.

When the bus finally stopped, nothing happened. An hour later the back door opened for a moment, a head count was taken, and then it closed. An hour after that, it opened again, and everyone was told to pass back their IDs. There were forty of them in that bus, and they all passed back their cards but for Pato, who'd left his wallet and keys and everything else when he'd stormed out of his house three days before. There was a claustrophobic girl who'd begun to lose her wits and, as if it was nothing, she was let outside into the night for a breath of air. Then, on second thought, the officer told her just to be quick about it and go, get lost, run home. The door shut.

Pato was his mother's son. He knew from his father how to disrespect authority; from his mother he'd learned to fear it. Seeing the girl released further unsettled his shaky calm. They were all in this together until they weren't.

"It's hot," Pato said.

"Nothing happens here," Flavia said, as if he'd actually said what he meant. "They're local cops. There are too many of us together. Anything that happens through the front entrance is fine."

"What's that supposed to mean?"

"It means if the local cops round us up and arrest us, they've pretty much got to account for us too. I mean if we go in through the front door of the police station, we likely come out the same way. It's the back door you've got to be afraid of."

Rafa liked conspiracy talk best. He drew a little crowd. "Accidents happen after you've been let go. A lot of people are getting run over as they walk out of the station. It's like living in a cartoon. Pianos constantly dropping on people's heads."

There were affirmations and corroborating stories. True or not, it's what everyone in that bus believed.

Pato said, "I don't feel so good."

"The paranoia that smoking reefer may induce is generally aggravated under these types of conditions," Rafa said. "It has been known to rankle."

Flavia kicked Rafa in the shin. "No worries," she said.

The door opened, and as with the return of their exam, names were being called in alphabetical order. One by one, A to Z, first Flavia, then Rafa, they were all—but for Pato—handed their IDs by a female officer and let go.

Rafa and Flavia waited across the street for Pato to come out. Pato waited alone in the bus and looked at the policewoman outside.

"Out of letters," she said. "The alphabet's done."

"Forgot my ID," Pato said.

Again the door shut.

The bus moved on, stopped, and the same policewoman let Pato out. He hopped down and the two of them stood face-to-face in front of a small police station that Pato had never seen. The policewoman looked deeply into his eyes. Pato stared at the holes in her ears where, off duty, she must hang earrings.

"Been smoking?" she said.

"Cigarettes," Pato said.

"Eyes mighty bloodshot for cigarettes."

"Allergies," Pato said.

She turned his face toward the lights on the building's façade. "It's dusty in the back of those buses," she said, and then took him inside.

An officer at the front desk looked up from a radio he was fiddling with, its front plate removed. There was another officer at a desk in the back. He didn't even turn as they passed.

She pulled Pato by his jacket, gave him a little shove into a holding cell, and locked him in.

Quite naturally, without even noticing, Pato took hold of the bars.

"Shouldn't you book me?" Pato said. "Don't I get to call someone and let them know I'm here?"

"Usually," she said. "Except you've got no ID. And without your ID you don't officially exist. It's kind of hard to process you in that case."

"That's why I need to call home."

"That's why you'll have to wait until tomorrow."

"Tomorrow?"

"Skeleton crew. The proper authorities are back at work in the morning. And then there's the backlog from the weekend. After that, we can see about finding out who you are."

"Then I can go like everyone else?"

"I don't know," she said. "That already was. The others have already gone."

She started to walk away. Now Pato, again, without thinking, pulled hard and pressed his face between bars.

"So Monday morning?" he called after her.

"So who knows?" she said. "Backlogged." Then, in a gesture so oddly friendly it doubled Pato's despair, the officer waved good-bye and left him where he was.

It was already late by then and, dozing a few seconds at a time on the benches, it didn't feel like long before morning. Someone brought him coffee on a tray. Toward afternoon a policeman on his way to lunch asked Pato for all his money. He took it and brought Pato a candy bar and a

Coke. Pato had expected every outcome, from torture to the guillotine, an amalgam of all the horrible stories and rumors and truths they spread among themselves. The only thing he hadn't planned on was to be fed, more or less, and left alone. After the Coke he felt comfortable enough to fall asleep for real and only woke up when woken by the same female officer, who—as if she'd never spoken to him before—gave him a pad and pencil and told him to write down all his information. In the interim, it seems, he'd slept through the introduction of another person to the cell. A middle-aged man in a suit (very worn) and running shoes (brand new), snored on the other bench. Pato could smell him from where he sat.

"Shouldn't be long," the officer said, when Pato gave her the pad.

Pato wondered if that meant hours or days, and it made the waiting all the worse. They'd left him his watch and he wished they'd taken it. He worried that the drunk might wake up, the least of his problems in a way.

At seven-thirty Monday night, the female officer took Pato out to call home. He was, previous to being locked up, dreading the inevitable first talk with his father. The idea became a lot more palatable under the circumstances. Pato still hoped—though it would scare her half to death—that his mother would be the one to answer the telephone. The worst part of this fiasco was that his parents didn't know he was in jail. It was only a night and a day, but had it already been a month they might still think he was over at Rafa's holding a grudge. It tightened Pato's throat in the dialing and he knew, if he didn't get another few seconds to control himself, if his mother grabbed at the phone right then, he'd burst into tears at the sound of her voice. Pato didn't want to cry in a police station. And not in front of the officer who'd waved. Eyes closed now, he pictured the apartment empty and dark, and the ring echoing around the living room and, faintly, out into the hall.

Then it stopped. Pato opened his eyes. With a finger to the cradle, the officer had hung up the telephone.

"We'll try again later," she said.

Once more, Pato thought he might cry. As with the claustrophobic girl and the roll call when Flavia and Rafa were set free, Pato knew this was another simple uncomplicated chance at freedom that would not necessarily repeat itself when later came.

[Fifteen]

THIS PERIOD OF INESTIMABLE LOSS and insecurity looked from inside Lillian's office to be a golden age. Those with real troubles were already afraid to make claims on them and the policies Lillian dealt with were more often from recent clients or the old ones who'd aligned themselves right. Gustavo's business reflected a fantastical era where new cars popped up in driveways and sometimes the driveway itself had a new house at its end. Women told stories of reaching up to find diamonds strung around their necks, while men laid watches on their bedside tables exposing sentimentalities whose provenance they couldn't explain. Sometimes there were surprises even greater than this.

Gustavo had kept the office open to receive a couple with a life insurance policy to amend. The couple was composed of a very powerful general and his very rich and powerful wife. Lillian had drawn up the original and, among other things that could have been done during business hours, there was a beneficiary to add. Lillian was taking care of it while Gustavo sat in his office straightening his desk blotter and arranging his pens. He was deeply embroiled for a man doing nothing. At any given instant he'd look euphoric, and then Lillian would catch him in a cold sweat so intense she'd wonder if his appendix had burst. He wanted the general's visit to go well.

The couple sat across from Lillian, radiating new-parent glow. The mother bounced a cooing baby in her lap, her bundle of joy. Answering Lillian's questions there was, at one point, a pause by the husband, a raised eyebrow from the wife, that fed into peals of laughter from the pair, a shaken rattle before the baby, and a chill down Lillian's spine. They'd stumbled on the date of birth. Their little angel: picked from a cabbage patch, flown in by the stork.

Lillian did not like the way this woman cradled a baby. She knew how an infant fit against its own mother's arm. Lillian had no credible reason to think anything was amiss. It wasn't the woman's first child; she'd held a baby before. Neither did stumbling on a date necessarily have any meaning. It was an insane thing for Lillian to think and even more insane that she had to fight herself not to say it aloud. Gustavo had good reason to sweat in that office. *This is not your baby* is what Lillian wanted to say.

She felt a bit dizzy. It was the same kind of disorientation she'd felt when she first saw her new nose—the very nose on which these people never once let their gazes fall. Saying good-bye, they stared at the top of her head.

And here was Gustavo out of his office. Here was Gustavo bouncing that baby, holding it up in the air. Passing it back to its mother, Gustavo put his arm around the father, slipped it around the small of his back. Gustavo with his arm around a general. Lillian had never seen him so happy before.

Gustavo returned with his briefcase in hand. He placed it on her desk and, putting the general's file in it, clicked closed both locks. "I don't know how you handle all these late nights. One is plenty enough for me. My thanks," Gustavo said. "Without you," he said.

Lillian wanted to tell Gustavo that it wasn't their baby. *I think that's a stolen baby* is what she was thinking, but the term didn't sound right even in her head. *Stolen baby* made the child sound like property. And *kidnapped* didn't relate to such a permanent thing. Also, it didn't seem possible. Where would a person find a baby to steal? She was as paranoid as Pato accused her of being. She let her mind run to extremes.

"I think we've signed on everyone in uniform but Videla" is what Lillian said.

Gustavo rolled his shoulders back. He nodded repeatedly at nothing in particular; it was his way of showing that he was entertaining a serious thought. "When was the last time you were out for a nice meal?"

"If you have to ask you have no idea how much you've been paying me." She tapped at his briefcase and the papers underneath. "If I did have the money, where would I get the time?"

"I'll close up with you after," he said. "Let's run out and get you a decent steak and a glass of wine. You'll talk me into a big raise for you and Frida, and I'll have you back here in a flash to finish up."

Lillian was at her desk deciding. She thought about that baby. She thought about a raise. She pictured herself going back to the apartment, the TV blaring, the cloud of smoke and the empty glasses, each one in its own little puddle on the floor. Kaddish would be on the couch, her husband whom she wasn't sure she'd tell about what she thought she might have seen, and—it hit her—what she had and had not done. If she'd pictured it differently, if she'd known that the apartment was dark and that she'd have the space to reflect, to sit in the comfy chair by the window with only a lamp on at her side, she'd have gone home. If Lillian had left right then she'd have made it, too; she'd have been there with enough space to doze off in that chair, enough time to drift and be startled awake by the second ringing of the phone.

Lillian took a bite of sautéed spinach. Garlic clung to the leaves in hunks. Reaching across, she stole a forkful of ravioli from Gustavo, who begged her to take more and lifted the plate. She pushed his arm down and raised up her glass, an acknowledgment that she needed a night out, and a fancy one too. Lillian sipped at her wine. Gustavo widened his smile. "Thanks for dinner," she said, and she ran a finger around the lip of her glass until the crystal hit a high note.

Kaddish had the occasional commission that took place outside the cemetery grounds. Though less public than the graveyard, the Benevolent Self's dilapidated house of worship still stood. As in any other synagogue, the prominent Jews of the congregation hadn't been averse to a little recognition for the donations they made. The standard bronze tree was affixed to the back wall. Silver leaves with donors' names were screwed onto bare branches in the days when the building fund bloomed. It's a tree that saw spring only once, Kaddish thought. Ever since it had been fall in the pimps' forest. The branches were almost bare.

Kaddish had no reason to wait until dark. The job was indoors. He'd arrived late in the afternoon and begun working by window light on what turned out to be a painstaking task.

Hanging at the front of the synagogue before an empty ark was the *parochet,* a heavy crimson curtain meant to give the ark a regal air. At its bottom there was an embroidered dedication—*In loving memory of Esther Zuckman*—with the dates of her life below it. The inscription had a lion holding it up at each end and was artfully rendered in gold thread. Esther's descendants had nothing to pay. They told Kaddish to keep the gold for himself.

Kaddish was far less sensitive about the rotting synagogue than the cemetery. He'd asked the family why he couldn't just tear down the curtain and be done? The Zuckmans wanted the curtain to hang as long as there was a building in which to hang it. They had twisted their faces at the very suggestion, unsure of his sensitivity, and Kaddish, who was thinking of gold, quickly added, "That is, it would be easy to tear it down if it hadn't been hung in your mother's name." With that they unscrewed their faces and gave him the job. Such was the balance he always had to strike between religiosity and superstition, pride and shame.

With cuticle nippers and tweezers lifted from Lillian's purse, Kaddish erased the name, thread by wire thread. When dark set in, he worked by flashlight. Kaddish was already pricked countless times by then, as if the name were a plant that didn't want to be picked. The brittle gold tips broke off and were buried in now red, now swelling, hands.

It was peaceful work for Kaddish nonetheless. The repetitive motion was calming, and the quiet of a crumbling synagogue had its own special feel. It set Kaddish to an odd mix of memory and daydream. He ignored his usual worries over mounting debt and Lillian's indifference, and the great weight of Pato's anger toward him. For a time Kaddish stopped his work and stared up into the darkness of the women's section, wondering where his mother had sat.

When he was done, Kaddish spread two handkerchiefs out on the floor. In the center of each he made a pile of gold wire and then compressed them. He looked at the treasure collected from his unraveling. He tied up the two handkerchiefs and, feeling their heft, he was satisfied at the deal he'd struck.

Kaddish stood up, put on his coat, and dropped one of the handkerchiefs in each pocket. There was a creak to his knees when he moved and a steel-wool sting to his hands. He stepped back to the pews and eased himself down slowly, trying to minimize the pain in his lower back. He smoked a cigarette and pointed the flashlight at the work he'd done.

The name looked worse. That is, *Esther Zuckman* looked better than it had in many years. The family hadn't considered this when they balked at the idea of the curtain's coming down. Protected from the light, from the air, cocooned in gold, the velvet underneath was unfaded. The pattern of the needlework outlined each letter. Kaddish had achieved the exact opposite of what had been intended. Esther's name had never before shone so brightly.

Kaddish didn't fret. He could be as savvy as his friend the doctor. He'd offered to remove the curtain and the family had resisted. If they wanted it disposed of now, he'd happily see to it for a fee. He switched off the flashlight and thought he could still make out the name in the dark.

Kaddish hadn't brought his car and, stepping out into a cloudy night, he began his walk home. All in all it was a successful outing. He mumbled a word of approval to himself and pulled his collar closed against his throat. His red hands, his swollen hands, were numb from the work. Holding them up for further study under a streetlight, a thousand gold splinters picked up a glint, and it was in his cupped hands as if he were looking at the stars.

[Sixteen]

WHEN THE PHONE RANG a second time, Kaddish was home to meet it. He tracked down Pato's ID and drove calmly to the police station they'd specified. He was adept at not confusing big trouble for small.

For Kaddish, there were two facts: The police had his son, and they'd called for him to come pick Pato up. Problem solved before the start. He'd only said hello to Pato on the phone, heard him say, "Dad," and then a woman had gotten on the line. It was the same as in the old days, a father's job to ferry his son. It would be like picking him up from a friend's house or fetching him from school. Pato would avert his eyes when Kaddish got there; he'd slouch his shoulders in front of the cops and sit huddled and silent in the car the whole way home.

Pato said nothing when Kaddish got there. He had indeed slouched and slumped and sat silent. When they arrived at the apartment he'd gone straight to his room. It was then that Kaddish felt the same terrible emptiness that Pato had felt when first locked in jail. His son had been in distress and Kaddish hadn't even known.

Kaddish called Lillian's office before pouring his drink. It was actually the kind of night Kaddish dreamed of—hard work, gold in his pocket, his son home and saved from some unknown danger by his father's hand. Tonight he'd be a hero. His wife would return. He'd trot out his son and pull the treasure from his pockets. Kaddish squeezed the handkerchiefs and decided right then he'd make Lillian a ring.

Lillian answered the phone at work, sounding happy herself. She was packing her bag and closing up. She was tipsy and well fed. Her own hard work had been recognized. She'd gotten a long-overdue raise.

And then Kaddish shared the news. For once, he'd told her in the way she'd always asked of him. Kaddish said, "Pato is fine. He's here with me. He's in his room and all is well." Then, after safety was established and good health was established, Kaddish explained about Pato's call and the police station from where they'd just returned. He managed this in such a light way that it came out as anecdote, something only a spoilsport wouldn't laugh off. When he was finished, Lillian said, "Thank you." She stressed and restressed the request she should have made on the day of the coup. Lillian said, "You keep him in the house, I'll be home soon."

"I'll sit on him if I have to."

"Superb," Lillian said. Kaddish had Pato's ID in his back pocket and knew, at least while the experience was fresh, that Pato wasn't going to storm out without his papers again.

There wasn't much time. Kaddish wanted things perfect for Lillian, and there was still some fatherly business to attend to. He wanted an explanation, a story to tell Lillian when she walked through the door. High with his success and with hers, Kaddish didn't want to find himself staring at the floor when Lillian asked for the rest of the details, he didn't want to tell his wife, "I don't know."

Kaddish went straight for Pato's room, entered without knocking and demanded his due from Pato, who sat, legs crossed, on his bed.

"The least you could say is thank you," Kaddish said. This was enough to get them right back on track, as if not a moment had passed, as if Kaddish had just set fire to the books and Pato had taken the swing that hit his father in the nose. Except now it was Kaddish who burst through the door and stood over his son. It was Kaddish who slowly flexed a red and swollen hand. The scales were finally set right.

"My room," Pato said.

"At the very least," Kaddish said, "is thank you."

Kaddish delivered the words like a threat. This wasn't his original intent but Kaddish heard the difference in tone and committed to it. He moved close and repeated, "At the very least," with menace.

There was a father in the room and a son. If Pato never wanted to acknowledge it again, he wouldn't have to. Tonight Kaddish was demanding capitulation. He wanted the boy to give in.

Pato clamped his headphones over his ears and dropped the needle onto an album. He flicked on the hi-fi at the end of the bed and closed his eyes. Such disrespect, as if his father weren't there.

Kaddish yanked out the headphone's plug.

Pato got up off his bed. "What do you want from me?" Pato said.

"What do I want?" Kaddish said. "I want basic respect."

"Then earn it."

"I'm your father. I don't have to. That's the whole point." Kaddish reached for the headphones. Plugged in or not, they were an affront.

Pato pulled them off on his own and threw them on the bed. "Fine," he said.

"Fine, what?" Kaddish asked him.

"They're off, is all. I'm agreeing with that. Nothing more."

After too long a pause, Kaddish said, "Nothing more?" It was another retort that was only repetition.

Pato shook his head, disappointed. He always found a way to condescend.

"You want to know what to agree on? You want something to agree with me about? I've got a list for you: Enough of the mouth and the bad behavior. Enough of the shady friends and the slinking around. Whatever you did to get yourself pinched, it's got to stop. Whatever you're involved in has to come to an end. You can't go on messing around."

Pato had been terrified by his quiet stay in a clean, quiet cell. He was happy to be back in his bedroom and couldn't wait for his mother to come home. He was happy, too, that his father had saved him and, over his dead body, he'd never let anyone know. He couldn't help but scream in response with his man's voice and little-boy indignation. "I wasn't doing anything. I didn't do it. I didn't do anything at all."

"For nothing? For nothing they pick you up. For nothing they toss you in a cell so I've got to go down there and fetch you."

"I didn't do a fucking thing," Pato said. "They grab us for no reason."

"Don't lie to me," Kaddish said.

Pato heard this and pressed at the sides of his head, a tantrum coming on.

"Fuck you," he said to his father. "We didn't do anything."

"Now it's *we*? Now the whole bunch of you is innocent? I want to know what you're into," Kaddish said. "And I want you out of it before your mother gets home."

"Fuck you," Pato said. "The only crimes I've ever committed are the ones for your whores."

"You watch your mouth," Kaddish said. "Not under my roof," he said.

The age-old responses, the words now only for rhythm. It was the eternal father-son fight. Pato rocked back and forth. To each threat from his father he responded with a hearty, "Fuck you." The thanks Kaddish sought had mutated into this. He redoubled his efforts to find out what Pato had done. "Not right or wrong," he said, "no one's accusing. Tell me, only, what did you do?"

It was a poor strategy, Kaddish's forte. How could he have known there was no answer for Pato to give?

Veins throbbed visibly. Teeth were clenched. And, as if they planned to butt heads, they scratched their feet at the floor. Kaddish and Pato stood chest to chest. So as not to tear each other to pieces, both knowing violence would go unrestrained, they found the only way out. They reversed course, giving their meaningless words all the meaning they could bear. They put the bite back into their yelling. They engaged all their socialized, civilized, higher human faculties. They barbed up their language and said what they meant and felt what was said.

With careful modulation and pitch-perfect sensitivity, Pato said, "Fuck you," to his father. He said it slowly and full of feeling and, tweaking, went at it again. "Fuck you," Pato said. "I wish you were dead."

And Kaddish, his father, stepped back at the words. How much, how much can one man take after doing everything he could and doing it wrong in the eyes of his son? There were tears in Kaddish's eyes. He thought he might cry. *Fuck you. I wish you were dead.* He'd heard it before. This time, though, the tone was right, the intonation was right, and he heard it personal. He heard it as truth.

Kaddish heard it and accepted it. He was bowled over by it and, wounded—that's all he could tell himself, that it hurt him to the core—he returned it to his son. Kaddish dished it right back.

"Fuck you," Kaddish said to Pato, his son. And—with all his might, with all his hurt feeling—"Fuck you," Kaddish said. "I wish you'd never been born."

He said it. And it left them both standing for a moment in silence.

Before there was time for either of them to absorb it, while the curse still hung in the air between them, there was, most clearly, a knock at the door.

And Kaddish went to get it. And Kaddish got his wish.

It was, in an instant, as if his son was never born.

[PART TWO]

[Seventeen]

A MAN IN A SHARP GRAY SUIT walked out the door into the darkness of the hallway, a book tucked under his arm. A second man followed, two books, like dead weights, one hanging from each hand. A third and a fourth man walked out the door with Pato, Kaddish's son, standing between them. They held him very firmly by the elbows, grasping tightly, so that his arms were bent and his hands straight in front. As he passed out of the apartment he smiled at his father, who hadn't moved from his place by the heavy door, holding it open (needlessly) with a foot. He said to Kaddish, "A very poor note to end on," and for this comment grips tightened and hands pointed higher in the air. They were not walking fast; Kaddish heard it all clearly. He also heard the elevator gate open and the hum of the old motor in the dark, since no one pressed the button for the hallway light. The gate to the elevator slid back, teeth caught gears, and then, along with the motor, there was the click of the release as the car lowered and the five bodies started to descend. Kaddish closed the door behind them and turned the key in its center.

The first man's suit had wide lapels. The second man had a windbreaker on between his suit jacket and shirt, mostly hidden, but Kaddish caught a glimpse of nylon: red and black, Newell's colors. Kaddish was a Boca fan.

Kaddish didn't read much but was sure the second man, the wind-breaker man, didn't either. It was the way he let the books hang in his hands as if there were nothing inside, nothing there at all but the weight of the things themselves. The book closer to Kaddish had a picture on the cover. He didn't recognize it then but would know the book and the photograph when he saw it, also in Spanish translation, on the shelf of a fellow Argentine living in Jerusalem ten years down the line. He would, in mid-sentence, stop talking and, remembering, ask to sit down.

There is no need to repeat that these books—all the books in the house, really—belonged to Pato. Kaddish and Lillian preferred the TV.

Lillian Poznan had tried to prevent this. She'd gone out and bought the door. It wasn't what she wanted kept out but what she wanted kept in. She had worried for her son.

Kaddish Poznan had also tried to prevent this. He walked down the hallway and into the bathroom. He closed and locked the door and sat down in the dark, leaning his head against his arm and his arm against the tub. He could feel with his fingers the rough enamel within. He smelled the burnt smell and saw, in his mind's eye, where the tub was black, where the paint on the ceiling peeled, which tiles were sooty in the grouting, and how the small window onto the air shaft was greasy black on the glass slats and around the edges where the wallpaper bubbled and warped.

Kaddish Poznan had burned his son's books in the bathtub. He just hadn't burned all the right ones.

[Eighteen]

KEYS JANGLING, SMILE FADING, Lillian's purse hung over her arm. She stepped into the middle of the room and put down her briefcase. She was calling for Pato all the while. The joy of coming home to her son, of the raise at work and her night on the town, still circled round her.

Lillian checked both bedrooms and the kitchen where, as usual, the split lemon sat. Maybe they were out in Kaddish's courtyard having a cigarette, the two of them stamping their feet against the chill. Lillian went out onto the service balcony, leaned over the railing, and yelled down. There was no answer from the bottom, only a half-deaf Mrs. Ordóñez with a, "Yes, dear" and an invitation for tea.

Kaddish lay on his side on the floor, his knees pulled up and pressed into his chest. He hung his arm over the lip of the tub and picked at the charred enamel. He was confused about exactly what had transpired. It had all happened so fast and yet, quick as it was, there was an enormous amount to absorb.

Here are the things that may have been said to his son: "We'll cut your little cock off and choke you with it, this is how they'll find you"; "Montonero, we'll cut out your tongue and sew it into your father's mouth"; and also, "We'll cut off your father's cock and plug your asshole with it." So many odd things he may or may not have heard. Kaddish thought, Why so sexual? In the moment it was happening he'd wanted to say, *Begging your pardon, is there any need to speak this way? Is it part of the job?*

Kaddish couldn't remember which one had spoken. Was it the wind-breaker man or the sharp gray suit? Oh, but there was a nice part. He remembered a nice bit that he could share with his wife. Such a tough boy, his Pato, but, in the moment, so sweet. On the way out, he'd said, "Fathers are always fathers. Sons always sons." Kaddish repeated it aloud. Lillian might like it, but he couldn't be sure.

Kaddish paid no mind to Lillian, mashing her fists, pulping her fists, screaming for him to open the door. At another time, in another Argentina, such a ruckus would have brought one neighbor running, set another complaining. There would have been a boot against a common wall, a broom handle in answer from Mrs. Ordóñez—ricochets and reactions and eventually police called in. Now it was assumed the police were to blame.

When people heard noise they didn't make more. They stopped what they were doing and turned their eyes to the floor. And, more and more, they kept on with their business. The neighbors heard nothing, no matter how loud.

Here was Lillian down on her hands and knees, her mouth at the space under the bathroom door. In her panic, she'd been calling for Pato. Lowering her voice to a whisper, she then called, instead, Kaddish's name.

Lillian not only said, "Kaddish," but also, "What have you done?"

That question, Kaddish heard. After a pause to consider the forked path of errors from the start of his life until that day and, from that day, the errors that led up until that moment, Kaddish raised himself up a bit. He hung his head over the slightly cooler emptiness of the tub. To Lillian's question, he formulated the best answer he could.

"I locked myself behind the wrong door."

Kaddish spoke into the hollow of the bath and the sound spread out, amplified by the tub, reflected by the tiles, filling the bathroom until it spilled out through the space Lillian spoke into, so that she heard Kaddish's answer less from him than from the house itself: *The wrong door,* carried out on an infinitesimal current of air.

"What is that?" Lillian said. "What does that mean?"

"I thought it was you," he said. Kaddish got up, unlocked the door, and, coming out, moved slowly past. Lillian followed him down the hall.

"You opened what should stay closed, what I told you to keep closed—"

"And closed what might as well be open," Kaddish said.

"And?" Lillian said.

"Three books," Kaddish said. "I missed three books. They took them along with Pato."

"God help us," Lillian said.

In the living room, Kaddish pointed to an empty space on the top shelf. "A place to start looking. From all the books in the world, I'm nearly sure one that we are missing went there."

"Lost your mind," Lillian said. "Lost our son."

"Yes," Kaddish said. "And I held it for them." Here his voice broke hard. "I held open the door."

Lillian then took Kaddish's face in her hands, and to get the attention of her addled husband, she squeezed that face as hard as she could. She pressed her nails into the side of Kaddish's head. But Kaddish didn't feel it. The pressure was already immense.

Lillian said, "Did you call the police?"

"Oh, my," Kaddish said. And he laughed. He laughed so hard his head shook and Lillian's nails, unmoving, broke skin. "No," Kaddish said. "The police," he said. "I didn't think to call them. I would have, my dear, my sweet." He kissed his wife on the cheek, leaning down, so that now her hands on his face resembled a grasp of great passion.

"I would have called," he said, "but I think—I'm quite sure—they only make a house call once a night. I think—I believe, my dear Lillian—I think the police have already been."

[Nineteen]

LILLIAN STOOD WITH HER FEET planted in the corners of the doorframe, hands clamped to the sides. She was watching Kaddish in the hallway outside Cacho's, her husband taking control.

Cacho, who was surely home at this hour, didn't answer. For this Kaddish deemed him involved.

Kaddish had never had to calm Lillian physically before. In the apartment he'd peeled Lillian's hands from his face. As if setting her loose, she'd stormed across the hall and again started banging, everyone in cahoots. Kaddish had hugged his arms around Lillian and moved her away. Then he'd replaced her.

Kaddish beat at that door, his swollen palms aching. Lillian said nothing. She stood in silhouette on their threshold while Kaddish backed up three steps and, charging, threw his shoulder against the door like the cops they saw on television. The door didn't give on the first hit or the second, and then it opened with Cacho hidden behind. He snaked his head around to find Kaddish with a foot planted for a third charge.

Cacho opened the door wider. He was wearing the same pajamas he'd worn on the day of the coup. "You'll have to excuse me," he said. "I was sleeping."

Lillian was already pushing at Kaddish's back. "Well, it's good you woke up," she said. "Lucky. Because, you won't believe it, but while you were sleeping Kaddish was breaking down your door. He was just this minute smashing it in so I could ask you a question."

"It must be important, if he was so driven."

"It is, it is," Kaddish said. "Baking," he said, squinting, studying Cacho's face. "And, believe it or not, we've run out of eggs."

"A cup of sugar," Lillian said, and stepped to Kaddish's side.

"You're kidding, of course," Cacho offered.

"Yes. Yes. We're big jokers, me and the wife. A comedy team. What we want to know—" Again Kaddish was squinting, and then he pointed at Cacho's face. A finger right up to his face. "Do you see that, Lillian? His eyebrow is bleeding."

"That's him," she said. "I've seen it before. He scratches the eyebrows until there's blood."

"Well, then"—Kaddish lowered the finger—"what about the mouth? Both his lips have been split. Do you think he punches himself in the mouth as well?"

Lillian doubted this. "Not likely," she said.

"That's why I was asleep so early, sleeping so heavily as to miss the knocking. Because of the accident. I've had a fall and I'm not myself."

"We understand," Lillian said. "We're no strangers to the recuperative. Kaddish is on his second set of black eyes."

"I was about to mention," Cacho said. "Both your noses have come out most lovely."

"Can we come in?" Kaddish said.

Cacho came out instead. He sighed as he did, knowing he was bringing his splinted arm along with him. He'd duct-taped a wooden spoon underneath his wrist; against the top, the tape held a spatula in place.

"Quite a fall," Lillian said. "To give you a fat lip as well as a broken—"

"Sprained at most."

"As well as a sprained-at-most arm."

"And the apartment a mess because of it, which is why I don't invite you in."

"We'll have you over instead," Kaddish said. He looked to Lillian for direction. He wasn't exactly sure about roughhousing a neighbor who'd been beaten and who hadn't really done anything in the first place, a passive crime at best. Taking all that into consideration, and glancing at his wife, Kaddish took Cacho firmly by his splinted wrist. Cacho screamed and then whimpered steadily as Kaddish led him across to their living room.

Cacho sat on the couch.

"They took Pato," Lillian said.

Cacho stared up in horror.

"No time for displays," Lillian said. "Kaddish thinks it was the police who took him. We're going down to the station to fetch him, and you can imagine how much it would help—"

"I was sleeping all night," Cacho said.

Kaddish sat down on the couch on his neighbor's bad side. "Did you dream any odd dreams, Cacho? Was there a nightmare where four men beat you for peeking out while they took my son away?"

"I didn't dream that," Cacho said. He looked up to Lillian, raising only his eyes.

"Dream it this minute," she said. "Go put some clothes on and get rid of that ridiculous splint and come with us to talk to the police."

"But I didn't see anything."

"I'll tell you what you saw," Lillian said. "You watched him grow up. You saw him from a little boy."

"I slept. I didn't dream. I didn't hear. I didn't see."

"Everyone losing senses these days," Kaddish said. He was truly disappointed. "When this is all over, it'll be hard to see these handicaps undone."

Cacho stood up to go. "It *is* everyone," he said. "Not just me. Everyone is sleeping deeply." He looked to Lillian, who looked away. "I'm sorry."

"For what?" Kaddish said. He pulled Cacho back down to the couch. "If you have no reason to come to the police station with us, stay here and babysit Pato."

"But he's gone," Cacho said. He cradled his arm.

"Then you'll have an easy job of it. You can call us at the station if anything comes up."

Cacho was desperate; his voice went high. "I don't understand. Who am I babysitting if no one's here?"

"How would you know that?" Lillian said. "Did you see?"

"I was sleeping, I told you."

"Then you'll have no trouble staying awake. And if you can't, feel free, stretch out on the couch. Read a book until you nod off."

Kaddish looked over his shoulder. "Don't touch the books. Television. Watch the TV."

"You can't make me stay here. What if they come back? What if they decide they want you two as well? Whole families. First one, then the others."

"Who's coming back?" Kaddish said.

"I can't do it." Cacho stood up cautiously. Kaddish didn't pull him back down. "I couldn't have stopped them even if I saw."

"We know that," Kaddish said. "Nobody thinks you could."

"A coward after all," Lillian said.

"I am," Cacho said, and his eyes turned narrow before—like a blink—returning to the width of his pleading. "But how did they get the boy past a man as tough as your husband?" He turned to Kaddish. "How did they get past you?"

"Go home," Lillian said. "We won't involve you, Cacho. Understood. We'll make sure it's stated clearly in the report: Cacho Barbieri is not involved. I'll tell the police you asked specifically for it to be recorded that you were witness to nothing."

"I'll stay," Cacho said. "It's fine."

Cacho sat. Kaddish blew his nose.

A threat from Lillian. Kaddish thought it as fine as any he'd given or received over the debt-filled high-stress bad-business years.

Lillian took a picture of Pato off the wall of family photos in the hallway. She put on her jacket and handed Kaddish his.

"I'll be here," Cacho said. "I'll wait until you get back with your son."

How many skinny boys work graveyard shifts on any given night? How many fathers approach these stringbeans knowing already that uselessness is why they've been put on the job? This was Kaddish's inspired observation as they entered Once's police station. The first line of defense for any corrupt dysfunctional system is an ignoramus guarding the door.

Young officer Rangel answered only, "Shorthanded," when Lillian demanded a senior officer again and again. She showed him the picture of Pato and he swore he hadn't booked a soul the whole night. "We've got two cars out on patrol, two at a fire, and the sergeant off doing sergeantly things. There's no one here but the three of us." The policeman had included Lillian and Kaddish in his count—such a polite young man. Lillian thought he could as easily have said *Just me.*

"Prove it," Kaddish said, as if the burden was on Rangel.

"We really don't do that, sir. Proving is frowned upon."

"My son," Lillian said.

He was new as could be, this officer, his judgment marred by inexperience. Rangel hiked up his pants and tightened his belt a notch. He took them to see the empty cells and, upon Lillian's request, opened the broom closet too. He even let Lillian look into the sergeant's office, putting out an arm to stop her when she tried to check under the desk.

"He's not under the desk. I've been here a double shift." He coaxed Lillian back to the civilian side of the counter to coincide with the sergeant's return. The boy told the sergeant what he'd been trying to explain. The sergeant wiped his hand across a creased night-shift face and, taking the frame from Lillian said, "Something official. I don't go by pictures off the wall. And we don't go by nicknames either. *Pato* is for home, I want what you wrote on the birth certificate when he was born."

"Pablo," Kaddish said. "On that it says Pablo Poznan, but we've never once used it."

"You'll use it here."

Kaddish produced Pato's ID from his back pocket. Lillian thought he'd planned ahead.

The sergeant scratched under his chin. He considered the ID, worn on the ends, the laminate peeling away. He put a thumbnail in the space and peeled it farther apart.

"It's against the law, this," the sergeant told them. "It's against the law to alter a government document in any way."

"It's not altered," Lillian said.

"It has been tampered with."

"You did that," she said. "You made it worse just now with your thumb."

"So you admit it's partially tampered with but accuse me of exacerbating the situation by investigating."

"She accuses you of nothing," Kaddish said.

"That's good," the sergeant said. Caught up in the tension, the string-bean revealed a fine case of rosacea, turning a deep red on cheeks and ears and behind his eyebrows. It reminded Kaddish of his neighbor. A fiery patch lit across Rangel's neck. "It's good that you aren't accusing. Or I might wonder why you have someone else's official documents in the first place."

"Because he's our son," Lillian said.

"It should be with him."

"We should be with him," Lillian said. "That's why we came."

"Well, you've come to the wrong place. This is a police station. We arrest those who commit crimes. Parents will not find innocent sons here." A scratch to the chin, a look at his watch. "I apologize if peon Rangel didn't make it clear, but your son isn't in custody."

"Thank you for your time," Kaddish said. They were finished there. He put out his hand for the ID.

"I can't return an altered document," the sergeant said, "especially to an individual who isn't the rightful owner. Send"—another glance at it—"send your Pablo to pick it up and explain its condition, and I'll return it to him."

Kaddish offered a second thank-you, like a curse under his breath.

Outside in the false dawn of streetlights, Lillian and Kaddish felt it simultaneously, though neither admitted it to the other. The sergeant had sent them out with their first shard of doubt. It reminded Kaddish of the fancy lady in the hospital with the splinter in her foot. Whenever he took a breath, tried to shift that doubt or bury it deeper, it was as the doctor had theorized. It splintered and splintered in endless directions.

[Twenty]

THE PICTURE FRAME WAS VELVET-BACKED and made both for hanging and standing. When Lillian extended its arm, a silk ribbon went taut, anchoring the frame on the officer's desk. Lillian had placed it where a loved one's photo would sit. In fact, she'd set it next to one of his own. After an interminable wait at the second station, Lillian and Kaddish had been seated in two chairs facing the officer at his desk.

The officer lifted the frame and the velvet arm fell forward against his fingers, a touch Lillian hoped familiar even if he studied an unfamiliar face. Then he raised his glasses and rested them on his head. Bringing the frame closer, he looked to Kaddish and then Lillian. She offered a warm smile.

Lillian believed deeply in the importance of these details. If she placed the picture in the right spot, he would reach for it and see the boy in a familiar way. If she was ready when he looked her way and smiled a warm smile during the worst moment she'd ever known, he would feel a bit of warmth toward her and in this way change their fate. He would walk off to some room and return with her son. The officer could stop it at the start. Lillian would hold no grudges and count this day as the happiest of her life.

The officer lowered his glasses and placed the picture face down. He took hold of the desk and rolled his chair closer until his stomach hit.

Kaddish and Lillian made the same motion. They wanted to meet this intimacy and better hear what he had to say. Except their chairs were not on rollers. Planted firmly, each made a subtle jerk forward and stopped dead.

"Maybe if you tell me again," the officer said.

"We've told you twice already," Kaddish said. Lillian pressed a hand to his knee and mustered another warm smile. The officer was unperturbed. "How many lady cops are there?" Kaddish said. "Call the one who released the boy into my care. I've already been here tonight."

"What you've told me is that you were having a fight with your kid and then the mystery police snatched him. Your local station has no idea what you're talking about so you figure, during a time of national crisis, that I sent my people across town to bust into your house and bring your son here. We're twiddling our fucking thumbs waiting for high-schoolers to roust."

"University," Lillian said.

"All this you back up with an absent neighbor's testimony."

"It's not my neighbor's word alone," Lillian said. "The police left their mark. He's waiting at our house right now nursing his wounds. Let's call him. You'll see."

The officer didn't reach for the phone.

"Fast work by those police, stealing boys and beating neighbors all before you could get home from work." The officer had taken some notes and he looked at his timeline. While he did this, he raised up the corner of his mouth, bearing teeth. "Yes? A matter of minutes for all that to get done. Efficient. Very efficient, those mystery police."

"Well, he didn't break his own arm," Kaddish said, his voice loud.

"No," the officer said. "Likely he didn't. And judging from your eloquently confused description, I'm sure it would take endless footwork to figure out who did. I'm sure it's a crime as inexplicable as your own black eyes."

"From my son. A different fight."

"Do you know what time it is?" the officer said. "You can't even get a pizza at this hour. If your toilet overflowed you wouldn't think of doing anything but bailing until morning. Yet you stroll in here looking for

Sherlock Holmes to solve what can't be solved. What I'm trying to be is polite. I'm trying to be nice in the middle of the fucking night."

"It is not unsolvable," Lillian said.

"It is with your husband's version. Come talk to me, Mrs. Poznan, when you find out what really happened before you arrived." Lillian knew with Kaddish that there could be another story, a new account introduced when they got back to the car.

"You took our boy once," Kaddish said. "Why wouldn't you do it again?"

The officer tore the back off the frame and pulled the photograph out. Raising his glasses again, he brought the picture up to his face and shook his head. "None of it makes sense, least of all the photo. This kid didn't come from either of you."

"Oh my God," Lillian said, absorbing, horrified.

"It's not my nose," Kaddish yelled, referring to his own.

The officer nodded, still staring at the picture. "At least you can be thankful for that."

[Twenty-one]

THERE ARE FIFTY-TWO POLICE STATIONS in Buenos
Aires, eighteen *secretarías,* and seven different ministries. There are
twenty-nine hundred registered lawyers working in the courts, three
military branches, and one Pink House—the seat of government down
the avenue, a palace where all answers lie. Lillian would find her way to
every one of these places. She'd show up on every doorstep and catch
every official by the collar.

Before heading home, Lillian and Kaddish made the rounds at four
more stations. They didn't corner the highest-ranked officers but the
lowest, stuffing cash into the hand of a kid emptying garbage cans and
slipping some bills to a mentholated policeman who smelled of alco-
hol poorly masked. Neither told them anything of value and Lillian
watched as the drinker spoke to them with his hand clasped over the
mouth of his mug.

Kaddish gravitated to the cheeks with burst veins, to the skinniest
men in the biggest uniforms, to the officers of rank with bitten nails or
bouncing legs. At the last of the stations he spoke to a nervous woman
in sunglasses who carried a dog out the back door at 3 a.m.

This was Kaddish's way they were trying. Already it had split into his
way and hers.

They woke Cacho when they got back to the apartment and sent him off without a word. Lillian hung her empty frame back up in the hallway. Kaddish lit a burner for tea.

He put out the butter. He called for Lillian and she didn't come. He poured the tea and poked around for bread. Kaddish found a baguette and split it. It made a cracking noise like wood.

The phonebook Lillian had taken off Pato's nightstand; a class portrait from high school she'd gotten off the shelf. In the front of his bag there was a list of contacts on a syllabus marked SURVEY OF SOCIOLOGICAL THEORY. In two different pockets of the same pair of jeans, she found the numbers of girls written on napkins in a round flirty hand.

Lillian woke them all: Pato's friends and their roommates and their parents, since most lived at home. She tried to sound upbeat, counteracting the truth and time of morning, contrasting the groggy, frightened voices on the phone.

They left her on the line to look in on children or wake up their folks. They hung up so that boyfriends could call girlfriends, and then Lillian would find the next number busy as Pato's friends reached out to others in turn. Half the time Lillian wasn't sure if she'd yet mentioned his name and already the conversation was over and the line gone dead.

With each call she became more desperate, and with that desperation her friends as well as Pato's seemed to understand less. So she said it more clearly. "Missing," Lillian said. "Kidnapped." The words generated their own static, Lillian forced to yell. Lillian called Rafa's and it was Flavia who answered. "Gone," is what she said. "Pato is gone."

Flavia let out a howl so deep it was the closest sound Lillian had heard to match what she was feeling. In response, Lillian let out a cry of her own. Lillian then heard Rafa advising. "Tell her we will call her," he said, and Flavia said, "We will call."

Worse than a lack of progress was a loss of ground. Lillian knew with each interaction she was saying good-bye. What she'd intended was to let people know that Pato had been missing one night. Lillian wanted group concern and group support, the horror that Pato was a few hours gone and the hope that he'd be a few hours back. What she hadn't expected was a detail spun out of control. It wasn't Pato taken they were hearing. In each telling it was as if her son had never been. The idea of absence had acquired its own fierce momentum. It was like snatching a ball from a baby and hiding it behind one's back—there was the initial shock and then, like that, Pato was no more.

The phone was on a phone table, up against the same wall that held the little scalloped shelf. On the other side of that wall was the kitchen where Kaddish was fixing breakfast. Lillian grasped what she'd done and stopped dialing the next number. She replaced the phone in its cradle and, leaning back in the chair she'd carried over, she banged her head hard against the wall. Kaddish came running out. He asked if she was all right.

Lillian said she was not all right. She'd spread panic. She'd set off a great rolling-over across the city—arms thrown over bedmates, loved ones clasped tight. No one was out looking for Pato, no one coming to help. They were otherwise occupied with forgetting him. And it wasn't only Pato—Lillian and Kaddish would be swept up in it too. Lillian had felt it over the phone, felt her own self turning tiny in their heads.

She apologized to her husband. She'd seen the family undone.

Kaddish wasn't sure he believed her.

"Try any of the numbers," she said. "Call anyone back."

Kaddish did. He took the list and called Rafa. The boy's mother answered, wide awake. "It's Kaddish," Kaddish said. The woman said nothing. Then he said, "Kaddish Poznan, Pato's father." In response there was some rustling, and eventually from Rafa's mother came, "Please understand." Kaddish couldn't. Though she'd answer him no further, she didn't hang up. Kaddish listened to her breathing for some time before putting down the phone.

"Try another," Lillian said.

Kaddish didn't need to. Kaddish got the point.

"You did the right thing," he said.

"I did it all wrong and I should have known better."

"Nonsense," Kaddish said. And unsure of where she'd bumped it, he rubbed the back of her head.

Lillian said, "Your expertise is finally being called into play. It's a situation tailor-made for the *hijo de puta*." She looked up at him, her eyes open wide. "Except this time it's on me, Kaddish."

Kaddish gave her neck a squeeze.

"I've taken us over another wall. I've dragged this family into the one graveyard that everyone in this nation has agreed not to see."

"It's not the same. And even if it was, look how they come to me now after twenty-five years. Truth can be denied but it can't be undone."

"I shouldn't have told."

"The price of doing nothing would be harder to measure. However much I suffer for keeping the Benevolent Self alive, at least I suffer whole."

"What about what Pato and I have suffered because of it? It's the price the rest of us have paid that I'm afraid of." Lillian waited for a response. "Maybe your truth would have done better had you held it dear, in secret and alone."

Kaddish thought about it.

"How true is anything that only one man believes?"

Lillian had no control over the hours stacking up since Pato was taken. Every instant, she knew, could move him farther, bury him deeper, place Pato in endless ways more distant from home. She was almost at the point where she'd have to abandon her belief in innocent outs: that Pato had been released, found unconscious by a stranger, or dumped into a gutter only to stumble disoriented to a friend's.

It was possible.

The officer had said, "Get the real story from your husband." With Kaddish she could hope for an actual course of events so far from his initial version that it would leave Pato free.

Kaddish came down the hall with a towel around his waist. Lillian still sat by the phone and Kaddish, his hand wet from the shower, placed it on her cheek. "It will do you good," he said. He puffed out his chest to show he was feeling rejuvenated and fresh.

"Fine," Lillian said, and shifted in the chair as if intending to rise.

"Starting a night without Pato is as terrible as can be. Finishing it with no one to help us is too much to take."

"How much worse for a family with no experience at being cast out? For everything there's a reason. We'll get Pato back. We'll keep our heads."

"The dead boy in the cemetery," Lillian said. "When it was another family's son—"

"We went back," Kaddish said, "and he was gone. Anyway, a dead body in a cemetery is a different matter. A boy with his throat slit is already beyond help."

Kaddish went to get dressed.

When she was young and the three of them were happy, in the days when Pato was still crawling around on the floor, Kaddish had said, "Let's have another." They were in bed in the dark when he'd proposed it, and Lillian had said, "Not now. In good time." "What if that time doesn't come?" Kaddish had wanted to know. And when Lillian didn't answer he'd said, "Two kids is better. What if one drowns?" Horrible. Such a thing to say.

In remembering, Lillian felt the last of her innocence ground down. She picked up the receiver and dialed Frida.

"What's wrong, sweetie?" Frida said, the first clear line. Lillian found herself heard before she'd spoke.

"It's Pato," she said. And Frida gasped, Frida knew.

Lillian said it anyway, because it was true, it was fact, because her heart broke.

"Gone," Lillian said.

Then there was silence. A new time started, a clock that ticked both forward and back. From then on, Lillian breathed twice as heavy, felt twice as hungry, and swore to fight twice as hard. She accepted then that to others Pato wasn't, and it was up to her to make it so Pato was. It was as if she were pregnant with a full-grown son.

Kaddish was thinking that Lillian should eat and she should shower. Then, Kaddish thought, they could go their separate ways. He had his own clock to keep to. If they didn't get Pato back soon, Kaddish believed his son would be dead. He'd seen the men in the suits. He'd seen the way they held Pato's arms. It was Kaddish who had listened to the sound of five men breathing as the elevator made its descent.

He had no more time to fiddle away in police stations. And he wasn't going to work his way through the system. Kaddish knew better. To believe their bureaucracy functioned normally was the same as believing the world was flat and that heaven started at its edge. There was no straight path. Bureaucracy in Argentina is round.

If they searched as Kaddish wanted, finding Pato could be as easy as spinning a globe. Continents and countries a world away are, on the other side, so close. So close, Kaddish felt, that it's amazing to find that the Russian and the Chinaman look different at all. Same with power. Top and bottom, high society and low. What is hidden from view, Kaddish knew, is where the hierarchy curves. Out of sight there is always a place where the two ends meet.

Kaddish needed to get out on his own, to search for the seam where the seedy underground was sewn to the seat of power. He'd find his way to the place where criminal and general, pimp and president, meet. It was not only that he believed it, what other choice does a man like Kaddish have?

Lillian was going to wash off the night—may it be the last one like it. She would scrub it away and see it run down the drain. This is how she'd live her own fairy tale. Every morning would be the first morning, Pato's presence fresh. This was the plan she came up with as night waned and day approached.

Lillian took off her clothes and looked in the mirror. She pressed at the bags under her eyes. "One night," she said out loud, this was the toll of one night.

The rest of the face she was used to, this other woman with her differently bad nose, a wishbone of a thing. Lillian was thankful then for Dr. Mazursky. Look at the tired eyes on this new woman's face. Lillian had wanted to be beautiful, it's true, but at least she'd come back different. Now she had the luxury of looking at the exhausted, worn face she saw in the mirror and pitying someone else. Poor woman in the mirror. Lillian was glad it wasn't her.

She stood in the shower with the water beating on her face and the temperature turned hot. She felt flushed and light-headed. Reaching for the soap, she noticed her hand shaking and felt it in her shoulders too. With the shake came a sound echoing off the tiles. It was the woman from the mirror, weeping.

She showered that way, body heaving, wailing unbroken.

She toweled off through racking sobs and, after managing toothpaste onto bristles, brushed her teeth. How it slowed a person down. Complications. It would further tangle up her day.

Her rib cage ached as she pulled on stockings and tried to catch the hook of a bra. She buttoned a blouse, zipped up a skirt, and sat on the edge of the bed.

It was her first real sitting that was not driving and was not waiting and was not the confrontation of search. Her blouse was already in need of changing for the tears falling and the open mouth running and the dripping of her nose. She reached for the tissues. Maybe it was best to allow this outpouring for a minute or two. Get it out and move forward, only a small recess for racking sobs, Lillian's chance to indulge.

Lillian rocked and wailed and felt her whole body running out of her face, through eyes and nose and mouth. She wondered if she could die this way, if so much of her could leak out that nothing remained.

It was not in the downward motion that it happened, as she cried her face into her hands and her head into her knees. It was in the return, in the great empty wail that she let out as she rose up for a new breath. Lillian cried so hard, rocked so hard, blew so hard that in the thumb pressing and tissue squeezing, Lillian felt her nose give way.

Her face went numb. The rest of her head was shot through with pain. The only point of focus was a viselike tightness in her two front teeth.

She cried on this way, ignoring the laxness in her blowing nose, ignoring the spotty blood turning fluid on the tissues, on her hands, and then reaching her blouse. It was simply one more thing to help drain herself dead. Ignoring the pain, keeping to crying, she made room only for the obvious conclusion. Her two-bit bad-debt first-time nose job seemed to have come undone.

What had she expected from such shoddy workmanship? What other outcome from such a rickety nose and a Kaddish-cut deal?

He made his way to the bedroom with a cup of tea and a slice of buttered baguette on a little plate. Kaddish is doing his best, Lillian thought.

"What is it?" he said, a ludicrous question considering their son's absence. Then, taking her in, he took a step back. It was something else entirely.

"It's the nose," Lillian said.

"I can see."

"No, you can't," she said, her voice nasal and gurgling, the crying continuing behind it.

"Something's not right with it, Lillian."

"Every time they look," she said, "when they see his picture—when they see both faces—already they don't believe." Lillian grabbed for more tissues and pressed them to those in place. "The first time I ever enjoyed my own reflection was after Pato was born. For a parent, from then on, when I looked in the mirror I saw myself and I saw him. We were the same, Kaddish. A son and a twin. Now he's gone from the mirror too. It is like murder, this nose."

"You can still see Pato in the mirror."

"I can't," she said, the blood running thick. "I can't find my own face in there anymore; how am I supposed to find his? My son is gone and the one way I always had him, that is gone too."

"Your nose, Lillian," Kaddish said.

"It bleeds."

"It more than bleeds. It's not right. It doesn't stand on your face," he said. "I think it's broken free."

"*My best student.* That was his promise. As with all your endeavors, Kaddish, a job well done." The crying slowed and then she laughed. "When the freezer went on your bargain off-the-back-of-a-truck fridge, when the engine gave out on your poker-game car, when the cabana in

Mar del Plata turned into the only one I've ever seen that wasn't near a beach—for these things I was always prepared. Even the nose job ending ugly was no great surprise. But to get a warranty on my face. To guess my nose was on consignment—this I couldn't have expected."

Kaddish came closer and did his best to follow. Lillian's speech was delivered in an ever more nasal pitch.

"Let's get you some ice and head over to Mazursky."

"Before dawn?" Lillian said.

"To his house," Kaddish said. "We'll pick him up and take him over to the clinic."

"And waste how many hours shuttling around and getting ready, each one amplified?"

As if she had to tell him. He had his own fears. "You'll be better off," Kaddish said. "It needs to be fixed."

"Get Mazursky to see me before the city opens or after the city sleeps. If he'll only work in daytime, get him to operate in the backseat of the car while we patrol the streets. Otherwise it'll stay until Pato is back. The only waiting rooms I'll sit in are those for our son."

"This is an emergency, Lillian. You have no nose."

"I do. It's just not connected to my face."

"You can't be of use this way."

"You just watch what I do without it."

"Mazursky will fix it. This time we'll see it done right."

"Not right, Kaddish. I want it wrong. Wrong in the old way, big in the old way, crooked in the old way too." She gave Kaddish a push toward the door, one hand still clasped to her face. "I want my big nose back, Kaddish. I want to see Pato when I look in the mirror. Go find me my old nose."

[Twenty-two]

KADDISH WENT OFF to get the doctor. Lillian went to the kitchen to put ice on her swelling face. She found the freezer completely frozen over, a solid block again.

We make adjustments, Lillian thought. We ignore things bit by bit until they've gone too far. Here was another encroachment that had slipped by her. She'd not be chiseling today.

Lillian tossed a dish towel into the sink. She turned the tap on high and let the cold water run. It was then that Lillian noticed what a mess she was. She took off her bloody blouse and the bloody bra underneath. She touched her hand to her chest, sticky as well, and took off the rest of her clothes. Leaning her head back, she placed the compress against her broken nose. Naked and poised and nearly blind with pain, Lillian made her way to the telephone.

The operator would help her. When all turns to loneliness how nice to know the operator is always awake. A woman answered, and she had a voice kinder than Lillian could have imagined. She placed Lillian's calls and stayed on the line while the telephones rang and rang and rang.

They tried the Army. They tried the Navy. They tried the Air Force.

Lillian had learned. She did not say to the operator, "My son has gone missing." She did not ask if the operator had heard other mothers asking to place three just such calls. The operator let the last one ring for what seemed like minutes before saying, "No one is picking up." She said it in a way that made Lillian feel like she knew everything and understood.

Lillian said, "Thank you." And then she said, "It's the perfect time to invade the country. The whole of the armed forces closed."

Lillian stood with her head tilted, eyes shut, and the compress in place. With uncertain steps, and unknown to her, Lillian followed a trail of blood to her bed. She lay down backwards, with her feet on the pillows and her head at its foot. Lillian turned her face to the side so she wouldn't choke. She'd told Kaddish she would manage just as well with a nose or without, but already Lillian knew it would be better if he came home soon.

She lifted the compress for a glimpse at the clock but couldn't focus. It was enough to see morning brushing up against the bedroom window. The sun would soon clear the building across the way, filling the street and flooding the bedroom; then it would reach the air shaft and daytime would invade their apartment from all sides.

Lillian's intent was to lie there another minute. She would not sleep, only collect herself until Kaddish or Pato came through the door. A little more light, a few more minutes, and she would muster herself, muster her work voice. She would start calling again, and this time she'd say the right things to the right people. She'd embark on her new business: the getting of her son.

It was the last thing Lillian thought before she fell asleep.

[Twenty-three]

"HANDSOME DEVIL," Dr. Mazursky said. "Look at the face on you."

Mazursky had followed his maid into his office, spouting a steady stream of curses and with his robe hanging open. He was about to start in on Kaddish as well, when he'd set eyes on him.

"This is why I get up in the mornings; this is why I do the work that I do." The doctor tied his robe, adding an air of formality. He let out a whistle, and his smile was all teeth. He stood there shaking his head and then coming up close, he snatched Kaddish's chin. "A Don Juan. A Romeo. You're beautiful as only the beautiful are.

"Come see, Silvia," the doctor said. The maid came close, as if all was forgiven. "A perfect job. I can't even tell you—damn me. Damn me." Here for a second the smile disappeared. "Why didn't I take a before picture? My best work yet."

As the maid left, the doctor called for coffee. "And breakast for two?" the maid asked.

"One," Mazursky said. "He won't be staying long."

Taking a seat behind his desk, the doctor said, "A pleasure to see you." Then the smile vanished. "A pleasure to look upon you, that is. To find you at my house unannounced and when we have no business, that's another matter. It's not in my best interests to associate with you. Fine specimen that you've become, you're an *hijo de puta* nonetheless."

"As are you, Doctor."

"Me? Show me proof." He showed Kaddish his empty hands. "All gone," he said. "So thanks for coming by. A day-maker, I'll admit. A beauty, Poznan. You came out nice." The maid returned with coffee for two, and the doctor took both cups.

"Lillian's nose," Kaddish said. "It's an emergency. That's why I'm here."

"I saw the nose she walked around with until now. That was an emergency and she lived with it fine."

"The kid's nose collapsed," Kaddish said.

"The kid's?"

"My wife's," Kaddish said. "The kid's work is no good. The bone—"

"Cartilage."

"It's hanging loose on her face."

"That's a different story," Mazursky said. And as quickly as he'd turned stern, a flash of empathy set in. He passed a coffee to Kaddish. "Was she hit?" the doctor said. "Did she walk into a wall? Frisbees— ever since the Frisbee made its way south, they break many a nose."

"Crying actually. She was upset and crying and it fell."

"It collapsed on its own?"

"Came loose, more. She feels—we feel—it should be under warranty."

"Crying is regular nose usage by any standard. I wish you'd clarified right off. It's Bracchi's bungle. We'll get him back in for the repair. These young doctors won't amount to anything if they don't learn from their mistakes."

"You'll do it, Doctor. And you'll make it right. She wants her old nose back."

"That's impossible."

"You work miracles. Work another."

"I don't even know what I'd use to reconstruct it. We'd have to fashion it from a rib. Maybe we can pull her femur if she doesn't mind walking with a cane."

"Not funny, Doctor."

"Then don't turn me into a joke. I'll make the fix. But you can forget about restoring that monstrosity. Have your wife call the clinic when it opens and tell the receptionist to put her in as a bump instead of the Fliegelman titties. It'll be tomorrow afternoon."

"Not tomorrow, today. Right now. Wake up your nurses and sharpen your knives."

"I have other emergencies ahead. There's a child with a hole punched through her cheek, what of her?"

"Let the little girl's ice cream run out her face for another day. I've got my own kid to worry about, Doctor. They've taken my son."

"God," he said. "I'm sorry," he said. Then the doctor pulled the top of his robe closed. "I've always heard you had no sense, Poznan. That your talent rests with the dead and not the living. But I can tell you, I've never heard a case pleaded so poorly before."

"Will this be a long lecture?"

"It's not a lecture, it's an offer. One hidden in a chiding." The doctor stood up and faced the painting behind the desk, his four horses racing. "You tell your story backwards. It should start with the missing son." He turned to face Kaddish. "If I can help in any way, I will."

"No one helps," Kaddish said. "It's only fate that returns them alive or dead, in whole or in part—or not at all." Here Kaddish's eyes misted over. "I didn't say a word to my wife, and an offer from you only further confirms it. I don't believe you make any deals you can keep."

"And here I am offering to assist."

"The last I'd expect."

"Kidnap and ransom is our gross domestic product," the doctor said. "But like everything else that ends up government run, they've sucked the profit out of it. They take and nothing comes back. That's why I'm offering, because what they've started is dirty in a new way. To kidnap the innocents, to take revenge on them—we've seen enough of that in this century. Too many are blameless. And too many are Jews." The doctor came around to Kaddish's side of the desk. "If there's one thing I learned from my dear forgotten father, sometimes, no matter how numerous or powerful the enemy, it's up to the individual to try and fuck those boys up."

"How can you help?" Kaddish said.

"I don't know yet. It's an imperfect plan. Come and ask when you need something specific, when you can make a better request than *Get me back my son.*"

"What other request could there possibly be?"

"There'll be something. You'll have to progress beyond that. Now give me a couple of hours, then meet me at the hospital with Lillian and I'll put her back right. And tell her not to eat, if she hasn't."

"Can I ask one more thing?" Kaddish said. He sounded almost shy. "No offense," Kaddish said, "dangerous as it is, and your explanation aside, why would you offer to help?"

"Penance," the doctor said. He put a hand on Kaddish's back and gave it a quick rub. "I have a new sin."

[Twenty-four]

A NOSE IS RESILIENT, it finds its own way. Lillian could feel it situating, somehow cozying up. There was the sensation of something calcifying, a sandy bond forming and a congealing elsewhere within. She thought her nose might have fused in place below the swelling. As she reached up to touch it and tried to open her eyes, Lillian recognized that she'd succumbed to sleep. She also recognized that it was the phone ringing that had woken her, and her nose wasn't the problem. It wasn't the nose that had her home in bed.

Lillian rushed to her feet. She moved down the hallway, steadying herself against one wall and then the other, propelling herself forward. She opened her sticky, murky eyes and made her way to the phone, knowing as she reached it and grabbed it and said, "Hello," that it had stopped ringing two steps before.

The pain then came back with a vengeance.

Lillian blinked her eyes. She pressed her fingers against them and sat down in the chair by the living room window. She couldn't believe how much it hurt. "You cannot know," she said out loud in the way that speech can escape us.

More than the pain, what Lillian truly couldn't bear was the transformation that came with first sleep. It's sleep that makes reality. She'd never have lain down if she'd known. She'd never have closed her eyes.

Lillian had lost control of the horror that had befallen them. She'd slipped into a world with no son.

She looked down into the street to see if maybe Pato was coming. She sat in the wingback chair and watched the corner. She tried to force Pato around it, tried to move him around the bend.

At the first sign of motion Lillian gave a start. It was only a dog. A dog and then a leash and then a man on the other end. She immediately wondered how many children the man had. She wondered if they were home. This is the world Lillian woke up into, a world of parents with children and those without.

There was a wisdom that came with her new position, and she couldn't believe she hadn't understood these things the day before. Here's what Lillian had come to understand: They wouldn't all get them back in such a place, they couldn't all get back their sons.

Lillian wanted to apologize to the man with the dog, to throw open the window and scream down to him, If indeed they've taken one from you, I apologize, because I'll be getting mine back. And this time it didn't slip out; she kept it in her head: *I'll get mine back.*

Lillian sat in that chair watching the street until Kaddish double-parked out front and stepped from the car. It was really something to see Kaddish this way.

When Lillian had wanted to bring Kaddish home to her parents, her father had asked, "Who is he?" and she'd had no answer. When they first got wind, they banned him from the house and then, heartbroken, demanded to know what she could see in such a man. Lillian told them. "I'm in love with what he'll become." Her father waved this off, her mother had *tfu-tfu-tfu*ed. "A golem," her father said. "A *shaygets,* a man unformed." He'd called him everything that day, everything but the one thing her Kaddish surely was. In that initial fight, *hijo de puta* wasn't said.

Now look at him, Lillian thought. Had her father only lived until this dark day.

Lillian stood and leaned her forehead against the window. She couldn't herself believe it. Her husband with his handsome new nose, the face after a lifetime finally right, and now, the final touch, his proper boundaries had fallen into focus. The man coming toward her was sharper, more defined, more perfectly and painfully her Kaddish than any she'd set eyes on before.

It was the closest to him she'd ever felt, the clearest he'd ever been. Kaddish stepped between cars and onto the sidewalk. He craned his neck to look up into their window, as if remembering something, as if he'd sensed he was being watched. Lillian waved with both hands, sliding them back and forth across the glass. Kaddish gave a sad half smile. He raised a hand and waved back to his wife. He paused for a second before disappearing into the building. Her husband, her dear Kaddish, a perfect fit. Kaddish Poznan, father to a missing son.

[Twenty-five]

KADDISH HADN'T WANTED TO WATCH. He stood outside the hospital smoking cigarettes. The nurse, his nurse, came out to get him. She led Kaddish to a recovery room where he found Mazursky smiling and Lillian bandaged up. Swaddled in blankets and still looking unconscious, Lillian cursed at the doctor in an unceasing mumble.

"*B'kiso, b'kaso, b'koso,*" the doctor said. "I didn't learn much in Hebrew school at the Benevolent Self, but this holds up. There are three things that show a person's true self: when money is involved, when speaking in anger, and when drunk. In this case, I stretch drunk to apply."

Kaddish looked over at his wife.

"A blue streak," Mazursky said. "It's good stuff too."

Lillian was in fine form. "Doctor Stinky Penis," she said. "Doctor Tiny Penis. Tiny tiny. Fat fat man."

The doctor put a hand to his belly.

"Fat, I think, is unfair. The penis, though, would be a matter of opinion."

Kaddish raised an eyebrow.

"The anesthesia occasionally makes for the foul mouth. The sentiments"—and here Mazurky laughed—"belong to her."

"Bastard," Lillian said.

"That could be either of us. For rambling it's rapier sharp."

"It went well?" Kaddish said.

"Wonderfully."

Kaddish dropped his voice to a whisper.

"You made it big like she asked?" Kaddish said. "The old nose is back? With the old bump? She wants to see our boy in the mirror."

"I guarantee this time that it will stay on her face. I've done my best work. There is a reputation to uphold."

"Mamzers!" This Lillian said loudly and, though pinched, with clarity. "Up," she said. "Let's go." Both men turned their attention to her, looking dazed and trying to pull herself from the bed.

Once was enough for Lillian. Two nose jobs she could handle, but waking a second time without thinking of Pato—that wouldn't happen again. The waking itself was just as bad, mind you. It was just as painful coming back to consciousness and accepting Pato gone. This time, though, nothing would stop her. If the nose was back in place, she'd had her last rest.

"Please," the doctor said. "Slowly."

"Is it fixed?"

"It's fixed," the doctor said.

"Then there's no time."

Kaddish looked to the doctor while rushing over to support his wife. Lillian stood herself up, but her feet wouldn't really hold.

"Is this all right?" Kaddish said.

"I won't stop a mother," Mazursky said.

Kaddish helped her dress and the doctor went off and returned with a wheelchair. "At least sit until you get to the car." Lillian sat and the doctor pushed her to the elevator. When the doors opened, Kaddish took the handles.

"Good luck," the doctor said. As Kaddish rotated the chair and started to back away, Lillian reached out and gave Mazursky's hand a squeeze.

Tired of begging, Kaddish banged and banged and banged. I should have been as vigilant, Kaddish thought. How hard was it to ignore someone outside your door?

If Lillian had been feeling better, if she wasn't leaning on his shoulder trying to keep on her feet, she might have said the same. He was glad she didn't; he wouldn't have been able to take it as they pleaded for Rafa's mother to let them in.

Kaddish knew the police would have broken down their door in the end. They would have gotten in regardless. But how much better, how much better for them all, Pato too, if Kaddish had at least held them at bay, if he'd at least forced them to make a little noise.

"I just want to talk to him," Kaddish said. "A word with your son." Kaddish did want to talk to him. He intended to do this while sitting on Rafa's chest and knocking his head against the floor. It was Rafa he blamed. However self-righteous the kids were, they were up to something. And Rafa was the instigator, Kaddish was sure.

Rafa's mother told them to keep their distance through a closed door. She told them to stay out of their lives. "You've done enough," she said. And Lillian was comforted. Whatever the accusation, Rafa's mother was the first of the opinion that Lillian had accomplished anything at all.

Eventually Rafa's mother opened the door. A look of concern spread across her face as soon as she caught sight of Lillian's. She didn't ask what happened or even say *Come in.* Rafa's mother hadn't seen Kaddish since his nose job, and it was only after absorbing Lillian that she focused on him. Had she bumped into them on the street, she wouldn't have known who they were.

Kaddish got Lillian to the couch and went, without pause or permission, into both bedrooms. In one a teenage girl did her homework and didn't bother giving Kaddish a second look. In the other an old man in heavy black shoes and two or three sweaters—with ample holes to see from one down into the next—was asleep on the bed. Kaddish walked back past Rafa's mother and then on into the kitchen.

When he returned, the two mothers were staring at each other in silence, Lillian still seated on the couch.

"Where is he?" Kaddish said.

"It's on your Pato," Rafa's mother said. "I loved him like a son, but this is on your kid."

"What is?" Lillian said. She did not like the word *loved*. "Love," she said out loud. "You love."

"I'm truly sorry," Rafa's mother said. "I was sorry to hear." She was about to cry but held it and, Lillian couldn't help but notice, her healthy nostrils flared.

"I welcomed him in," she said, "made him a home. He lived here when there was no place else."

"There was always a place," Kaddish said. "Whatever he liked to believe."

"Pato didn't so much think so. He spent a lot of his time with us."

"Discipline," Lillian said. "Often the children mistake discipline for cruelty and so they congregate in the homes with no rules."

Rafa's mother bent at the knees and screamed in Lillian's face, which to Kaddish looked all the more desperate with Lillian's bandage, and that bandage stained with blood. "A single mother," she screamed. "A single mother!" She straightened up and Kaddish was surprised that neither the old man nor the girl came out of their rooms. "I slaved to make them a place, killed myself for these kids and now"—she raised up her voice again—"gone."

"Who is gone?" Kaddish said.

"Rafa," she said. "Flavia."

"Arrested?" Lillian said. "The police?"

"No," Rafa's mother said. "They ran off. They took your call, took a few things, kissed me on the cheek, and left. 'You don't know us anymore,' they said. What kind of good-bye is that from a son? And then Rafa said, 'If they press you, if they torture, tell them exactly what happened. Tell them about right now. Tell them we got up and walked out the door.'" Rafa's mother grabbed at the shirt on her chest and pulled as if she intended to rip it off with the skin underneath. "How am I supposed to live with that?"

"You're lucky," Lillian said. "They left on their own, and they can come back the same way."

"How is that lucky when they won't—when they can't because of Pato?"

"The daughter," Kaddish said. He had his own answer. "You're lucky enough because there's still the girl."

"Get out," Rafa's mother said.

"Unfortunately, we can't without answers." Kaddish said this politely. "We need to know what the kids were up to. We need to know why Pato was taken. Tell us and we'll go."

"Up to? Don't you know?" She studied them, incredulous. "You don't even know about your own son."

"What?" Kaddish said. "Are they Zionists? Is it communism?"

"I know what they're guilty of," Rafa's mother said. She shifted her eyes to the left and the right. She leaned in to whisper. "Our children were deep into growing up."

"That's it?" Kaddish said.

"Nothing more."

"There's always more," he said. "Things don't happen without a reason. Maybe you too are missing a secret." Kaddish gave Rafa's mother a slow once-over. "You know where they are," he said.

She ignored him.

"Please," Lillian said. "Anything. You must have some idea where they went. An inkling."

"No more than you," Rafa's mother said. "Go check their hangouts. Go ask around there."

Lillian looked to Kaddish, and he slipped his arm behind her back.

"You don't know," Rafa's mother said. "You really don't have a clue."

Kaddish didn't move to speak. It was for Lillian—this had been placed before Lillian and Lillian, accepting, surrendered.

"We do not know about the children," she said.

Rafa's mother sat down. She sat and explained, telling them all she knew of the kids' comings and goings, where they bought their beers and their books, where they ate and danced, on which blocks and against which streetlights they leaned.

It was wonderful to hear, like meeting a different Pato. How nice it sounded. It was a good and vibrant life. Their surly son sounded like a happy child, like the boy Lillian knew he was. They were a gift, these stories. New memories, new pictures, whole new dimensions to beef up the boy in her head.

"Thank you," Lillian said when they left. She went to hug Rafa's mother, who stepped away. She wouldn't have it.

"I love him like my own," she said, "but Pato's the one that drove them out."

"It could have been any one of them that got taken," Kaddish said.

"That," Rafa's mother said, "is my fear."

Lillian remembered playing her childhood games and all the ways in which they'd mimicked a sophisticated world. As she and Kaddish went from police station to police station, she wondered if Videla and the other generals had played those games the same. Maybe in their version the patient lifted the doctor's shirt and, if the doctor resisted, the patient split her tiny little head with a rock.

Maybe all people are set in their ways that far back and it served to explain everything. Maybe that's why she and Kaddish so differed in how best to respond. Kaddish also remembered games from his childhood, except Kaddish's games were played by adults. If you asked him he'd tell you: when the policeman comes for the criminal, Talmud Harry offers him a drink, and some cash and lets him have his choice of the finest ladies in the house.

He'd tried explaining this to Lillian, as well as his beliefs about government offices and hierarchy and why he didn't want to go along. "Make me a promise," Lillian said. "We do this through proper channels. No more headstones, no more deals. No underworld contacts and no bright ideas. You're a model citizen until we get our son back."

At each station, as with the first, Lillian demanded to see holding cells and in more than a few the officers obliged. Kaddish was convinced that being led to the cells they'd never be led back, and one policeman looked at him with real violence in his eyes. Kaddish was doing his best to try Lillian's way. Lillian mistook his acquiescence for like-mindedness. This was partly because she believed this to be the single logical path and partly because she assumed Kaddish knew, deep down, that his pursuits were often futile. When night had settled in and there was literally nothing left to her, she said to Kaddish, "Even for me, it's time to go home." She was caught off guard when Kaddish proposed they try his way for a stretch. "What way is that?" Lillian asked.

"Roundabout and wrong-headed. But to me it looks right."

There's no reason to whisper in a parked car on a deserted street. Still, Lillian kept her voice to a hush.

"Only owls use the night better, Kaddish. I don't know, though, if slinking about under cover of darkness will help Pato's case. It seems the wrong message could be sent."

"We don't know yet that he's innocent," Kaddish said, keeping his own voice down. "And we don't yet have a case to prove. As much as you blame me—"

"I don't blame you."

"As much as you do, I lay it on Rafa. He's behind whatever trouble Pato's in."

Lillian didn't care to share her opinion. She looked out her window into a rundown courtyard with a FOR SALE sign hanging over the gate. It had one of those checkerboard patios she'd always dreamed of. With a little money, someone could do it up nice.

"What about the fact that his best friends ran off?" Kaddish said. "It means they did something, no? It means they're guilty of something?" Kaddish gave Lillian a chance to respond. When she didn't, he broke off whispering and yelled. "You must agree, because you're here, right? You're waiting with me? Agreed? You wouldn't have come if not."

Lillian, still in a hush, said, "I make the best of things. At home all I'd do is sleep."

Kaddish flipped on the headlights, illuminating the all-night bookstore they'd been watching on the next block. He pulled the car out and headed for a bar by the Obelisco, where Rafa's mother said her son often sat. When they got there he put an elbow out the window and got himself comfortable. He dropped his cigarette in the gutter and let his hands go limp on the wheel. Kaddish was waiting—and waiting was now the order of their lives.

"How's your face?" he said.

"I already feel like I shouldn't have fixed it. How much better would it serve us if I'd left it a horror, putting fear into everyone we meet? Our own little junta—me and my nose. The pair of us broken, going around and spreading dread."

There came the boy around the corner of Suipacha, pushing his way along. He walked with hands in his pockets and shoulders hunched, as if that noggin was weighing him down. Lillian recognized him first. She'd fed these kids, with their bottomless stomachs, on countless occasions—and still so skinny, every last one. As soon as Lillian pointed, Kaddish was out of the car and crossing the street.

Kaddish looked this way and that to see if anyone else besides Rafa was around. He crossed the street at a slant, the way one works in open spaces, on water and ice, in wide-open fields. The boy was oblivious. It takes effort, Kaddish thought, not to notice such purposeful steps, a coming-right-at-you walk on an angled path.

Kaddish had sacrificed stealth for speed, so different from the careful way he moved when erasing names. Stealth, though, was his regardless. Considering all the time these kids wasted talking about energy and auras, Kaddish felt Rafa should have been more sensitive to the very negative, very angry vibrations directed his way. Rafa didn't pick up on Kaddish's approach until it was impossible to miss and too late.

Kaddish hit into him low, head turned to the side to make full use of that heavy bull shoulder. Hitting and straightening and throwing his weight, Kaddish catapulted the boy hard and high up against a brick wall. Doing the best he could without standing on tiptoes, Kaddish reached up and pressed Rafa's face against the wall.

"You know Pato Poznan, you his friend?"

"No," Rafa said. He spoke through a squished mouth compressed into a kiss.

Kaddish was milking the fear out of this boy and it felt good after the constant frustration. It was the first chance he'd had to unleash some rage. Maybe that's why Kaddish was so rough, why he pressed hard against the face until he heard the rasp of skin against brick.

"You don't know him," Kaddish said. "But I know you." Kaddish could feel the boy's pulse in the palm of his hand. He could make out an Adam's apple bobbing around. It was hard to keep hold, scared as the boy was and sweating so hard. "It's me," Kaddish said. "Pato's father." Kaddish was about to lose his grip.

"You sure you're his father?" Rafa said. "If you're really his father, ask me again."

Kaddish let go and the boy slumped forward, face-to-face with Kaddish before straightening up. Rafa touched his jaw tenderly and said, "You sure you're you?"

"It's dark," Kaddish said.

"There's enough light to see that you don't look Poznan. You sound like you, though," Rafa said. He stared at Kaddish's nose. "Pato told us you guys had yourselves fixed, that you'd gotten yourselves neutered and spayed."

Kaddish hadn't asked. He grabbed the denim collar of the boy's jacket and dragged him across the street. He forced the boy into the back of the car.

"Can we just clarify something?" Rafa said. "Because dragging folks into cars is an unusually sensitive matter these days. If you're a Pato's-dad-sounding cop and you're going to kill me, I'd like to know right now so I can have a fucking heart attack in the backseat. I can feel the fucking pains in my arm already."

"I'm his father," Kaddish said, "for real. And I still might kill you. His mother you also know, and she will be assisting in killing you if need be." Lillian turned and nodded. The boy seized up, even more terrified, and actually clasped a hand to his chest.

"Jesus Christ," he said. The boy looked to Kaddish. Whatever recognition he was working on was wiped away. Lillian smiled warmly but it only pushed at the bandage, forcing closed swollen eyes. Rafa read it as a wince. Something dripped.

Lillian turned on the inside light. "You don't look so great yourself," she said.

Rafa leaned forward to see his cheek in the mirror, scraped raw. There were also beads of blood forming two neat lines. Rafa wiped them away.

"We have questions about Pato," Kaddish said.

"You could have called me," Rafa said.

"We did," Lillian said. "You were supposed to call us back."

"Your mother is distraught," Kaddish said.

"You talked to my mother?"

"We visited your mother. We were looking for our son's best friends, but they seem to have run away."

"There's nothing I can tell that you don't already know. Nothing since Pato called me from jail."

"When?" Lillian said.

"It was before," Rafa said. "After the concert and after the weekend, but before they took him again. He said you were coming to the station to get him. He was supposed to meet up with us later and he never showed. We called your house and no one answered. We went over last night to pick him up, and your freak neighbor wouldn't open the door."

"You see?" Lillian said, interrupting. "You see the locked door?"

"I see that idiot Cacho didn't tell us anyone came by."

"We went back to my house to decide what to do. And then you called, and there was no other choice. We were worried—we are—for our friend. We had nothing but the worry and we ran."

"Not very far or very well," Kaddish said. "It was pretty easy to find you. A pitiful fugitive. You only made it one day."

"I was hiding just fine. I only came out for a game of foosball and a Coke." Rafa looked into the rearview mirror and blinked. "If I knew where Pato was, I'd take you. I'd give my life for your son."

"If we can arrange the trade, we will." Kaddish watched the boy in the rearview mirror. He passed back a cigarette and lit another for himself.

Flavia sat on the carpet in the middle of the room. She had the front of her hair tucked behind her ear. Her knees were pulled to her chest and she wore a modest peasant skirt that was spread out around her. She'd always been friendly to Lillian in the past. She wasn't now. She sat there looking scared.

The walls of the apartment needed painting and there was no furniture in the room but for two park benches facing each other in the center. There was a clump of grass still clinging to one of the feet. It was clear no one had lived there for some time.

Lillian and Kaddish sat together, bodies touching. Rafa was stretched out on the bench across, with a leg thrown over the side.

Flavia got up and went into the kitchen to turn off the water before it reached boiling. She brought back the kettle and put it on a burnt spot on the rug where the acrylic fiber had melted down. She again set her skirt around herself. She passed the maté to Lillian and then hit Rafa so that he sat up.

"Pato has done something wrong," Kaddish said. "You've done something wrong. Somewhere, somehow, you and your friends have broken a rule."

"Pato has *not* done something wrong," Rafa said. "We have not."

"There's a reason," Kaddish said.

"The reason is no reason."

"How about you make one up?" Lillian said.

"I think they took Pato because it sounded right to them, because he followed the last person and set up the next. That's how it spreads, like a virus. It's enough to get sneezed on by the wrong man."

"Nonsense," Lillian said.

"Don't be a fool," Kaddish said.

Rafa took the maté from Lillian. The *bombilla* clinked against his teeth as he drank. "Do you really want to know what we've been up to?"

"Yes," Lillian said.

"During uncertain times Pato and Flavia and I discussed a government so paranoid that it would one day hunt us for fearing such a situation would come to be. We're conspiracy theorists who've been stripped of our conspiracy. Fearing this would happen is our biggest crime."

Flavia shook her head in disappointment, as if she'd been supervising until then and Rafa had just failed. "This boy here, sadly, is the closest we have to a radical. Does he sound like a mastermind of anything to you?"

"No," Kaddish said. "He doesn't."

"We can't help you," Flavia said. Her face was expectant and Lillian took note.

"But we can help you," Lillian said.

Flavia didn't hesitate. She launched right in. "You have to get rid of his address book and his pictures and find his diary and any letters he wrote. You have to destroy everything that ties anyone—any of us—to your son."

[Twenty-six]

RHYTHM AND REPETITION had no effect. Neither did choreo-graphed motion, the flexing of specific muscles, or meditative chal-lenges such as staying completely motionless or staring at certain objects until reality fell away. Lillian spent the dawn hours with a teaspoon cradled in her palm, focusing on palm and spoon, spoon and palm, until the lines were blurred, and still no one called. She had come to the con-clusion that it was all nonsense but the numbers. Nothing but the count-ing seemed to make the phone ring. She sat in the wing-backed chair, counting up to thirty and then back down. The call came on nineteen, Pato's age—another sign. She was out of the chair, the telephone to her ear, saying, "Hello," and then "Hello," again. When she heard no answer, she held out the receiver with both hands and yelled "Pato," into the mouthpiece.

"It's me, Gustavo," Gustavo said. There was confusion in his voice. He hadn't intended to draw out Lillian's desperation. It was an intimacy he wasn't meant to hear.

Confused herself, Lillian looked around for a clock and then to the watch on her wrist. Finding it, she understood it wasn't the time but the day she was looking for. It was Friday. Friday with Gustavo, her boss, on the phone.

She hadn't spoken to him in a week, hadn't been to work in a week—and then again to the watch—or was it only four days? When had they been out to dinner, eating spinach, drinking wine?

"How are you, sweetie?" Gustavo said. "How are you doing with it all?"

"Fine," she said. "Bad."

Lillian looked out the window and after, for comfort, at Pato's shelves. Such a smart boy. And kind. And full of surprises. She came up with a nice memory to calm herself. She thought about Pato staying out all night with his friends, and stopping at the bakery on his way home. He'd bring back a dozen *medialunas* wrapped in patterned paper and warm to the touch. Lillian would wake and smell them from bed, and know her son was home safe. In high school, before he turned surly, he'd still get up in the mornings and drag himself downstairs. It was the first errand Kaddish sent Pato out alone on, the list and the money pinned to his shirt. He couldn't have been more than five. When he didn't want to go, when he didn't understand how this responsibility had fallen to him, Kaddish had explained it simply. "That's why we had you," is what Kaddish told him. "To get pastries is why you were brought into the world."

Lillian remembered one thing and forgot another. She was on the phone with Gustavo. She should have been listening; Gustavo was always full of advice. Lillian tried to pick up a thread but he'd already stopped talking. He might have hung up.

Out of the silence, Gustavo said, "How long have we been friends?"

"I don't know," Lillian said.

"It wasn't easy to get you in," he said. "I had Frida calling people all day. No one's willing to help, and definitely not a lawyer of Tello's caliber. You're fortunate he's agreed to get involved."

Gustavo stopped talking again.

"Thank you for calling," Lillian said.

"You just feel better," Gustavo said, as if she was home sick. Lillian held the phone tight. "And don't worry about the bill. It's taken care of."

"Where am I going?" Lillian said.

"Where are you going? What does that mean, Lillian?"

"I lost the address," she said. She looked around for a pen. "And the name, and"—she started crying—"I don't know what you're saying. I'm having a very hard time."

"All right," Gustavo said. "Fine, Lillian."

She put the phone into the crook of her neck, raised up a shoulder, and tilted her head. She scratched a pen against the back of a pad, testing her readiness, listening as best she could.

We not only discover who our real friends are in an emergency, we also discover who we consider, in our hearts, to be our real friends. Lillian honestly hadn't thought about Gustavo until she'd answered the phone. And she didn't expect any more from him than what he'd offered. Gustavo wasn't Frida. He wouldn't risk his life for Lillian any more than she'd risk her own to save his. The limits were mutual and clear.

Kaddish didn't see things the same way.

"Who hasn't passed through that office since the coup? A top lawyer—what's that worth?" Kaddish said. "A top fucking general is what we need."

"Don't," Lillian said.

"I will," Kaddish said. "You've been there for a dozen years, and the best he comes up with is a shyster? Now that he's got you dealing with stolen property and stolen babies, you'd think, for that alone, better favors were owed."

"Never out loud," Lillian said. She put her hands over her ears. "Once I whispered it to you. Don't ever say that out loud, Kaddish, you'll see us all dead."

"Who says the outcome will be any different?" Kaddish said. "You gave that man the best years of your life."

"No," Lillian said. "Those I gave to you."

"And mine went to you and Pato. And whether Pato wants to be or not, he's my son too."

"Who's saying different?"

"I think you are. All the decisions are getting made like you're in this alone."

"I don't have the strength for this, Kaddish. You promised me."

"No. You promised *for* me," Kaddish said. "Now I want an assurance of my own. I want to know you understand that almost a week has gone by and we've gotten nowhere. Visiting every police station in the country won't make a difference and Gustavo's lawyer isn't going to tell us anything we don't already know."

"What is the point of this?" Lillian yelled. "What does this do?"

"The point is for you to understand that if we keep going this way, we'll end up roaming that building with the rest of the hopeless people who aren't getting their kids back. You're driving us toward the Ministry of Special Cases and I want you to know it. The system doesn't work for anyone, Lillian, and it definitely never has for me. I still think, if we look the right way, we can find our son."

"You don't want to start pointing fingers," Lillian said. "It's a losing proposition."

"If you blame me for opening the door, then say it."

"I'm trying to find Pato the only way there is. If you have one of your schemes at the ready, tell me. If it's something concrete, let's do it right now. I'll help you search the nursing homes for the last Jewish pimp with a policeman in his pocket and a marble in his head. You lead and I'll follow. We'll exhaust all your big connections. Go get a shovel and we'll dig up one of your heroes tonight." Kaddish said nothing. He didn't have a scheme. All he had was what he knew, that the government wouldn't help them. "If your plan isn't ready, then put your coat on and let's go. Otherwise we'll be late for the lawyer—a lawyer we'd never get to without Gustavo's name attached."

Kaddish put his coat on, and finding the gold in his pocket, he dropped the two handkerchiefs on the shelf by the door. "That Gustavo's an *hijo de puta*," Kaddish said. "A lawyer is a pitiful best from your best friend." Gustavo wasn't her best friend, he was her boss. Kaddish was coming with her so Lillian let it pass.

· · ·

The lawyer's name was Alberto Tello, and there seemed to be a huge misunderstanding about what exactly he'd been hired to do.

"New York," Alberto said. "Paris. For Jews there is Israel. If you want Spanish spoken, there's Mexico. There's Uruguay if you want Spanish spoken and to be close, but I don't recommend it. This government has reach. Too many people go missing in the countries nearby."

"You want us to leave the country?"

"I'm offering help."

"Does Gustavo know this is what you're doing?"

"He's very concerned. He asked me to take care of you."

"New York?" Lillian said.

"I mentioned it as an option. I told him I could get you on a plane today, get you settled. He said to arrange it if you decide."

"That's insane," Lillian said.

"Often the families disappear as units, which makes it not very insane at all. It makes it actually smart. As for your estate, I'll handle all of it. I'm to see that the transition is smooth."

This was the funniest thing Kaddish had heard since their lives turned bad.

"Our estate?" he said. "Yes, Lillian, who will look after our holdings while we're gone?"

"I know you have limited means," the lawyer said. "I apologize. These are the terms we use."

"I can find a travel agent on my own," Lillian said. "What I need is a lawyer. If you're willing to see us, you must be willing to help."

"Yes," Kaddish said. "Here's your chance to tell us you'd help if only you didn't have your own family to worry about. Then send us to the Ministry of Special Cases and we'll be on our way."

"I do have a son, and I do worry," the lawyer said. "But that's not the reason I won't start a dossier for you."

"Then what is it?" Lillian said.

"It's that there's one of me and every day more people like you. I'm not smart enough to win these cases and I don't have heart enough to keep losing them again and again. My talent lies in getting families out and finding them countries where they can stay. That's the compromise

I make. I offer small comfort to a lot of people in the time it would take to do nothing on a grand scale for one."

"You have tried, though?"

The lawyer nodded.

"And the ones you fought for, did they get their missing back?"

The lawyer shook his head.

"I had a married couple abducted from their apartment. The army secured three city blocks before they went in. Dangerous a mission as it was, they remembered to bring a moving truck. They took the couple and then they took everything else. They stripped the place to the floorboards. Do you know how many people see such a thing—how public that is? They closed down a neighborhood and then carried the people out along with their couch, the radiators—they took the kitchen sink. And still the habeas corpus was refused. The army said, 'Not being detained.' That's how all my dossiers came back: 'Not being detained,' no matter how absurd."

"What about witnesses?"

"I haven't had a decent corroborating witness outside the family yet."

"And you never got anyone back? Not one?"

"One," the lawyer said. "And that was by fluke and still a sad story. The habeas corpus was refused, a 'Not being detained' like the others. It was the father who tracked the body down at the Forensic Medical Corps morgue."

"Dead?" Lillian said.

"Yes," Tello said. "That doesn't mean there aren't stories where the opposite is true. I've heard of people released in all manner of ways and a habeas corpus issued to a person who hadn't asked. The one thing I can tell you is that this government runs on paper. If they want they can erase someone in a day, everything—birth certificate, diplomas—all of it expunged, co-workers swearing they'd never met. They'll undo a future and a past in one blow. What you need is to make your son exist on paper. You need to get something official written down. If they own up to arresting him, they may also own up to the possibility that you're due him back and in one piece. That's really the key."

Kaddish said, "What goes in must come out?"

"Paper is proof. They'll lie about everything and make up the rest. The only thing they cower in front of is the filled-out form. If you build up to something, if real progress is made, I'd try for the habeas corpus. Otherwise, as you already said, it's the Ministry of Special Cases. A success can be had there, but it's like getting water from a stone." The meeting had ground down. Kaddish and Lillian stood. "If you change your minds," he said, "you know where I am. Bring a packed bag and a passport and I'll see you both safe."

Lillian spent Friday night in her chair by the window, watching the corner around which Pato might turn. Kaddish watched TV too loudly, drank too much, and smoked until the taste in his mouth went stale. He went into the kitchen at ten-thirty to freshen his drink and only came out again just before midnight, carrying a salad in a bowl.

"I've mashed potatoes," Kaddish said. "I've burnt you a steak." His own he took bloody, touching it fleetingly to the griddle.

"I'm fine," Lillian said.

Kaddish laid out place settings and served the rest of the dinner. He said to Lillian, "Come eat."

"If we're having Friday night, let's have it."

Lillian put three candlesticks in the center of the table. Two candles for Shabbos and the third a *minhag* from Lillian's house. Some mothers light an extra candle for each of their children. Lillian's mother had lit one for her, and Lillian did the same after Pato was born.

At least she had for the first weeks until Kaddish had used them to light one too many cigarettes, until he'd made her feel it was nothing but superstition, nonsense to light candles when they did nothing else.

Kaddish hadn't felt like he was being a brute. He had no use for laws that saw him a bastard, and less so for traditions passed on. Let them take the rules that made him *mamzer* and outcast and use that extra candle to push them deeply up their collective ass.

"You have to do that before dark," Kaddish said.

"Now you're a stickler for things you don't believe in?"

"It's the one Jewish tradition I keep—a hypocrisy that traces back."

Lillian held his gaze. "It can't hurt to light a candle for Pato."

"No," Kaddish said. Lillian put out a hand for his lighter and he gave it to her. "Sounds more Catholic than Jewish, but no."

Kaddish stood quietly while Lillian lit the candles and then covered her eyes. Because of the bandage, the whole of her face was hidden but for her mouth. She mumbled the blessing and she made a wish. They sat at the table and Kaddish had to admit—strange compliment though it was—that he'd not seen her looking better since Pato was taken.

"I added a layer of gauze," Lillian said. She smoothed the ends of the tape down against her cheeks. "A bit of clean dressing on top always brings out my eyes."

Kaddish went and opened a bottle of wine, trying to maintain the spirit. He poured for both of them and quickly drank. He wasn't about to say a prayer.

"It's not hypocrisy," Lillan said of the candles. "It's what lapsed Jews do in times of trouble. They make amends and beg help from God."

"I'm not going to, if that's all right."

"To ask?"

"To beg," Kaddish said.

"That's all right."

Kaddish ate and Lillian didn't. She sat with her lips pressed tight as if Kaddish might try and feed her off his fork.

Kaddish said, "Please, Lillian."

"What if he walks in right now and finds us like this, having a feast, drinking wine?"

"He'll think we were keeping up our strength so we could find him, and it will be the sweetest moment of our lives."

"But we won't have found him. It doesn't look right. I'm not even watching from the window; he'll take us by surprise."

Kaddish nodded. He stood and went into the kitchen. He returned with another place setting, the wineglass rolling in an arc around the plate.

"There," he said, and set out the dishes, folding the napkin, putting the silverware in line.

Lillian's bottom lip shook. This is why she had long ago married him, these were the things he could do.

Kaddish sat. Lillian took the wine bottle and filled Pato's empty glass.

"He can't really surprise us," she said. She pointed to the scalloped shelf where Pato's keys rested next to the gold. "What if he gets back when we're out looking?"

Kaddish got up again and went to the front door. He turned the key in its center, unscrewed the knob, and pulled the door open a few centimeters. "Who's left to kidnap with our son already gone?"

Kaddish sat down at the table and cut a piece from his steak. He reached over to set it on Pato's plate.

Lillian stopped him. "I won't ask you to take it that far."

"And the door? You'll be able to sleep with it open?"

"Better, if anything. Better if I manage to sleep at all."

This time Lillian stood up. She went around the table and kissed Kaddish on the back of his neck, lingering there.

Kaddish stayed frozen. He was trying to keep that kiss in place. It was the same kind of energy with which Lillian tried to move her son around the corner time and again.

After dinner they had coffee, Lillian in her chair and Kaddish in front of the TV. They stayed up until the candles went out, with Lillian glancing over, watching to see which one would go out first, praying it wasn't her son's.

When Kaddish turned off the television and went to the bedroom, Lillian followed. When he sat down on the corner of the bed, when he unbuttoned his shirt and pulled his undershirt over his head, when he leaned down with a grunt to pull off his socks, he was hoping in the least selfish way he knew how that Lillian might replace that kiss.

And she did. She pressed her lips to his neck.

It was like it had been when Pato was a newborn, like making love with Pato's bassinet by the side of the bed. It was a mix of passion and wonder and, for Kaddish, recognition of responsibility and consequence in the world.

[Twenty-seven]

THE CRY WAS SO STRONG, Kaddish sprinted down the hall to meet it. He found Lillian in the bathroom with the bandage in her hand. It was clear from the side as he stared at his wife in profile, clear before she turned to face him head on.

Again Lillian screamed with despair and, when she said it, Kaddish only nodded. What was there to do but agree? How else to respond when Lillian said, "I'm beautiful!"

Mazursky had done a magnificent job by Mazursky's standards. The swelling and the black eyes did little to hide it. Lillian was transformed. Transformed, and even in Kaddish's imaginings he'd never pictured this. He'd thought so always but now, to look at her, Lillian was right. She was nothing short of beautiful.

"Murder," Lillian said, her old nose gone, Pato missing from the mirror. "To change a face it is murder."

Lillian stopped at the fountain as she crossed the Plaza de Mayo. It was turned off and empty even of rainwater, so that when she threw her coins in she heard them hit and watched them roll. Lillian wasn't sure of the rules, if it was the fountain or the water that counted, or, as a homeless woman walked toward her, if the money had to sit for any length of time. A wish is a wish, is what she decided. On her way to the Ministry of Special Cases, Lillian would take what she could get.

That she was going to the ministry didn't mean that what the lawyer said or what Kaddish said or what Cacho feared was right. Maybe people waited too long to go because of the rumors, and, having missed their window of opportunity, the building's reputation proved true. Maybe the other families were making spurious claims and that's why they found no recourse—it wasn't for Lillian to judge. And if what the lawyer said was accurate, if it was like getting water from a rock, so be it. She wasn't trying to find all the missing. She was trying to get one son back. Kaddish thought she was afraid to face reality when it was the other way around. This was the place the parents, the husbands and wives, the children of the missing went. And Lillian was headed there alone.

She looked at her watch when she got to the building. The Ministry of Special Cases didn't open for another hour.

Except that it did.

The door was open and the lobby was packed with people. They pushed and shoved, all trying to reach the lone security guard behind the counter. He stood on his chair, then up on the counter itself, yelling at the crowd.

Lillian worked her way into the mix. "It's not supposed to open for another hour," Lillian kept saying, a form of apology as she pushed and was pushed back.

"It's the numbers," a lady told her as they were pressed up against each other. "They give them out ten minutes before one hour before." And then they were separated and then they were back. "But only the first fifty. If you don't get one now, you better hustle when they open. We wait outside and then there's another line upstairs." They were pushed apart and the lady was gone. Lillian was by then close enough to the guard to see better and understand.

He wasn't yelling *Order, please,* or *Line up,* or *Who was here first?* He was picking people at whim, saying, "You," and, "You there." He was feeding the frenzy. It was a cruel game.

By the time Lillian grasped this fully, the crush of people was thinning out. The guard climbed down and Lillian watched the last of the stragglers race back outside. When she looked over her shoulder, the security guard met her eye. He said, "We're closed until eight."

Lillian exited the lobby. The guard locked the door behind her, and Lillian saw, stretched out and down the block, a line. She didn't need to look for the slip in each hand to know when she'd walked by the last of the chosen and on to the dry faces that followed. She didn't see the lady who'd explained so as to offer thanks.

Lillian didn't quite understand why they were all in line now, or at least, if they were, why those with numbers stood in the same one. Still, it was orderly and purposeful and so she stood at the end and waited.

When the line began moving slowly ahead, Lillian followed. When the pace picked up, Lillian picked up hers along with it, and when those from behind, first one and then another, rushed past, she too broke ranks and ran the last steps.

It was too late. Back again like before, everyone pushing toward a single door beyond the counter and off to the left side.

This push was more suffocating than the last. It was pandemonium until one man, right at the street entrance and a few meters behind Lillian (she'd made some forward progress), began to call out in a confident but harried tone. "Can't a man get to his office?" he said. "Coming through," he said. "Late for work." And in the midst of what seemed like complete chaos, now, so easy, a path was made. The man—smoothing down his mustache and mumbling insults—slipped right through the crowd.

When Lillian reached the door, it led into a narrow stairwell. This was the reason for the jam.

There was a smaller lobby two flights up and another counter, this time with a woman behind it. Mounted on the wall next to the counter was a battered red-metal ticket machine. From this the numbers were pulled.

Lillian pulled hers. Number 456.

She followed the others into the adjoining hall and found a place to sit among the fixed wooden benches and folding chairs. The clerks faced them from a row of desks on the far side of the room.

Lillian sat holding her number tight with two hands. She'd look to it and look toward the clerks. Eventually one stood and called out, "Nine."

"Nine," he said again. There was rustling up front, and a woman in a kerchief stood. Lillian looked around to see that she and the woman in the kerchief were the only two who'd paid it any mind.

Lillian looked at her number again when they called for ten and eleven and twelve. She then asked her neighbor, "Do they stay open until they're done?"

The man laughed.

"So tomorrow?" Lillian said.

"What do you think?" the man said. "Take a guess."

"One," Lillian said.

"Yes. A natural. The day begins with one."

Lillian thought she might weep right then and would have if not for a distraction.

"He has one-sixty-two," an old man said. "*El desgraciado* has one-sixty-two." The old man drew the attention of another couple, who also began to curse, which brought another lady into the fray. "Monster," the lady said. And the man she called monster, the one the couple leered at, the guy the old man raised his cane at, was the very same man with the mustache who'd arrived "late for work."

He was, like them, waiting. He did not work there and had been late only for the line. He'd lied and, like suckers, they'd made him a path. There had to be another entrance for workers. How, in all that time waiting, could only one need to use the front door? How had they not caught on—caught him—on their own?

The rage was unbelievable; Lillian thought they might kill the man with the mustache for real until the old man struck him in the mouth with the hook of his cane. As hard as the old man could hit was not hard enough to do much. The man with the mustache spit blood, though, and this seemed to satisfy the crowd. The man sat for the day looking ashamed but he held on and was called with his 162.

Lillian had no book and no papers beyond the few documents she'd put together that related to her son. She spent the day staring at a very large woman in a very small chair who held a bottle of fizzy water and sweated the whole time. The woman was not a delicate woman but she did have a delicate bird's tongue. This she'd dab into the neck of the bottle, never once sipping from it or tipping the bottle back to drink. Only, like a hummingbird, that tongue darting into the neck, dabbing endlessly, the whole of that woman spreading out from that point.

Lillian thought the woman would die of thirst. She'd never get anything that way. Lillian wanted to run over and grab the bottle and drink it down herself. She wanted to push that woman's giant head right into it, to shove her inside and set the bottle back on her seat. It was too much: the waiting and the sweating and the numbers not moving and that woman, with her tiny private purpose and flicking tongue.

Lillian watched the whole bottle disappear, one dab at a time.

That this woman's blank face and her sharp raspberry tongue could so fill Lillian with hate unsettled her. They were all of them waiting, all in this together. Lillian still couldn't stand her, but she forced herself to wish the woman well in her mind.

When the ministry closed, Lillian still hadn't been called. She did not know if that day was special or if they'd closed earlier than on most. Her own office was still open and, reminded of it, Lillian decided it would be good to go by. On her way out, as had the others, she let her number—worn through—flutter to the floor.

Gustavo approached at the start of their embrace but Lillian and Frida didn't let go. Lillian wept on Frida's shoulder, and Frida whispered into Lillian's ear. "No, you don't," Frida said. "Not from me." When it seemed the embrace was about to end, one or the other would give a good squeeze and shore it up. "Hide all you want," Frida said. "But this is the longest you go without seeing me again."

"I swear," Lillian said, and then they moved apart.

Gustavo pulled Lillian by the shoulders and kissed her on both cheeks.

"A visit?" Gustavo said. "What a nice surprise."

"I thought I could do a couple of hours' work," Lillian said. She motioned, shocked to see it, at the mountain of files on her desk. "I've got to keep the job in order," she said. "I've got to keep the job."

"Don't be silly," Frida said.

"Don't be silly," Gustavo said. "The important thing is Pato. Are things moving along?"

Frida took one of Lillian's hands and held it between her own.

"Poorly," Lillian said.

Being back in her office, stepping into what was so recently her day-to-day, was enough. Answering the question was too much. It unmoored her. Lillian didn't consider it to be crying, but when she said, "Poorly," the tears began rolling from her eyes.

"Things will normalize," Lillian said. "When Pato is home—exactly as before. I won't let things slide too far."

"We are very busy without you," Gustavo said.

"Don't be ridiculous," Frida said. "You shouldn't come in at all."

"Yes," Gustavo said. "We're doing fine."

This was followed by silence. Lillian was trying to maintain composure. Gustavo and Frida didn't know what to say. Certain observations simply aren't appropriate to certain moments, but neither can they be ignored.

It was Gustavo who spoke. "You look, Lillian, absolutely gorgeous."

"I have a new nose," she said. With that, she went to her desk and set to work.

Lillian arrived earlier at the ministry the next day. Kaddish had offered to come, his face buried in a pillow. Lillian told him to stay home by the phone.

Again Lillian failed to get a number in the first rush. In the second— toward the stairwell—she fared a little better but still found herself back on the benches holding 401. Lillian did not see the lady with the raspberry tongue or the man who was late for work, but already many of the faces were familiar. The lady who had told Lillian "ten minutes before" passed by. She smiled at Lillian but did not stop.

Lillian brought food. She brought one of Pato's books from the shelf.

She sat and read and did not look up when they called numbers. The ministry stayed open a half hour later than the day before and still they didn't get to Lillian. She called home from the corner. Kaddish answered. There was nothing to say and she stood there in silence feeling the weather, until Kaddish finally said, "I'll cook."

They were whispering by the extra desk when Gustavo came out. "Two days in a row," he said. "Such dedication, Lillian, it really means a lot. This is the last thing to worry about."

"I can't lose this job," Lillian said. "Look at milk. Look at butter. How much with inflation will it cost to get my son?"

Gustavo smoothed his tie.

"Who is talking about lost jobs?" Frida said. She gave Gustavo a threatening look, as if he'd raised the idea. Gustavo threw up his hands. He took a step back.

"Your position is safe," he said.

"For how long, really?" Lillian said. Gustavo smiled. He blushed. "Considering how much I do here, Gustavo. Considering I do most of your job, give me a number." Lillian's voice turned sharp. "How many days or is it weeks or is it months, how long is safe, how long is paid, how long is this place my home if I don't show up? How long will the paychecks come?"

Gustavo started to speak. Lillian actually reached out and put a hand over his mouth.

"Don't say it," she said. "I know you, Gustavo. I know you well. A date. Something real. Until when will you pay me for a job undone?"

"Lillian," Frida said, but she wasn't sure why.

The hand came down. Gustavo buttoned his jacket, he straightened his cuffs. Today he was the one with tears in his eyes.

"Honesty is all I have left," Lillian said.

"You have more than that," Gustavo said. "The lawyer—how was Tello? Do your best, I told him. Send me a bill."

"Is there a date?" Frida said. "Tell her if there's a limit."

Gustavo, who could not look at Lillian, hissed at Frida through clenched teeth. "You know who's coming," he said. "There's no time for this." Only then did Lillian notice his good shoes, his good cuff links: Gustavo dressed to the nines. "They can't walk in and find a scene."

"Then tell her," Frida said.

"I'm telling you, not Lillian. Go to your desk and look busy. Right now all our jobs are on the line."

"Tell her she's safe forever," Frida said. "Tell her you'll pay her forever."

Gustavo looked at them both, his jaw tight.

"No one gets paid forever," Gustavo yelled, and then he smiled a beautiful smile that went right through them. It was meant for the venerable, the powerful, Judge Ocampo and his wife. They were as important a pair of clients as one could wish for. To insure even the scraps from their table would keep a man afloat.

"You asked about the lawyer," Lillian said, as Gustavo greeted his clients. "You asked about Tello."

Gustavo was the picture of calm but for what was left of his blush. He said, "Excuse me for a moment," to his clients and turned to Lillian.

"Tello," she said. "Your lawyer was useless. He offered no help at all."

"I'd wondered," Gustavo said, getting back to his welcome, the matter dealt with.

The judge, who was not deaf, couldn't resist.

"It wouldn't be the first instance," he said to Lillian. "Useless lawyers I see by the bucketful. Enough to fill the whole of Río de la Plata so that we could walk over them to the other side."

Gustavo laughed too loudly. The judge's wife laughed just the right amount. Lillian and Frida pursed lips and tilted their heads in the woman's direction. The men followed suit.

Celia Ocampo then asked, "And what happens to the most useless of the lot?" Her husband smiled and kissed her on the cheek—yes, a family routine, a set question. After the pause, he chucked Gustavo's chin and answered. "Those are the ones who are chosen to judge."

All laughed, Lillian too. The color began to even out in Gustavo's cheeks, and the meeting continued in his office. Lillian and Frida sat outside at their desks. Framed through Gustavo's doorway and on

display for the clients, it looked like just the kind of boutique business
to do delicate work for a judge.

When Gustavo walked the couple out to their car, Lillian grabbed her
coat and her bag and announced that she was done for the day.

"Can you wait a minute?" Frida said.

"Not even for a second."

"Well, then," Frida said, "I guess I'm ready now too. Can I walk you
home?"

"That would be lovely," Lillian said, and she went into Gustavo's office.
She held her bag between her knees and bent over Gustavo's Rolodex.
Frida followed her in.

"Whatever you're about to do, Lillian, I guarantee it's beyond what
Gustavo can handle."

Lillian spun the wheel.

"Let it spin," Frida said, "and let's go."

"The general," Lillian said. "If he and his wife can produce a child out
of thin air, they can do it a second time for me."

"Babies are easier."

"Then it will be a challenge for them," Lillian said. "Let them muster
a full-grown son."

"The general—" Frida said and stopped. They both knew these were
dangerous people and that Lillian didn't care. Frida thought about it and
then said only, "Gustavo." Lillian knew what she meant.

"I've been the provider long enough," Lillian said. "Kaddish can be
the breadwinner for once."

Lillian continued to spin the wheel one way and, against the momentum of the deck, used a fingernail to slow the cards in the other. She
pulled the general's loose.

"Just copy it down," Frida said, "and let's go."

Lillian dropped the card into her bag.

"No one left to stand by their actions in this country," she said. "No
secrets for me. Lillian Poznan leaves a trail."

[Twenty-eight]

THE ELEVATOR OPENED ONTO A HALLWAY that led into a foyer. This is where they were left waiting, at the foot of a vast staircase with marble stairs and an oriental runner held down with polished brass bars. From the top, behind the balustrade, peeked a boy with slicked hair and a monogrammed silk robe. It was past his bedtime. He had sneaked out without his slippers. Lillian and Kaddish pretended not to see.

A butler came and they followed. There was a glimpse of the general's wife in the sitting room as they were led past. The living room beyond offered another entrance to the sitting room with the sitting wife, but they were taken through the far door into a library, whose ladder was affixed to a rail curved expertly in the corners so that, perched on a rung, one could circumnavigate the whole of the room. A servant disappeared through a section of wall as they entered a connecting hallway. The butler finally deposited them in a formal dining room and was gone.

The room was vast and chilly. A tapestry, faded, chosen clearly for its width, was hung on one long wall. The opposite wall in this endless apartment was one of windows, with a narrow balcony beyond. In the center of the room but favoring the windows was a long table, wooden and medieval in its design. It wasn't apparent in any particular touch, only that the deeply polished, deeply worn wood made Kaddish think he could still feel the tree in the table. It was accented by eight high-backed chairs placed along one side. There were two more, these with arms (the rough plugs of the pegs sticking out of the armrests), one at each end. Along the window side an upholstered bench ran the length of the table. It looked even stiffer than the chairs. This is where Lillian and Kaddish were deposited, in a room that swallowed them up.

Lillian adjusted the strap to her dress. She ran her finger along its edge to make sure her bra was hidden underneath. A single small diamond on a thin platinum chain hung around her neck. It was reset from her mother's engagement ring, her heirloom, the family jewel. Lillian centered it below her collarbone.

"You look elegant," Kaddish said.

"If a woman can't have a new dress, at least she should have a new face to jazz things up."

Kaddish sat at the head of the table.

"We could have become used to a life like this," he said. "Servants trotting around with gravy boats. Us waiting for the echoes to reach the end of the table to hear what was said. If things had worked out differently, we wouldn't need a favor. We'd be granting them. If Perón hadn't come back, if the governments didn't swing as they do, who knows?"

"But it's inevitable," Lillian said. "It's like betting against nature, Kaddish. You take odds every fall, betting the leaves will stay on the trees. There's no deal you touch that doesn't sour. A thousand nose jobs and each would fall."

"Mine hasn't," Kaddish said, looking around. "It's Perón who soured me. He should have come back from Spain like Evita, in a nice glass-topped coffin and doing no harm."

"Why do you always put on the same show? Enough of the old problems," Lillian said. "You want to remember Perón? Then take a lesson from him."

Kaddish stood up and went over to Lillian. "What lesson from him?" he said in a whisper. "What lesson from that man?"

"Never to give up," Lillian said, whispering back, no distance between them. "They stole his wife and hid her grave. They stole his country, and banished him from it. And he didn't give up," Lillian said. "Do you understand me? There's no sea you need to cross, no country to conquer. Only one thing: Get the boy. You want to stay vengeful? Then one-up Juan Perón. Outdo your made-up nemesis. Not just the body, Kaddish. Go bring your son back alive."

"And what does it matter if I try when I have a wife who forever bails me out? Here we are at the top and it's all your doing. As always, I promise and you come through."

"And still it's not enough. An insult to be left stranded in this room. You want to see me do something, Kaddish? I'm going to find that woman as if at a friend's. I'm going to kiss her on both cheeks and then we'll talk about our children."

Lillian started toward the tapestry, going back the way they came.

"Don't," Kaddish said. "Their rules in here, Lillian. Their signals."

She stopped and looked over her shoulder, but left her body set toward the hall. "No one will help us without dignity."

"There is dignity in staying put—more, even. These are the people of the measured pause. They'll stop mid-sentence for a drag of a cigarette and look out the window for half an hour, forgetting to exhale. But they are watching, Lillian. There's only to be unruffled and uninterested."

"You think I don't know? I deal with them for real, not during dream business. You're all big talk and contracts sealed with the dead."

"With you, with tension, it always turns into blame."

"It's not your fault, Kaddish."

"Then trust me. And wait."

"The whole idea of this room is to make us feel small." Lillian put her arms across her chest and hugged herself.

"Sit down," Kaddish said. He felt a rage building toward Lillian, for no reason toward Lillian except who else could he be mad at, who else was there in this giant room to focus on? He knew what this rage was. It was helplessness and here was Lillian, still holding on to the notion that they were in a position to expect anything.

"I'm going to find his wife."

"The wife is not our contact. He is our contact, he is the favor. Now wait as if you weren't. Suffer over your son while waiting without a care in the world."

As if in defiance of Lillian, Kaddish lit a cigarette, shook out the match, and—no ashtray—placed it on the corner of the table. A few puffs of smoke, the gray cloud between them, Kaddish stepped around the long bench to the windows. He bent and pulled two brass latches from their grooves in the floor, reached up and pulled two down from the ceiling. Kaddish pressed brass door handles down, popped open French doors, and stepped out onto the balcony. He leaned over the edge and smoked, taking in the night.

All these years married to his inappropriateness and bad judgment, to an unearned confidence and boundaries ignored, and here Lillian thought maybe she'd been enlightened. Kaddish had managed to explain himself. A first.

The breeze blew through the doors. It blew over her husband and brought with it smoke, and Lillian saw Kaddish as her hosts would, cigarette in hand and elbows to the railing—a man enjoying the evening. It was a guest receiving his hosts, his ass stuck out to greet them. Kaddish could, she thought, set their most important meeting off on the wrong foot. But if you lived your life wronged, if you already felt the world was upside down, discourtesy might seem like your only chance at respect. And you may be right. Lillian was starting to understand, too little too late.

Also, honestly, Lillian didn't want to go storming through the house after that woman. She sat where Kaddish had and crossed her eyes, trying to get a look at the tininess of her nose.

Still no one came.

It was too much for Lillian to fake ease while waiting for this man who would or wouldn't deliver Pato, who would rescue their son if his mood was right, who might see that he stayed missing solely because of Kaddish's attitude, or just as easily join Kaddish for a cigarette and a breath of fresh air, and that the sole reason he'd offer any support at all.

It was too much for a son's life to rest on whim.

Lillian's pulse beat hard and the room, in sharp focus, turned brighter. She was feeling a bit faint. If someone didn't show up right then with a glass of lemonade or tea. If Lillian didn't get some ice to chew on, they would find her on the floor. Kaddish would surely approve of a position so relaxed.

Lillian would help herself to a glass of water. She was dying of thirst and in any other strange home she'd do just that—she'd happily drop dead in sight of the sink before opening cabinets in search of a glass and turning the tap. Today she would trust him. She would join Kaddish in his ease.

They'd entered through the only door. It was a dining room with no kitchen in sight. On the short wall behind the chair she'd sat in, Lillian spotted the cuts in the thick molding that ran waist-high around the room, the delineation of a hidden door from where the servants might pass. Lillian pushed it inward and the door pushed back on double hinges. Maybe Lillian would do this at home, add to her heavy front door a dense coil of springs.

Another push and Lillian held the door open. Light from the dining room cut a swath across copper pots suspended from the ceiling. Lillian let the door close against her arm, her hand in the kitchen, fumbling for a switch. Fingers spread, she reached in farther, feeling her way along the wall. Nothing. She pulled out her arm and searched the dining room side. If the door was so well hidden, maybe the light switch was hidden too.

How does Kaddish do it? Lillian thought. How to be entitled. A glass of water, a simple thing, and even about this she made a timid display.

Lillian pushed through into the darkness and let the door swing closed behind her. She tried the same wall again. She waved her hand in the air to check for a chain. You would not, she thought, put a switch behind a swinging door but she passed to the far side. There she was in the pitch blackness. A fit place for her, she thought, blind and searching an unfamiliar wall in an unfamiliar room, looking for and not finding what must, what had to, be there.

Lillian was relieved when the door cracked open, happy that Kaddish had come looking. She felt more kindly toward him, and said, "Rich people have no lights."

"By and large, we have whatever we want," was the response, and then as blind as she was from the darkness she was blinded by the glare. That calm, calm voice wasn't Kaddish's at all.

Prior to embarrassment, prior to introductions, Lillian was still looking for the switch. She wanted to know where it was. When her eyes fell on the general, a strapping man in a fine suit of clothes, he smiled and tilted his head back, signaling with his chin.

Across a vast kitchen—full of steel and butcher block, with a giant island for cutting and rolling in its center, and an oven with a dozen burners that was long enough to roast a man—there stood a wisp of a woman with a doily on her head and wearing a maid's uniform. The woman stood with her hand on the switch, right where Lillian would have reached if positions were flipped, right where it belonged but all the way down there, on the other side, by the maid's quarters and a butler's pantry that led into the next hall.

"There isn't one on this end," the general said. "No switch. I should hope in a properly run house I shouldn't have to be digging about for spoons."

"I just wanted some water."

"We can probably do better than that," he said.

Lillian tried not to, but she couldn't resist. "Excuse my poking around," she said. The general ignored the comment and led her back to the dining room on his arm. The maid was already there with a glass of water, a sprig of mint floating. She presented it on a tray. Lillian was so thirsty she couldn't help but drink it down right then, eyes wide and staring up into the general's. The maid, as if expecting this thirst, remained. She extended the tray.

Lillian felt safe for the first time since Pato's disappearance. These people could help. A man who never needs to turn on a light can see to great things.

The general motioned toward the table, and Lillian was surprised to find candles set out. Kaddish was already seated, a drink in his hand. There was a bowl of fruit, a plate of cheese, these things had somehow beat her back though she'd blocked the kitchen door.

Kaddish slid over on the bench and Lillian sat next to him. The bench was too low and the table hit her in the middle of the chest. The general's wife sat at the head of the table with her chair angled away from them. She held a glass of white wine.

Though Lillian had handled their file, though they'd sat at her desk bouncing that borrowed baby on a knee, all earnest and kind, it was as if they'd never met. Full introductions were made. The wife said to call her Teresa. The general, it seemed, felt his title was enough.

"Something stronger than water?" he said. He placed a hand on the wine bottle, and Lillian nodded.

Lillian looked back toward the kitchen and out came the maid with a tray of oysters. Another servant, wearing a vest, was right on the maid's heels with another tray. The butler came last with a third.

"Had we been expecting you for dinner," Teresa said, "the table would have been set."

"Yes," the general said, his own apology. "You get a glimpse into our quirks. It's a most informal version of ridiculously formal. If there's something else you want, a sandwich or a salad? I'm sure we could rustle up an omelet and toast."

The trays were unloaded. Deep dishes of oysters on beds of crushed ice. Half were on the half shell and the other half closed. As the servant in the vest put out a stack of small plates, the lemons and the sauces, Teresa signaled to him most subtly with a look. Lillian caught it as the servant understood, displaying a silent shock and picking Kaddish's cigarette butt and match off the corner of the table. He tucked them into the pocket of his vest.

Kaddish poured an oyster into his mouth.

"Now I remember," the general said to Lillian. "Gustavo's girl. The one we worked with at the office. I thought it was you but, if you can forgive my rudeness, you look different, much younger and—"

His wife continued for him. "More Argentine in some way."

"Less ethnic," Lillian offered.

"If you say so, yes," Teresa agreed.

Kaddish took a sip of his drink and took a long look at the general's wife. Teresa turned a bit farther into the angle of the chair.

"I've noticed it myself," Kaddish said. "She does look younger. Taller too."

The general liked this. He laughed. "If only it were possible at this age. Maybe she found the centimeter I lost."

"Would it be all right if we got right down to business?" Lillian said.

"Business?" Teresa said. She held a tiny silver fork. With it she freed an oyster and aimed it at her mouth so that the brine dripped toward the table, landing, of course, on her plate. "What business could there be? What business would we want to discuss at our table, in our home?" At that, she tipped the shell and Lillian watched the oyster slide onto her tongue.

The general looked to his wife as if there was explaining to be done. "A turn of phrase, I'm sure," he said, and then addressed his guests. "I'm admittedly flabbergasted by your presence. I was led to believe—by you yourself—that it was Gustavo who would be arriving." The general stood and stepped behind his wife's chair. "And now to receive his assistant in his place. We don't much like surprises, and we don't conduct any business in our home."

"It's not business," Kaddish said, his heart racing. He had no idea Lillian was capable of such a thing. He couldn't believe that it would cross her mind to put them all together in that room with a lie. "It's more of a favor."

"You are here to do us a favor?" the general said.

"To ask one," Lillian said.

"Why would we owe you a favor?" the general said, his voice now harsh.

"Owe?" Kaddish said. "God forbid. Favors aren't traded. Friends don't cash them in like poker chips at the end of the night."

"But we aren't friends," Teresa said.

Lillian pressed her lips together and set her jaw. "But you may find that you'd like to help us anyway because you feel we're good people to have in your debt." She assumed that such rarefied conversationalists didn't miss to what she referred.

Teresa had an amazing amount of poise. Lillian felt her seething, yet there was no identifiable outward sign, no motion or move, only a simmering hatred of which she was sure.

The general's composure seemed to crack when he looked toward his wife. "You're here already, let's make the most of a misunderstanding. Have a drink, have an oyster, no damage done."

"Yes," Teresa said. "Eat up, as who knows when the opportunity will arise again."

Lillian pushed her plate away. "I ate at home."

"That's a shame," the general said, "as this is the perfect month for the perfect oyster. These we harvest ourselves."

In the painful silence that followed, Kaddish reached for oyster after oyster. He swallowed them as fast as he could. "Delicious," he said, "incredible," trying to fathom how he'd gotten into this position. He'd never had to cover for Lillian before and wondered if this was what it was like for her, raising a husband for all these years.

Kaddish slowed down, running short on superlatives, and feeling green. He wanted this to work. He agreed with Lillian, this man could produce their son. "A rare treat," Kaddish said. Then, summoning up enthusiasm, he said, "Did you say you grow them?"

"Not grow," Teresa said. "Harvest."

"My father-in-law's legacy," the general said.

"When he first sailed to North America," Teresa said, "he was horrified to find that they rinsed the brine from their oysters."

"Think of that," the general said. "Washing the flavor right off. It ruins them. It's the Yankees," he said, conspiratorially. "Their influence. In mixed company let me say it as delicately as possible—the Yankee doesn't like anything to taste of the sea." Lillian put her hand on Kaddish's knee. "From that trip on, they never made a voyage without their oysters. If you keep them in their own sand and flush their water, you can fool them into staying alive the whole trip. When he moved here for good he shipped the whole operation over. He made the final crossing with his precious cargo as if he had his own ocean belowdecks."

Here came the single bit of life shown by Teresa.

"A funny man, my father," she said, with actual sweetness. "He hated the passage and did everything for his comfort but was always jealous of the food. He always said, 'First class passage is first class passage, but my oysters travel in their own beds.'" She held out her wineglass and a servant filled it. "As ridiculous as it sounds, it's more natural than bringing along the livestock. There's nothing more pitiful than a seasick cow."

"At the end of the war, when the United States was storming every beach in Europe with their amphibious crafts, her father would scream back at the newsreels about the churning up of the shallows. 'Those barbarians won't stop at the Nazis,' he'd yell. 'The Yankees will put an end to decent dining so as to protect the democratic way of life.'"

Kaddish pried open a belon. "Again, they're a rare treat."

"Yes," Teresa said. "They transplanted to our bays very well. As good an acclimation as any Italian or Jew."

"At least as well as the general takes to new governments," Lillian said.

He didn't seem insulted. "It's my loyalty to the uniform, which is a loyalty to the state."

"As long as it leaves you in good stead," Lillian said. "It's of the uniform that we need a favor. My son has been abducted. It's been more than a week," she said. She looked at Kaddish. "And we've made no progress in getting him back."

The general gave the wine in his glass a turn and watched it swirl.

Teresa reached for an oyster and piled it high with horseradish. She swallowed the oyster and the horseradish and then looked right at Lillian, her face flushed. "Your son has disappeared?"

"He hasn't disappeared," Lillian said. "He *was* disappeared. The government did this to him."

Kaddish sucked on a wedge of lemon. He watched the exchange, eyes darting between them.

"Taken by the government?" the general said. "Arrested is very different than vanished. Where is your son being detained?"

"If I knew we wouldn't be here."

"You shouldn't be here anyway," Teresa said.

"But you know they have him?" the general said, his face full of concern.

Kaddish popped the lemon from his mouth, and his front teeth felt as if they'd been dried down to the roots. "There were agents," Kaddish said, "four men in suits." He ran his tongue along the front of his teeth, "One with a windbreaker underneath."

"Agents?" the general said. "Insurance agents like your wife?"

"Cleaning agents?" Teresa said, catching on. "Like Odex or Ayudín?"

"It happened very quickly," Kaddish said.

"You were there?"

"Yes," he said. "They took three books. They beat up our neighbor."

The general gave a sniff. "Who did they say they were when they arrived?"

"They just knocked," Kaddish said.

"Well, why didn't you accompany these agents when they took him? Wouldn't you ask where they were headed with your child?"

"You know it's not like that," Kaddish said. "They would have killed me—killed my son—in a heartbeat." Now Kaddish looked to Lillian. "There's nothing that can be done."

"You attend these home invasions regularly, then?"

"No, but I've heard."

"They pointed their guns at you? Did they threaten to shoot?"

"No," Kaddish said.

"How about we stick to what is verifiable?" the general said. "We are fortunate to live in the best nation on earth, and yet, the more I hear, the more I'm convinced we destroy ourselves with gossip. It's a fifth column in itself. If we aren't careful, idle chatter will be this country's downfall." The general shook his head, looking gravely disappointed.

Teresa spoke up. "There are many wild ideas that the hopeless grab onto," and she reached over and patted Lillian's hand. "I'm sure my husband is interested in helping. But to believe such rumors? It's just not so. This band of missing, it's made up. They don't exist."

"I think you might mean that," Lillian said. "It's even scarier to think that the people who run this country believe their own lies."

"That's too far," the general said. He was on his way to standing when his wife stopped him.

"I *do* believe those lies," she said. "What I want to know from you is, if everyone believes the same lie, isn't it, maybe, the truth?"

Lillian didn't pause, not even a beat. "That's how the world stays balanced. You can never get everyone to believe the same thing."

Kaddish wondered if a lie could become truth even if everyone agreed. But there was a consideration more pressing. He wasn't sure there was anything that he couldn't be made to believe.

"There is lying going on," the general said, "and there are young people missing. But they aren't in secret jails or fighting alongside the leftists. They are on drugs, they are lost. They're a bunch of hippies who've run away to the beaches of Brazil and Uruguay to chase after sex. The lie this government tolerates is that it's political. The people aren't disabused of the notion that these drug addicts and ne'er-do-wells are up in the mountains planning revolution. A generation of youth hasn't been raised right, which is as much the government's fault as it is the fault of the family. Why not let the parents believe their children are off somewhere fighting for a cause? The only secret being kept from the people is that a whole generation is being lost to selfishness and bad behavior."

"What could you possibly be saying?" Lillian went white.

"Admittedly, it's hard to put ourselves in your shoes," the general said. "I do understand how you'd interpret that as a denial of whatever trouble your son may be in."

"This meeting is actually our greatest accomplishment yet," Lillian said. "You're the first official to admit I have—that I ever had—a son."

"And sadly this in an unofficial capacity. There is one other bit of information I can offer. It doesn't help, but it may make you feel less alone. This problem is not limited to Argentina. We talk to our neighbors. There is a wanderlust, and it's as bad in Chile and Bolivia and Peru. For every one of our kids who crosses those borders, another is on his way here to get lost the same way. I don't want to be the one to tell you that the child you've done all you can for has run off without a good-bye. The clerks draw straws at the Ministry of Special Cases. No one wants to tell the parents these things."

"Our son didn't run off," Kaddish said. He rushed it out, hoarse. "I told you what happened."

The general sighed. "I'm a military man. This kind of hand-holding is not my forte."

Kaddish couldn't wait any longer, he held a cigarette to a candle until the tip burst into flame. Blowing it out, he took two quick pulls, the paper of his cigarette scorched black.

"There's really nothing more forthright that I can offer," the general said. "I wish you success. And if you want to achieve it, I recommend a large dose of self-control. Rabble-rousing will get you nowhere and only see your son farther away."

"That's an admission," Lillian said, pointing a finger. "That means the two are related, that what we do affects Pato—what we do to you. You admitted it just now, that there's a link." Lillian looked to Teresa as if she'd feel obligated to support her.

The general said, "I made a point about preservation and about silence."

"You made a point about cause and effect. You can help us. I'm begging you. Use that uniform for someone else as you have for yourselves—"

"What does that mean?" Teresa said, angry.

"Use it to get back our son," Lillian said. She spoke to the general. "You're a powerful, powerful man and I beg of that power."

"This excess energy would do better if it was focused on restraint," the general said. "Silence saves lives. If there's to be any chance for you or your son, you need to go home and behave and be quiet. Go home and wait. The boy will return when he is ready, probably with a tan and a pregnant revolutionary on his arm."

"There were four agents," Kaddish said. "They took three books."

The general looked at Kaddish as if he were a madman.

"Do you see?" he said to Lillian. "This kind of protest does him no good. Your husband sounds as if he's coming unhinged."

"I'm fine," Kaddish said.

"Please," the general said, "such a tough-looking little man. You think

I don't see it? I could make you cry right now with half a word." Kaddish took a drag of his cigarette to hide the fact that what the general said was true.

"Go home," the general said. "Wait quietly. See it as a contribution to order. We are all making sacrifices to mend the torn fabric of this country, to put the economy back on track and build ourselves up. Do you know officers holding government positions have had their salaries wiped away? Do you know I now serve for free? We all must do our part. I only request you don't feed the hysteria. It's easy to set a whole society on its head. Panic spreads worse than wildfire."

"You're not going to help us," Lillian said. "You will look us in the eye and do nothing."

"I can't say I'm convinced anything has happened that you can be helped with."

Lillian said, "Children don't just vanish as if they never were. The same as they don't just appear."

Teresa, working at an oyster, slipped and pricked her finger with a knife. She rushed her finger into her mouth and then, pulling it out, studied the droplet of blood that formed. "There's always something rotten inside when they are locked that tight."

She reached under the table and, with the corresponding finger of the other hand, she pressed an invisible button connected to a bell they could not hear. The maid arrived, walking at a clip, and reacted as if her mistress' head had been cut off. She then, sweetly, kissed the cut. "Patch me up in the drawing room," Teresa said, and she left the table without even a nod good-bye, her arm raised above her head.

"You can do this," Lillian said to the general, as soon as Teresa was gone. "You are the only one who can get him back."

"Go home, Lillian." It was the first time he'd said her name. "Powerful as I am—I admit it—I can't undo what's not been done. I can't make your son from nothing. You are Jews," the general said. "Go to the river and mix him from clay. People from nothing is a Jewish affair."

"That's what I came to hear," Kaddish said. He stood up and slid past Lillian on the bench. "My wife expected help. I came looking for clarity." Kaddish offered Lillian a hand, addressing her. "When you want to see which way the wind blows, always talk to a frightened general. You won't find any bravery but at least you'll learn the truth."

And then it was Lillian who was shocked by Kaddish. She didn't believe that what he said was inappropriate or rash. She thought it was strong.

"I can only pity you," the general said. "It's hopelessness that makes you talk this way."

"I'm not hopeless," Kaddish said. "Everybody better pray that it doesn't get to that." The general, amused, leaned back in his chair.

"You go on my list," Kaddish said. "The government has its list. You go on mine."

The general was holding his stomach as Kaddish threatened him, his eyes welling up. He was afraid he might fall from his chair. The general watched the tough little man leave with his tough little wife, and he laughed and laughed and laughed.

[Twenty-nine]

KADDISH JOINED LILLIAN at the Ministry of Special Cases on the day her number was called. Kaddish had come late. He'd slipped out to buy cigarettes and then again for the papers, and finally to fetch them lunch. Still, when the number hit in the afternoon, he was by Lillian's side.

On the way to the front of the room, a woman thrust her number out at Kaddish. "Trade," she said. "Please." Kaddish sidestepped her and walked on with his head turned, keeping an eye on the lady. The woman kept her eye on Kaddish too. When he sat down in front of the clerk, the woman stood up and, a final try, waved her number back and forth in the air.

Lillian gave him a pat and acknowledged their good fortune. She said to Kaddish, "You're a charm."

They sat across from a young man who didn't bother to look up. He was sharp-faced and bespectacled, and Kaddish felt he was staring down the blade of a knife. After some time the clerk raised his eyes long enough to say, "Number?" Lillian handed him the slip of paper, which he dropped into the wastebasket without a glance.

"Passports," the man said, this time without looking, only the hand outstretched.

"We don't have our passports," Lillian said.

"No passports?" he said. "Is this travel related?"

"No," Lillian said.

"Then let's see the letter."

"Which letter is that?" Kaddish said.

And in the way the weary bureaucrat fills his days so he'll have something to be indignant about when reflecting at night, he said, "Sir, I will not sit here and argue with you."

Kaddish, honestly confused, looked to Lillian.

"We don't understand," she said.

"The letter. The letter from the Ministry of Special Cases, what did it say? In relation to what issue was your presence requested? Have you been abroad in the last six months? Have you requested a visa for travel within the Soviet bloc?"

"No letter," Lillian said, "no travel, no visa. We've come on our own. We were told—we have heard—"

"Stop," the clerk said. He pressed his fingers into his eyes as if to relieve a headache, but he pressed so hard, Lillian thought he might have been trying to give himself one or worse. "I already know," he said, dropping his arms and engaging Lillian properly for the first time. "I swear the others make sure it works out this way. I don't know how they manage it. A thousand, thousand things to deal with, and always they send the parents to me. Am I right? Someone's flown the coop? Someone's missing at home?"

"Disappeared," Lillian said.

The clerk looked at the other clerks, as if they really had it in for him, as if he were the butt of some joke.

"Rapscallions," he said, referring to his co-workers.

The man then shook it off and extended a hand.

"Habeas," he said.

Lillian kept her own hands on the bag in her lap. She blinked. Kaddish pulled at the legs of his pants and exhaled.

"Do not threaten me, sir," the clerk said. "This is not a barroom, it's a ministry of the government. It's the same as assault, the threat. It's exactly the same as far as I'm concerned."

Again Kaddish turned to Lillian.

"He means nothing by it," she said. "We have no habeas corpus. Our son has disappeared."

"A police report," the man said, clipped.

Lillian just shook her head.

"Room two-sixty-four," he said. "Down the stairs, back to the lobby you entered but on the other side, another door, another stairwell, to this floor on that side." The man then sneered at his co-workers, giving them a look through hooded eyes. In the quickest turnaround Lillian had witnessed, he then waved at the man who called numbers and another number was called.

Lillian and Kaddish found themselves going down and across and up, then opening a stairwell door onto the narrowest of corridors. There was a desk, its drawers facing them, directly in their path. Had someone been sitting at it, they'd not have been able to enter. This also was likely the reason that the gentleman on the right side of that desk, on its short side, had placed himself there. His feet, invisible from the stairwell, were up on the desk's corner and the man had a brown Borsalino tilted over his face, ostensibly to aid in sleep. There was a fan of three short feathers, blue as a bluebird's, arranged in its band.

Kaddish and Lillian stood on the left side of the desk. Before they could clear their throats, the man righted his chair and tipped back his hat. At first glance Lillian thought he was a woman, so fine were his features. She imagined this was why he had cultivated a sparse mustache—to help nudge people toward the right guess.

"We have been sent to room two-sixty-four," Kaddish said.

The only thing on the desk was a stapler. Before answering, the man tapped out a nervous little rhythm on it as if he was answering them in code. He then pointed behind them. "Down that way and around." He tipped his hat forward again and pitched back his chair. Lillian thought, This is why he wears the hat. Even more than the mustache, the hat made her think, Man.

When they found two-sixty-four, the office was locked. They knocked on the door and its neighbors. They gave it a few minutes, tried again, and then slowly made their way back to the corridor with the man in the bird-feather hat.

They'd somehow entered the hallway from the other direction, coming up behind him. Lillian and Kaddish slid by, pushing a desk drawer closed to pass. The man neither gave a start nor acknowledged them. He held a wide slice of provolone in one hand and a pair of scissors in the other. He cut it in half and then reached for a ruler and a slice of bread.

"It's locked," Lillian said. "No one's in room two-sixty-four. No one answers the door."

"Of course not," the man said. "It's my office, and I'm sitting here."

"You didn't just—" Lillian said.

"Didn't just what?" the man said, spreading butter unperturbed.

"Send us," Lillian said. "You didn't send us to find your office while you were sitting here?"

"I work hard!" the man yelled. "I've earned citations for hardness, for temerity!"

He replaced the top slice of bread on his sandwich. Kaddish half expected him to staple it closed.

"Are you on lunch break?" Lillian said.

"It's a snack," he said. "Would you eat lunch in a hallway? I should hope I'd be able to do better than that."

Lillian wanted to scream at this man. She wanted to tear into him. Kaddish pulled out a handkerchief and wiped the whole of his face.

"So you'll be returning to room two-sixty-four?" Kaddish said.

"After my refreshment."

"And we should wait for you there?"

"No," he said. "You shouldn't." He took a bite of his sandwich and with his mouth full, said to Lillian, "You should really learn to hate from inside. It is very off-putting when it's all there on the face to be seen."

"You misread me," Lillian said.

"I'm sure," he said. "Nonetheless. Let's deal with the matter now." He aimed his sandwich at them. "Is this in reference to compulsory military service?"

"No," Kaddish said.

"Is it about your tax assessment?" he said. "I don't handle tax assessments, either new cases or existing complaints. Not military-service deferments either."

Lillian left Kaddish to answer the questions. She was looking across the span of the desk and wondering how every interaction of even the most minor import took place with a desk in between, as if without a desk keeping people apart, every meeting would end with the weaker party strangled dead. And it might, Lillian thought. She would strangle this man.

"It's none of these things," Kaddish said to the clerk. "Why would it be?"

The man looked baffled.

"Because I don't deal with them," he said, "and because this is where they're always sent."

"We are here about a disappeared child," Lillian said.

"That we deal with," the man said. "That is here."

"And you're going take care of it in a hallway, with nothing in front of you but a sandwich?"

"Better on a full stomach than empty."

"Then, sir," Kaddish said, as polite as he got, "we're asking for your help."

"The child," the man said. "How old?"

"A son," Kaddish said. "Pato. Age nineteen." And then, remembering where they were, he said, "Pablo Poznan."

"Has he been gone more than seventy-two hours?"

"Yes," Kaddish said.

"If, indeed, a citizen is incarcerated for matters relating to national security, a file is made, a copy comes to me, and it's held for forty-eight hours to allow for legal intervention through the Ministry of Special Cases, which is separate from the Ministry of Justice and the courts (it's a copy of their file that we get). Then—and this taking into account the twenty-four hours it could take to be delivered—after three business days then, the file is closed and sent down to the archives. This part I shouldn't tell you, but I do—you see the advantage in talking to me on break? It eases me up; I feel like a regular guy. The archives are under this very building, and this building runs deep." He stopped and took a bite. "So to get it back is like in the National Library. Like any place with underground stacks—we are the same."

"I've never been," Kaddish said.

"You've never been to the library?" Kaddish nodded. "There is a slip to be filled out. The slip you put in a tube, the tube goes down, and it is dealt with by some extremely pale clerks who are consigned to the archive." Here he laughed. "If you weep over a trip to a locked office, let me tell you, this is the promised land up here. We are the bureaucrats of goodness and light; down there is the bureaucracy of the netherworld. Down there, who knows how long until a file is located. If it turns up, there is a little elevator, like for people but tiny, just for files—VIPs the files. We may abuse people at the ministry, but the files we treat right. They don't ride with riffraff. They don't take the stairs. They have their own private elevator, where they'll be left to themselves."

"So when—" Lillian said.

"If the slip is in by eleven in the morning, the file is often up by eleven the next day. But slips sent down this late in the afternoon are often lost."

"So tomorrow we should—" Lillian said.

"Nothing tomorrow. That's my job. I'm explaining my part. You give me the habeas corpus—"

Here Lillian interrupted. "We don't have one," she said.

"You don't? They sent you over without it? Nobody is supposed to be up here without a habeas corpus, and even those people aren't allowed up anymore."

"Why," Kaddish said, "would we even be here if we had one?"

Lillian looked at her husband. He was right. Why would they?

"It has happened that both files exist, the original and the copy, that the police report is submitted, the habeas corpus issued, but it is the detainee that is misplaced. That's not my job, but those people are some-times sent this way."

"So what do we do?" Lillian said.

"What do you do? You get the right paperwork, or you fail to get the right paperwork in the right way, and you open a file. You don't come empty-handed and expect results. You don't come here with nothing, and you don't come to me during lunch," he said. Then, correcting, he said, "Snack." He pulled open the bottom drawer and pulled out a Coke. "Either way, it's the other clerk's fault. Next time they send you, ask first if it's right."

"Every last one of you will end up in hell for this," Lillian said. It didn't sound the least bit aggressive. It was a simple statement of fact, and the man seemed to receive it as such.

"This country is at war," he said. "There are things that are done to ensure victory. Right things." Here he put the cap of the soda bottle against the edge of the desk and brought a fist down on it. The cap rolled off and the bottle gave a hiss. "When the country is safe, the vic-tors will choose their own fates. And I don't think, as compensation, we will choose for ourselves hell. We'll choose better for ourselves. Some-thing nice."

"Whatever's been started, you won't be in power at the end. Nothing lasts in this country," Lillian said. "This won't either. You'll have to answer, all of you."

Another bite, another sip, and, mulling over Lillian's comment, he reset his hat on the top of his head.

"You're right that nothing lasts in this country. But you also must know that in Argentina there is no reckoning. Here no one ever pays."

[Thirty]

THERE WENT KADDISH TEARING out of the store, the string of bells tinkling in his wake. The sole of his shoe flexed as he caught the opposite curb and, lifting himself, pumping a fist, the package he held, in its festive wrapping, tumbled out of his grip. It flew end over end and burst open against the sidewalk, pastries spreading over the street.

Kaddish raced on toward his building, into it and up the stairs and through their front door.

"It's Pato," Kaddish said. Not Pato himself but word of Pato. It was, for Lillian, enough. She pulled on her pants and grabbed for a shirt. Kaddish tried to relay what he'd heard.

He had gone to the bakery. A woman in a corduroy blazer and smelling of perfume was finishing off a joke as she pushed past. The baker was up on her ladder, stacking *facturas* in a pyramid on a shelf.

"Flaco," she said, to Kaddish, "where have you been?" She didn't say another word until he took out his wallet, not another word until she was behind the counter, the register closed. She handed him his package. "I can't take your money today," she said. "Everything is free today."

Kaddish accepted and was leaving, looking back over his shoulder as if she was going to change her mind. Then she said, "Come back with your wife." Kaddish told her that Lillian wouldn't. There was no way.

The baker climbed up the ladder; Kaddish tucked the package under his arm.

"Tell her," the baker said as she returned to her stacking, "I was up in the office when they made your son gone."

"I almost didn't tell your husband," the baker said to Lillian. "I saw him and almost didn't say a thing. They'll kill you for less. Your son isn't my only customer gone. Oh, God," she said, "I almost didn't tell." She turned to Kaddish. "If I'd let you go once, I'd have made it."

"It's all right," Kaddish said.

"It's not all right," said the baker. "Not all right not to tell, and not all right now that I have. I'm a dead person. I'm involved and I will be dead." She pulled her apron off and blew her nose on it.

Kaddish shook a cigarette out of a pack and offered it. The baker took two.

"I have my own kids," she said. "How could I not say anything when I'm a mother? And as a mother who will leave orphans, why have I said a word? These, mind you, are the most sober of thoughts." She blew her nose again and then leaned toward the flame Kaddish held. "At night, full of sorrow, I picture myself dead and think, Who will take the cookies from the oven when they're done?" She snorted at herself and smoked.

A customer came in and the baker waved the balled-up apron at him. "Closed," she said. "Closed for an hour." The man looked from face to face and left.

The baker flipped over the OPEN sign in the window, turned the lock, and all three went behind the tallest display case, where Lillian sat on a footstool. She leaned her head against Kaddish's hip. He rested a hand against it, moving only to light cigarettes for the baker or himself.

On the night of the abduction, the baker had been upstairs in the office doing her bills. It was late for her to be working, later than she liked to stay awake.

"A baker rises early," she said. "I saw a couple making out in the back of a car. I figured with parents in both apartments and no money for the *telo,* they've got the backseat. They were wrestling around, and I was smiling. I've got a good angle from upstairs, a view straight into the car. Right as I'm going back to my bills, giving them their privacy, the boy rears up for second, pulls back an arm, and gives the woman a few quick punches to the face. Businesslike punches, not from anger." She stopped to demonstrate for them. "It's then I see the boy is very much a man, ten years older than I'd thought. He sits up higher, not rushed at all, and he starts punching these longer, lazier punches. I could see that the man was explaining something with the slow punches, admonishing the girl."

"It was a girl?" Lillian said. Her stomach dropped.

"I still say girl," the baker said. "I thought even through the punching that it was a girl, but that was leftover from the making out, from the first glimpse. It was," the baker said, "a boy, a shaggy-haired boy."

"Was it Pato?" Lillian said. It was an odd mix of feelings, Lillian wishing that it was her child hit in the face.

"I couldn't see that much, but owning a shop is peculiar that way. Your customers, there are so many—yet you know them from the subtlest things, a bit of hair, a familiar motion. The shape of a head."

"Of a nose," Kaddish said.

"How many times have I seen Pato make his way in here, rubbing the sleep off his face? It was dark and there was the other man blocking, but I knew. I spent many hours pretending otherwise. I spent a few days trying to convince myself. And I'm sorry for that."

"My God," Lillian said.

"When was it?" Kaddish said.

The baker showed them the dated stubs from the checks she'd been writing.

"I stayed on my knees all night in that office. The whole of it wishing that your son would come in."

"There was only one man?" Kaddish said. "There had to be more."

"There were more," she said. "The punching one got out and spoke to a man in a hat. I couldn't tell if they were arguing or not, but the one with the hat waved his hands a lot, as if excited, and then he put his hat on the roof of the car. That's when three others came over."

"Four altogether?" Kaddish said.

"Five," she said. "Five, plus Pato, beaten in the car. The one who did the hitting got back in, and the three who arrived last got in the other doors."

"And the hat," Lillian said, the bird-feather man still in her head. "Were there feathers?"

The baker looked baffled, and Kaddish caught her gaze.

"Where is Pato right then?" Kaddish said.

"The floor, I think," the baker said. She looked deeply ashamed when she said this, as if this was the worst part. "I think under their feet on the floor. That's when I figure, if I can see them they can also see me. It's also when I notice that the car is a Falcon, a green Falcon, and I duck. When the car started up I peered over the edge of the window. The man, the fifth man, reached for his hat. He didn't lift it so much as hold it as the car drove out from underneath, so that he was left with his arm sticking out and the hat in the air."

"And then?" Lillian said.

"Then nothing. He put the hat on and walked in the other direction, in the direction of your building. He just walked off down the middle of the street like anyone."

"And you?" Lillian said.

"I was working with a banker's lamp. I yanked out the plug and stayed on my knees in the dark, and—I told you already—I wished until morning that your son would come in."

[Thirty-one]

KADDISH RAN HOME AGAIN to gather up the papers, to grab
Lillian's purse, and to call Tello, the lawyer, to see if he had any advice.
Lillian stayed back with the baker; she wouldn't leave her side.

When the baker went for a new apron, she brought two, and together
they reopened the store. Lillian was happy to try out the baker's fantasy,
to pretend, with every swing of the door and sound of the bells, that it
was her Pato shuffling in. Lillian took orders and wrapped up pastries
while she waited for Kaddish to get back. It was as she pressed down a
piece of tape and sent another customer off with his breakfast that she
understood how part of their problems came to be. Everything in the
whole damn country comes wrapped up like a Christmas present, cotton
balls, a bar of soap, the *medialunas* with which she'd sent the customer
home. "The land of pretty paper," Lillian said. "Everything full of promise until you peel the wrapping away." The baker only nodded and
opened the register to make change.

The Ministry of Justice was peopled with brittle, unfriendly workers
who had actual answers to questions posed. The workers gave off
the impression that information might be communicated to them and
that such information might merit eventual consideration. It was still a

government office, but a level of efficiency was apparent. Lillian saw people working everywhere she looked. And one spinsterish clerk was, in answering her, actually kind. The mood among those waiting was no cheerier than over at the Ministry of Special Cases, but there was a marked difference in how those assembled waited. Missing from their faces was the flat affect of those who know there's no hope of getting anything done.

Before the baker had turned the sign in the window of her shop, she'd packed a hard leather case with thermos and maté and wrapped up enough pastries for a family of ten.

"You have high hopes for our appetites," Lillian had said.

"There will be other people there. It does no good going stale."

The baker hadn't said a word since they'd arrived at the ministry. She didn't offer a single stranger a pastry. She sat stock-still, the leather case hugged to her chest. At the bakery, she'd seemed liberated by her admission, excited to be free of her secret and to have done right. At the Ministry of Justice, Lillian thought she might be slipping into shock.

Lillian wanted to tell the baker to pace her panic. It would be days, she expected. The baker might be forced to join them for some time before she could do her part.

Lillian was surprised then when a stern-looking man in an undertaker's suit approached them and quietly led the baker away. "Thank you," Lillian said, reaching out just in time to touch the small of her back.

Lillian's fingers tingled the whole time the baker was gone, so intense was the idea that Pato's story was being told, that a case was being built, and that Pato might, as the bird-feather man explained, be moved from darkness back into the white world. She sat there and shivered. Kaddish stayed planted at her side, a crushed and empty pack of Jockeys clenched in his fist.

Kaddish was having a stretch in his seat when he caught sight of the baker rushing across the room, giving them a wide berth. Even at this distance, Kaddish could see the sheen of sweat on the woman and a distinctly gray pallor to her skin. He tapped Lillian and, taking his cue, she turned. Lillian found what she was supposed to be looking for as the baker, who could not resist, stole a glance their way. The baker caught herself caught by Lillian. She put a hand to her mouth and rushed off, nearly in a sprint.

Lillian begrudged her nothing. The baker could turn into a stranger like all the others. She could deny Pato ever was for having remembered him now.

Kaddish pulled off the leather top of the maté case the baker abandoned, as if he'd just been given it as a gift. Before Lillian could even figure out what to do next, the man in the dark suit returned, carrying a clipboard.

"I want to go over something," he said, matter-of-fact. "And there are statements for you to fill out and sign."

"There is a case?" Lillian said. "There's a habeas corpus?"

The man lowered his clipboard and gave Lillian a hangdog look.

"There will be an investigation into the claims. If there is merit, a writ of habeas corpus will be issued."

"Just like that?" Lillian said.

The man turned the clipboard toward her. "Fill these out," he said, "and sign."

It appeared to Gustavo that all they did was hug. If Lillian was in the office, she and Frida were locked in an embrace. Gustavo had returned from a lunch meeting with a bit of a tilt to his step. He'd walked in to find the two of them pressed together and Frida cooing, "A good sign. It will end well."

"Is he back?" Gustavo said.

The women separated. It was baffling to Lillian that Gustavo needed to ask. How could the answer ever be anything but obvious? Frida would bolt upright in bed, she'd know in her sleep if Pato was home. Frida went back to her desk and Lillian started for hers. "So much to catch up on," was all Lillian said as she sat down.

Gustavo scratched at his ear.

"Lillian," he said. And Lillian looked up.

"Hard to believe the sea change it makes. It's only a nose, but you come in here more stunning each time." Gustavo kicked at the leg of a radiator. "Could we talk in my office?"

"What is it?"

"It's a private matter," he said.

"Then I'll only have to repeat it to Frida after. You know we share everything between us."

Gustavo gave another kick to the radiator and rubbed at his neck, doing his best to emphasize that he was torn. "Then stand up," he said. "At least stand up and come over here."

Lillian stood up and went over.

"What is it, Gustavo?"

"It's not a time for messing about." Gustavo paused, expecting Lillian to interrupt him. "We have powerful clients, some of them."

"Yes," Lillian said. "You've built up quite a reputation. Many delicate situations handled well. Top-notch."

"It's not just your own life at stake," Gustavo said. "You'll get us all killed."

"I will?" Lillian said. "That's what you think?"

"I've had a call from the general. You stole his number. You took it from me, Lillian."

"They stole a baby. Someone stole my son."

Gustavo shook his head. "You knew there'd be repercussions."

Lillian didn't even blink.

"You must have," Gustavo said.

They stood there, the two of them, staring.

"You're going to have to do it by yourself," Lillian said. "It's the one time I can't do your work for you."

"I promised him," Gustavo said.

"I need this job, Gustavo. My family won't be able to survive without it. We'll end up on the street."

Gustavo looked to Frida. She held his gaze and he turned back to Lillian.

"I won't understand," Lillian said. "It's wrong. Don't do it."

Gustavo pursed his lips. "You're fired," he said.

Frida gave a sharp, awkward cry. Gustavo went into his office to get the severance check he'd already written—generous, he thought, as generous as could be. Lillian stood there, not even stunned. She felt relieved. One less thing to think about.

Lillian needed all her time for Pato, to see to his return and, when he got back, to be by his side. If she missed an opportunity because of this job, what good was money anyway. And when her son was with her she could live off the joy. From looking at Pato alone, Lillian knew she wouldn't starve. She'd eat the boy up for a lifetime. Gustavo came back and handed Lillian an envelope. All she could think in the moment, all Lillian could manage, was to note that first thing in the morning she must rush to the Ministry of Justice and remove her work number from the forms.

[Thirty-two]

KADDISH BREATHED THE FUSTY BREATH of the two offi-
cers flanking his chair. He made no attempt to stand. Still, they each
kept a hand on a shoulder, pushing him down. There was no excuse for
such treatment. He wasn't a criminal (or, at least, if he did break certain
laws, he wasn't in the police station because of them now). If he had to
take some responsibility for his current predicament, he'd concede only
to souring the overall tone.

Kaddish had maybe driven a bit fast en route to the station, upon
arriving he might have expressed his concerns a touch too loudly, and,
when the policeman out front had been unwilling to facilitate his request, Kaddish might just have seen himself into the *subcomisario*'s office,
already familiar with the way.

It was Lillian's optimism he was bearing. She'd been energized by the
Ministry of Justice and convinced that with the baker testifying to having seen the police, the police might admit to having been seen. If Kaddish didn't feel as upbeat, he was still ready to try. He'd offered to go
back on his own to the station that had first held Pato.

"You do not barge into my station and make a scene," the officer
behind the desk said. "You do not demand anything, especially an audience with me. I remember you," he said. "I know who you are."

"That's more than most," Kaddish said. The policeman on Kaddish's left gave him a shove.

"What," the officer said, "could possibly have brought you back here?"

Kaddish, who didn't care about a shove and didn't care to be bullied, who feared more deeply and differently for his son's death than ever before, did not feel like being polite. "Why the fuck else would anyone show up at a police station except to get help? That's your fucking job."

"Sometimes they come to turn themselves in," the officer said. "We've had a huge run of guilty conscience. Is that why you're here? To confess to something?"

"I came by to see if you wanted to do the same," Kaddish said. "If there's something you'd like to tell me, now is your chance."

The officer looked bored. He took off his glasses and placed them on his desk next to Kaddish's papers. "It's probably unwise to keep talking this way. If you want to commit suicide, it would be simpler if you went home and shot yourself in the head."

"And if I die in this chair won't I end up at home and listed a suicide just the same?"

"You wouldn't necessarily end up anywhere."

Kaddish leaned as far forward as those restraining him permitted. "I know what you do," Kaddish said. "I know how you do it."

The officer picked up Kaddish's ID. "Mr. Poznan," he said, reading from it, "what could you possibly know?"

"Really, I only came for assistance in locating my son," Kaddish said. "I have a witness now. Somebody saw you. If you're ready to admit your part, then it's best I don't say anything, as you've advised."

"Too late," the officer said. "You missed your chance to kiss and make up."

"You arrested my son," Kaddish said. "You released my son—you released him to me, in this station. And then you came over to my house and took him right back."

"We took him back?"

"Forget that part," Kaddish said. "If the lady officer will come give testimony, or if you'll give me the page from the logbook, we are in the process—we are very close to getting a habeas corpus. It would be useful if you would tell the truth."

"You say your son was released into your custody."

"I do."

"So what kind of habeas corpus do you want? Do you want one that says your son is with you? You could issue that yourself. I'll have one of the men take dictation if you'd like."

"You took him back. That's how it works. You release them so you can snatch them right up again. It's one of your tricks."

"My tricks?" the officer said. "Since we didn't rearrest your son, and since we didn't have him in the first place—"

"You did," Kaddish said. "That's the frustrating part. You can't deny what I know, what is fact."

"I deny it."

"I know how it works, even. I know about the phone books, I know what you do."

"What is it we do?"

"You use phone books and class lists and anything that links two people. You take them for nothing and that's why you don't charge them with a crime, that's why it's secret. This government has started a crazy war of association. You've made up a national threat. I didn't believe it myself," Kaddish said, "but now I do. You take one, and then you take the others without reason."

"Using phone books?"

"Yes," Kaddish said.

"Theory aside," the officer said, "there's a hole in your reasoning. If you're under the impression that I have your son here, aren't you afraid of what such a visit will cost him?"

Kaddish considered before answering. "I'm not afraid. And I'd rather not consider why that is. I'd rather not worry about why I don't worry."

"There is one part of your claim that touches on reality, and even that you got reversed." The officer stood up. He unbuttoned his uniform jacket, removed it, and hung it carefully on the back of his chair. He lifted a thick, worn Buenos Aires telephone book off a file cabinet and held it with both hands. The officer stood before Kaddish and the policemen at Kaddish's sides put more weight onto his shoulders. Each pulled back on one of his arms. "It's not what's inside the phone book that's most useful—" and here, with two hands, he raised it high—"it's the information that the phone book draws out." Like that, he swung it down onto Kaddish's head.

In that first instance Kaddish wondered if his neck had broken and was only happy to register the pain from the policemen pulling at his arms. If it's possible to be surprised in such a manner twice, Kaddish couldn't believe how much it hurt the second time the phone book was brought down on his head. The blow was delivered with such force, Kaddish thought his eardrums had burst outward from the pressure generated within. Kaddish meant also to say something, to request that the officer stop. Opening his mouth, he found it shut with another blow, his teeth driven deep into his tongue.

Right then the officer stopped on his own.

Kaddish used the break to great effect. He freed his teeth, retracted his swelling tongue, and set himself up for the next series of blows, which came quickly.

"Do . . . not . . . bother . . . me . . . again," the officer said. He brought down the phone book once with each word, punctuating. Kaddish saw endless points of light and heard a great roar each time he was struck.

After the next round, the officer said, "All right, then." He followed it up with such a wallop, Kaddish heard a crack. He took a deep swallow of blood.

"You want to know our secrets, Mr. Poznan. This is one: I can beat you to death with a phone book and it won't leave a mark. I can see you've bit your tongue," he said, studying Kaddish's face. "Otherwise what you feel inside doesn't show. Do you get it? Now do you see why the phone book is our greatest investigative resource?" The officer patted the book and gave Kaddish a moment to agree.

"Do you have my son?" Kaddish said.

The officer let loose with a pounding so relentless, Kaddish was sure it would not stop until his head, like a nail, was driven into his chest.

The officer stopped and waited to see if Kaddish had anything smart to say. When Kaddish didn't, the officer gave him the handkerchief from his own pocket. "Wipe your mouth," he said. "There's blood." The policemen at Kaddish's sides released him. Kaddish could still see and could still hear, but he was so disoriented he wasn't sure how to process what it was that he saw and heard. It took him some seconds to connect his brain to the burning in his arm and to move the handkerchief to his lips.

"That was three short minutes," the officer said. "A little bit more or a little bit less. There are five hundred such periods in a day. Think of that, Poznan. Think of that day after day, and imagine what can be done if delicacy were not a factor, if I was not interested in sending you back out as pretty as when you came in." The officer put his jacket on and began to button it up. "I do not have your boy here. But now I promise you, my own search begins right now. I'd very much like some time alone with him. All this to tell you, Mr. Poznan, you and your wife do not help anyone. You make things worse. And no parent should be out making things worse for a son."

Kaddish wanted only to sleep this day off. With small painful steps, with a grinding headache behind his eyes and a feeling of sickness that he couldn't isolate, Kaddish pushed through their always-open apartment door.

Lillian stood with a drink, facing him. Kaddish had the sense that he'd stepped into a conversation they'd already started. She took a sip. He wiped his lips against his sleeve. Kaddish didn't think he'd ever seen her holding a whiskey in her hand.

Kaddish wanted to tell her everything, to tell his wife that he'd been tortured at the police station, and tell her what the officer had threatened to do to their son. He wanted to bend his stiff neck and lean his head on Lillian's shoulder. If he did that he knew he'd tell, and if he told he didn't think Lillian would live through the night. She wouldn't survive, Kaddish thought. Not three times three minutes of considering the fate that had befallen their son.

He kept his lips pressed together and tried to communicate as best he could by looking into her eyes.

"I got fired," Lillian said. She took another sip. "Gustavo let me go."
Kaddish felt his legs start to shake. He didn't say a word.

"That's it?" Lillian said.

It seemed that it was. Kaddish walked right past her, down the hallway, his mouth full of blood.

[Thirty-three]

NOT SINCE THE NIGHT of the abduction had Kaddish stood so solemnly before Pato's books. He first tried to bring to mind the three missing volumes, the ones that had disappeared down the elevator shaft along with his son. Then he went about trying to cull with new eyes. He wasn't after contraband. He was looking for anything that might link Pato to one of his friends. Kaddish found a humor magazine with a classmate's name written on the back. He found the class portrait where Lillian had left it and placed it on top of the magazine in his tool bag. This he lifted with a moan, so sore and stiff was he from the beating, and carried into Pato's room. He didn't know how he'd swing his hammer in this state, let alone climb over the cemetery wall. Kaddish had managed to get a new job.

It wasn't yet midnight and he hoped when the witching hour came he'd feel a touch better. He took a deep swig from a glass of Lillet he'd left by Pato's bed. A few more hours of drinking and he could at least guarantee he wouldn't feel as much.

Kaddish found the address book on the stereo and then gave the room a thorough turning over. In the sock drawer he found a tiny black book with first names and phone numbers inside. He found one albumless album cover among Pato's records. It had a lump in its center. Kaddish stuck his hand in and came up with a bag of marijuana, half a joint, and a pipe. He pocketed the joint and put the rest back. Kaddish figured if something was made to be smoked he'd likely be good at it, and if it eased any of his sufferings he'd be thankful for the help. There was a stack of photos of Pato and his friends in a shoe box. Kaddish could hardly bear to add it to the pile. Taped to the wall next to the bed was a picture of Rafa and Pato hanging from a goalpost. That one he left where it was.

Kaddish fished out the joint and smoked it. Everything still hurt, but it all hurt a little less. His troubles stayed the same, though he did sense that the world they took place in was neither as cruel nor as ruthless as before. And he felt tired. He thought hard, trying to focus, wondering if he could trust himself not to pass out for the night. He decided he couldn't and then tried to find a comfortable position on Pato's bed. His left side was no better than his right. If he turned his head either way his tongue would bleed. He ended up planting two feet on the floor and lying with his shoulders pinned against the mattress, as if he'd been sitting on the edge of the bed and someone had put a hand to his forehead and pushed him straight back. In this position, if there was still blood it seemed to take care of itself. Kaddish got up to put a record on. He spent the next few hours listening to Pato's music through the headphones and trying to make heads or tails of it, to glean even the most basic meaning from the words.

Wary of the clanking from his tool bag and the sound of his lumbering step, Kaddish was almost at the front door when Lillian gave him a fright. She was in her chair in the living room, awake in the darkness, not asleep in their bedroom as he'd thought. "Be careful," Lillian said, leaving him doubly surprised. It was a sentiment she'd never expressed when he went off to the cemetery before. She didn't say anything about the fact that he'd taken a job.

"You're still awake?" Kaddish said.

"You wouldn't believe the subtle changes that take place on our street, even when not a thing moves."

Kaddish put down his bag and stepped in front of it, an extra measure. There was no way Lillian could see what he'd stuffed inside.

"You didn't tell me," she said, "that you got a new customer."

"The woman swore she'd pay cash," he said. "Tomorrow we'll have money to line our pockets. And I still have to figure what to do with that gold."

Lillian shifted in the chair. She didn't mention her severance. Her tin was full again; she'd gone straight from Gustavo to the bank. The freezer had frozen over so Lillian wrapped the tin in a rag and put it under the sink. There were other hiding places as well. She'd spread the money about.

"We don't have to be ruined," Kaddish said. "My business will take off."

"Even when Pato's back, I doubt the delicate sons of whores with something to lose will seek out your services. They pay you to avoid drawing attention to themselves, not for you to put them in harm's way."

"A quiet time, is all," Kaddish said. "It has nothing to do with Pato. It's like the street outside. All kinds of things happening in the silence."

"Go do your chiseling, Kaddish. Just know that news of Pato must have made the rounds. Word always spreads among the Jews."

"It will pick up," Kaddish said. "I will take care of us."

"I'm not complaining either way. Once we have Pato we'll start from nothing. We've done it before, haven't we? It will be a new beginning for all of us. I can hardly wait for morning with no job to worry about and only the Ministry of Justice ahead. I'm going to read through Pato's novels while I wait for the good news. A literary mother to talk to, that will be some shock when he gets back."

Kaddish picked up his tool bag.

"I see why you thrive on the nights," she said. "I'd always thought it was depressing. It's hopeful, though. It's the body defying nature, too excited to give up on the other half of life."

"There are things missed while the city sleeps."

"I'm going to stay up and keep an eye," Lillian said. "Who knows, maybe the wheels already turn at the Ministry of Justice. Already tonight those cowards could let him go."

There was a bottle of turpentine in the super's crawl space off the lobby. Kaddish poured it over the pile he'd made on the grate in the center of the air shaft. He mixed the day's newspaper in with Pato's possessions and lit the edges. He then retired to his Moorish bench.

Lillian was right, they had nothing left to lose. Without Pato to protect, there was no reason for Kaddish to hide out in the bathroom burning books. And even if he set himself on fire and sang the national anthem while he cooked, his neighbors wouldn't dare see. Lillian was the only one who'd look down.

Kaddish knew she wouldn't understand what madness had driven him to do what he was doing. It was a fire for the others, not for Pato or Lillian or him. If Lillian thought he was heartless, let her stand by her own logic. She shouldn't care about a few keepsakes when they'd soon have Pato home. Back to your chair, he'd tell her. Watch your street. You don't want to miss Pato's nighttime return.

Before heading off to the cemetery, Kaddish stood with his tool bag and admired his little fire. The smoke rose straight up from the courtyard, not a twist, not a bend, a perfect column of smoke rising straight up into the sky. He checked a broken nail on his thumb and bit at its end. Then he took a last look toward their balcony. Let her come out, Kaddish thought. Let her see the kind of sacrifices he made.

[Thirty-four]

WHERE WAS KADDISH for such a moment? Lillian didn't think she could handle the joy of it alone. Two days at the Ministry of Justice and the man with the clipboard was back. He came up to her and offered a perfunctory greeting, an interaction mirroring those between normal people who've already had dealings within the framework of a normal world. "Mrs. Poznan," he said, "your paperwork has come through."

"I got it?" she said. "It's not a 'not being detained'?"

The young man, straight-faced, straitlaced, looked neither happy nor sad. He put Lillian's purse on the floor and sat at her side.

"You have been issued a habeas corpus," he said, "in regard to the arrest attested to by . . ." and here he paused, flipping through the various papers for the baker's name. Then, as he had the previous time, he asked her to sign and sign and sign.

"What do I do now?" Lillian said. It was a protocol question, no desperation to it.

"Generally," he said, "nothing."

"There must be a next step," Lillian said.

"Not for the petitioner, really. It's more of a government matter—it's up to them to respond, to provide an answer or a person."

"Will they?" Lillian said. She began to shiver. "Will you?"

"Me?" The clerk seemed genuinely taken aback. "Not my decision." He looked at Lillian, whose shaking was prominent. He puffed out his cheeks and blew the air out slowly. He made eye contact with the woman sitting across from Lillian. The woman, who had been pretending not to listen or look, got up and walked away. "Usually I wouldn't know, not a detail."

"But this time you do? In my case there's something irregular?"

"In this instance there was a small hang-up, a complication to settle. Curious as it was, I made some calls personally."

"And?" Lillian said. Now she was desperate, now her voice was that of a woman losing control. She could tell she was supposed to say something to the clerk. She had no idea what it was. And then she got it. "I didn't hear it from you," she said. "I swear on my life," she said. It wasn't enough. "I swear—I swear on my son's."

"Police Station Number Forty-six."

"By the Railway Hospital?" Lillian had already learned them by heart.

"Yes," he said. "They gave no explanation. For some reason the girl will be released into your custody there."

"Girl?" Lillian said. "What girl?"

"The one arrested." He showed Lillian where it was typed unevenly on the page. "Mónica Álvarez," he said.

"Who is that?" Lillian said. "What nonsense is this?"

"It's all written here. You can check. You can read." He handed the clipboard to Lillian. She took it from him and she read.

It was the right date and the right time. It was the right description of Pato's abduction at the right address. All was exactly as it should be but the name.

"This is a lie," she said.

"What's a lie?" he said. It was that much more frustrating for Lillian to talk with someone who gave the impression of understanding. "You're not saying the arrest you reported was a fake?"

"No," Lillian said.

"I wouldn't think so because it has produced an individual. A habeas corpus has been granted you and the turnaround has been amazingly fast. Beyond that," he said, "it wouldn't be an exaggeration to say that receiving one is rare."

"It's supposed to say Pablo Poznan," Lillian said. "You can't expect me to believe this girl was taken from my block, from my home. You can't expect me to accept that I've lost my mind."

"I make no judgment," he said, taking back his clipboard.

"A hang-up, you said. A curiosity. It's because you know what's right. That's why you made those calls. That's why you located the girl and are telling me to go get her."

The clerk separated Lillian's copies from his. "Thanks to your dogged-ness there is a woman, a Ms. Álvarez, who is waiting to be released. Waiting on you."

"It's supposed to be my son."

"That, Mrs. Poznan, would be an issue for the Ministry of Special Cases. Such appeals are handled there."

She wouldn't go back there. This is not how the day was going to end.

"You're the one who's mixed up," Lillian said. "My Pato will be wait-ing at that station, and at another station, with another wrong form, another mother—Mrs. Álvarez—will find her girl."

"Whoever it is that you wish, Mrs. Poznan, I wish also for it to be true. Would you like," he said, "a manila envelope?" He blew into the envelope and, smiling, slipped her papers inside.

It was the sergeant who addressed Lillian as she stood on the threshold of the open door. "Would you mind coming a bit closer so we can have a look?" He motioned toward the envelope Lillian was brandishing. "Can you at least open it a little and give us a peek?"

The sergeant was making a joke of her. The station house was bigger than any she'd been to, and there must have been a dozen policemen standing about, watching her make a scene.

"There's nothing to peek at," Lillian said. "It's a habeas corpus on behalf of Pato Poznan, fresh from the Ministry of Justice."

The sergeant cupped his hands around his mouth, as if his voice needed to carry a great distance, though Lillian was only a few meters away.

"We have someone to release," he yelled. "But that's not the one we've got."

Lillian yelled back, "Bring out my boy," at the very top of her lungs.

The policemen looked at her as if she was a crazy lady. Lillian pulled out the habeas corpus. "Right here, it says Pablo Poznan," and she pointed at the name.

"I'm going to have to see that," the sergeant told her.

Lillian looked at all the people looking at her. She marched up to the counter and, when she did, most everyone watching went back to their business. It wasn't much of a show. They'd see better before the shift was through.

Lillian slammed a page down against the countertop, her palm pressed flat to it. The sergeant pushed delicately at her fingers, trying to read. He wasn't a cruel man.

"You've scratched out the name," he said.

He looked up at her now with a serious expression. He took the manila envelope and went through the rest of the papers. "You've changed it on all of them," he said, incredulous.

"It says Pablo," Lillian said. "That's who I'm supposed to get." She pointed to where she'd written it in.

"We have our own copies," the sergeant said. "You're Lillian Poznan and we've got a girl, sixteen years old, a Mónica Álvarez to release to you."

"I don't want her. I want my son."

The sergeant held one of the papers up to the light. "You can still see where it says Mónica," he said.

"Where's my Pato?" Lillian said.

The sergeant said, "Not here."

Lillian opened her mouth to yell again and was silenced with a stare. The sergeant wouldn't have it. "Do you want the girl or not?" he said. "You can take her or leave her. Decide quickly before we scratch out her name on our forms too."

Lillian's chest heaved. From a place of such deep hatred that it curdled the blood to hear it, she said, "I'm not going to leave that child."

The sergeant scanned the room until he caught someone's attention. "Get the girl," he said.

While a policeman did, Lillian turned angrier and angrier. By the time the policeman came back, Lillian's huffing had built nearly to a growl. It was to this woman, to a Lillian Poznan looking positively out of her mind, that the cowering girl was released.

Lillian grabbed the girl's elbow and gave her a shake. "Tell them," she said. "Tell them you weren't taken from my house, from my block. Tell them it's a lie, that we've never met."

"It was your house," the girl said. Lillian drew back, startled by the claim and by how sharply the girl smelled of pee. "From the top floor," the girl said. "Your house. And a bakery. There was a bakery and a beating in a car."

Lillian first believed the girl meant it and, thinking her somehow bewitched, she pushed her away.

This was surely a nightmare that Lillian was having. To prove it, Lillian crossed her arms and pinched at her biceps as hard as she could. While Lillian did this she also tried to turn the girl into Pato. If it was a dream, let her see her son.

The girl wouldn't change, and Lillian knew this wasn't anything but another disappointment. All she'd be getting was this child, with her sallow face and cracked lips and a hollowness to her eyes that only got worse when Lillian saw them straight on. This child was empty inside. Lillian let her hands drop. What the girl had said wasn't a lie. Certain things at certain times are always truth.

Lillian understood then that they must go.

"Turn the music up," Lillian said. "Keep it up and listen to it."

The cabdriver turned up the music and drove on.

Lillian hugged the girl in the back of the cab. She held her close, and the girl let her.

"Not my house," Lillian whispered. "Tell me it wasn't. Not my bakery.

Not my block." The girl pulled away. "OK," Lillian said. "*Shhh,*" she said, and pulled her back with more force than delicacy. Lillian stroked the girl's hair, all stiff and matted. "*Shhh,*" Lillian said. "I'm sorry. I will not ask." The girl lived in Belgrano, a fine address. In the station, she wouldn't tell Lillian where and the policeman had been forced to write it down.

Lillian watched the city go by.

She said, "I have a son, like you. I have boy somewhere within." She rocked the girl, cooed at the girl. "Did you meet a Pato? Did you hear of a Pato? A skinny boy with too much hair?" Lillian smiled. "And a nose. A huge big nose."

Lillian bent her neck until it hurt. She wanted to hold the girl while keeping an ear next to the child's mouth—in case she should whisper, whisper under the music.

"You are free, my sweet," Lillian said. "You can tell me, my skinny."

Lillian held the girl and for some minutes kept the girl's warm lips against her ear.

"You do not know the things they put inside you," the girl said. "So many different things, so many people."

"What are you saying?" Lillian said. There was so much this day that she couldn't comprehend.

"Electricity," she said. "All up inside you." The girl took Lillian's face in her hands. She put her nose to Lillian's nose, her forehead to Lillian's, and blinking into her eyes, she said, so strongly, so absolutely—she said, "I'm pregnant with electric shock."

Lillian couldn't understand. Not what the girl was saying and not how, around that warm mouth, so much coldness came off her. Lillian felt that inside this child something essential had been knocked loose. Such a cold girl, but at the same time Lillian could not help loving her. She pulled the girl closer, rubbing with both hands, trying to get the rest of her warm.

"My daughter," Lillian said. "Lean back, my girl."

The girl leaned, going soft, and Lillian only squeezed tighter. "*Shhh,*" Lillian said. "My daughter," she said. "Not long, almost there, almost home."

[PART THREE]

[Thirty-five]

A SUCCESSFUL NIGHT and a successful day, Kaddish had finished the job, collected payment, and made a neat and goodly stack of bills on the table for Lillian to admire. It was on top of this that Lillian had thrown down the forms.

"Do you see what's being visited upon us?" Lillian said.

Kaddish took up a page and could see, as had the policeman, where the ghost of a name was still visible.

"It's just punishment," Lillian said. "All those Benevolent Self bodies buried in no-name graves. And for us the name is all we have left. That job is a curse," she said. "You brought this on our house."

Lillian had never indulged such hopelessness, not even, Kaddish was sure, in her thoughts.

"It's only a bit of stone chipped away," he said. "That's all that's been done."

"With his first words, you two started your first fight. Really, though, I didn't believe you hated him back. I thought it was aggravation. I thought you fought from sadness. Now I know better, Kaddish. You did this. You brought a curse on our house and then you opened the door. You wanted it and you got your wish."

She couldn't know that—from what he most didn't believe in, from her world of curses and superstitions, of spilled salt and stepped-over legs—there was one thing Kaddish held true. He'd wished on that last night that his son had never been born. "Shut your mouth," Kaddish said.

To ensure that she did, Kaddish put a hand over it, closing it for her. While he squeezed her mouth shut, he tried to appease her—to appease himself—with his talk.

"A new plan," he said, the hysteria in his voice at a pitch. "Trust me, Lillian. We'll turn this around."

Lillian took hold of Kaddish's wrist, and the hand came down.

"How will we manage that?" she said. "Back to the Ministry of Special Cases? I'll die."

"The girl, Lillian. She's real proof, much better than a baker's word or a big-nosed photo. You'll see. She'll tell the truth and save us." And then it dawned on Kaddish. "You should have brought her here," he said. "And you let her go."

"The girl is at home where she belongs. Go get her yourself if you want. She's ruined. There's nothing left to her."

"For part of this you have to own up. For today's heartache and today's horror, you're guilty too."

Lillian didn't entertain any blame.

"My only mistake was ever letting you and Pato out of my sight."

"No," Kaddish said. "Now we also have on our heads a crushing disappointment. And that's your doing; it's you that got us swollen with hope. We've done it your way from the beginning, Lillian. So why not tell me what's next."

"The Jews."

Lillian rarely managed it. Only Pato was expert at tailoring insults out of Kaddish's deepest fears. Here Lillian had pulled it off, and as with Pato it left him with no other words but the ones that conveyed his feelings without thought. "Fuck you," Kaddish said.

"It's only from them we'll get help finding our son. The only safe place in the world for a Jew is with others." Then, with a real sadness to her voice, Lillian said, "I never should have let you put me on the outside."

"It's them who put us. You can't give them the satisfaction."

"What kind of pleasure will they take? Who do you think these people are? We're alone in this, Kaddish. Who else at this point will claim us?"

"You think there's only one answer, but I'm telling you that answer is wrong. Pity is not acceptance. And pity is all you'll get from the Jews."

"They'll help us."

"They'll pretend to grieve when really they think there's a reason why misfortune was delivered upon him. Somewhere deep down, Pato will have deserved whatever he gets. They save all the innocence for their righteous."

"Don't talk like he's lost, Kaddish. Don't ever talk like we have no son."

"We don't," Kaddish said.

Lillian, with great speed, slapped Kaddish across the face.

"It is not a sin to admit," Kaddish said. "Until we get him back, he's gone."

"You listen," Lillian said. "He's not anything but ever-present, he is not anything but on his way home."

Kaddish went to speak.

"I'm not finished!" Lillian yelled. "We are Jews, Kaddish. You can choose not to be one yourself, but you are to them. You are to the government and to the people who have our son."

"I've never been anything else. It's the community of which I'm not part."

"You are," Lillian said. "You're their pariah, and that's a special role. Let's offer you up. Let's go to them with our heads bowed. I know they can help, Kaddish. What our enemies say about us is true. The Jews have connections; they'll have their ways. And they'll take us in like family. Play by their rules only until we get Pato back."

"It'll be for nothing, Lillian. Conditional loyalty is worthless. And we're going to need more than charity asks."

"Who can talk to you? You're broken."

"From them—they broke me. Or so they'd have me spend a lifetime believing." Kaddish knocked at his chest, a show of solidity. "I'm good, Lillian. I'm not broken at all."

"You're broken in so many places for so long that, like your nose, it has come to pass for beauty. It's no wonder you only get along with those stones."

"Run to them," Kaddish said. He took up the habeas corpus and the page with the girl's address and some money from underneath. "Only don't call whatever they give us loyalty. Loyalty needs to be absolute. Argentina needs to be loyal to all Argentines. And the Jews to all Jews. Never is it so—that's the problem." Kaddish stood up to leave. "It's always conditional. This is the poison of man."

Kaddish sat on his bench in the courtyard and tried to catch enough moonlight, enough balcony and bathroom light, to read the habeas corpus they'd been given. It was—Lillian was right—a curse.

Kaddish checked the girl's address. He looked at his watch. Then he folded up the papers and wrapped them around the money. Let the girl have until morning. Let her have a good night's sleep.

Kaddish smoked cigarette after cigarette, trying to keep his mind clear. He didn't want to piece together the habeas corpus with the other dark facts he knew. Neither could Kaddish picture himself at the United Jewish Congregations building, standing in the president's office and asking Feigenblum for help. The thought of Lillian turning to the Jews in his name was already too much. They'd kept him on the other side of the wall his whole life, and now Kaddish wouldn't have it any other way. That's where he'd stay forever; it's where he'd go into the ground.

Kaddish had done his best to follow Lillian's lead. He'd thought of Pato as both alive and well. On this night, on his bench under the sky, Kaddish only managed to see his son dead. Kaddish licked his fingertip and tapped quickly at the coal of his cigarette, putting it out with a sizzle.

He then went back into the building and walked right out the other side. He walked by the Pink House and the ministries. He strolled on past the Liberator's Synagogue, where the hypocrites and loyalists prayed. And without a thought he stepped right under the window from which the admiral was thrown. He walked the streets of the city for hours. Eventually he stopped at the sealed gate of the Benevolent Self Cemetery and peered through the bars.

When he was so tired that his body would have to let him sleep, Kaddish made his way over to the old shul. He went up to the ark and yanked down the curtain he'd left hanging. Here in an instant he'd done the rest of the job for the Zuckmans, once and for all and for good. Kaddish lay down on the first pew and used the curtain for a blanket. He made a pile of prayer books, soft from reading, for his head. He gathered them together and he slept.

Lillian didn't think her body could take it, not one more disappointment, not one more dashed hope or dead end. She'd made it to the bedroom and was lying on top of the covers in her clothes. Her skirt was unzipped halfway, and the same with her boots. She'd never in her life felt so tired, not even on the day Pato was born. She stared up into the light fixture. Lillian was too tired to close her eyes.

As Lillian gave herself over to sleep, her eyes did close. She lay there watching the lightbulbs' impressions changing colors in her mind, and drifted off imagining the only two things that seemed to calm her: Pato walking into the bakery, accompanied by a tinkling of bells, and the feeling of that girl in her arms. The girl, Mónica, sometimes turned into Pato in the bakery, and sometimes Pato leaned into Lillian in the back of the cab. The images wove and unwove this way. For Lillian it felt so good, both the fantasy and a crawling sleep so deep that she began from somewhere else in her head to fear it. It was so nice a feeling and so strong a sleep, she began to worry that she'd not wake up from it, that she wouldn't want to. Holding the girl, holding her son, hearing those bells tinkling with Pato's arrival, it was—she couldn't have asked for more—the dream of all dreams.

Harder than waking from a nightmare was trying to wake herself into one. Lillian forced herself to part with Pato and the girl. She willed herself awake. When she succeded—feeling like she'd lost her son again, feeling so physically exhausted that she couldn't make herself move—Lillian got herself out of bed. She could hear herself whimpering as she dragged heavy feet down the hallway and settled down in her chair with a view of the corner.

She knew then she could not trust herself to sleep. She wouldn't let herself lie down again until Pato was at home under her roof.

Lillian reached over to turn off the lamp and to shut her reflection out of the window. She had her hand on the pull chain beneath the lampshade. She hesitated; the back of that hand looked so familiar, but it did not look like hers. Coming through from beneath was a weathered skin. Creams and potions applied for a lifetime, and all that attention undone by these last days. She looked at how high and heavy her veins were. She'd missed this, their turning prominent. And also the dull blue flow underneath, a tired vein. Lillian had seen these hands before. They were her mother's. That's where she knew them. It is not like reading a palm, Lillian thought. There's no future in it. The back of a hand is all past.

The concierge was taller than Kaddish and broader than Kaddish, but with his hair oiled and his poor-man-in-a-fancy-suit look, he seemed smaller in some way. That's why when Kaddish punched him hard in the face he'd thought the man would go down. The concierge partially sidestepped the blow and Kaddish partially abandoned it when something sharp and painful happened in his neck. Though Kaddish only grazed his victim, he did manage to cut the man's lip. The concierge was apparently unconcerned about this injury since he first tended to Kaddish, laid out on the lobby floor.

"Call the police if you want," Kaddish said. "I'm sure we'd both enjoy a visit from them."

"I was thinking an ambulance might be better."

Kaddish tried to get up onto his elbows and, with a wince, let himself fall back down. The concierge took off his jacket and put it under Kaddish's head.

"You're very nice, considering," Kaddish said.

"Thank you," the concierge said. "It's my job to be pleasant. Though if you get back up I'm going to kick the shit out of you."

"I'll keep that in mind," Kaddish said.

"I was serious about the ambulance."

"Give me a minute," Kaddish said. "An old football injury is all."

"I still can't let you up to the apartment," the concierge said. "I'll lose my job."

"I'll let myself up," Kaddish said.

"I have instructions from the family. They don't want to be bothered."

Kaddish took in the fancy coffered ceiling and the tops of the potted trees. A rich person's building. Whatever he could try and bribe this man with, it wouldn't be as much as he got every time he flagged down a cab.

With the help of the concierge, Kaddish got into a seated position. "Sorry about the punch," Kaddish said.

The concierge helped Kaddish to his feet. While he still had his hands on him, he aimed Kaddish toward the door. "I think you did more damage to yourself," he said. "Let's call it even." He gave Kaddish a little push, some momentum to help with his exit.

"I have to talk to them," Kaddish said. "I need to talk to Mónica."

"The answer is no," the concierge said. "If you remember, we already got to this part. That's when you whanged me in the jaw."

"I remember," Kaddish said.

"You want to make another pass at it?"

Without his jacket the concierge looked even bigger, his arms filling out his shirt. Even ignoring Kaddish's physical disadvantage, they both knew he didn't have enough left in him to try.

"They've taken my son," Kaddish said. "That's the reason I've got to ask her some questions."

The concierge ran his tongue against the cut in his lip. It didn't bleed much. "I'm sorry to hear that," the concierge said, "but she doesn't want to talk."

"You're not going to give in, are you?"

The concierge shook his head.

"I'm going to get up there," Kaddish said. "I'm going to stay here in this building. I can't leave until I do."

The concierge motioned to two long couches.

"Help yourself," he said.

Kaddish glanced toward the elevator. He wouldn't make it if he ran.

"If it wasn't for my wife," Kaddish said, "that girl would still be missing. My wife got her out." Kaddish reached into his pocket for the papers. "She's the one who brought her home."

"That's your wife?" the concierge said. "Mrs. Poznan?"

"Yes," Kaddish said.

The concierge led Kaddish to the elevator. It was as the doctor had said: Kaddish had told his story backwards again. When the elevator man opened the gate, the concierge said, "Six." When they got to the floor, he said, "Do me a favor, Pulpo. Watch the lobby for me until I get back." The elevator man gave a whistle.

Kaddish was surprised when the concierge took out a set of keys and let himself in. The apartment had a big open living room. It was modern looking, nothing at all like the general's, though you could sense the money inside. It was messy too, Kaddish thought. Messy for rich people. There was too much clutter for a place that looked like it was designed to be empty. There was a dress over the back of the sofa and, on the floor at Kaddish's feet, a belt. Kaddish stepped over it, and looking farther in he saw a silver sugar bowl tipped over on the sideboard and sugar on the floor. Kaddish was about to ask in which room they were hiding, except it was clear that they were gone. His next thought, and it choked him up, was that the police had been, or the army. That they'd done exactly what they had to Pato, letting the girl loose so they could claim they'd released her—or claim nothing—and then snatching her right back up. They'd snatched up the whole family, it looked like.

But something in those first seconds was different; it changed Kaddish's mind. The house was not so much ransacked as it was disheveled. Kaddish looked around the room. All the expensive stuff was still there, and all the things you'd break stood unbroken. The place was only victim to a rush. He was about to follow the trail of clothing toward the bedrooms when he better understood. Kaddish faced the concierge and now felt small; he felt tiny, so sincere was the look of pity in the man's eyes.

They'd left. The Álvarezes got their daughter back and ran.

[Thirty-six]

BEFORE FEIGENBLUM GETS A CHANCE to establish him-
self, his office makes it clear: Here is a Jew of import. On side tables and
shelves, on pedestals and windowsills, on the walls and across his desk,
from any angle that a visitor might face are visible the honors and acco-
lades, the statuettes and Judaic symbols that those in power procure and
acquire and, most often, award among themselves.

Hung in a grouping was a selection of antique *channukiot,* with their
fingernail wells and Roman design. Freestanding was a large brass
menorah, seven-branched as in the Holy Temple. And if a visitor could
not picture the glory of that place, on the pedestal to its right was a die-
cast replica of the Third Temple itself, just as it will be lowered down
from heaven. Next to it a shofar rested like a samurai sword on a fork-
armed stand.

Closest to Feigenblum's desk—to keep him full of humility and lest
he never forget—was a yellow Jude star, pinned to velvet in a mahogany
case. On the other side, in bas-relief, a representation of the Western
Wall was hung so Feigenblum also might never lose his cunning.

Between the threshold and the desk, one wall was covered with photos of Feigenblum and personages of import, proof of his connections to
the outside world. There were many grinning handshakes on display
and a couple of images, in Lillian's quick survey, that seemed more

questionable, as if Feigenblum had jumped in before the flash. There was also a large portrait of this President Feigenblum with the original President Feigenblum, his father, who'd help found the United Congregations of Argentina and who stood by so long ago while the cemetery was divided.

Feigenblum sat behind his desk, marking up a letter. He was very very not-busy with this letter. He was so deeply and ridiculously not busy with marking it up that Lillian, who had admittedly been nervous about the meeting, was put at ease. As Feigenblum moved the nib of his pen along a line, Lillian wanted to tell him, *I have sat across from the masters, Mr. Feigenblum. I have been to the ministries already.* To see such a tepid stab at self-import, to be confronted by a man so obviously aware of her presence and his own, whose faux thinking smelled of thought about thought. It was not only rude, it was funny. Lillian let out a sound that could only be described as a guffaw. Feigenblum redoubled his efforts. He left her standing.

When ready, he pressed the letter to his desk blotter and moved a paperweight in the shape of a dove of peace atop it. He placed this artifact over the intended recipient's name.

"Mrs. Poznan," he said.

Lillian sat. Feigenblum cocked his head, ready to listen. He arranged his hands on the desk, one resting on the other in a way that complemented his welcoming clean-slate expression. She thought it downright aggressive. It was graciousness as a weapon.

Lillian waited for him to talk, to commit to a position as detestably gracious. She would hold him to everything from word one.

"I'm surprised to see you," Feigenblum said. "Let me say, though, that all are equal in my office. Any unpleasantness that has arisen because of your husband—past or present—is today as if it never happened."

"Agreeing to forget would be less than prudent," Lillian said. "Not when this is all the junta asks of us. Not," she said, "as the mother of a disappeared son."

The gasp and sigh from Feigenblum, the sudden smell of empathy in the air, the quickness with which he was around that desk, comforting Lillian, offering an arm, leading her over to sit with him on the couch below the photos, underneath all those powerful watching eyes—it was real. In his haste, Lillian noticed, he'd even knocked down his little dove.

Lillian had been waiting for this, waiting for anyone at all to do as Feigenblum had, to rush, literally, to her side.

"You didn't know?" Lillian said.

"So much whispering," Feigenblum said. "A nexus, this building. Every bit of talk makes its way through."

"Then you did hear?"

"I'm hearing what you tell me now. And I swear to you—not even promise, Mrs. Poznan, a Jew swearing—on my honor, I will do my best to bring him back. And all the missing children along with him."

That was it. All these days, this was the promise she needed. Lillian was suddenly and deeply consolable.

"I should have ignored my husband's wishes from the start," she said. "The moment Pato was taken I should have run to the United Jewish Congregations, to you, President Feigenblum. This isn't about defending Kaddish's pride. This is about larger ideas of family. You should be aware that I've already brought this to the top. I've sat with generals." At that Feigenblum gave a nod. "Nowhere have I witnessed such courage; no one else has said it straight. We have to bring the children back," Lillian said. "Pato and the others."

"That is all I work toward."

"And how else to do that if we don't admit they're gone."

"Absolutely," Feigenblum said. "It is the first step in the battle."

"You'll help, then?" Lillian said.

"I won't stop until every Jewish boy and girl is returned home."

This was good, Lillian thought. This was family. If being Jewish brought extra trouble onto their heads, why should it not bring extra help.

"Every child the same," Lillian said. "You will fight just as hard for each of them, yes? Even for the son of Kaddish Poznan, for the *hijo de puta* who is also a Jew."

"Old talk, old tales," Feigenblum said. "Why bring back the rumors of long ago? As my grandmother always said, there's no such thing as a

Jewish whore. Let's leave it at that. Children are children. All the same."
This was already too much for Lillian. But Feigenblum couldn't resist.
"Since you bring it up, my problem with Kaddish has nothing to do
with his claims," he said. "It's the actions that are at issue. He is a vandal,
your husband. He takes money to desecrate the dead. I don't want to
make comparisons. Please don't push me to say what sort of people top-
ple and smash Jewish graves."

Lillian felt a surge to the pulse in her neck, the blood pushing with a
shush past the temples and into her head. She felt the fury and speed of
it must be apparent to Feigenblum. She dropped her gaze to her hands
for a glimpse of those slow, steady veins.

"It takes too much to understand how you keep my husband on the
outside for a lifetime and in the same breath deny the very reason that
you do. The grudge against us started long before the names began disappearing. For a people so dedicated to remembering everything, how
is it that my husband is punished for doing just that?"

Feigenblum sat as rigidly as he could against the give of the couch.

"Nothing is being denied. There is a wall in our cemetery over which
is buried a defunct congregation. All the world over, there are such sep-
arations among Jews. There are breakaway shuls and breakaway schools.
This one calls kosher what another calls *tref.* It's in our nature. There are
always two synagogues and two cemeteries. This one belonged to the
Synagogue of the Benevolent Self, a renegade shul."

"Not shul," Lillian said. "The Caftan Society is what it was. Pimps and
whores, why not say it? How can I trust you to take on this government
if you employ their tactics?"

"There are no tactics involved, Mrs. Poznan. I simply refuse to do to
these people exactly what you accuse me of doing to your husband.
There's a wall, yes. But it's all the same cemetery. What is the point in
stressing differences? These people put themselves on the other side,
same as your husband. Sad as that is, it's a choice." Feigenblum gave her
a warm smile. "To me, all Jews are one. And I feel equally responsible for
them all."

"It's not good enough," Lillian said. "Not when we're dealing with
Kaddish Poznan's child."

"What more can I tell you than I already have? Would you have me agree to bring back the Jew with horns as I would the one without? You dredge up old prejudices. Leave them where they are, Mrs. Poznan." Feigenblum put his hands on her shoulders and turned her toward him. "I'll do everything that's in my power," he said. "The same as I would for my own son."

With that statement, whatever trust Lillian had mustered slipped away. She knew Feigenblum's boy, younger than Pato. Looking at the father, seeing Feigenblum as parent, not president, she knew—however far he might go for the community, however much he believed he would champion their sons—that saved up in this man was a secret absolute, a single call, an only favor. He was ready for the day when they might take his child, and Feigenblum in his heart knew that's when he would do the real getting back.

"The list," Lillian said, getting up, pulling him along.

She led him to the bulletin board in the hallway outside his office. It was the place where they pinned up the flyers for cultural events and holiday services, for WIZO meetings and Israeli folk dance, and for all the other groups that no longer dared meet. The board was behind glass, in a metal case the putty color of file cabinets and hospital equipment, of functional things meant to last. It would hang there as long as a wall stood up behind it and—Lillian gave it a try—it would also stay locked.

The case had lately been assigned another use. In it hung the list. Double-spaced and single-columned, it already ran two and a half pages long. These were the names of the Jewish missing typed up in alphabetical order, posted for easy confirmation and to keep people like Lillian right where she was—on the outside of Feigenblum's door.

Lillian gave the metal frame a solid yank. It didn't move. So she brought her beautiful new nose right up to the glass. She hunted with a finger, locating the spot where Pato would fit, nestled between Néstor Lewin and María Rabin.

"There," she said to Feigenblum. "Right there is where his name goes." She tapped her nail against the pane. "Let's open it and write it in now." She steamed up the glass with her breath and stared with such agony, it was as if the children themselves were right there on the other side.

"Soon enough," Feigenblum said, lifting his eyes past Lillian, a silent greeting to a colleague going by. "The moment Pato makes the list, we'll add him to the rolls. Not in pencil, either. We will type him into his rightful place."

"What does that mean, *make the list*? How to make it except to be added?"

"Nothing is simple these days," he said.

"A million times I've heard that," Lillian said. "A million other places. Only once, only here, have I gotten, *I'll help, my best, all I can*. Only from you, Feigenblum, has it been uttered. From your mouth alone have I heard, 'I'll bring the Jewish children home.'"

"It's my sworn duty."

"Then what could be simpler? It's silly even. A little concession so a mother feels good."

"It would take nothing to add it," Feigenblum said, agreeing. "Not a bit of effort."

"Yes?" Lillian said. "And?"

"It doesn't help if we add every name in the world. This is a list as registered with the government. There's a protocol. They approve every name on it, even if they don't agree or actually note the same names themselves. But they know we have it right out in the open, for anyone to see. It's a protest. It's a list that contradicts and calls the government to task—of this I'm proud. Our staff does the research, working in tandem but independently. We use the government's very resources to challenge its claims with our own official roll."

"So it's their list," Lillian said. "A farce."

"It's ours. And it's more than anyone else has managed," Feigenblum said. "We negotiate the names, and it's a fight to get each one. The government still denies that these people are in their custody. It's through perseverance and pressure, through finagling and back channels, that we have reached this watershed. We have gotten them to admit that these are the people we accuse them of incarcerating."

"They admit that you accuse them?"

"Yes," Feigenblum said.

"What's that worth?"

"Everything," he said, "when it's official."

"That's your best?" Lillian said. "That's the most the officers of the Jewish community can do?"

"Do you think more would get done if we chained ourselves to the doors of the Ministry of Special Cases? Aggressive tactics, rudeness and tough talk—that would leave me feeling satisfied at the end of the day, but where would it leave us?" Feigenblum gave a sweeping gesture to include Lillian and the United Congregations and, she imagined, all the rest of Once's and Argentina's Jews. He raised his eyebrows and made a point of staring. "Why cut off our noses, Mrs. Poznan, only to spite our face?"

"As worthless as Kaddish swore," Lillian said.

"Does that mean you'd prefer I don't submit your son's name?"

"For approval?" Lillian laughed. "You work with them, Feigenblum. You channel the grand tradition of Jewish diplomacy: Never acknowledge catastrophe until it's done."

"That's a preposterous accusation."

"Afterward you'll raise up a tall building around it. You'll enlist a great Jewish after-the-fact army to fight with all of hell's fury over how it is to be remembered."

"This is a fantasy."

"You'll deal with the very same officials," Lillian said. "You'll fight bravely over how many of our dead they'll agree to list on the monument." Lillian gritted her teeth. "What it means, Feigenblum, is that I want my son, my Pato, home alive. Not the Museum of the Jewish Disappeared."

"How dare you," he said. "I risk my life, and my family's, advocating for this cause."

Lillian shook her head. "I can see already in your eyes, I can see how you plan to mourn."

"You're crazy," he said.

"And you're worse than them," she said. She meant to wound Feigenblum, she felt his betrayal was great.

"Selfish woman!" Feigenblum grabbed Lillian by the arm, the delicacy gone. "How many mothers make their way here, acting as if each child is the only one?" Feigenblum sighed and let go. Then he smoothed the lapels on his perfect suit, adjusted his collar, and centered the dimpled knot of his tie. He pulled at his cuffs—his cuff links, in the motion, gleamed—and pressed carefully against his hair so as not to muss its perfect part. "There is a plague upon us," he said. "On this community more than the others."

"What shock do you think you can give? My son has been disappeared. I know that when there's death in the air the Jew is more susceptible, more likely to catch it."

"My position brings with it an elevation that affords its own particular view. I'm privy to things. And I'm convinced you wouldn't speak to me this way if you were responsible for more than one son."

"If it were your son missing, neither would your best efforts ring so false. If it were your boy he'd be back in a day, wouldn't he, Feigenblum? There is a different *all*. There is a *most* that you save for him."

"Honestly, I can't tell you until it—God forbid—should happen. Right now, though, the resources must be shared."

"Do the undoable, Feigenblum. Reach out as if Pato were your own."

"I'll get his name added. Despite this visit, I'll try."

"You're a weakling," Lillian said. "You want to lead the Jews while they come for our children, and all you manage is an incomplete list. You want to talk plagues, Feigenblum? In Egypt they took the Jewish children, and do you know what they got in return?"

"That was miracles," he said. "That was God."

"No, that's what we say now. Who better than you should recognize the whitewashed version of the story. Do you really think there were frogs, Feigenblum? Do you really believe an angel came down from heaven and took our enemies' firstborn? There was a leader, Feigenblum. It was Moses and his Jews who rose up and did the slaying."

"This is the talk of a desperate woman, God help you. You should wish for rescues as sweet as in Egypt. The waters don't split for us anymore. I'll tell you, without metaphor or rumor or lie, there are terrible things happening. There are crimes the Western Hemisphere has not known. You must open your eyes and look up, Mrs. Poznan. Then you won't expect so much of anyone. It isn't angels you'll see. Those are bodies raining down from the sky."

"You don't look so good," Dr. Mazursky said.

"Always seeing beyond the surface," Kaddish said. "It's touching, that kind of sensitivity."

"Better than mentioning the smell." He gave Kaddish a pat on the back. "Any news of the boy?"

"You sound concerned for a man who won't let me get near him."

"When have I turned you away?" the doctor said.

Kaddish tilted his head toward the pillar he'd been hiding behind. He'd loitered there for more than an hour, waiting for the doctor to walk the few paces from office building to waiting car. The doctor turned and looked at the pillar. He gave a big shrug.

"Considering our dealings were most secret," Kaddish said, "your people are very good at identifying me. The maid at your house is one thing. Here I can't even get into the lobby."

"You exaggerate, I'm sure," the doctor said. "Either way, it's not about you. It's a global tightening of security. These are volatile times."

The doctor's car pulled forward and the driver, seeing Kaddish, seemed to be in a panic as he got out and came around the front of the car.

The doctor held up an open hand and the driver stopped mid-stride.

"Leave the engine running," the doctor said. "We'll just be a minute or two." The doctor looked to Kaddish and Kaddish nodded. "Should we take a walk?"

"That would be good."

The driver got back into the car. Instead of idling as instructed, he put the car in gear and drove slowly, keeping a car's length behind the two men.

"If it's not about me, why don't you take my calls? I must have tried a dozen times this afternoon alone. It's not like I'm not also a patient. How strange would it be to have me back for an exam?"

"Some very important titties up there today, patients that not even by face should be able to identify a tit such as you." Mazursky pointed toward the Botanical Garden, and they started to walk that way. "It's really nothing personal. I don't know how better to prove it than by strolling with you now. It's riskier to be seen with you outside than in." The doctor looked up at the sun disappearing behind the city. "The air today is very nice. I should sneak out more."

"Not enough fresh air at the track?"

"Plenty. Except all I breathe in there is horseshit, and it smells like money to me." Mazursky stepped off a curb and, nearly clipped by a taxi, stepped back up. His driver honked the horn.

Kaddish popped a cigarette into his mouth and followed the doctor across the street. He smoked quickly, feeling unsteady. "I've got some business," he said.

The doctor shielded his eyes.

"Do we have any left?"

"A question," Kaddish said. "You said when I had the right one that you could maybe do something."

Mazursky sucked in his cheek. "If I said I could maybe do something, that would be a very unbinding promise. Not much to cash in on."

"It wasn't even a promise. It was a kindness that you offered. And it wasn't with a maybe. Definite. You said you would."

"Well," the doctor said, his second shrug of the day. "As you know, I'm a man of my word."

Kaddish dropped his cigarette to the ground.

"I wanted to know," he said to the doctor, stepping on the butt and staring down at the grinding tip of his shoe, "I wanted to know," Kaddish said, "if my son, Pato Poznan, whether he's alive or dead."

[Thirty-seven]

KADDISH HAD TAKEN TO SLEEPING under the front pew instead of atop it. He'd told himself the bench was too narrow for a man of his bulk. It was really that the synagogue was too wide. He was amazed at how easily a man adrift could make himself feel at home. Only, he'd discovered, the space in which one could manage it got tighter and tighter.

He piled the prayer books in stacks right in front of the pew, each stack with a pair of bricks on the bottom so the books wouldn't touch the floor. Kaddish left a space by his head and closed himself in. Should he ever reconcile with Lillian, should he have the good fortune of a dignified death and the foreknowledge that the end was near, Kaddish would ask for a coffin cut extra tight to his body. Let the worms find their own place to sleep.

It was not two days after Kaddish had made his request of the doctor that he woke with a start. He guessed from the light that it was barely yet dawn. As he blinked his way to focus, careful—in his shock—not to bang his head, what came into view right in front of his eyes were two feet and two legs planted in the space he'd left open. He was a little bit afraid and a little bit curious and felt a rising sense, in his cozy space, of being trapped.

Apparently there was a man sitting above him. Kaddish did his best to keep silent, which was no easy task for a lifelong smoker. He tended to greet each day with a racking fit of coughing. Kaddish studied the fine silk socks the man wore and thought of sinking his teeth into an Achilles tendon and then making a graceless scrabbling escape.

The heel of the left shoe rose up and then came down with a clack, sending a swirl of dust right into Kaddish's face.

"I know you're awake, Poznan. A terrible actor." It was Mazursky. Kaddish's heart beat heavy; Kaddish should have known. "You're either awake or dead, Poznan. Both the snoring and farting have come to a stop. You've got to breathe from somewhere."

Kaddish stifled a cough, keeping silent.

"We've got to get a look at those sinuses again. It really is an ungodly noise. The other end I won't touch. You'll have to find a braver doctor to stick his nose in that."

Kaddish wasn't sure what to say. "Are you going to let me out?" was all he came up with.

The feet came together and slid over. Kaddish pushed a pile of prayer books out of his way and slipped through, taking the curtain he used as a blanket with him. He stood up and dusted off, a hand now holding two corners of the *parochet* to his chest. All the red velvet draped around him added a touch of the kingly to an otherwise undignified moment.

Kaddish sat next to the doctor. He threw the excess curtain over his legs to keep away the chill and fumbled for a cigarette.

"How did you find me?" Kaddish said.

"It's your son that's disappeared," the doctor said. "The condition you suffer from is completely different. With you, Poznan, no one is looking."

"Still, this a very odd place at which to arrive."

"It's not the first spot I checked. Trust me, though. I didn't go far. You're a man avoided mainly for the fact that you might end up here. I'd have walked right back out, if not for the snore."

Kaddish knew what question he'd asked of the doctor, and, as much as he wanted an answer, he was afraid of what it was.

"I appreciate the risk you've taken in showing up here."

"This is the synagogue, not the cemetery. If it was to save your son's life, I can't promise I'd have come to find you there."

"Is it to save his life?"

"I don't know," the doctor said. "I spoke to a gentleman who spoke to a gentleman who's willing to meet. I was making a different point. It's that Toothless' name wasn't screwed into the wall over here." The doctor put his elbow over the back of the pew, looking around. "There was never a leaf on that tree for my father."

Kaddish took the opportunity to have the coughing fit he'd fought off underneath. The doctor watched as Kaddish's eyes bulged. He listened as whatever was sticking to Kaddish's lungs came loose in an amazingly audible sound.

"Time to go," the doctor said, when Kaddish recovered.

"Like that?" Kaddish said.

"Just like that. And it was no small feat to arrange such a rendezvous."

"With who?"

"The only man I've ever heard of that's more pitiful than you. But you've got to get going, he's not easy to pin down and even more rarely coherent."

"He sounds like a prize."

"Have mercy. It's difficult to live with the answers to the questions you ask."

"Is he close by, this man?"

"Jesus," the doctor said. "Did you walk out on your wife without taking the car?"

"With nothing," Kaddish said. "Why else would I be sleeping under a bench?"

"I still can't understand why you'd leave." The doctor took out his billfold. "You're a man with a hard life. Why on earth do you go around making it harder? The top of the bench would do you better." The doctor handed Kaddish three American ten-dollar bills. "I'll drop you by the golf club."

"You want me to go golfing with him?" Kaddish said.

"Your man is at the Fisherman's Club. The golf club is for me. If I'm up this early, I might as well get in a round."

"The pier is a good three kilometers from there."

"You're enough of a prize your own self, Poznan. I don't need to be spotted near the both of you together. Anyway, you look near death. A brisk walk down Costanera, a bit of park time, a stroll along the river—it'll cure what ails you."

"What about the rush?"

"I wouldn't stop for breakfast on the way," the doctor said. On second thought, he gave Kaddish another ten. "Treat the man to a meal."

Lillian stood outside the Ministry of Special Cases deep in a line that ran the length of the block and snaked around the corner. She'd sworn that another visit to that building would kill her. With the habeas corpus fallen through, she'd returned without pause. She would show up at Feigenblum's the same way, just as she'd visit police stations and hospital wards, roam the parks and misery towns, and stand in the morgues of the city, not looking for Pato—as he was alive—but to count the bodies herself, to rule out each one with her own eyes, the dead *porteños* that were not her son. She added to this roster the foreign amnesty groups and the Israeli embassy. If they could find and kidnap and sneak Eichmann out, how much harder could it be to track down Pato? Let those commandos roll her son up in a carpet and spirit him off, too.

When she got to the hall it was packed worse than she'd ever seen it. They were in the aisles today, sitting on the floor. And why shouldn't it fill to overflowing, Lillian thought, if people kept disappearing and so much work went into getting even one boy home?

Lillian spied an old couple who'd staked a good claim. With their knees together and backs turned out, a bag between them and one each on the outside, there was room for another person on that bench, maybe two. The woman moaned as she took a shoe off, so that, staring at a swollen foot, her neighbors did their best to shift farther away.

Lillian was over, Lillian was pointing and reaching, a hand on a bag. "On the floor," Lillian said. "I could sit if you move them."

The old woman took Lillian's hand off the bag. "I'm getting settled," she said. "I can see how crowded on my own."

The woman took her time getting off the other shoe, a heavy thing with a heel that looked as if it were cut from a two-by-four. The husband went into the middle bag and produced a pair of slippers and then went back to ignoring Lillian and his wife.

"Bad circulation," the woman said. Then she shifted and organized and Lillian sat down.

It was when Lillian checked the crumpled number from in her pocket that the old woman spoke. "How high?" she said.

"Too high, I'm afraid." Lillian put the paper back and pressed her pocket closed as if to signal that their conversation was done.

"Is it your husband?" the woman said. She stared at Lillian's wedding band. Lillian stared at it too. It had been so long since she saw it as a symbol of any tie to Kaddish.

"No," Lillian said. "It's my son."

"Snatched up?" the woman said. She inquired with great concern.

Lillian answered. She told them what had happened and was surprised to find that she was happy to talk and be listened to, to have her story—to have Pato—believed by strangers. When she finished the husband said, "Hardship all the way."

It was as Lillian wondered why they didn't all share their troubles that she learned her telling would warrant a listening. The woman told her their names—Rosita and Leib—and launched into the story of their own absent son. Lillian wasn't sure why she didn't see this coming or, more curiously, why she thought it so unfair.

"It's killing us for real," Rosita told her. "It's killing Leib."

"I've been in the hospital," he said. He pointed to his heart.

Lillian didn't feel generous, and she didn't feel bad. What she did feel was repulsion, visceral and sharp. The buffer was there for a reason. The customs of silence and solitude for a reason. The Ministry of Special Cases didn't need, with all its other tortures, the mixing of hopelessness and hope.

"Until this, he was always healthy, and now he has heart failures all the time. Not even attacks," she said. "It's different. The heart doesn't try anymore. We're packing it in. We're moving to Jerusalem before Leib dies. The strain can kill us over there just as easy."

There was a look of horror on Lillian's face.

"We'll come right back if there's a miracle," Leib said. "It doesn't help our son if we die from the waiting. It's time to move on."

"Yes," Rosita said, agreeing. "How many ways can they tell us to give up? For how long?"

"If we don't protect ourselves a little."

"A good boy," Rosita said.

"A scientist," Leib said. "We have letters on his behalf from Britain, from the United States. One was even sent from the Technion in Haifa. A name, our son. We weren't the only ones working. Others have tried."

Old as they were, frail as they were, Lillian passed judgment. She held her tongue between her teeth, so strong was the urge to say, *If it's killing you, the waiting, it's nature's wish. Then it's a person's time to die.*

"We fought long," Rosita said. "First in Salta, from our home. Then we came to the capital, to be near the government and near where Daniel lived, near the scene of this crime."

"We've been staying in his apartment," Leib said. "Parents sleeping in a dead son's bed."

"We've lived away from home so long," Rosita said, "there's no reason to go back. At our age when you've been uprooted, when you've broken the routines of a lifetime, what difference is it to keep on to Jerusalem? It's the same thing for us, ten kilometers or ten thousand."

"My heart is no good," Leib said.

If they can run from their son, Lillian thought, why couldn't she run from them? Lillian bent to separate her bag from theirs, to get her things and move on.

"The intent wasn't to burden," Rosita said. "You go," she said. "Be well."

"I'm not judging," Lillian said, unnerved. "I'm just going. You be well," Lillian said. "You have good luck."

"You're new," Rosita said. "I understand, I remember. You shouldn't know from it," Rosita said, "but two years on this bench is enough."

Lillian was in the midst of backing away. This stopped her, Rosita's *You shouldn't know.* Who more than her? How could anyone claim more than Lillian, to suffer?

"Two years?" Lillian said, angry now, ungenerous. "It's hardly two months since this nightmare has befallen us. There's no need to make it worse than it is."

"She's all piss and vinegar," Rosita said to her husband. "It's the only way to start out."

"You can fly away if you need to," Lillian said. "But you don't suffer any more than me."

"Maybe you suffer more, maybe less. Either way, it's the same two years for us. You can't imagine yet—no matter your claim—what two years will bring. In '74 our Daniel was taken."

"The troubles go back a ways," Leib said. "Before the junta, before Isabelita, still with Perón it started."

"Not true," Lillian said. "Then it must be something else. A different matter than disappeared."

A sweet, sweet smile from Rosita, at Lillian and then at her husband.

"Even now," Leib said. "Even still, it is hard for us to imagine that maybe, before our Daniel, there was another."

"We know how it is," Rosita said. "Everyone is like that. The troubles always start when they start for you."

Lillian did run from them. She ran out of the hall and down the stairs. She wasn't going to sit there turning into that woman while the hours ticked by. She knew full well that a marred habeas corpus with names scratched out was neither a document issued on behalf of her son nor proof of the rejection of such a request, either of which—according to the clerk in the hallway—was the province of the ministry's other side. And even that she no longer had. Kaddish took their copy when he left. She'd find the bird-feather man regardless; she'd make him help. Lillian headed for the stairway on the right.

The door was locked and Lillian tried to force the knob. Then she began banging with her fists. The lobby was empty except for Lillian and the guard. He came straight over to ask what it was she thought she was trying to do.

"To get upstairs," was her answer.

"That part I figured," he said. "Except I'm not really interested, because you're not allowed up there, not without special permission—and if you'd been given it, they'd have called me. I'd have been the one to escort you."

"It's not nice the way you give out the numbers," Lillian said. "It's cruel. You could make a line and hand them out, one to fifty, in the order in which people arrive."

"I don't think that's what we're discussing."

"We are discussing sadism. It's sadistic the way you hand out the numbers and a further indication of that trait when you come over to harass me instead of simply unlocking that door."

"No one gets up there without approval and without me leading the way."

"I've already been up," Lillian said. "My husband and I were there together. I'm returning to finish the business I've already started on that side."

"Take it back," he said.

"What?" Lillian said. She blinked, and was honestly startled, so perfectly infantile was the request.

"If what you said was true, I'd get in a lot of trouble—serious trouble."

"But it is," Lillian said.

"But take it back," the guard said, dead serious. "If you'd been there I'd have a record in my log and a note to put in the file that goes to the archive that lists all the citizens who've been up there that week, except that I haven't had to send the file or use the log this quarter, because no one ever goes."

"I spoke to a man in the hallway. He was eating his lunch." Lillian knew she should stop. If she had to keep coming to the ministry every morning, she'd never get one of the good numbers. "Let me up this time," Lillian said, "and I'll take them both back, this visit and the last."

"You've got two seconds to take everything back before I thwart your attempt to enter a secure area."

Lillian took this to mean that he meant her harm. But she really couldn't imagine that he did. That's maybe why she said, "Only the truth. That's all anyone gets from me."

She really didn't see it coming, that first swing. It wasn't aimed at her but it made such a crack, and the crack, in that empty lobby, set off such a boom, Lillian actually screamed and jumped, and couldn't in the intervening seconds get rid of the shakes. The guard had pulled his baton and swung it with all his might against that door. He raised it again and this time it was poised above Lillian.

"You weren't up there," he said. "Take it back."

But Lillian couldn't take it back, because she'd been there. It seemed insane even to her not to just say it when she knew a single blow would break her bones. "I was up there," she said. "And you were here, like always, and didn't stop me."

She tensed as she spoke, curling her shoulders and tucking her chin, preparing to be hit. All the guard did was slip the baton back in its loop. For an instant Lillian thought that the strength of her resolve had won him over. And then she straightened up, understanding that they weren't alone.

Lillian felt the man's presence behind her. Then a hand was clasped over her shoulder in a kindly way, and—the strangest thing—he said, "Candy?"

"No, thanks," the guard said. "Not today." He kept his baton hand by the baton, and the other one he raised, to wave the offer off.

"Come on," the man said. "You're the only one in the building with a sweet tooth worse than mine."

"I'm working," he said.

"From what I heard, it sounds like you need a break."

At that the guard's cheeks turned red and he said again to Lillian, screamed it in front of this man, "Take it back!"

"Have a piece," the man said. And an extremely long arm reached out past Lillian, crossing the space between her and the guard. A chocolate coin wrapped in gold foil was pressed into the guard's hand.

"She's lying," the guard said. "She was never up there." The guard seemed to be trying to frown, but only one side of his mouth turned down.

"As expedient as caving in this woman's skull would be, would you be amenable to another solution as a favor to me?"

The guard nodded.

"And you?" the man said. He was talking to Lillian. She already knew, from the length of the arm and the height from which the voice came, to look up when she turned. Still, Lillian fell short. She first saw his jacket and then, at his neck, the collar around it. He was a military priest. In those first moments she didn't raise her eyes from there. "Yes," she said.

"This is excellent," the priest said, and returned his attention to the guard. "Not to upset standard procedure too much, how about I give you a second piece, which we'll call a bribe?" Again the long arm was extended and the coin, this one silver, was passed to the guard. "My version of events goes like this: This woman was never on the other side as she claims," he squeezed Lillian's shoulder to stop her before she spoke. "She never stood here right now, and I never gave you the second chocolate, only the first was given as a courtesy. Since nothing transpired, it would follow that there'd be no reason for bad blood between you, and there'd definitely be no reason to approach a stranger and ask if she ever was where she shouldn't be—to which, being a stubborn stranger, she'd surely answer yes, starting a cycle that ends with a split-open head. Now that outcome doesn't have to be. Problem solved."

"Yes, Father—sir," the guard said.

"Yes," Lillian said.

"Excellent," the priest said. "You eat your chocolate," he said to the guard. "You come for a walk with me," he said to Lillian. "And when we get back, a test for everyone, we will see how good we all are at keeping a promise."

"You should be more cautious," the priest said. "Is it really worth it to die over that?"

"I don't think he'd have killed me right there in the lobby."

"It's not conjecture. I've seen someone beaten to death in that lobby before."

The priest had a talent for listening and Lillian wondered if receiving confession was an actual skill. Lillian spoke more openly to him than she had to anyone other than Frida and went as far as sharing her dream of an Eichmann-style rescue, which she'd never said aloud.

"The Eichmann abduction was a more complex operation than you make it seem. Let's say there were people who looked the other way so that it could be such a well-publicized success."

"Those are the people I'm trying to get to," Lillian said.

"They don't do favors," the priest said. "And they can't be bought with a cookie."

"But they can be bought?" Lillian said. She thrust out her sheaf of papers. The priest stepped back and Lillian only reached out farther. The priest's arms were nothing; Lillian would reach across the city if need be.

The priest took the papers and began patting himself down. Lillian, preempting, offered her own glasses. Testing them out, he moved them forward and back on the bridge of a perfect triangle of nose. "More or less," the priest said. He crossed his eyes and took the chain that hung below his chin like a bridle. He lifted it over his head. The priest *tsk-tsk*ed and pulled out another chocolate coin. He unwrapped it, snapped it in two, and offered Lillian half.

Lillian took it. "Is this your cure for everything?"

"In this case it's about all I can do." He licked his thumb. "I'm a military chaplain in a Catholic army. I split my loyalties between God and country. Even if God takes precedence, I think yours is beyond my jurisdiction."

"It's all the same when it's about saving a boy."

"In this world, maybe. Most of what I do is focused on saving people for the one to come."

"Now is when I want him. Save the boy in this life and you can have his soul in the next."

"I wish I could," he said. "I can't."

Lillian didn't believe him. "Then you wouldn't have gone this far," she said. "I've learned enough in these last weeks to know good Samaritans don't just materialize. Priest or no priest, there's something in it for you."

"That's an extremely cynical view of the system. We should get you into a uniform. I think you'd do well."

"I only want one thing from it," she said. "Whatever your deal is, if it's guilt or God or dirty money, anything you can do to keep my son out of his grave, I'll take with me to mine."

"I really can't help you," he said. And then, handing Lillian her glasses, "I really shouldn't."

Kaddish walked through the park to the water. Not a great naturalist, while looking at trees Kaddish was reminded that there were trees, and heading out to Avenue Costanera to walk the promenade he saw the great river, and acknowledged—even with cars passing by—that it was something to behold. Kaddish rubbed his hands together. It was still very cold.

Walking along the river, Kaddish couldn't help but see it as an ocean. It was an idea Talmud Harry had put into his head as a child. Harry would say, "Take every river and lake from the Bible, gather them up and drop them into our Río de la Plata, and guess what? They wouldn't even make a splash. Tell me though, little Poznan, if God himself isn't afraid to have His storied seas look like puddles upon inspection, why must the Argentine fake a river that is a sea?" Kaddish, of course, had no answer. "Hubris," Talmud Harry would always say. "It is dirty pride and hubris that spur such a deception." Practically fifty years later, Kaddish still thought it every time. Who wants the planet's tiniest ocean when he can have a river that makes men weak in the knees?

Fishermen began to dot the path, and planes from the airport nearby took off, rippling the air behind them with the heat off their engines. Kaddish was surprised that the fishermen didn't look up as the jets roared overhead. It's amazing what people get used to.

A woman pushing a stroller stuffed with blankets veered toward Kaddish and said, unasked, "It's the only way to get her back to sleep." Kaddish nodded and walked on until he saw the Fisherman's Club hovering on the mist above the water. In the dawn, with the pier hidden below, it was like walking into a fable. It was just the place one might approach when seeking answers from strangers to unknowable things.

As Kaddish got closer and the mist lifted and the wind slowed, the pier came into view, stretching out a solid half-kilometer into the river. The club building appeared to be clamped onto it. It was broader than the pier and jutted from it on both sides. The building was constructed right on top of it, maybe fifty meters from shore. It was a handsome wooden structure, with high arched cupolas and fine detail. It looked all the finer for the functional pier it straddled, naked pile and beam.

There was no one fishing in front of the building. Here and there he could see a rod visible on the other side. Walking through the club Kaddish tried to look purposeful, which was made more complicated by his lack of rod and tackle. And even for an early morning fisherman Kaddish's stay at the Benevolent Self had left him differently rundown. Two separate people asked who he was going to meet. Without a name he said, "Out back," pointing and following his finger and heading for the exit. Both stepped out of his way.

The doctor had promised that Kaddish was expected, that he'd been described to the man. Kaddish assumed the man had been given a report as kindly as the one he'd received: *Fatter than you but not so short, and with a bulldog's face.* So Kaddish searched for a stocky bulldog of a man, which covered basically each and everyone out there, including Kaddish himself.

He was oddly unconcerned. Kaddish believed one look would be enough. Despite the litany of things that went wrong in his dealings, Kaddish believed his instincts were still spot on.

At the end of the pier there was a small lean-to, and right before it Kaddish found his man: a *corcho* in a winter parka with one foot up on a rail. He had a mustache and, from what looked to be a general lack of grooming, also nearly a beard. As soon as Kaddish saw him, he did indeed know.

Two fishing rods were fastened in place and the man stood between them drinking his coffee, the cup hidden in a meaty hand. It was a look the man had, familiar to Kaddish from his own face, that was the giveaway. It was the broken-man look that said, had Kaddish walked right up to him, grabbed his ankles, and tipped him over the edge, he wouldn't have resisted for an instant—the acceptance that if his life came to an end it would simplify many troubling things.

They nodded at each other and, taking his foot down, the man took up his thermos and refilled his cup. So much steam came off it, Kaddish wondered if all the haze he'd seen on the way had risen from there. He offered it to Kaddish. It was a tiny tin cup covered in chipped white enamel, a beloved thing.

Kaddish said nothing, only staring back into the man's bloodshot eyes. They were big and yellow and much larger than they seemed for being set deep behind heavy cheeks. They stood there sizing each other up and Kaddish, not uncomfortable even with a silence as painful as this, turned with the man back to the rail.

The water below the pier was thick with oil and gas and industrial runoffs that gave it a glassy sheen. Every ripple and wave sent through it lifted up layers of purple and red and a yellowish runny-egg blue.

Kaddish thought it beautiful. Though, following those fishing lines, he wasn't sure he'd want to eat what was pulled from that water. There was the call of a horn as a tugboat limped along, steering a barge into an invisible lane.

Kaddish passed back the cup and lit a cigarette.

He smoked some and then flicked his cigarette out over the edge, half expecting the water to catch and the river to go up, the whole of Buenos Aires lit with a shimmering chemical flame.

The man shook his head as if to say, It won't light; he'd tried it before. Then Kaddish decided he couldn't possibly know what the man was thinking.

It was enough of an interaction either way, and Kaddish reached out to shake hands. The man had a strong grip. He held on and said, "What's your name again?"

"I thought maybe I wasn't supposed to," Kaddish said. "That you wouldn't want—"

"Victor Wollensky," he said.

"Kaddish Poznan," Kaddish said. "It's more your name I thought we were protecting."

"Not at all," he said. "A guilty man can't get himself killed in this town. Only the innocent need to watch out."

"Is that so?"

"I'm living proof," he said, "by virtue of the fact that I should be dead."

"You escaped?" Kaddish looked back toward the club. The end of the pier was a good place to stand for a man who wants to see who's coming his way.

"Escaped what?" the man said, an eyebrow raised.

"The junta," Kaddish said. "Their clutches."

"The junta?" The man laughed. "A naïf," he said. "Can't you tell by looking?"

Kaddish looked. While he did, his teeth began to chatter. It was cold over the water with hot coffee swishing inside. Wollensky took off his parka and handed it to Kaddish and Kaddish put it on.

Left in a heavy wool sweater, Wollensky pushed up the sleeves, revealing stretched and faded tattoos. "I'm to be escaped *from*. That's the kicker: You spend a life chasing and when you want to run, you're stuck. The one who chases can't get away from himself. I tried. I hid all over. And guess what?" He closed those big eyes and then popped them open, first one and then the other. "Take a peek and there I was."

Kaddish listened. He nodded and kept glancing at the tattoos.

"You're a sailor?" Kaddish said.

"Navy," Wollensky said. "And what might a man in this upside-down country end up doing in the navy but flying on planes."

"A pilot?"

Wollensky pulled down an eyelid. "*Ojo*," he said. "I've got big eyes for giving big warnings, but they don't see so good." He freed one of the rods. "Good enough to be a navigator. Good enough to see too much. I wish I was blind."

"A dark wish," Kaddish said.

"Not when you've seen what I have." There was no tension to the fishing line beyond the pull of the current. Wollensky began to reel it in. The hook came up baited, and the navigator cast it back out.

"What could be so terrible?" Kaddish said. He put his hand on the second rod and Wollensky nodded. Kaddish pulled it free.

"I know what happens to the children," Wollensky said.

Kaddish took a step toward him. "How are you the one to know?"

"By doing it," Wollensky said. "I'm the monster who tosses them into the sea."

The fishing rods were again fixed in place and the two men stood at the rail, staring out over the water. Kaddish reached into his pocket. He took out a snapshot of Pato and slid it along the bar to the navigator.

"Pato Poznan," Kaddish said. "My disappeared child."

The navigator didn't look. He turned his head.

"Please," Kaddish said. "He might be familiar. If not the name, maybe the face."

"It won't matter," the navigator said.

Kaddish, pleading, said, "It does to me."

The navigator took it up, stared at it, pushed it back Kaddish's way.

"They all look the same and they all look like this. *All in the same boat* is the saying. But they don't have one. They're all at the bottom of the river."

"How can I be sure?" Kaddish said. "As a father, how do I trust?"

"You want someone to swear for you? You need it to come from outside?" The navigator waited as if he expected a real answer from Kaddish. "You look like you already know the truth."

"What do I know?" Kaddish said.

"That once they're disappeared, it's already done. None of them will ever come home."

"That can't be," Kaddish said. He couldn't believe what he'd heard.

"I've killed many. I may have murdered your son along the way."

"You wouldn't admit it to me. You'd never say it."

"I told you at the start, I can't get myself punished. I've tried to tell my story to the world, and you're about the only one who'll listen."

"If it was true they'd disappear you also."

"It seems to be the opposite. They've left me as the town crier. I'm a fat, ugly drunk and a general disgrace. There will always be truth that escapes, and when you make lies into truth and truth into lies, people like me serve a purpose."

"What purpose is that?" Kaddish said, still not sure what to think.

"Exactly the one I'm serving now. So far-fetched, so impossible and unbelievable a claim, made by such a foul, stinking man"—here he smiled so his puffy gums showed—"and, more so, one who sleeps on the streets and lives off the fish that feed on the children, eating myself mad." He scratched furiously at his ear, as if he'd been bitten. "The government sees me as a treasure. I'm the man who tells their secret and out of whose mouth it sounds like a lie."

This Kaddish understood. "Then tell me how it's done."

"I'm not the only navigator. There is more than one plane, just as there is more than one prison or one city or one son. I can't tell you what goes on in their dungeons, I don't know what goes on under-ground beyond torture. I would wait in a plane on the runway. At night a bus would come, and off it marched the young people—they were almost always young, they were always naked, and they were drugged and on their way to passing out cold."

Kaddish gave no cues. He did not shake his head in disbelief or *tsk-tsk* or purse his lips. He waited for the navigator to go on.

The navigator stuck out his hand. He pushed it out over the railing and then swooped it right up toward the sky.

"We would take off," he said. "We flew out over the river. The pilot piloted. The navigator, which is me, has no real job when there is no real journey, so I'd go back into the hold, where there was a different guard each time—a single guard but always different, a way to put blood on a different person's hands. All in it together, all guilty just the same. It's harder to pass judgment when one must pass it on oneself."

Here Kaddish responded. "Yes," Kaddish said. "Then?"

"Then we'd throw them down into the river."

"All of them?" Kaddish said.

"Every last one. In the night. From the air to the river below. You couldn't see anything or hear anything over the engines, and they were always asleep. Sometimes I'd pretend to hear screaming. Always I'd believe I'd heard the impact, the breaking of bodies. From that height it isn't drowning that kills them, just hitting the water from that altitude at that speed—it pushes back with such force—it's water but it's like they've hit a brick wall."

"But you couldn't see?"

"But I know they're dead even without seeing, same as you."

"What if one were to wake?" Kaddish said.

"Wake and what?" he said, laughing, though it wasn't funny at all.

"What if one were to hit right and hit awake? What if one were to land in the cold water and land awake and swim away?"

"Wake and fly is what is needed. It's too far down and they fall too fast. If one of them knew how to fly, I'd say it's possible he's alive. None I ever saw was a flier, and only one awake. A very tough girl who did for me what I did for her. She ended any life I might have had left."

"Not in the same way, I'm guessing," Kaddish said. "She is not now standing on another pier with another father telling this same story."

He took out a cigarette. The navigator reached for one of his own but Kaddish was wearing his jacket. Fuck him, Kaddish thought, and shook another from the pack. He wasn't buying him breakfast but neither did he want a favor from this man. Kaddish would buy the story of his son's death for the price of a cigarette. He struck a match and slipped it between the navigator's cupped hands.

A puff, and the navigator said, "Pushing them out, it was terrible but it wasn't murder. It felt like discipline." He paused and gestured with his chin. Kaddish had nothing to add. "That girl, maybe she was stronger than the others, maybe she got a smaller dose of whatever they give them or had better resistance. My guess—not so scientific—is that she sensed death upon her. But then every one of them should have woken at the hatch. When I was pushing her out, her eyes opened up like she was startled. Her legs out, her body half out, and then the eyes, bigger than mine," he said, "they opened. She was practically airborne and she grabbed hold of my arm, she snatched my arm, and I screamed with holy terror, half out myself and on my way farther. The guard, he grabs my legs, and the girl has my arm, and it's life or death for both of us." The navigator gave his own cues. He stopped and shook his head. "I pulled those fingers, I broke her fingers, yanking them back—and then, like that, she drops. There was a flash, though, the two of us staring at each other, the girl in the air. And then gone. I was flat out on the floor of the plane, my arm hanging from its socket, my shoulder on fire, and I knew."

Kaddish made a questioning face. It was as much as he felt like giving.

"Sharing that stare, seeing her eyes, I knew—logical, a navigator by trade—rate of flying, rate of falling, wind and visibility, it couldn't have been an instant, definitely not long enough to see her judging, though I swear I did." The navigator put a hand to his shoulder and demonstrated its limited rotation, giving the shoulder a poor half turn. "I knew my arm would never go back right and I knew the same for my head. Both no good for anything past fishing. *That* girl, I murdered. I had to kill her before she killed me and it would follow, would it not, I had troubles, heavy troubles, trying to keep the lies as truth and the truth as lies and not recognizing what I was really doing from then on. Because I was sure of one thing: I didn't want to go out that hatch. Each time after, I knew."

"You're a murderer," Kaddish said.

"Yes," the navigator said. "A killer and a monster, and I can't live with it."

"I should kill you myself to put things right."

"I'd be obliged. A murderer, and yet too cowardly to take my own life—it makes me that much more guilty. Still, I'm braver than I was before. It's hard to admit such crimes."

"I can imagine," Kaddish said.

"Can you?" the navigator said. "It's only the first minutes."

"The first minutes of what?" Kaddish said.

"Of hearing the sound of them hitting," Wollensky said. "Your first minutes living life with that terrible noise in your head."

. . .

Rushing down the pier, raising his gaze higher, it was already as if the news had come from another place, so incongruous and overwhelming was the view of Buenos Aires spread out before him, tall buildings rising up, a span of city as boundless as the river. For this reason, to remind and solidify, to keep knowing what he knew, Kaddish kept shooting looks over his shoulder, Wollensky still in sight and backed by emptiness, vast unframed water and sky. Kaddish pushed a man out of his way and pushed into the Fisherman's Club. Picking up his pace, he felt someone's grip slip off him as he ran the last two steps and was out the front door and back into his city.

Kaddish stopped for a moment to catch his breath. He took hold of the wooden railing and watched a carpet of gray clouds, lined silver, roll reflected on the water. The clouds moved one way and the current faster in the other as it slipped under the pier, the sky losing ground.

A skinny old man in a raincoat dropped his bucket by Kaddish's feet and jammed a fishing pole in a space of rot between two planks. He held the hook in one hand and came up with a tiny *mojarrita* in the other. It was the raincoat that reminded Kaddish; he stuck out his arms, turned over his hands. The navigator's parka—he still had it on. Kaddish looked toward the club building and then, with a confused expression, looked at the old man. The old man gave Kaddish a friendly nod and then pulled the hook through the fish's eyes.

"They biting?" Kaddish said, the small talk surprising even him.

"Don't know yet," the man said. "What does it matter? The fisherman fishes whether they bite or not."

"I guess so," Kaddish said. The old man took up his rod and cast his line with a whistle. Kaddish thought of the hook and the navigator and the girl who snapped awake. He hugged the rail and tried to catch his own face in that mirror of water, but it was too far down. He turned his gaze back to the city rising up behind him. One day it's all fingers, Kaddish thought, and another everything is hook and eye.

[Thirty-eight]

KADDISH'S GOOD SUIT no longer buttoned but it still fit nice. He was showered and shaved, his shoes polished up with the shirt he'd spent the last days in, and, right before he hung a sheet over the bathroom mirror, he used its reflection to adjust his tie.

In the kitchen he took up a knife and went after the block of ice in the freezer, just enough chipped off to cool a drink. He toasted the air, drained his glass, and poured another full. He then took up the knife a second time and aimed it—with no intention of stabbing—at his heart. Lapel in hand, Kaddish made a cut with a sawing motion. He put the knife down and rent the fabric, giving a good tear.

This is how he did it, this is how it's always been done: a sign of mourning. He smoked a cigarette and waited for Lillian. He had a vague memory from a lesson of Talmud Harry's, and at one point, feeling foolish, he ashed the cigarette onto his head.

There was the thud of a bag dropped, heavier for having been dragged around all day. Lillian let out a groan as she hung up her coat. Neither the sound of the thud nor the echo of her despair came back with anything other than an empty-house feel, this despite Kaddish's presence there.

Lillian didn't start at the sight of her husband seated behind the little table in the kitchen. She noted the hair combed down and the clean-shaven cheeks, the smell of soap, and the suit he wore. "Have you wrapped yourself up like a gift for me to take you back?"

Kaddish, with head dropped, stared down at the table.

"Is it a party, then?" she said. "Should I get dressed up to celebrate your coming home?"

Kaddish raised his eyebrows and, as if that had generated the momentum, followed with his chin until his head tilted back.

Lillian looked down at him. There was a laxness to his skin that undermined all the grooming, and wet bloodshot eyes that were nothing but sad. With an open view of his broad chest, Lillian saw how the lapel hung down.

"No," she said.

"Dead," Kaddish told her. "I've spoken to a man."

Lillian stood up straighter, raised her own chin high. "Show me," she said. "Get up and take me." She grabbed the little table and pulled it to the side. The only thing on it, a glass, fell to the floor. Lillian covered her mouth. How sad Kaddish looked in the little chair. Not since their wedding, Lillian thought, Kaddish in a suit and a broken glass between them.

"There's nothing to show," he said. "Disappeared, the man said, is as it sounds. The children are gone for good."

"Who?" Lillian said. "What man?"

"The navigator," Kaddish said. "The man who tosses them from the planes."

Lillian forced her mouth into a smile.

"Now I get the suit," Lillian said. "Now I understand the celebration. With a husband who's forever wrong, with a man whose every promise comes apart, whose word is no good, whose beliefs always bring the opposite, and, if they don't, he's been telling lies . . . I get it now," Lillian said. "You're celebrating. Because even if you really think the worst has befallen him, it can mean nothing more, my Kaddish, than Pato is surely alive."

"Dead," Kaddish said. "I believe it."

Lillian brought her face right up to his.

"Not under this roof, husband. Under this roof Pato is still alive. In this house," Lillian said, "live a mother and a son who is soon to come home. What is hazy, what is still unclear, is if a father lives here too."

"How will it turn clear?" Kaddish said.

"If I can picture him with the mother waiting. If he is not waiting for the son to return, he is not not-waiting here."

It isn't fair, Kaddish thought. She couldn't be asking this of him.

"I'm in mourning," he said.

"No," Lillian said, waving a finger. "No, we aren't. I'm not. I'm not and you must decide. Waiting is the only option for under this roof. Waiting and wishing and helping to bring him home."

"You can't expect," Kaddish said. He stood to face her.

"I can," Lillian said. "I do. I've let you fail for a lifetime. And it's a lifetime's worth of expectations I've saved up. All for this, all for now."

Kaddish breathed the short breaths that precede tears.

"Don't," Lillian said. "Forbidden. You've already said what you believe. And I want you to know, you're thinking sick thoughts. Guilty thoughts. They contribute. They contribute to making real what is a lie."

"I spoke to the man," Kaddish said. "The navigator."

"Invisible claims," Lillian said.

Kaddish missed his son so dearly it was as if he hadn't been feeling a thing before. He didn't know what to do with Lillian's ultimatum, he only knew he couldn't face that pew again tonight, he couldn't wrap himself in that curtain and make it through until dawn. Of all the bad odds and long shots Kaddish had bet on, of all the good enterprises gone wrong, it seemed this was another deal he was making. Another deal with no other choice. So Kaddish leaned over and kissed his wife on the cheek, whispered into her ear. "Your roof, your rules," he said.

"Nothing less," Lillian said, kissing him back. "Only alive, Kaddish. It's the only way to keep it so."

Kaddish didn't know in that instant if he could believe a dead son alive, but he was sure he wouldn't make it without Lillian. And in a country where everyone was forced to live one lie, what did it hurt—for Lillian, for her sake and for his own—to try and live another?

Kaddish made his way to their bed and lay down fully dressed. It was worth it, he thought. He could manage it if, when Lillian slept, he could lie beside her, his arm around her, and think the truth. This is what he told himself, not knowing that Lillian did not sleep, that she'd never return to bed without her son.

Lillian went to the sink in the bathroom to brush the taste from her mouth. The sheet over the mirror startled her. She grabbed it in her fist and was about to tear it down, when, staring into the whiteness, she decided it was better. Pato's face, Lillian's face, they were both gone from that reflection. What was left for her to see that memory didn't better serve.

[Thirty-nine]

LILLIAN PRESSED MONEY into Kaddish's hand and rolled her fingers closed around his. She said, "You and I can live on our worries. A guest might need more to eat. Frida's coming by. How about we have steaks?" When Kaddish nodded, she said, "Make sure at least one is a decent cut."

They were already behind on rent. They didn't have a single job between them. And the night after he'd come home declaring Pato dead, she was digging into the money he'd left on the table and catering for a guest. "A bottle of wine," she said, as the elevator dropped. Kaddish kept his eyes straight ahead. A voice from above.

Kaddish went to the butcher's and the butcher wasn't there. His daughter, who sometimes worked the register, wore his apron. It nearly wrapped around her twice.

Kaddish had been shopping there forever and he'd never found the store open without the butcher, Julián, there to greet him, plodding over, a pair of giant flat feet slapping around behind the counter.

What to say in these days when nothing was said, when health or holiday were not assumptions, when only one conclusion was drawn? Kaddish couldn't imagine what trouble a butcher might have got himself into. No more or less, he figured, than had his son.

Looking at her face, looking around the empty place, it seemed the situation was as he'd thought. The butcher disappeared and his customers along with him. And how many, like Kaddish, coming in, taking note, still walked up to the counter as if this always was?

Kaddish listened to what—even to his ear—sounded like a dull cleaver, the woman fracturing bones as if by malice. Her lips were pressed tight as she hacked. Kaddish knew what was in her mind. Each one a general, he was sure.

He peered over to see the cuts of meat, terrible and rough. He thought the steaks might come apart before she got the wax paper closed. Another student for Mazursky, this one. Ready for her first nose.

Kaddish nodded to the daughter. He ordered three steaks.

As he turned to leave, he had a change of heart. Maybe an attempt at solidarity was in order, maybe he could say something nice. Kaddish did nothing more than stand there. It wasn't that his mind went blank. It was that, after the navigator, the only thing he could say to her was, *He's dead. Your father's not coming home.* That wasn't Kaddish's job. He wasn't the grim reaper. Once a day, announcing death, was already too much.

A car ground its engine in the street. Kaddish clenched the change tighter as if Lillian still held his hand closed. He opened the door with his hip, the bottle of wine he carried banging hard against it.

The walk home was used for hating Frida. What kind of person would let herself be fed by those left desolate? What kind of friend would let the mother of a disappeared son—without money or prospects—treat her to steaks and a bottle of wine?

Kaddish wore the navigator's parka and his suit jacket underneath. The torn lapel no longer hung down. Lillian had made him stitch it back right. Only the sheets stayed over the mirrors, which was good for a man who couldn't look himself in the eye.

For all Kaddish's thinking that Frida should know better, he got home to discover that Frida did.

"You're our guest," Lillian was saying. "A pleasure, when pleasures have gone rare."

Frida was shaking her head and unpacking what she'd brought. The smells had already reached Kaddish and his stomach growled.

"Steaks," Kaddish said. He lifted up the wrong hand, showing them the wine.

"You save those steaks for another night," Frida said. "Make another meal out of it. Maybe Pato will be back in time to join you."

"Let it be so," Lillian said. "Amen," as if it had been a prayer.

With Frida there and food brought, Kaddish felt like it was a condolence call. It pained him physically that it wasn't. He stepped forward and kissed Frida on both cheeks. They had always loved each other, Kaddish and Frida. They hugged and it was warm.

Lillian reached into one of Frida's bags and came up with a deep dish of chicken and rice. Uncovering it on the table, she plucked a green pea and popped it into her mouth. "Who comes to dinner with dinner?" Lillian said.

"A much better cook, that's who."

Frida brought out a bottle of milk, two-thirds empty and still cold.

"For my tea," she said.

She went back to unpacking, unchallenged. Batata and pickles, a dented pear, and, from the bottom, a tray of empanadas, one with a bite in its side.

"I got hungry wrapping it up," Frida said. She rubbed at her belly. "It's a dangerous thing to be impressed with one's own cooking. There is a price to pay."

Lillian took the empanada with the bite missing and, considering it, sunk her teeth right on top of the ridge Frida had left, bite over bite.

With Kaddish's chair pulled up to the table, a glass of wine before him, and sweet Frida putting a buttered roll on each of their plates, Kaddish already thought he would break. His shoulders rose and fell in two quick heaves. He tried very hard not to, though he thought he might cry.

Lillian, who would not brook it, raised her voice louder, told her story faster, pulling Frida's gaze. Kaddish sniffed and wiped his nose. He was fine being boxed out of the conversation, absorbed as he was in marking the end of Pato's first day passed. Kaddish took a sip of his wine. And thinking of his son, surely dead, and picturing the navigator, who knew it was so, and staring at Lillian, who hadn't believed him, and hating a government that would deny Pato had been, Kaddish recognized also that this was the end of the first day for him alone.

Lillian's fork scraped against her teeth. Frida ate an empanada, catching crumbs in a palm held under her chin. How much different was this dinner, he thought, than the one at the general's? Was it any better to sit here and talk of Pato in prison or swallow that man's oysters while he claimed Pato was sunning on some beach? It filled Kaddish with such rage and so much guilt he thought to flip the table. Not wanting to, knowing also that what Lillian did was out of heartache, Kaddish only wished he'd slit the general's throat when he'd had the chance. He should've taken the knife that pricked that woman's finger and used it to split her in two, exposing the black pearl she must have instead of a heart.

"I'm going to hold Feigenblum's feet to the fire," is what Lillian told Frida. "The Jews will put Pato on their list. And then there's the newspapers. Each and every one will come to our aid. A front-page story on Pato disappeared, and let them run a banner when there's news of his return."

The thought of a Poznan begging favors from the Jews put a shame on top of Kaddish's sorrow. He finally had something to add. "If the other Jewish council had flourished," he said, "if the Benevolent Self had made it instead of Feigenblum and his friends—and it could as easily have happened—this would have been over and done with at the start."

"The other Jewish council?" Lillian said. "Yes, I'm sure a board made up of pimps and alfonses would have an amazing amount of pull."

"If Talmud Harry were alive, or Shlomo the Pin, if Beryl Brass-Balls or any of the caftans who ran the Benevolent Self were around, there'd be broken knees between here and Ushuaia and enough dirty secrets to put the whole junta down. Pato would've been back the first evening," Kaddish said. "If it was the other way, I'd have fixed it in an instant. A single call. All I would've had to do was pick up the phone."

Frida smiled into her plate.

"But it's not the other way," Lillian said. "It's this way. And I'm going to get to everyone but the doctor. The one useless man with power, I leave for you."

Kaddish had been brought low by this dinner. How much worse if Frida also knew that to keep his wife, to keep his home, he'd been made to betray his son? He tried to read his secret on her. What else of his name-chipping *hijo-de-puta* life had she been told?

"Do you know?" Kaddish said to Frida.

Frida said, "What?"

She waited for an explanation while Kaddish stared at her, looking for a sign. When he turned to Lillian he found her jaw set forward and a rage to match his own. "I can't do this," he said.

"Fine," she said, so quickly Kaddish wasn't sure he'd even spoken.

He looked back to Frida. He was going to tell her the truth. Let Frida hear what he had to say about Pato, and let her decide which one of them she wanted to believe. But Lillian had been his wife a long time. Lillian knew him better than anyone else in the world.

"Don't say it," she said, "don't dare." Lillian reached out and grabbed his wrist. "You can't take certain things back," she said.

Kaddish nodded and went to the bedroom for his tools. He put a sweater on under his suit jacket and over it he put on the navigator's coat. The suit was tight already. With the sweater underneath and the jacket above, Kaddish's arms didn't touch his body.

Seeing Lillian's purse on the bureau, he couldn't help himself. Kaddish rifled through and took a few hundred-peso notes. It was only fair, this dipping into her wallet. He was leaving her the apartment (at least until they were tossed out) and the money from the last job, and he trusted that Lillian always had cash squirreled away. On his way out, Kaddish stopped at the table. Lillian didn't interrupt the conversation to acknowledge he was there. She wasn't going to give him a second chance to announce that Pato was dead. Anyway, pretending Kaddish wasn't there was no great feat. It was the easiest thing in Argentina to effect.

"I bet Gustavo doesn't lose any sleep," is what Lillian said to Frida.

"No," Frida said, "not a wink." She laughed nervously, and gave Kaddish a sidelong glance.

Kaddish reached right in between them. He took the bottle of wine from the table. Lillian didn't acknowledge this either. So Kaddish shuffled off with his tool bag and headed out their always open door.

Kaddish stopped at his kiosk on the way to the car. He put the bottle on the counter while he fished out some cash. It was a windy night and the tears in his eyes—for Pato and for Lillian and for the thought of leaving—could easily have been from the weather. Kaddish raised four fingers, the money pressed into his palm with a thumb. The kiosk man nodded and Kaddish shifted the weight of the tool bag, keeping it close to his body.

The kiosk man moved the bottle of wine over and plunked down four packs of Jockeys. Two and two.

He said to Kaddish, *"¿Qué tal, Flaco?"*

How's it going, Skinny?

And, as always, Kaddish answered, *"Bien."*

It's going good.

[Forty]

DESPITE BEING CALLED A LIAR, despite feeling like a failure, despite the terrible things that had driven him back to that Benevolent Self pew, Kaddish wondered if his intentions shouldn't count for more. He'd always meant well, even if lacking motivation and short on success. Thinking this thought through, he had to admit his logic was shaky. The navigator, Kaddish knew, would claim the same. A man who'd meant the best with each one, with every last body he'd fed to the sea.

But this wasn't his real concern. It was a momentary deception natural to a man already in the midst of what he couldn't bear to do. To act brought with it a great dread for Kaddish. It was a shame that much more shameful when it forced him to betray the principles that protected him and to break with the picture that defined him. He found himself driven to take comforts he swore he'd never seek.

Kaddish Poznan dropped off his pew and dropped to his knees. He pressed his forehead to the floor of the Benevolent Self and, banging his fists, raising up dust, Kaddish let out a wail. . . .

And he prayed.

[Forty-one]

THESE ARE THE THINGS Kaddish did not pray for: He did not pray for permission or for guidance, he did not pray for forgiveness or for help, he did not ask for a sign or for solace, he did not beseech on anyone's behalf. And though Kaddish turned to a God above, he did not wish for a heaven to house Him. For there is shame also in man's weak imaginings, always eyes and eyes and eyes endlessly peering, as if there is no privacy to be had, as if entering heaven would bring no greater understanding, no context or comprehension, as if every motion of every earthly being is eternally scrutinized by every dead mother and dead son.

This is why a man in deepest despair might fight it, why Kaddish— born into a world for the sole purpose, it seemed, of being kept out— would never dare turn to God as he currently did. Because he did not want to worry that the doctor might walk in and tease him, that the rabbi might walk in and own him, that all the dead from all time, all those with chipped names and those without, might hear his supplications and think that Kaddish Poznan had suffered so much he'd finally seen the light. It's a bully's heaven we have been given, a coercive place where all the self-righteous float around judging, voyeurs with wings.

All in all, it was not very much and not very long, and—in the way the head works and the way grief works and the way Kaddish himself worked—barely a prayer at all.

With knees on the floor and head on the floor and fists at his sides, all that passed, all that was directed, the little bit aimed at God (if it were even spoken) would have sounded like nothing more than this:

"Pato, my Pato, my son."

The guard wasn't supposed to acknowledge Lillian, and yet when she tried to file into the ministry that next morning, he stopped her at the door. "You're not supposed to," she said, and her jaw went so tense there was an audible pop. The guard put the heel of his hand against Lillian's chest. He gave her a shove that served to spin her around and motioned to the café across the way. "He said to wait for him there." Lillian rubbed at her chest, and when she looked back the guard had melted into the crowd.

Lillian and the priest strolled along the avenue that fed into the Plaza de Mayo. It reminded Lillian of her mornings before the tanks rolled in and the boy soldiers were posted to the corners, clips loaded in their guns. They'd been walking for some time and Lillian wasn't even sure if she was leading or following. When she could, Lillian chose a turn that led to the ministry, and then on one street or another she'd found they'd turned back.

"May I ask," Lillian said, "if we're headed in any particular direction?"

"I'm a clergyman," he said. "I've got countless homilies at the ready when it comes to choosing a path." He steered them toward the center of the plaza. He chewed at his lip.

"I used to love this place," Lillian said. "Crossing it was my favorite part of the day."

"And now the buildings have turned sinister for you?"

"It feels like a Roman coliseum," Lillian said. "And the government has taken all the seats. They've left the whole country in with the lions."

"I'm part of that government," the priest said. "At best, in your analogy, I come out of it a lion."

"It can't hurt to have one on my side." Lillian tried to catch his eye. "I'm assuming you're on my side. Why else would you be here? Unless you plan on eating me yet."

"That's the catch when dealing with a dangerous creature. It all boils down to trust."

"You have mine," Lillian said, without hesitation. "I'll do anything. I will."

"You shouldn't make such a promise until you know what's being asked."

"For my son, I'll do anything. You can't ask too much."

"Go home," the priest said.

"That's it?"

"Write down the boy's name, write down your address, and go home and wait for me there."

The priest studied the pictures on the wall in Lillian's apartment. Again he had her glasses perched on his nose. Lillian thought it sweet, the way he pointed at her likeness or Pato's, mumbling to himself, his head darting round.

"It is a lovely apartment and a warm home that you've built."

"It doesn't feel so warm these days."

"That doesn't disappear. It lingers for your son to come home to." The priest smiled. "Is this where he was raised? Did you buy it long ago?"

"We should have. We've been renting for twenty years."

"Renting?" the priest said, and turned back to the photos, pointing at one. In it Pato had his feet and hands spread apart, reaching across the narrow corridor in which the priest now stood. Pato was literally climbing the walls of the apartment.

"Always up to mischief," Lillian said, and then she led the priest to her chair. She served him tea and put out a plate of cut sausage and the last of Frida's empanadas. They were the only viable things in the kitchen and she'd arranged them as best she could. The priest shifted in his seat. He held the tea but didn't drink. Lillian thought the fidgeting was hopeful, a sincere sign of a person feeling torn.

The priest looked out the window. "If you were a couple of floors higher, you'd be able to see the Pink House from here."

"The very heart of the city," Lillian said.

"Can I ask you a Jewish question? I've always been interested."

"I'm not too well versed but you can try."

"Why do you live here?" he said.

She was wondering if he meant Argentina and, already insulted, she said, "Where? I'm not sure what you mean."

"In the heart of the city," he said. "I'm not an expert on Jews either, but I know enough of your history. We live in a vast country that reaches to the very end of the earth, and most of the Jews live in this neighborhood, meters away from the seat of power, at the mouth of the basin into which this whole country flows."

"Why wouldn't we?"

"You tell me. For a people that doesn't want to assimilate, that wants to avoid vice and temptation, for a nation formed while roaming forty years in the desert, why didn't you walk a little farther? Why did the Jews of Buenos Aires drop their bags and build their lives wherever the boat dropped them ashore? It wouldn't have been so hard to join your gaucho cousins in the North. There was a fine Jerusalem being built there, an uncontested unmolested Jerusalem in Argentina where the Jews might have thrived. Staying here makes no sense when trouble seems to find you too easily as it is."

"You don't really think that," Lillian said.

"I do indeed. So many times nearly destroyed, one would think you'd look for a place where you wouldn't draw attention, and always you choose a place where you will."

"You think we suffocate the Pink House with our presence? Do you think the generals turn their own selves pink trying to breathe while we suck all the air up with our giant collective Jewish nose?"

"I wanted to know and I asked. You get yourselves mixed up in politics and the newspapers. It's either the heart of the city or the heart of the matter. What doesn't make sense to a bystander is this Jewish hunger, this compass like a pigeon's for putting yourselves in the center of things."

"I'm not really sure it's the fly's fault when it gets eaten by a frog."

"You make yourselves proximal, and for that there's no one else to blame."

"If others court tragedy, let them. Get me my son and I'll move to a mountaintop tomorrow. I'll take him straight to Jujuy."

"Yes," the priest said. "Let's talk about Pato. You should be warned that everything I offer can come to nothing. And even if there are good people involved in this enterprise, many are not. Some are as hungry for money as you are for your son. Think of how far they'll go."

"There are people to deal with, though?"

"There are, for a fee. Every last cent of it will go toward a bribe. It's all dirty dealings from here."

"I understand," Lillian said.

"There's one more thing. Engrossed as we are with your problems, I maintain a set of worries of my own. If we're to do this, I can't have you around. That means you stay away from me completely and away from the ministry where I work."

"I can't go to the Ministry of Special Cases?"

"I've never met anyone yet who was upset to hear that. But, no," the priest said. "If you want me to help, then for everyone's sake you need to stay away. At this stage, even if I manage to get some information it'll be very little. If the money gets into the right hands, it may be possible to find out where your son is and how he fares and no more."

Lillian's mouth fell open. She tried not to scream. She went over and grabbed the priest's face in two hands, squeezing as she had squeezed Kaddish's on the night Pato was taken. She did it with the same fervor—but, happy now, with joy—and she leaned in and kissed the priest on both cheeks. "How much?" Lillian said, letting him go.

"It's always too much, and that's how it will be every step of the way."

"Anything. I'll pay any price."

"You mustn't say that," the priest said. "They'll ask. And negotiations can be long." Here he stopped himself. "It's better that you don't hope. It's better that we first find out where Pato is and confirm he's alive."

"More?" Lillian said. "There are other steps? Other hopes to have?"

"Let's first do this," the priest said, patting the air, trying to be calming.

Lillian knew every last peso she had in the house and imagined that it still wouldn't be enough. She made the rounds collecting. There was a stocking with a roll of bills in the bedroom and, in the kitchen, the tin under the sink. In the living room, she pulled out one of Pato's books, money fluttering as she shook it from the leaves. Finally she went over to the scalloped shelf and brought over Kaddish's gold. This the priest put right into his jacket. Then they sat on the couch together and counted.

"Not enough?" Lillian said.

"No, not really," the priest said.

"It's all I have," Lillian said. And then remembering, slapping her head, she emptied the contents of her purse. "I can call my friend Frida if you need more this second. She'll be able to get."

"I hate to say this, but maybe we shouldn't bother starting. I'd assumed that a Jew would be a homeowner—that there'd be collateral of some sort. Tactless as it sounds, if you're already emptying your purse, what do we do if things progress afoot? What if we were discussing, say, buying freedom, how will you get more? We're talking about serious sums."

"It could go that far—where we could buy him back?"

"It could," the priest said.

"I'll manage anything. Truly." Lillian knew she was being tested, and she knew she had to lie. "My boss is very powerful now," Lillian said. "You wouldn't believe the business he does. He has resources. From him I could get any amount—we're like family. He thinks of Pato as his own son." The priest looked skeptical, and Lillian began naming the new clients: factory owners, diplomats, the general, and the judge.

"For now, though," Lillian said, "for this part, is it enough?" She pointed at the money.

The priest waved her away. "I'll make them take this. I'll make them understand."

"Thank you," she said. "It's really everything. Please tell them it's the truth."

Lillian picked up the money and put it in order. She then pressed the fat roll into his hands. The priest stood up to receive it. He pushed the money down into his left pocket. As he did so, he pulled his own wallet out from his right.

"Let me give you something to tide you over," he said.

"No, I couldn't."

"I insist. You'll pay me back one day, I know it. I'll come," he said proudly, "and collect it from Pato if need be."

"You're too generous," Lillian said, "too kind."

"A small contribution," he said, handing her two crisp green American twenties. "We must all bear this burden together."

[Forty-two]

KADDISH DROVE TO THE UNITED JEWISH Congregations building intending to punch Feigenblum as hard as he possibly could in the face, this somehow as a message to Lillian, though Kaddish would have been hard pressed to say what the message was. Feigenblum, lucky for him, didn't exit the building while Kaddish was idling outside. From there he drove to Rafa's mother's, thinking she could answer the difficult questions he had. When she wouldn't let him in, Kaddish leaned his head against the doorframe, and didn't exactly heave, nor would he say he cried, but made some ugly motion, a broken breath and whine. He'd run out of cigarettes and didn't have a cent to buy them, and the maddening craving further aggravated his despair. All together Kaddish had the distinct sense, maybe the only thing clear to him, that he was losing his mind.

Kaddish went back to the car. He turned the key and pumped the pedals and couldn't get the engine to turn over. Out of gas and out of money, he abandoned the car and walked to his apartment. Kaddish paced in the street below, looking up at the window where Lillian always sat. He wanted her to look down and take comfort in one of her boys coming home. He wanted her to see he was no longer taking liberties. He was waiting for an invitation, nothing at all assumed or believed beyond the one thing that couldn't be undone.

Kaddish cursed at a passing car that forced him from the center of the street. He stood on the sidewalk looking wounded and then went around the corner to peer back with stealth; Lillian might show herself if she thought he was gone. And she did. Kaddish saw her immediately. That is, he saw a sign of her. The lamp in the living room was now off, and only a moment before it had been turned on. Though, thinking about it, he couldn't really remember seeing it lit and might even remember noting it was off. He still took it as proof of Lillian's presence, reconciling the disparity with the knowledge that he was going mad—the awareness of which filled him with a kind of ease. It neutralized the confusion in his certainty that he'd seen two opposing things. How nice to hold in his head both the belief that he'd seen the lamp turned off and at the same time the one-hundred-percent conviction that it hadn't been on. How easily accommodated he was.

Hands shoved into pockets, Kaddish rolled up onto his toes. He gave a whistle and tried to appear nonchalant as he returned to his original position in the middle of the street. He could tell Lillian was watching him from her chair, watching and ignoring, watching and cursing him. When it became too much, he cursed back up at her and, because Frida might well be up there, he cursed her too. Kaddish threw pebbles at the window. Never once hitting it, he managed to draw some of his neighbors to their own. They pulled curtains aside, and not one of them waved. All of them fuckers. "Fuck you," he called. "Sister fuckers," and "Mother fuckers," and, oddly, cursing those fuckers felt like the least crazy bit of it all, because those blind and silent and complacent motherfuckers couldn't see him or hear him just like they hadn't seen his son. But Kaddish had no time to focus on them. He had a question for Lillian, the same one he'd wanted to ask Rafa's mother, and Feigenblum (after he punched him hard in the face), and the doctor, and the navigator the same. It was critical that he ask it, and he wished any of them had answered. Kaddish more than anything did not want to ask the one man who knew best.

A neighbor too cowardly to show himself screamed down to Kaddish, "Poznan, come in already or go." Rude as it was, Kaddish accepted it as sound advice. He knew Lillian wasn't home, that she wasn't either watching or teasing or sitting in her chair at the window ignoring. He also knew she was and that she'd never call down.

It took madness, he felt, for two conflicting realities to exist at once. For Lillian and Kaddish in Argentina, it also did not. Everything and its opposite. As in the case of a son that is both living and dead.

By prying up the staples that ran along the baseboard and unscrewing the jack, Lillian had freed enough cable to get the telephone to the table so she could join Frida there. Frida had protested when Lillian was down on hands and knees pulling staples up with a screwdriver, but Lillian kept saying, "A celebration," tempered as it was. Lillian had asked Frida to bring over ham sandwiches and beer. That's what she wanted, actual cravings. Lillian hadn't wanted something for herself in so long.

Aside from the telephone and the beer, Lillian had put what little jewelry she had out on the table. There was also a small bronze statue from India that Gustavo had once given her; she was convinced it had some value though Frida wasn't sure. "You can sell it all for me," Lillian said. She added her wedding ring to the pile and put her car keys on top. "I don't know where the car is, Kaddish has it. You hold the keys, though, and then, if I find where it is you can go get it and sell that too."

"That's a plan," Frida said, thinking that it wasn't. She opened her mouth two different times, trying to figure a way to say it and missing the opportunity. Lillian launched into the story again.

There was the short version of the priest's call, as well as the walls-have-ears rendition, full of "*my* friend" and "*your* friend" and meticulously avoiding any damnable phrasing regarding money or detention centers or contacts inside. Both of Lillian's accounts ended with the critical, "He's alive." Frida practically swooned at the news each time, while Lillian repeated the story in a loop, giddy with the telling. That part was pure delight. It was the rest of Lillian's response that Frida wasn't sure how to process. The priest had told Lillian to stay by the phone and she'd agreed. That Lillian was willing to turn her whole brave search into cradling that phone in her lap and hiding out at home, Frida couldn't believe. This was what she most wanted to say, and she knew Lillian wasn't going to let her.

Lillian could see the way Frida was seeing her. So Lillian fed Frida sensible, grounded thoughts at intervals. At the end of each telling, Lillian expressed either skepticism or concern. "I know he's not safe yet," Lillian would say. Or, "These are very shady people. I don't even know where he's being held."

Shady people, Frida knew, did not include the priest.

When it was time to leave, Frida gave Lillian everything she had in her wallet. Lillian didn't hesitate in taking it, a sign of their friendship. Neither did Frida protest about taking the jewelry and the statue and the keys. She left the ring for last. "Are you sure?" she said. Lillian was. Frida slipped it on her finger, pressing it up against her own wedding band.

Frida hadn't said enough and—her last chance—she did no better than asking Lillian, "What's next?"

"Pato home," was her answer.

"The priest said that?"

"No, I'm saying it. The priest said he could maybe do more and maybe he couldn't."

Frida wondered how, in a hundred tellings, this part had escaped untold.

"Then why sit and wait like this?" Frida said.

"It's nothing to worry about. That's how he talks. No promises made, no results guaranteed. Even if nothing happens, he said to be by the phone—because at nothing we might only get one chance."

A beautiful girl with a skirt to the floor led Kaddish through an apartment not much different from his. A granddaughter, Kaddish supposed, or maybe "great" even; it was possible when he considered all the years gone by. He couldn't believe the girl let him in looking as he did, though, sweeping her skirt behind her, she kept an eye.

The girl poked her head into what looked like a study. She stood on the threshold nodding and then answered in Yiddish. Not since childhood had Kaddish heard a lovely young woman speak it so well.

The rabbi stood in the study's entrance, practically panting with upset.

"Vandal!" the rabbi said. "How do you come into my house?" The statement gained gravity as the rabbi stared and sniffed and took a step back, further startled by the condition of the Kaddish in front of him.

"I have a request," Kaddish said.

"Do you want me to hire you? Are you off to Europe to knock down my parents' graves? Done already, I promise. The job done free of charge." The young girl looked fraught. The rabbi signaled to her and, obedient, she retreated down the hall.

"A second favor," Kaddish said. "I've come to ask it."

"A second favor? From me? I don't even know about the first."

"For my mother. You came to Talmud Harry's. You gave me my name."

"That favor was for her, not for you. Even if—how do you merit a second?"

"Merit?" Kaddish said. "You're a rabbi, not a king. A Jew comes to you respectfully—"

"Not any Jew," the rabbi said.

"No. A Jew you punished for the sin of being born and then excommunicated for refusing to forget from where he came. Now we're going to balance the scales. I need your advice," Kaddish said, "that's the favor. I don't know what to do when one is without."

"Without what?" the rabbi said, no patience from the start.

"Without a body," Kaddish said. This was the question he'd wanted to ask all day, a version prepared for his wife and Rafa's mother, for Feigenblum and the navigator, for each one a different facet of the problem that was eating at him. He wanted to know how to make a funeral when there wasn't a son.

The rabbi took a better look at Kaddish's face, at the scruff and dirt, and, under his filthy parka, the worn and filthy suit. Here he saw the lapel Kaddish had torn a second time, and he looked back up into Kaddish's eyes.

The rabbi stepped aside and motioned into the study. Kaddish went. It was a room like Pato's: narrow, a desk where the bed would go, and, covering half the window at the end, a bookshelf full of books. What Kaddish wouldn't have expected, what he hadn't noticed, was the music. Behind the rabbi was a turntable spinning and an opera playing. There was no second chair in the room and the rabbi offered his. Kaddish fell into it and stared, bewildered, toward the music as if he could see it in the air.

"It's to be appreciated," the rabbi said, reading Kaddish's surprise. "The overture to *Die Meistersinger*. A gift from God"—and he held up a finger—"a gift from God through man. The music is not the person, I also deeply believe. But that's a discussion for another time."

Kaddish nodded, as if to say it was for another time, or to acknowledge the beauty of the music, or simply a reflex, utterly numb.

"I'm in mourning," Kaddish said, "for my son."

The rabbi rushed out the blessing, *baruch dayan emes*. What else but death could have brought this man into his home? He said, "I'm sorry. I hadn't heard."

"Would it have made a difference?"

"It would," the rabbi said, fully somber. "I would have made a shiva call if I knew you'd been sitting."

"I have nowhere to sit," Kaddish said. "I carry the grief around with me."

Already confused, the rabbi didn't think this an actual physical claim. He was more interested right then in learning where the grave was. He hadn't heard from the burial society and wondered if Kaddish's son was laid to rest as a Jew.

"Where's the boy buried?" he said.

"The junta," Kaddish said. "They are murdering the children. This country runs out of control."

The rabbi straightened up and lifted the needle from the record and whispered, "You're forbidden to hear music at such a time." He twisted and retwisted the tip of his beard. Letting go, it held its form for a few seconds and then untwined. "The wife," he said, "your Lillian. I can still make a visit if the shiva is done."

"There's no need to visit," Kaddish said. "She wouldn't appreciate it."

"There is an unfortunate history between us," the rabbi said.

"Not because of that," Kaddish said. "Because to her the boy, our Pato, is alive."

"Alive?" the rabbi said. What other choice was there but flabbergasted? This was not a conversation of which one could make sense. Reformulating, the rabbi asked, "How can a mother deny that her son is dead?"

"It's very sad," Kaddish said. "I feel the same way."

"At the funeral," the rabbi said (still curious about where the boy was buried), "she must have acknowledged the loss in some way."

"It's about the funeral that I'm here. We haven't yet had one. And I'm unsure," Kaddish said, "exactly how to do it. I turn to you, painful for me as that is."

"How no funeral? Where's the body?"

"Disappeared," Kaddish said. "They toss the bodies—" and here Kaddish bit at his thumbnail, looking distraught. "Not bodies," he said. "Still living, they toss them from airplanes down into the river. There will never be a body, but a funeral is his right."

"I don't understand," the rabbi said, no judgment in it. "If there's no body, how do you know he's dead? How," the rabbi said, slow and careful, "how do you know your wife is wrong and you are right?"

"How do I know?" Kaddish said. He hadn't expected such a question. "The navigator told me—the fisherman. I spoke to the man who did it, the one who throws the children from the planes."

"A fisherman did this to your Pato?"

"He might as well have," Kaddish said. "Of those he murdered, it's possible Pato may have been among them."

"So there's no proof?" the rabbi said. His voice rose up in the asking. Again, it was without judgment. The rabbi was trying only to grasp.

"This is the way in which it's Argentine," Kaddish said, now animated, eyes open wide. "It's neat and it's clean and, more than anything, it's well-mannered. The whole country turns away, as if they've caught the government with something in its teeth. It's become crass even to acknowledge the loss," Kaddish said. "You don't think it impolite, I hope, that my son has been made dead?"

The rabbi began to mutter a *baruch shem kavod.* It wasn't a second *bracha,* it was instead the line mustered to undo the erroneous blessing. The rabbi dared not let a prayer over the death of a child stand when he thought the boy might live.

What other conclusion could the rabbi draw, listening to this madness, talking to this madman, a son of a whore who always made trouble, who was born to it and now stood before him, filthy and stinking and wearing—Vashti-like—all his ugliness on the outside?

It was no struggle choosing whom to trust between Kaddish and his pitiable wife.

"She waits for him?" the rabbi said. "Lillian believes you're wrong?"

"She doesn't wait. She searches and searches. Admirable behavior," Kaddish said, "if Pato were alive, if there were a boy to find."

"And there's no way you can see her side?" the rabbi said. "That it is good what she, as a mother, does?"

"The way in which she is right is that she demands to see a body. And the way in which she's wrong is that there isn't one to find."

"Maybe," the rabbi said, "you're wrong in not waiting."

"Me? I'm the same as always. Not right or wrong, only deficient," Kaddish said, "forever falling short. But this one thing, a father to a dead son without a son to weep over. This is an absence that's not right and not fair."

"What am I to do?" the rabbi said. "I can't produce him."

"I'm not a fool," Kaddish said. "I'm not asking for a miracle. Only advice. How without a body do I make a resting place for my son? You tell me not to leave my house during the first week of mourning, and I tell you, without a grave, the mourning never ends."

"Abandon the mourning," the rabbi said. "Go back to your wife. She's a sensible woman, Poznan. It sounds like she does the right thing."

Kaddish wanted to scream.

"How do you perpetually side against me, Rabbi? I come here alone and I give you the facts. I tell you my story and that Lillian is wrong and, as if it's the only conclusion that can be drawn, you tell me she's right."

"Maybe you tell a different story than you think."

"A grave," Kaddish said. "A funeral."

"Are you going to persist with this? You can't leave the dead alone and now you fiddle with the living. When will you turn serious, Poznan? You've said it yourself already, there can be no funeral without the son. Be thankful. Be thankful that you don't have him, that there's still hope."

"How much more serious can I be," Kaddish said, "if I'm willing to come to you?"

"Serious or insane? I admit, I'm distressed at the sight of you."

"Isn't that proof enough? Isn't this exactly how I should look in my predicament? Have mercy on me, Rabbi. I'm not asking you to agree, only to tell me how to make a funeral without the son?"

The rabbi put a hand on top of his big black yarmulke and slid it forward. When he could formulate no conciliatory answer he dropped his hand. The rabbi looked down his nose at Kaddish, the silk edge of his yarmulke reaching to the middle of his forehead.

"You can't dig a grave," the rabbi said, "without something to put in it. Beyond Jewish law, it's basic logic. A grave must hold something if it's to be a grave. Otherwise it's just a hole filled in."

"You can do better. There must be more."

"You would need—" the rabbi said, and then stopped himself. He was not, God forbid, talking about Pato specifically, a boy who possibly lived. "*One,*" the rabbi said. "To have a funeral, to dig a grave, *one* would need something to put in it. Not even a whole body. Even a finger is enough."

Kaddish raised an eyebrow and leaned in as if trying better to hear what had already been said. He rolled his eyes as if considering and then the lids above them began to flutter. The rabbi was convinced it was some sort of attack and pressed a hand to his own heart in the witnessing. He then called Kaddish's name so loudly and with such panic that, at the sound of it, his granddaughter came running.

When she arrived she was startled to find her grandfather beside Kaddish gently stroking his hair. "*Shhh,*" the rabbi said. But Kaddish wasn't hearing. He was very busy thinking. He was right then remembering what he'd had and what he'd left: Pato's fingertip as if it were reaching, sticking up out of the sand. The one time God had blessed him and Kaddish was too blind to see it. Had he kept that fingertip, Kaddish would have had his one miracle and Pato his grave. Everything always done wrong.

The rabbi kept on with his shushing and, with a glance to the girl, said, "It will be all right." The girl moved back into the hallway, still watching, and the rabbi said to Kaddish, "But you must go home."

"I can't," Kaddish said, shaking his head, shaking the rabbi off.

Even if Kaddish was willing to go home, the rabbi didn't think anyone, even Lillian, could be expected to take such a specimen back.

"When did you last eat?" the rabbi said.

"Cigarettes," was Kaddish's answer. The rabbi arched his head, catching the eye of the lingering girl.

"Go get cigarettes," he said.

The girl looked at her grandfather, her face blank.

"Jockey," Kaddish said. "Any kiosk. All of them sell."

The girl didn't acknowledge him.

"Go," the rabbi said. "Do what he said."

The intensity had waned and the rabbi couldn't say why he felt another touch was in order. Still, he reached out.

"You must eat," the rabbi said. He turned and dropped the needle back onto the album. Kaddish ignored the message in this, closing his eyes and listening to the music. "You can sleep it off," the rabbi said. "We'll put a blanket and a pillow on the floor in here. Rest tonight and tomorrow you'll go home."

Kaddish rocked forward and back in the chair. He squeezed his eyes so tightly they burned and he ground his teeth together to keep back the tears, because never ever had he not been sent away.

In the morning Kaddish stood before the rabbi, fed and cleaned and rested. Even in his beaten suit and stocking feet, he was much improved.

The rabbi was slipping his tallis back in its bag and offered Kaddish his tefillin. Kaddish shook his head, no.

"You've had enough to eat?" the rabbi said.

Kaddish nodded.

The rabbi pointed at Kaddish's socks. "We wear shoes in this house," he said. Worse, catching sight of that re-torn lapel without the parka to cover it, the rabbi knew it would not do.

"Let me give you a change of clothes."

"I'm fine," Kaddish said, but the granddaughter was called and given orders. She stared openly from her grandfather's stomach to Kaddish's gut.

"It'll be a tight fit," she said. Then she went off.

The rabbi affected a stern expression. "Jews don't abandon their missing," he said. "It's best that you go back to Lillian. One can't ever know who will return from war."

"It is a war, though?"

"I think it might be," the rabbi said. "But your worry is your son."

"I won't live as if Pato does. I already need his forgiveness for too many things."

The rabbi stuffed his tefillin inside the tallis bag and zipped it up. "It's Lillian's forgiveness you should be getting."

"I know what it is to be a husband," Kaddish said. "I want to make peace with my son."

"Why do you come here asking questions if there's only one answer you'll accept? If you want forgiveness from Pato, join Lillian and pray he returns. Forgiveness can only be asked in person or, God forbid, at the grave, both of which—"

"Call for a body," Kaddish said. "Living or dead."

"Yes," the rabbi said.

The granddaughter returned with a black suit jacket and a white dress shirt. Kaddish thanked the girl and took the clothes down the hallway to change.

Kaddish came back wearing the jacket over his own shirt. (The rabbi's was too narrow to button.) He put the navigator's parka on over that, ready to go.

"For the food, for the clothes, for your kindness, I thank you," Kaddish said. "Your advice, though, leaves me as always on the outside."

"It's the law," the rabbi said. "I can't change it for you."

"I'm pretty sure you could," Kaddish said. "I'm pretty sure you could read it in a way that would fit with my life, instead of forcing my life into the law."

"That's your opinion," the rabbi said. "And I already gave you mine. I've told you only what I think to be right."

Kaddish shook his head.

"It's not enough," he said. "It's coldhearted."

The rabbi shook his own head, disappointed in turn. What was left for him to give this man? Everything Poznan does is wrong and the only comfort he will accept is to be told he's right. The rabbi had done his best. He'd opened his home to this vandal, this—forgive him—son of a whore, and it wasn't enough. And still, in this instant, the rabbi found more.

"If the boy is dead," the rabbi said, "if the body is recovered, it would be my honor to perform the funeral myself. I will make you a beautiful ceremony, the first Poznan on the right side of the wall."

"There's only one right side," Kaddish said. "I'll help you climb over the wall myself. Otherwise, I don't see any charity in dressing and feeding and housing a Jew who came to you desperate only for wisdom. No more than offering bread to a man dying of thirst."

"I gave you an answer," the rabbi said. "It wasn't the one you wanted to hear. For that you fault me. And after I welcomed you into my home."

"A funeral," Kaddish said. "A grave. All I need from you is to know how." Here Kaddish's voice dropped and, the rabbi felt, turned threatening. "You can't understand how excruciating it is for me that I even care. Mistreated by you forever, Rabbi, and still I want to do what's right."

"What's right, Poznan?" the rabbi said. "Forget a funeral. You're forbidden in these circumstances even to mourn."

[Forty-three]

HATEFUL, A HATEFUL PREDICAMENT: fearing one's neigh-
bors. Apartments, vertical living, it's unnatural. Never meant to be. This
is what Cacho thought, rushing in and pressing the button for the lobby
while he pulled the gate closed. Worse, he could never tell when one of
them was coming or going, that door always ajar.

Then, what else to expect, Lillian calling, "Hold the elevator, hold it."
Cacho winced. He could pretend he hadn't heard. Except Cacho could
not pretend. He felt guilty. Innocent of wrongdoing and guilty, guilty
inside. The latch was a hair's breadth from locking and he slid the gate
back.

Cacho stared at his grip on the handle. Lillian stepped in and he
could feel her facing him, feel the proximity of her crossed arms. Every
floor down, Cacho believed, would shave another year off his life.

The elevator started and he gave Lillian a sidelong glance and nod.
He couldn't help but acknowledge her, torturous as it was.

Surprisingly, Cacho didn't register any hatred. As the elevator de-
scended he found that he was getting a fairly friendly response. Cacho
let his shoulders relax, rolled them back, and turned to face her.

"Any news," he said, "about Pato?"

Cacho thought he might pass out. He'd received a grimace or maybe
a flash of a grin.

"All good," Lillian said. "He's been located. Someone has found him. It won't be long," she said. "Home soon."

Let's make it clear that it's a girl from the start. There should be no expectation of its being Pato when we see the body, long and lank (and living still). It would be an easy mistake. The boys so much like girls these days, all long hair and slouchy posture—and posture anyway irrelevant in her position; the space cramped and suffocating, the girl lying down. She, the girl, shifted a knee, rolled onto a hip. The cell is so low and narrow it's like being laid out on a morgue tray. It's like already being dead.

The prisoner, the girl, is in a man's bunk. She can feel this, smell it, sense the occupant before. It's not Pato's smell alone that she's smelling. It's that the traces of the one before her and all those before him have melded and been breathed up and breathed out and that breath grown into mold and those molds into heat, making an air, generating an actual feel. If we see things as a continuum, if, at this time of unbroken murder and unbroken torture, we see it as a chain, then it is fair to say that Pato somehow lingers even before she finds what he has left.

The girl does not yet know where she is or where she is headed. Where she came from has broken down and simplified itself only to *before* and *now, above* and *below.* That is, she does not connect herself to her name and her life, to her studies and her friends, to her family and her dog and the last book she read. The girl wouldn't have guessed that in being disappeared she would find it easier, better, to disappear herself—complicit in her nonexistence. It is too much to be as was. For her it was like being terribly old, when there is nothing left but the body, nothing to concentrate on but am I cold or am I hot, hungry or full, and, most importantly, how much does it hurt.

When the girl says, out loud, "I wish I was dead" or "Let me die" or "Kill me now," it holds no meaning. It's reflex, a tic. She only manages a little emotion to it if she is up on the torture table, if they've got her out in one of the cinder-block rooms, if they've got her strapped down and she believes that specific torturer might do it, that if she says it good and strong or says it properly hopeless, her tormenter might turn up the knobs, turn up the current until it all just ends.

The previous place she was held was more like a house than a dungeon. There was contact and chatter and the occasional group meal, all under watch. She slept on a cot in a tiny room with a window and once, for an hour, she was allowed to stand outside with her face in the sun. Everyone there knew more than her, and the other disappeared, always changing, whispered useful information when they could. Almost every fact she was told she then heard in a contradictory version, every truth with an opposite truth spread throughout that place. So that one prisoner, wide-eyed and flat-stomached, told her she'd been nine months pregnant when they arrested her, and another, who looked to be nine months pregnant herself, swore she was brought in a virgin and was a virgin still. Word was—and the girl had believed it—that no one is ever freed, until they brought in a man twice freed and twice rearrested. It was from him that she picked up the jargon, and when she was transferred she already knew the torture table would be stainless steel and that her cell was called a tube. The only constant was that everyone claimed innocence. Innocent her own self, she could not believe that for all these people, that for each and every one, such a nightmare could be true. She lived like an amnesiac inside that tube and managed this mostly well until she'd found the notes.

It was the same man in the last place who'd told her the notes were called caramels, this because they were swallowed when they were to be moved. She'd thought maybe it was caramel because when one is suffering from greatest isolation, to find such a treasure—there could be nothing more sweet. She wasn't sure how one knew when to swallow them, how she was to judge if she was being moved from the tube back to the house, or the tube to freedom, or on to death—which would mean destroying the notes herself. Since the dead never returned, she didn't know how it might come.

During the endless hours locked away, her fingers had found their own boredom, their own energy, her body breaking down into its own animal parts. They went off searching. They found a hole in the foam pad she lay on and, exploring it, burrowing inside, they came upon something. In her brain, in her head—with its own separate work-ings—she seized on the thoughts of caramels and figured what to do. The fingers kept working as she pulled out caramel after caramel, balls of paper wrapped in plastic, and it was hours, she'd guess, hours of con-sidering before she connected with her own self, before she connected up all the disparate parts of herself and unwrapped them and read.

There was a small vent at her head. It wasn't the only source of air, as she'd covered it with her wet undershirt for a good long time and did not suffocate. Through it came light and sometimes noise, and it was up against that vent that she held the notes. Each one had a name at the top: PATO POZNAN written in block-letter print. It was exhilarating to see.

From PATO POZNAN there came into existence a boy to go with the name. For that alone there came a gratitude mixed with yearning, infat-uation and admiration and love. It was such a civilized act, writing one's name, a concrete act. It made her think she could leave a history herself.

She pictured Pato easily and pictured him all wrong. She saw him blond and hazel-eyed, with freckles across his nose. She saw a man more like her brother and father if the two were melded and then mixed with her last other-world crush.

When she dreamed of being freed—which, with Pato's notes, she now did—she imagined finding his family. She did not picture the right neighborhood, the Jewish neighborhood, or the right block. Nor did she imagine an apartment where the mother would already be waiting, fixed like a gargoyle and staring down. She saw herself outside a gate where a father (just like the son but white at the temples—and also, in a way, now her own father) would come to greet her, taking the notes from her and, before reading them, giving her a hug.

There was another smell that lingered in the cell, this one distinct from the people who'd amassed it and so dominant that the girl didn't understand how she'd ignored it until then. It was the smell of fear. And it helped her imagine the worst: Pato gone, Pato dead, and she, carrying a message, his final and only link to the world, doing for him this good deed and, by accident—the accident of her own death—erasing his name from above.

What she could not know was that (as far as we are concerned, as far as those caramels are concerned) as much as the girl lived for Pato in that moment, she was linked to Lillian and Kaddish in equal measure. This is the point where the three of them came together, symbiotic, and the point from which they all three diverged.

While the government did what governments do (taking ownership of the present, laying out visions of the future), this one also reached back into the past, to change what was, to deny what had been. And this was the junta's great success—recognizing that to truly take control one must move back with the same fervor that one moves forward (infinity reaches both ways). Taking this into account, it was no small matter that, over what happened in the past, over what happened to Pato, this girl and Lillian and Kaddish all agreed. It was Pato abducted, Pato imprisoned, Pato in a cell.

In the present is where things came apart. Lillian alone was convinced of Pato alive and Pato well and Pato held in some other place. Kaddish alone believed, beyond the shadow of a doubt, that Pato was at the bottom of the river. Then there was the girl.

She embraced, quite neatly, the conflicting positions of Lillian and Kaddish. She saw both their truths, believed ardently both their absolutes. By virtue of inhabiting a cell where Pato once was and now was not, Pato was to her as living as he was dead. There was, related to this, a decision to make. The girl had to decide the fate of the caramels by figuring her own, a future that was equally split.

She thought about it and, inspired by the notes themselves, decided she would live, that she would go free. She memorized the notes, six in all, in case, for some reason, she survived without them.

She rewrapped the caramels and pondered where to hide them: whether to stick them up and inside herself, where her tormentors were always probing, always checking, so that it seemed the only place on her body where anything should be put, or whether to take them by mouth, where she worried that in the swallowing, they might be swallowed-up, the caramels more easily lost.

In the end, she pressed them into her mouth one after the other, partly because they were less likely to be found this way and partly in deference to the name. Where else would a caramel go?

An obvious omission. It's fair to wonder about the contents of those notes. It's true that the girl got to read them and memorize them and swallow them down. It wouldn't be right, though, to share Pato's message when neither Kaddish nor Lillian will hear it, when neither parent will learn that those notes ever were.

By the time Kaddish was trying on the rabbi's jacket and Lillian was descending in the elevator with Cacho at her side, the girl's body had already been settled in the silt for some days under the pressure of a trillion liters of Río de la Plata. The notes were still protected in her stomach, still readable below all that water, hidden inside that girl, herself swallowed up in all that dark. There was no perverse miracle in the days that had passed when that poor girl's body could have been caught in a net or snagged by a troller's line, the moment in a thousand Jewish fables where the diamond appears in the fish's belly, where the notes would be harvested (maybe by the navigator himself) and handed to Kaddish or delivered to Lillian in her chair.

The memory is the girl's alone, and that's how it will stay. Still, in this horrible time when the junta would weave a nation's truth from lies, Lillian would have been happy and Kaddish would have been happy that, independent of them, one fine girl for one fine day believed in Pato Poznan—both living and dead.

Drugged and naked and slipping further into her own self, the girl thought about Pato and the short history in the notes that she carried inside. She wondered if he'd been taken on this same route or was right now on another, wishing for the best. All this took place before they reached altitude and before she lost consciousness; before the hold on the plane was opened and before the girl, who had already long ceased to exist in Argentina, was dropped, unresisting, from above.

[Forty-four]

JUST AS A CURRENT SHIFTED and a bubble moved and a note protected was flushed and eaten by the sea, Lillian Poznan stepped into the Ministry of Special Cases. She was looking for her priest. Had she known, Lillian wouldn't have missed observing that the notes—as they shifted and wetted, opening out like fronds before disintegrating wholly—were until then protected in the belly of someone else's daughter, whose parents right then waited and worried. Or didn't. Or, like Kaddish and Lillian, split, did both.

Four days he'd left her, another four days by that phone. Lillian sat there waiting for it to ring. When she couldn't bear it any longer, when the thoughts she'd sworn never to consider threatened to be believed, Lillian got out of her chair by the window, went across the hall, and came back with Cacho, seating him in it. Then she went where she'd sworn she wouldn't go.

Lillian caught sight of her priest as he caught sight of her; what could be more fortuitous than that? He was right there in the middle of the lobby. Lillian's exhilaration didn't last through to the end of her head tilting and to the conclusion of her grinning. Her hip hadn't fully locked and her hand hadn't reached it, leaving Lillian's where-have-you-been and there-you-are stances less than fully expressed.

It was the priest's face, a frown forming, and the guard that was standing across from him, also turning, eyebrows crossing, and the man between them, a father—who Lillian was in the process of recogniz-ing—whose eyes were widening; it was taking in the whole picture, three men watching Lillian watch them, that it was communicated back to her that she'd done something wrong.

So similar was the man's position to the one she'd held, Lillian wasn't sure if she'd seen a flash of silver foil in the guard's reaching hand, or if she was remembering the priest's intervention on her behalf when she'd tried to get up to the ministry's other side. Lillian didn't have time to check as her attention was drawn to the guard's far hand rising, the baton above it, and then focused on the priest rushing toward her. It was more than a rush. The priest, yes, he was running, and the guard (in the background) already swinging and the father—she'd missed that, he wasn't falling but fallen, curled on the floor. Lillian remembered the dis-tinctive crack from the baton striking the door back when she'd stood where the father now lay. The noise was just as loud in that great empty-but-for-them lobby when the baton hit against a man. Among the cracks that followed while the priest grabbed her and pulled her into the street, Lillian couldn't differentiate which were new blows and which the echoes of the last, all of them intermingling with the unearthly and terrible screams. As scared as she was in that whirlwind moment, she couldn't get the eyes of that father out of her mind. It was bewildering for Lillian to see on another parent that kind of fear.

Already holding Lillian roughly, the priest jerked her toward him, lifting her off the ground. An apology wasn't on the way.

"How dare you," he said. "You've no right to come chasing."

"The same thing—I saw the exact same thing. You gave him a choco-late. That's why you keep me away. So I shouldn't see."

"You think it's the same?" the priest said, furious. "The same would be me successfully defusing, instead of that man being brutalized, possibly beaten to death. That would be different from your experience, wouldn't it? It would also be your fault."

"Not mine. I only came looking. And good that I did. What were you doing with that man? How do you leave me to rot?"

"What do you think happens in that building? Parents figure out there is another side and the guard goes mad, and I do my best. What did I tell you? Stay by the phone and stay away from the ministry. Look what it does to you, two seconds here and already you're full of accusations, as if I didn't do my best."

"You did, and then you left me, forgotten. You've given up on Pato and didn't have the decency to call."

"A permanent victim," the priest said. "Why not add me to your list of disappointments and be on your way. I said we shouldn't start down this route and I should have listened to myself. You're not to be trusted, Mrs. Poznan. I'm better off trying to help someone else."

"You can't do that. I'll stop you. I'll tell." Lillian didn't even know what to threaten. She pointed toward the ministry. "I'll tell them what I saw." And then, frantic: "If you help anyone it has to be me—you were already helping."

"Go tell whoever you want, you have my blessing. They may even believe you," the priest said, "but they won't admit it and they'll despise you for taking witness. These are the things this country wants desperately not to know."

The priest made a big show of being dumbfounded by Lillian. It was meant for an audience and Lillian peered up into the buildings around them to see if the generals were looking down.

"I apologize," Lillian said. "I'm sorry for coming down here and sorry for accusing. Your help, that's all I'm after. I trust you. I won't question anything again."

"Be thankful for what I already gave you. There's no more to be done," the priest said. "Sometimes one should be thankful with less."

"Please," Lillian said. She wanted to beg. She looked to the sidewalk and the priest looked with her. She was considering getting down on her knees.

"Why don't you go home with the confirmation that Pato is alive and with an honest-to-goodness military priest to loathe for your troubles. This way you'll sleep at night like everyone else. This way your life will go on."

Lillian couldn't help it. She had to ask. "Is he dead? Is that why you're acting like this?" Lillian gritted her teeth, pressed them so hard she felt one break.

"Dead?" he said, and seemed confused. "No, that's not it. He's alive, I already told you. It's enough to be thankful for. Now go home."

"He can be freed?" Lillian said.

"What does it matter when you have no one to help you do it? I'm done, and there's no one else who'll try."

"I'm begging," she said, "for your help, for the truth, for whatever it is that you're keeping from me."

"It's not me you'll hate if I tell."

"Is it my husband?" she said. "Is it Feigenblum, who speaks for the Jews? Did he mess things up with his list?" Lillian thought her head might break like her tooth, so sharp and quick were the swings between hope and hopelessness, a hot-cold leap she was sure would kill her.

"It's you," the priest said. "You'll hate yourself."

Lillian yelled so loudly that passersby turned. "What could that possibly mean?"

"It means, better that this rests on me than on you. That's my only motivation. If your son doesn't make it, you'll live better hating me. I've seen it before," the priest said. "They don't recover. The mothers who know they failed their children are never the same."

"I won't fail," she said.

The priest sighed. "One can arrange to get a son freed from a secret prison even in the middle of a secret war. The apparatus is imperfect; it can be gotten round."

"How do you not call me with this? How do you not give me the option?"

"Because I know," the priest said. "Because I took all your money to buy one question. I know your situation, and it's too much for a mother to bear. It's better that you believe yourself abandoned."

"Tell me what I need to do."

"Nothing. That's the horror. All you have to do is pay. That's why I didn't call and didn't tell, that's why it's painful to share. You could free your son right now, Mrs. Poznan, except that you can't. Except that now you must sit and wait and pray, knowing you failed him, knowing there was a price to pay and you couldn't manage it. Now it's on you, Mrs. Poznan. Your burden to bear."

"I'll pay it," she said. "Just tell me a number."

"You won't," the priest said.

"How much could it be?"

"More," the priest said, "than you'd ever imagine."

[Forty-five]

KADDISH WAS HUNCHED FORWARD on his bench in the courtyard, smoking butt after butt, cigarettes of strangers pulled from public ashtrays and picked off the street. His tool bag was at his side.

Mrs. Ordóñez peered down from her balcony and called into the dark, "Who's there?"

"It's Kaddish," Kaddish said.

"You don't look like you," she said, and, with a huff that carried down, she moved her giant body back inside.

Kaddish wasn't wearing his own clothes, and he had what was almost a beard. Thinking of it made his face itch and he scratched it. Neither of these changes was so drastic that Mrs. Ordóñez should call down to him as if to a stranger after all these years. Destitution was enough, he figured. The sight of him set women to clutching their purses and crossing the street.

Kaddish leaned his head back and took in his patch of stars. What he hadn't expected to discover was that he could survive hungry and survive filthy and live while feeling so cold. Without a peso in his pocket, he could manage. It was without Lillian, he'd discovered, he couldn't go on.

It wasn't about love.

If Kaddish had a body to bury and Pato's grave to visit, he might be able to take it all on his own. To be without his son and without his wife, and to be alone in his belief, this was too much.

He couldn't will Pato back any more than he could make Lillian believe him gone for good. The only thing within Kaddish's power was to draw on his powerlessness. He could live as Lillian asked. He would live a lie for the right to return home.

Kaddish fished out another butt and lit it with the last. If he'd smoked a touch more, tried a little harder, he maybe could have struck a single match when he was a boy and kept that flame going until now.

Kaddish took the stairs in the dark and reached for a key out of habit. He could see the chink of light from his apartment as he turned on the landing from the third floor. When he pushed at the door, the door pushed back. Lillian stepped into the open space. She was forcibly blocking his way.

"Have your senses become so attuned?" he said. "Did you pick up my scent?"

"I heard you call up from the air shaft."

Kaddish took a step forward, and Lillian took one back, though she planted a foot behind the door.

"You look—" she said, and Kaddish finished for her.

"Like a rabbi. I know," he said, thinking it was his beard and (under the navigator's parka) the rabbi's jacket.

"No," she said. "Like a bum. Like a real one."

"That's because I am," Kaddish said. Lillian seemed to hear it as an admission and Kaddish rushed to add, "That's not what brought me back."

"I'm sure that's exactly what brought you. You'd starve to death before taking honest work, and now you've tested it to its limits. Whatever the reason, it doesn't matter. I'm not taking you in, Kaddish. This is as far as you go."

"I'm not back out of laziness," Kaddish said, "and not out of hunger. I'm back because I can't do this without you, Lillian. Your roof, your rules—I said it before. Now I've learned my lesson," Kaddish said. "I've even been to the Jews."

"Who?" Lillian said, not believing.

He showed her the jacket.

"I went to the rabbi, Lillian. He said I'm wrong. That it's a sin the way I live. He said I should do like you, that the waiting is right."

"The old rabbi said that?"

"He did. And I thought about it. And I'll try."

At that Lillian started closing the door.

"I won't try," Kaddish said. "I'll do it. I'll wait with you for Pato to come home."

"You're a man who needs to be saved," Lillian said. "Unfortunately, I'm no longer capable."

"I honestly don't think I can make it."

"That's a shame," Lillian said, "because I can't take you back anymore."

"I'll beg if I have to," Kaddish said.

"A truly brokenhearted man would already be begging. You raise the option. Always it's the least that can be invested, the minimum at stake."

"Then I beg you," Kaddish said.

"Don't," she said. "It's not up to me anymore. While you were with the rabbi, I went out and found myself a priest."

"A priest is in charge?" Kaddish said. "A priest deciding? It's hard to say which is more shocking, your visit or mine."

"Together they're no shock at all. Forever at cross-purposes. What did you expect when you showed up here ready to see things my way? It's too late. I've come to see them in yours."

"About Pato?"

"God forbid!" Lillian said. "I'm talking about money, Kaddish. If you're really here to wait on Pato, I'll take you back this second. The problem is, I can't let you in for nothing. Entry into this house now has a price. Living here is no longer free."

"I don't have a cent," Kaddish said. "And I've no way to get money anymore."

"A shame," Lillian said.

"That's it?" Kaddish said. "Everything a shame?"

"How long have I believed in you, Kaddish? Through how many schemes and get-rich-quicks? Through how much of your gimme-six swagger and it'll-be-OK talk? All of it. I saw you through everything, believing when I didn't. Now it's your turn. Go out and find us a fortune, Kaddish. Not what comes from chipping a name off a headstone. If you leave that cemetery blank, if you wipe every grave clean—that's the kind of money they're asking to get Pato back."

"How am I supposed to manage anything," he said, signaling his current condition, "like this?"

"If it's really life or death, your survival or Pato's, I'm sure you can manage it."

"Please, Lillian. This is madness."

"Good," she said. "You're a wellspring of that. From the million plans you've had over the years—every one a winner—you can't tell me there's not a single flimflam left. Go back to your underworld and talk to your cronies. I give you my blessing. Seek out all the people I begged you to stay away from since the start of our marriage. Don't look so confused," she said. Then she went off, vanishing into the apartment. Kaddish stayed right where he was. Lillian brought back a piece of notepaper. "A new nose won't do it this time," she said, and pressed the paper into his hand. "Your way, Kaddish. Everything as you like. All you have to do is succeed."

Kaddish looked at the sum. He was stunned.

"The way you like to do business," Lillian said. "Figures written down."

A pair of dogs strained at its leashes trying to get at Kaddish through the doctor's fence. It was night, though there was plenty-enough light for Kaddish to make out the doctor in his robe—open and revealing the doctor naked underneath. On his feet he wore a pair of unlaced boots, the tongues hanging out, lolling.

"If you're so hungry," the doctor said, "why don't you reach that head around and take a bite out of your ass. That should feed you for a while."

"If I want to feast on my own fat ass, it appears I'll have to get in line." Kaddish pointed at the dogs. With his arm that much closer, the dogs reared up like a pair of horses, front legs scratching at air. The doctor wrapped the leashes tighter and leaned back, his heels dug in.

"Since when do you have guard dogs?" Kaddish said.

"Let us say things have deteriorated."

"My report," Kaddish said, "is more or less the same."

The doctor gave a yank to the leashes and the dogs responded instantly, as highly trained animals do. One dog heeled on each side of him, looking as if carved from stone. "I tried to get rentals," the doctor said. "Apparently that's not the way they do it. And I have to say, I've become attached." The dog on the doctor's left lifted its head from between its paws and stared back at its master. The master, following the dog's gaze, tied the front of his robe. The dog sneezed and put his head down. "Loyalty is loyalty," the doctor said. "Still doesn't mean I should dangle my *pija* in front of them."

"Is that why you don't invite me in?"

"Because you'd bite off my penis?"

"Because you don't trust even those you trust."

"That makes my head ache, Poznan," the doctor said. "I'm not going to unravel it. The reason I didn't invite you in is because it didn't cross my mind. What I was mulling over was whether to release the dogs on you or not. I'd have called the police and been rid of you forever but I no longer have the luxury of acting the good citizen. They might just take us both."

"If you didn't begrudge me every visit, if you weren't so downright nasty, I wouldn't believe your love was heartfelt. I appreciate it, Doctor. For a pair of fuckups, it's a very special thing we have."

"First of all," the doctor said, "*you* are a fuckup. *I'm* fallen. It's a very big distinction. It means, at some point in the past, I achieved something. That can't be taken away." The doctor made a gesture, and the dogs jumped to their feet looking fierce. "Second, you look absolutely terrible, Poznan. You've taken what we call, in medical parlance, a turn for the worse. Now, make this leap with me if you can, follow along: The madman always thinks he has some deep bond with the focus of his manic obsession. That's what makes him a madman. All the visits, the stalking, the loitering outside my office, it's unwelcome. I'd rather have Toothless' name back up and be a son-of-a-whore surgeon than a surgeon who hangs out with a son of a whore."

"Now you're making my head ache," Kaddish said. The doctor didn't respond and Kaddish felt sick with the size of the favor he'd come to ask.

"Even the rabbi let me in," Kaddish said. He opened the jacket, trying to show it off. The lining shimmered. "The rabbi let me sleep over. He gave me his suit."

"Then there's someone else who loves you, Poznan. Go back to him."

"I recognize that you're the last man I should turn to during my time of need," Kaddish said.

The doctor nodded. "It's for the nose I do it. If I could take that and leave the leftover Poznan outside, I would." He unlocked the gate and, loosing the dogs off their leashes, led Kaddish around the back of the house, through a patio entrance, and into a wood-paneled den. There was a card table set up, and a deck of Spanish cards out on it, four hands dealt, as if Kaddish had interrupted a game. There were fresh logs burning high in the fireplace and a book was open facedown on the leather couch, a transistor radio stuck between the pillows at the side.

"Couldn't sleep," the doctor said. And, following Kaddish's gaze, "You think I don't read? Nothing like a novel to knock a man out. Been reading the same two pages of this one for a year."

The doctor motioned for Kaddish to take a seat at the card table. He went over to warm himself by the fire. He crouched down and rested on his heels. "Was my man at the Fisherman's Club to meet you?"

Kaddish picked up a card, the ace of swords, and tapped its edge against the table, turning it over and over again in his hand. It couldn't be that he hadn't spoken to the doctor since that morning. Kaddish pictured the doctor's socks, his view from under the bench.

"Yes, he was there," Kaddish said, "Thank you for that."

"Then it was good news?"

"No," Kaddish said. "It was bad. The boy is dead."

"I'm sorry," the doctor said.

"Me too," Kaddish said. "I miss him very much."

"I'd been wondering. I wanted to know what happened—I was hoping for good news." The doctor stood up and joined Kaddish at the table.

"It's actually a good-news question that I came over to ask." Kaddish spoke while staring at the face of the card. "I need help paying a ransom. It's for Pato's release."

He looked up at the doctor. The doctor looked back at him, displeased.

"Is it shock value you're after? You can't want that to make sense."

"It's Lillian," Kaddish said. "She thinks the boy is alive. She's found someone who swore, if a bribe is paid, that Pato could be gotten back."

The doctor took the card from Kaddish's hand as if ending the game. He swept the others up and shuffled the deck, contemplating what Kaddish had said.

"I have nowhere else. No one at all."

"That's readily apparent," the doctor said. "Tell me, though. You're sure the boy is dead?"

"Do you know about the flights? Do you know what they do with the missing?" The doctor stopped shuffling. He put down the deck. Kaddish wasn't sure if he was acknowledging the flights or not. "They push them from airplanes high above the river. Unless there's any way to survive it, I believe Pato is dead."

Again the doctor said, "I'm sorry," and then, looking toward the ceiling, "It's hard to believe."

"The navigator, the man at the pier, he said it's the impact that kills them, that the water is like a brick wall when dropped from that height. Do you think," Kaddish said, "is there any way a person could survive?"

"As a doctor," the doctor said, "I think you're asking a physics question."

Mazursky got up and walked to the window. He put his hands behind his back and stared into the yard, though from Kaddish's vantage point, and with the night outside, all that was in the window was a reflection of the fireplace and his own sad figure behind Mazursky's.

"I can tell you this," Mazursky said. "Assuming a great ability to swim or something floating by to grab onto; assuming also an extreme amount of strength and resilience—and tolerance to cold; beyond all that, and there are probably many more factors, just regarding the falling and the speed and the resistance of the surface of water, it would come down to the perfect dive. Water is not a brick wall; it can be forgiving to a great degree. I think—and this all very rusty—I think the molecular structure is very similar to that of glass." And, as Kaddish had tapped the card against the table, the doctor tapped at the window with a fingernail. Kaddish could hear the dogs run up from outside. "Have you ever looked at an old windowpane? Have you seen how the glass warps?"

Kaddish nodded.

"It's the glass running, like a liquid. It happens over time."

"That's hope?" Kaddish said.

"It's possibility, is all," the doctor said. "Technically, or maybe theoretically, and maybe that doesn't even hold, but if I were to get the timing right, the pressure right, the angle of entry—and maybe it would take all of eternity—I should be able to push my finger through, to dive through glass."

"And?"

"And likewise, if everything were perfect, it would be possible to dive from a great height and cut seamlessly through the surface of the water, to rise up, and swim off."

"Nothing is ever perfect, though," Kaddish said.

"No," the doctor said. Then, turning, smiling, he closed one eye and studied Kaddish. Kaddish knew the doctor was looking at his nose, that he was going to say, *Except for your nose, the only perfect thing,* but the doctor didn't make that joke again.

"I still need the money," Kaddish said.

"For what? To let your wife pay a ransom for nothing? You're going to give it away?"

"Yes," Kaddish said. "It's Lillian's turn. A thousand fortunes promised her and none delivered."

"Touching," the doctor said, "and not at all sensible."

"It's my own ransom that I'm paying. The price Lillian exacts for forgiveness. And it's only fair. Why shouldn't she have her chance? Everyone deserves one hopeless scheme."

"If you recall, I didn't pay when I owed you money. You can't expect me to come through now." The doctor rejoined Kaddish at the card table. "It's bleak, Poznan, the coffers are empty."

"Then feed me to the sharks," Kaddish said. "Put me in touch with the people you gamble with and borrow money from. Help me get into the same high-quality rich-man debt as you. That's all. A fair shake when it comes to self-destruction. Class fucks both ways, Doctor."

"Two problems," the doctor said. "The first is that the people I deal with will kill me when you don't pay, either after they kill you, as interest, or before, as a warning. Both possibilities leave me dead—something I've been working tirelessly to avoid. The second is, you have no value. They don't want to get paid back, they want debt to accrue and assets to seize." The doctor motioned to the room and the house around them. "There is no value to you, Poznan. A fortune lent to make a claim on a chisel and hammer isn't going to do."

"If my wife were here, she'd say, A man who's made so many different fortunes over the years must be able to point us toward one."

"Actually, it's how many you lose that matters, and I'm a fortune in the hole." The doctor rubbed his face in his hands to wake himself up and then turned his bloodshot eyes to Kaddish. "Your expectations are too high. I'm a plastic surgeon. A specialist. I think you're looking for the country doctor. Marital troubles and bunions and toothaches no longer come in one man."

"No," Kaddish said. "But you're a stubborn *hijo de puta,* and they generally know how to survive."

"Is it a pep talk you're after, Poznan? Tell me what it is you need that I can give you. Otherwise let me fall asleep on my book."

Kaddish took out the paper from Lillian and laid it on top of the cards.

"Jesus," the doctor said. "Even the greedy have gotten greedier. That's a lot of money to ask when they won't deliver you a son."

"Wouldn't it be great if they did, though?" Kaddish said.

"Enough of that," the doctor said. "We're figuring now. Practical. What is it you can do?"

"I can get the money," Kaddish said.

"If you had a way, you wouldn't be here," the doctor said, frustrated. "We need to deduce, to think from the abstract to the specific. The money is the end point, not the start. Back up in your head, Poznan. What is it they're asking?"

"For ransom," Kaddish said.

"Fine," the doctor said. "And if one needs to pay a ransom, what would be the best way to get it?"

Kaddish snatched back the paper.

"Tell me what you want me to say," he said, "and I'll say it. If you're hinting, I don't know."

"How did we end up with this government in the first place? Not the coup. The coup is like saying money when you mean ransom. The people of our beloved country, why did we let it happen?"

"Did we?" Kaddish said.

"No government can do anything to a nation when the whole nation wants it otherwise."

"I guess, terror," Kaddish said. "Before they took Pato, I think I'd have said it: Worse than this government was the violence and the terror. If it hadn't touched my family, if they'd stayed out of my home, I'd say we were better off now."

"When the rebels were running wild and making chaos, how did they finance it?"

"Kidnappings," Kaddish said. "Kidnapping and ransom."

The doctor leaned back and clasped his hands behind his head.

"You want me to kidnap someone?"

"I don't want anything," the doctor said. "I haven't even said the word. It was your idea."

"That's the government's dirty business. For me to disappear someone," Kaddish said. He couldn't.

"Do not confuse the two," the doctor said. "This disappearing is an evolutionary refinement, a political variant to an industry Argentina has always held dear. It's the junta that destroyed the kidnapping trade. They think they're idealists, and evil always follows when people stop taking cash. It's a capitalist truism. Beware when your leaders can't be bought. If they really were ransoming Pato, I'd give a sigh of relief. I'd say there was hope for us all."

"It's too big," Kaddish said. "I couldn't do it."

"Not to save your own son?"

"It's *not* to save my own son," Kaddish said.

"Your wife believes it is."

"I was born into a house where people were bought and sold. You come from the same place."

"It could be over in a day," the doctor said. "It's a simple transaction."

"Nothing goes simple with me. To tear a hole in another family, even by accident," Kaddish said. "A kidnapping gone wrong is murder."

"Murder is a category of intent," the doctor said. "You think I don't end up with bodies of my own? They come in for their noses, their tits. I could tuck tummies, if I wanted, all day and all night. Do you think I haven't buried ladies, mothers of small children, who only wanted a little less crinkle to their smiles? Does that sound like murder to you? Come, Poznan, such risks are part of every undertaking. People kill every day just driving their cars."

"I really can't risk any life but my own," Kaddish said. "Worthless as it is, it's all I can gamble. I don't have the stomach for this."

The doctor held up his hands. "I was asking, not advocating. No one is recommending that you commit a crime. I was simply making a cultural observation. If you're after easy money, it's my feeling that the sole resource with guaranteed value, the only thing a good Argentine won't piss away, is family. We'll burn down all our forests and drown ourselves in lakes of cow shit; we will rape this blessed land of plenty until we've squeezed out every last peso and not give a fuck. But for sisters or sons, for our dear mothers, a ransom will be paid."

The doctor turned toward the fire. Kaddish followed his gaze and both stared at the logs, at the flames dying down and the fitful burn to the coals.

"What is it, then," the doctor said, "that your delicate constitution can handle?"

Kaddish stared, Kaddish thought.

"Cemeteries," Kaddish said. "Bones."

The doctor knit his brows and, considering, nodding slowly, he brightened up. He reached across the table and gave Kaddish a good solid pinch on the cheek.

"Where else but in Buenos Aires would such an idea make sense?"

Kaddish shrugged. He wasn't sure any idea had been proposed.

"Well done," the doctor said. "In this city the dead are worth more than the living. In Buenos Aires bones will work just as good." The doctor smiled a warm, almost loving, smile. "Here bones can be ransomed too."

[Forty-six]

HOW IS IT THAT A MAN who'd strolled down Avenida del Libertador countless times did not once in his life end up visiting the Cementerio de la Recoleta, a treasure in Buenos Aires and one of the most famous in the world?

For Kaddish, it was a sense that he'd had since boyhood. It was a matter of pride. He didn't need to see how much better the dead lived than the living. He had no reason to pay any notice to the opulent city they'd built within that cemetery's walls. The tops of the soaring monuments and mausoleums were enough for Kaddish. With a wall between himself and the rest of the Jews for most of his life, Kaddish had always felt he should be allowed his own graveyard to deny.

When the doctor had asked Kaddish, "Whose bones?" the answer was at the ready. The general was the first person Kaddish mentioned; when that garnered no reaction, Kaddish suggested the wife.

"There's a fortune behind her," the doctor said. "You couldn't pluck a better name from the society pages if you tried."

"Her father's dead. He'd have a grave in this town for sure."

"Now I believe you haven't been to Recoleta. Everyone in Buenos Aires knows that crypt. This is high profile, Poznan. If you don't get killed doing it, it's turning into one hell of an idea."

"You think this can work then?"

"If you're going to do such a thing, I don't think you could dig up a better man."

Kaddish swung his stiff leg forward in a counterclock step. He held one hand to his chest, as if his heart might go, and the other to the small of his back, as if it too might fail him and was causing great pain.

He stayed close to the wall even in darkness; he hung in the shadow when the moon broke cloud.

A healthy man (more or less). The chest, the back, the gimpy step deceiving. Back in the Benevolent Self shul, Kaddish had pressed a shovel face to his chest and a pick head to the small of his back, girdling them as best he could with a canvas sack. He'd given his steel chest a knock, remembering a tough guy's youth. Then he'd slid the wooden handle down a pant leg—clutching the grip between arm and ribs like a crutch—before buttoning it all up under his shirt.

Kaddish was out after bones, aristocratic bones made hard on heavy cream and caramel and coddled unbroken through brittle age. He wanted well-behaved picture-perfect bones that would lie like an anatomy-class skeleton in their coffin and clink like castanets when poured into his sack.

Moving away from the Iglesia del Pilar and sneaking in between the trees along the cemetery's outer wall, Kaddish looked for a place to enter. When there was enough streetlight or moonlight or headlight from a car going by, he caught glimpses of the bits of statue and mausoleum that stuck out above the wall. He saw outstretched wings and haloed heads. There were many raised fists, holding aloft crosses and laurels and giant bronze swords. Kaddish stopped alongside a barechested lady who looked inspired and sturdy and like she might support him on his way down.

Kaddish reached into his shirt and slid out the wooden handle that had hobbled him. In the night, by the cemetery, it looked as if he were pulling some central structural bone from his own chest—as if, with its removal, he would collapse into a pile of ribs and limbs, clinking (as he'd imagined the skeleton would) to the ground.

If there had right then been a guard roaming near, Kaddish's caper would have been finished before it began. For all the effort he made disguising himself, hiding his tools, and limping along, he made a ruckus clambering over the wall. There was grunting and huffing and more than one curse, drowned out by the wooden handle hitting and the shovel face clanking when he dropped them down. His chisel tumbled from a coat pocket along with the flashlight, which didn't break (all Kaddish needed was to do this in the dark). While he reassembled himself on the cemetery side—all except for the wooden handle, which he held like a staff—Kaddish found he was calmed by the sloppiness of his crossing. If there was room for one error, maybe the night would forgive a few more.

The first thing that overtook him was the presence of all those Gentile dead. This was not his cemetery. When a cat's eyes glinted as it slinked by and there was a distant creak and lonely whistle as the wind blew through, it all seemed loaded with meaning, as things must, Kaddish decided, when one is in a foreign cemetery to rob a grave.

Kaddish took out his flashlight and did not, as at the Benevolent Self, keep it cupped in his hand. He couldn't resist—with a sense of jealousy and wonder—seeing this glorious city in the center of his own.

Knowing the cemetery's boundaries hadn't prepared Kaddish for what he found within. In the rashness with which he'd steeled himself and embarked on this plan, he hadn't dreamed of what it would be like to face an avenue that stretched into the distance and was lined on both sides with tombs.

He set off down an alley of smaller monuments. It opened onto a broad thoroughfare edged with memorial statues, the flashlight's beam spilling past to light stained-glass windows and reflect off polished stone. Kaddish considered that he might not find the bones that night with nothing to guide him but a name.

The monuments were more castle than crypt and the statues often so lifelike Kaddish experienced a feeling he'd thought lost to him—a regular graveyard fright. He even screamed once when his flashlight lit on a muscled back, a lone figure of a man in the middle of the lane. The figure was frozen in a crouch, a statue dropped down to one knee atop the single modest grave Kaddish had seen. He then turned down a peaceful tree-lined avenue that, he noted, its residents never roamed.

When Kaddish passed the tombs of the revolutionary heroes and the Guerreros del Paraguay, it was the kind of history he'd expected. What surprised him was the personal history and the great flurry of memory that came with it when he saw President Yrigoyen's name. He would have sworn that his mother's burial was the only funeral of his childhood. Seeing the grave, Kaddish remembered standing in the rain alongside his mother as the coffin of the president was driven by. He had so few memories of his mother, Kaddish couldn't figure—so precious—how he'd lost this one: the rain, his mother's skirt, the president's coffin, and a parade. Talmud Harry always called Yrigoyen the last good man. He'd say, "We are fucked as a country from here on in." The statement had held true.

Among the giant monuments there were a few, as one would expect, that stood out, dwarfing the others in size. Kaddish used them as beacons, navigating by them like stars. There was one tomb the size of a chapel, with a statue of, Kaddish felt, great beauty rising from a domed roof. It was initially his farthest marker, the statue no more than a solid black line sticking up in the distance. Kaddish had thought it was an obelisk, and then, as the night drew on and he drew closer, the statue came into focus. It was a Jacob's ladder with an angel perched on top and cherubs somehow flying, literally circling above.

The nearer he got, the more confused he became. Whatever alley he turned out of, whatever avenue he chose, Kaddish found, in orienting himself, that the statue was facing his way—so that walking south, he was sure he'd gone north, and righting himself he'd be convinced the Iglesia del Pilar, forever east, now faced west. It was an illusion, Kaddish found, a four-sided statue, with four sleeping Jacobs at its base, and four ascending angels mounted face-to-face, their wing tips welded, so it appeared that they were stepping off the top rung into the sky.

Kaddish would forever say he knew this was the grave he was after, that the statue had beckoned him all night, a sign. Of course, if this were so he might have gone straight to it instead of gawping and gaping while he circled, lost for hours.

There was a brass plaque set into the mausoleum's front wall. Kaddish brought the flashlight up to it, and when he saw the name he'd been searching for, it felt to Kaddish ordained, nearly religious—the mission felt right. What he could not believe was that it was the only name there. Such a huge mausoleum must hold more than one body inside.

Kaddish slipped on a pair of gloves and touched his fingers to the name sticking up in relief. It was a beautiful cast. The raised letters, each one ridged, stuck out a solid centimeter.

Kaddish tried the double doors without real effort, knowing they'd be locked. He slipped his chisel in the gap between the doors, rocking it in place against the bolt and—the only real noise he'd made since clambering over the wall—he hammered and hammered until the bolt gave way. He waited outside to see if any alarm had been raised. Hearing nothing but a distant bark, Kaddish opened the doors and quickly closed himself inside.

With his flashlight pointed straight up at the domed ceiling, and before he'd gotten his bearings, Kaddish was convinced that the mausoleum was ten times larger than it looked to be from outside. The doors he stepped through seemed tiny upon consideration. He couldn't remember—an instant before—if he'd bowed his head to get in.

Taking a step forward there was a rasp, along with the sensation of sinking, as a flagstone settled under Kaddish's weight. The echo built on itself and the sound picked up, growing louder and louder before fading away.

Kaddish moved forward and back, planting his heel, testing the sound, and calming himself (he wasn't sure against what) with the thought, *It's only the drop and rise and rasp of loose stone.* He aimed the flashlight at his feet. He circled the whole room, with that echo rolling back at him after each step. Weather was all he could come up with. Only weather that finds more energy before petering out. Then he came up with longing and loneliness and, feeling himself turning maudlin, Kaddish— annoyed—shook it off. Like the four-faced statue crowning the roof, it wasn't anything but an illusion, a trick of the room. Kaddish battled the same feelings nightly when he slept under his pew. These hallowed halls and holy places were all erected to make us seem small, so that we should always feel as if we're in the belly of a whale. It was nothing more than a geometry applied so one couldn't help but turn inward, to fear God and fear death.

More importantly, Kaddish hadn't found a place to dig. He feared, right then, another plan gone wrong. What if this whole massive monument was built because there *was* no body? What if this man had suffered a fate similar to his son's?

Kaddish turned back toward the doors and began to scour the walls centimeter by centimeter, wondering if, as at the general's house, they'd built a servant's entrance behind which the coffin was hidden, a butler mummified along with it to serve in the world to come. What Kaddish found unfolding before him was a mural covering the walls. It was, he thought, a twisted history of Argentina. The family had built itself a pyramid painted in nationalistic style. There were bodies and babies and heaps of people clawing and climbing over each other toward some totalitarian ideal. There were mothers nursing and old people dying and funeral pyres burning so that Kaddish, picturing the man cremated and sprinkled over his oyster beds, again worried that he'd find nothing that night. Pointing his flashlight toward the ceiling, he saw now that the gray was mottled, it was part of the painting: a sky blotted out with smoke. Passing the light's beam over it as he'd done with the floor, the gray gradually brightened into the purples and oranges of dawn. Breaching these colors from the side walls were horns of plenty and overfed cattle, smokestacks floating above assembly lines, missiles flying and military men saluting below, all the signs of prosperity and might. It culminated on the far side with an enormous sun painted half on the ceiling and half on the wall. At the base of this giant sun, in the middle of that back wall, was an alabaster panel, marbled through with pink. It was so fine and delicate a specimen that, in the light, it was nearly transparent, so that Kaddish could separate out the veins in front from those spreading behind. The name was chiseled in the panel's center and four brass bolts held it to the wall, each one rounded and smooth. Kaddish couldn't figure how they'd been screwed into place or how he'd pull them free.

Considering his options, Kaddish felt hot with shame. Only a son of a whore from the Benevolent Self would bring a shovel to such a place. How was he to know that the rich bury themselves in the walls, that they don't touch the dirt even after they're gone? Kaddish pulled at the panel with his gloved hands and couldn't get a grip. Without pliers or ratchet, Kaddish tried to force the bolts out with his chisel. They wouldn't budge. Even if they had, the panel itself wasn't even the size of the front of a coffin. What if they'd built this place around it and bricked the body in?

Kaddish affixed the head of the pickax to the shovel handle, a wobbly affair he should have tried before. He put the flashlight in his mouth and attempted to fit the blade's edge between the plaque and the wall. His intent was to leverage it by pressing up on the handle and delicately prying the panel away. Kaddish worked at this for some time until he'd burrowed in behind it and the pickax caught. Kaddish bent his knees and gave a good even shove.

The sound of shattering stone as the panel gave way and smashed against the floor was greatly magnified in that tomb. It was as if Kaddish had brought the whole place down around his feet. Before he dropped his pickax, before he reached into the nook to see what was inside, Kaddish felt terrible about one thing. He harked back to what the rabbi had accused him of; it was never before true, but Kaddish had finally done it. He'd vandalized his first grave.

There was a cubby cut out of that wall and in it was a wooden box. Too small, Kaddish thought. It wouldn't even hold the remains of a child. He pulled it out carefully and placed it on the floor. Working at the top with two hands, Kaddish lifted it off with ease.

He'd found what he was after. Here was his man, disassembled. There was a skull on top and below it two hands—the man taken apart and, it seemed, lovingly and carefully arranged. Kaddish lifted out the skull, feeling its heft. He put this in the bottom of his canvas sack, and then, lifting the box and holding the mouth of the bag to its edge, it was very much like what he'd dreamed of as he poured the bones inside.

It was not yet dawn when, on the other side of Recoleta's walls, a man—straight backed and head held high—walked along with a sack thrown over his shoulder. He carried a staff and planted it against the sidewalk with a click as he made his way down the street. Had anyone been watching from the start of the night and seen that stiff-legged man hobbling alongside the cemetery walls, only to witness the spring in the step of our friend with the sack, our observer wouldn't have connected that poor specimen with Kaddish Poznan, full of pride and feeling, after a lifetime of failures, that he'd finally pulled off his first get-rich-quick.

[Forty-seven]

THE GENERAL'S WIFE WAS RIGHTFULLY CONFUSED.
Each night she wrote out her list for the next day on a piece of sta-
tionery with her date book open in front of her. This way she could slip
it into her tiniest bag. It was late morning and she was expecting to hear
from the florist. This was the call she was supposed to receive at eleven
o'clock. There was no one but the servants around, and when she'd finished her grapefruit she'd used her list as a place mat, putting the bowl
on top so as not to leave a ring on the side table.

With the telephone in one hand she stretched across the couch to
push at the bowl with her fingertips, sliding it over until the entry
marked *Florist* was revealed. It was as if she was confirming that, no,
indeed, she had not scheduled for this. She straightened up, feeling irri-
tated, and moved back toward the base of the phone.

"You've kidnapped my father?" she said.

"For ransom," Kaddish told her, already the third time.

"And you're sure you've got the right person?"

"It's not a joke," Kaddish said. He was on a pay phone near the
Benevolent Self shul. He tried to keep his voice deep and threatening—
this despite feeling frenzied by the unruffled tone of the general's wife.

"Because I thought it might be a joke," the general's wife said. "My father is dead, you know? Dead and buried, for—what year—it has been some time."

"Bones," Kaddish said. "I've kidnapped them."

"You stole my father's corpse?"

"The skeleton," Kaddish said. "I've got all the pieces right here."

"You mean you took them from the grave?" Here the first crack in her voice, the first sign of panic.

"For ransom," Kaddish said. He wasn't sure if he should start discussing the exchange before she'd fully understood. "If you ever want them back—"

"You'll have to excuse me," the general's wife said, interrupting. "It's shocking news. And frankly, I'm finding it hard to fathom."

"Oh, believe you me," Kaddish said.

"You'll have to excuse me if I don't," she said, "if I choose not to believe you. You being the type of person to do such a thing—or claim to. But," she said, "it's easy enough to check."

"To check?" Kaddish said.

"The grave," she said. "You be careful with what you have there, if you have it, and I'll send someone round to Recoleta—"

"Trust me," Kaddish said.

"I don't," she said. "Since you already have the number, it's fairly simple. Why don't you give us a little time and then call back."

"Call you back?" And here Kaddish couldn't help it, his own voice had risen. He figured it wasn't much of a slip on his part, because the general's wife had already hung up.

[Forty-eight]

LET HER SEND SOMEONE. Let her butler or driver go, let one of her staff run off to check. A businessman himself, Kaddish understood. Who wouldn't want verification when so much money was about to change hands?

Kaddish used this limbo period to descend into a full-on panic. He became certain that he'd taken the wrong set of bones. He pictured himself misreading the brass plaque and then doing it again with that beautiful alabaster panel bolted to the back wall. Kaddish would hear the sound of it shattering against the floor and see all those scattered pieces, the gypsum letters and half letters spread about. They'd reassemble themselves in Kaddish's memory, forming in the flashlight's beam, as if on stage, wrong name after wrong name.

When the right name held steady, Kaddish convinced himself that the bones themselves were lost. He'd return to the Benevolent Self shul and find that they were gone. Kaddish broke into a sweat at the thought. He walked and then ran back to the building. He ran to the front of the sanctuary past the bench under which he slept and yanked open the ark. This was accompanied by the dull jingle of the curtain rings left hanging after Kaddish tore the *parochet* down. Reaching into the ark, Kaddish opened the bag and found the bones just as he'd left them. He cinched the sack's neck tight, closed up the ark, and—feeling momentarily relieved—backed slowly away.

Take pity on him. It wouldn't bother Kaddish in the least. He'd gone to his kiosk to beg a pack of cigarettes on credit and the kiosk man shook his head and *tsk-tsk*ed. He handed Kaddish a carton and made no move to mark it down. A gift and a good-bye, Kaddish figured. He walked off, his chin tucked into his chest, mumbling *Bien, bien,* though the kiosk man hadn't asked him how he was.

Thankful for this bounty, Kaddish headed to the water by the Fisherman's Club. He wended his way through the park and went through his pockets for the hundredth time, making sure his last phone token was still there. It was the same panic he'd suffered over the bones—the sense that what he needed most would simply disappear. It was, even to Kaddish, a woefully obvious fear.

A pair of soldiers approached as he fed the token into the phone. Kaddish wondered how they'd known. The soldiers slowed when they got near and, giving him the once-over, kept on their way. A burst of laughter trailed back. Kaddish knew it was at his expense.

Never had the silence between rings lasted so long. Kaddish looked out over the water and waited until a maid finally answered the phone. Kaddish asked if he could speak to the general's wife.

"Who may I say is calling?" the maid said. Kaddish hadn't run into this last time. The general's wife had picked up the phone herself. "Hello?" the maid said, and Kaddish responded with the only thing that came into his head.

"It's the criminal," Kaddish said. "Please tell the lady I've called back."

The general's wife got on the line and said, "You've put me in a pickle. You've done something unconscionable and here I reward it by paying you mind. There's nothing worse than grave-robbing. What has this country come to when a person would sink so low?"

"There are lower things happening," Kaddish said.

"It doesn't justify such intolerable behavior. It's a disgrace."

"One that can be undone. Pay me and all gets put back as it was. A grave unrobbed and a father at rest."

"I don't know," she said. "I need to think."

"You've had time to think."

"I'd like to discuss it with my husband, is what I meant. He's away until evening. It's a very big decision to make on my own."

"This won't wait until evening," Kaddish said, with appreciable fury. "I'm a desperate man taking desperate measures. I swear, it will be over by then—one way or the other." He'd again attempted his most threatening tone. Kaddish assumed the silence that followed was one of acquiescence, the general's wife cowed and ready to comply.

After an interval—and Kaddish was no judge of how long—the general's wife said, "Well," and went silent again. Kaddish worried about the line going dead, his token swallowed with a chug.

Then she said, "It's not like you can make him dead twice."

"What?" Kaddish said. It was barely a croak.

"Time is not the issue, really. Not on my end."

"It is," Kaddish said. "This is your last chance."

"You've got my father—and I'm sure you've thought this out," she said, "but it's not really a your-money-or-your-life situation. We're talking about an exchange; a retrieval of, for want of a better term, my property."

"Today," Kaddish said, "or it doesn't happen. Desperate measures," he said, and feeling he'd already said that, stopped dead.

"I believe that's why this type of thing is usually done with the living. If you'd taken my son, for instance, instead of my father, you'd be in a better position to make demands. I've spoken to people missing sons, and apparently it causes great distress."

"You've spoken—" Kaddish said.

"In my own home," she said. "I feel like I *know* them and understand their plight. Bones, on the other hand—"

"Your father's," Kaddish said. "I'll toss them into the river. You'll never see them again."

"I'll tell you," she said, "and it's rather personal—private business. Aside from my father's blue-blue eyes and vast-vast fortune, I've been made to understand that I've also inherited his ice-cold heart. As a family, we are not sentimentalists by nature. I feel as I have from him all that I need."

"You don't want them back?" Kaddish said. As he said it, he regretted it. He didn't mean to raise the question.

"Oh, no," she said, "I do. I'd love to have my father back. What I don't want is to pay a fortune for what is mine. And it's silly to pay so much for one, when I'm in the market for two."

Kaddish couldn't help it; Kaddish asked again.

"Two?" he said.

"A second set of bones," she said. "Feel. Spring is around the corner. There's a touch of warmth in the air already." Kaddish listened and felt and thought, yes, maybe there was a hint of spring. "It's nearly time for planting, and I thought it might be nice to have my father back in his crypt and your bones for my garden. A little keepsake, unsentimental as I claim to be. Either way, it will be good for my roses, and at the very least it will keep the dogs entertained."

"I won't be bullied," Kaddish said.

"Then it's mutual. Now let me give you fair warning: It's much easier in this country to get disappeared than to stay hidden. They are two very different things."

"You're not going to pay?" Kaddish said, turning hysterical. He couldn't believe it and screamed into the phone. "You really won't," he said, now quiet, totally dejected. "You're going to let me keep him."

"Absolutely," she said. "You've finally got it. Well done. A greater mastermind there surely never was."

[Forty-nine]

KADDISH WAS IN THE BENEVOLENT SELF shul as darkness set in. He sat in the front pew, where he slept, and stared into the open ark at the sack of bones. He kept his eyes on that spot even after night came, staring steadily ahead.

What is left for a man to think when he was raised for ruin and it comes. Kaddish had fought against it, striven always for greatness, and not let any of his endless unbroken string of failures drag him permanently down. Knowing what he knew now, he would have lived better. He'd never once have let himself worry about ending up as he had. A lifetime of fearing it, and yet to find himself ruined still came to Kaddish as a surprise. If there was any wonder left in him, he spent it on this.

Whether it was minutes or hours he sat there in darkness, Kaddish couldn't tell. He was busy mulling over all the things that had gone wrong in his life that he might have seen as right. None of those failures flipped fully in Kaddish's mind, but nearly every incident shifted for him toward some central point, neither ruined nor right. In a lifetime spent striving, Kaddish had never before considered that, somewhere below greatness and high above where he now found himself, all could have turned out, simply, no better or worse than fine.

One thing was sure, however he'd come to see it: Life hadn't been fair. If there was a God for those who visited the Benevolent Self shul, that God had not favored him.

This would be his opportunity. Kaddish decided right then. Of all the chances gone sour and schemes gone awry, it was this one that Kaddish would make right.

It was bones for a reason, Kaddish decided. It was ransom for a reason and the same with everything gone wrong. From here, from now, he would turn it into favor. Even if he had to force his own God into heaven and hold His face steady, Kaddish would make Him smile down.

Trying to figure what he could settle, what he might fix, it was about Pato that Kaddish felt worst. He never should have tried to bring Lillian that money. He never should have let her try and buy back a living boy that he was convinced in his heart was dead.

As dead as the man before him.

Pato as dead as those bones.

Lillian held her foot behind the door and Kaddish tried to edge his way in.

"Do you know what time it is?" It was the middle of the night.

"No," Kaddish said, with utmost sincerity. He really was having difficulty keeping track.

"What couldn't have waited until morning? For a visitor, that would be the appropriate hour."

He looked down at the doorsill and pressed a toe against it.

"I've come back to put things right."

"Right is with Pato. Right is him safe. Tell me that you've managed it, that you've proven yourself the hero you always swear to be."

Kaddish stood silent. He couldn't produce for her the fortune that she'd asked. And he knew by her tone that she didn't expect it.

"How do you show up here empty-handed? That's what I don't understand."

"I'm not," Kaddish told her. He wasn't. "I've brought you something else."

Now it was Lillian's turn to stand silent, waiting for Kaddish to show her something when all she wanted was the money to rescue her son.

"I've made a decision," he said. "For both of us."

Lillian blinked. Limitless was her husband's ability to misconstrue.

"You weren't supposed to do that, Kaddish. A decision was already made. You were supposed to be off helping me with mine."

"I tried that," Kaddish said. "And I nearly succeeded. I think you'd be proud. Only, you can't make a murdered son live. That can't be done no matter how hard even the best man tries." Kaddish lifted his foot and gave a little kick to the sill. It was white when they moved in and the stone was now black, the threshold stained with a million comings and goings, the crossings from the three separate lives lived within.

There was nothing to do but to say it, and so Kaddish did. "If not for your sake or for mine, then for Pato's alone we owe him a grave. It's time to bury him, Lillian. A dead son is all I have left to give you. That's why I'm here. That's what I've got. I brought you back his bones."

Lillian had seen him through everything and stood by him through everything and couldn't know him any better. Looking at him right then, there was nothing left for her of the Kaddish that was. There was no sense to be made of him now.

Lillian was in the midst of recoiling, and Kaddish, who'd been pressing on the door, found himself stumbling forward and, regaining his balance, standing inside. How nice it felt to be home, even in the midst.

The door—heavy as it was—struck the wall with its momentum and knocked from it Lillian's scalloped shelf. Lillian looked down at the shelf as Kaddish had at the doorsill. She was thankful for something concrete to process so that she might gather her thoughts, find the tongue in her mouth, and try to comprehend the stranger before her.

"Bones?" she said, her face open with the asking.

"Yes," Kaddish said. He motioned feebly behind him toward the hall.

"You can't mean it. You can't have done this. It would, Kaddish, top all."

"I swear," he said. "I'll show you." He glanced at the clock. "We should hurry, though. This is the best time for the Benevolent Self, the best time to climb over the wall."

Lillian did not beat at his chest; she did not raise her voice; what she did was stand in the doorway and look over her husband's shoulder into the darkness of the hall.

Kaddish craned his neck, looking with her. Again he pointed. "Come," he said. "Come see."

Lillian did not move and Kaddish did not try to lead her. The only noise was the broken exhalation as she let out, in a thousand steps, her breath.

"A mother knows," Lillian said. "A mother knows her own son and when he is near. I've no idea what you've got out there, Kaddish, but I'll swear on my life that they're not Pato's bones. If they're another man's, God help you. Take them and do what you need to set yourself right."

Kaddish nodded. Kaddish understood.

He backed away from his wife, keeping his eyes on her as long as he could, and then the door closed in front of him. Kaddish picked up the sack from where he'd left it and started down those stairs, two bodies descending. He didn't bother with the hallway light. He knew every step.

This was indeed the best time for the cemetery, and the plot next to his mother's belonged to One-Eye. There was a lovely stone on it and Kaddish had already chipped away the name. A chisel works both ways, he figured. He could add another just the same. As for the bones, there'd be plenty of space alongside One-Eye's. The old man always was a good sport. Kaddish was sure he wouldn't mind.

In the house, Lillian stood with her back to the door. She let out a long slow wail and, for the first time in a long time, she let herself cry. She cried about Kaddish and the bones, about the fortune she'd never muster, and about the priest's call she knew would never come. When she was done, she wiped her face on her sleeve and made her way to the chair by the window. She sat down and settled in. She set her gaze on the corner Pato would come around. And as she did every night, Lillian thought, He will turn.

ACKNOWLEDGMENTS

The author gratefully acknowledges the support of the Bard Fiction Prize, the John Simon Guggenheim Memorial Foundation, and the Dorothy and Lewis B. Cullman Center for Scholars and Writers at the New York Public Library. Over the years, there were many people whose kindness and wisdom were invaluable to the completion of this book. A sincere thank you to all of them; and to Jordan Pavlin and Nicole Aragi, thank you for your ceaseless dedication. The following sources proved helpful during the writing of the novel: *Nunca Más,* The Report of the Argentine National Commission on the Disappeared; *A Lexicon of Terror* by Marguerite Feitlowitz; *The Flight* by Horacio Verbitsky; *The Disappeared and the Mothers of the Plaza* by John Simpson and Jana Bennett; *Circle of Love Over Death* by Matilde Mellibovsky; *Prostitution and Prejudice* by Edward J. Bristow; *Sex and Danger in Buenos Aires* by Donna J. Guy; *Making the Body Beautiful* by Sander L. Gilman; *Seven Nights* by Jorge Luis Borges; the article "The Gray Zone" from *The New Yorker,* by Seymour M. Hersh; and the testimony of survivors and relatives of *desaparecidos* at the Foreign Ministry in Jerusalem in March 2001.

A NOTE ABOUT THE AUTHOR

Nathan Englander's short fiction has appeared in *The Atlantic Monthly, The New Yorker,* and numerous anthologies, including *The Best American Short Stories* and *The O. Henry Prize Stories.* Englander's story collection, *For the Relief of Unbearable Urges,* earned him a PEN/Malamud Award and the Sue Kaufman Prize for First Fiction from the American Academy of Arts and Letters. He lives in New York City.